CARL HUBERMAN

A freelance writer for fifteen years, Carl Huberman lives quietly in Cheshire with his wife and family, four cats and his conspiracy theories.

His first novel, *Eminent Domain*, was greeted as 'a potent mixture of sex, violence and intrigue . . . a real page-turner' (*Midweek*) and was followed by *Firefall Taken*.

Also by Carl Huberman

Eminent Domain
Firefall Taken

CARL HUBERMAN

Welcome to The 51st State

PAN BOOKS

First published 1999 by Pan Books

an imprint of Macmillan Publishers Ltd
25 Eccleston Place, London SW1W 9NF
and Basingstoke

Associated companies throughout the world

ISBN 0 330 36777 3

3 5 7 9 8 6 4 2

A CIP catalogue record for this book is available from
the British Library.

Typeset by SetSystems Ltd, Saffron Walden, Essex
Printed and bound in Great Britain by
Mackays of Chatham plc, Chatham, Kent

For my agent, David Grossman,
and my editor, Peter Lavery,
for all their advice and guidance

A man's character is his fate.

Heraclitus

Three months ago

Dale Cresdee was walking cheerfully to his doom. Dressed, as ever, like a backing singer for Earth, Wind and Fire, he was middle-aged, middle-spreading and bald. Despite the heat of the Vermont afternoon, and his consequent perspiration, Dale was in a good mood. Those damn kids down the block were in school, he'd had a two-pound rack of ribs at the Bar-B-Q Bodega, and his inside pocket bulged with the latest rolled-up copies of *Hawk* and *Barely Legal.* The afternoon looked set for some serious stroking. And then, tonight, the Red Sox and Toronto were on TV, followed by Sally-Anne, who, when she got off work at K-Mart, would gladly get on to his smiling face.

So happy was Dale that he even waved at Mrs Hootkins, who was tending her lawn, knowing full well that she would ignore his greeting. Like many, she regarded the glittery flamboyance of Dale, and the lilac-painted house he had split into studio flats, to be as welcome in their quiet, residential neighbourhood of Lewisville as a crackhouse. But Dale didn't mind; he was anticipating the spread legs and open orifices in his pocket. Life didn't get much better than this, he thought. Unfortunately, Dale's life wouldn't be getting much longer either. Dale was going to be murdered in four minutes.

With just three minutes of his life left, the blissfully

ignorant Dale unlocked the front door of 105 Fairdale Road and let the cooler interior of the house embrace his hot face. He spotted an envelope on the hall table, picked it up and opened it with his pudgy fingers. Several ten-dollar bills peeked out and Dale smiled. Luanne McGhee, Apartment 4, paid her rent weekly and in cash. Why, he didn't know, but he wasn't about to argue. He pocketed the cash, pulled out his notebook, scribbled a receipt and slipped it back into the envelope, replacing it on the table. He then opened the door to his own apartment, No. 1 – with two minutes left to live.

The room was like a refrigerator, the air-conditioning set at 11. He slipped off his coat and hung it on the door, then extracted his skin mags and laid them reverently down on the couch before going to the windows and drawing the drapes. A little privacy was called for. However, as he let go a satisfied belch and tasted the barbecue sauce anew, he decided to head for the bathroom. Then, bladder emptied, hands washed, he came back into the living room, with just thirty seconds of life remaining.

He pulled off his shirt and unbuckled his pants, but instead of dropping them, he walked into his small kitchen. He needed a Schlitz to help rinse away the meat trapped between his teeth.

It was as he bent to open the rattling Kelvinator that someone stepped out of the shadows by his kitchen door and plunged the ice-pick into his back with sufficient force to penetrate through to his heart.

And even before Dale Cresdee had fallen to his knees, wondering why he couldn't breathe any more, his murderer had slipped out of the apartment, bloody weapon still in hand, and closed the door on Dale's life.

ONE@Chapter

Fergus Kintrey leaned back in his chair and stared at his computer screen. It was Sunday afternoon and he had spent the last couple of hours in the upstairs office of the Ryecatcher Bookstore, checking the accounts. But his real reason for being there was to see if he could discover anything about the mysterious e-mail he had received the night before.

He had been working late, trying to track down some wandering Wilbur Smith invoices, when an e-mail had arrived. Clicking it open, he had found four pages of close-set names and addresses. Strange, but it had become even stranger. After scrolling through the entire list and pressing HOME to get back to the start, the damn list had disappeared – and no amount of key-punching would bring it back. Nor could he trace who had sent it. And today's efforts had proven just as fruitless.

Puzzled, Fergus had finally decided to dismiss it as just another computer glitch. After all, how many times had he talked to Cathy Farrelly, the bookstore owner, about upgrading her accounting system? And how many times had he let the subject drop when she suggested they discuss it over dinner? If that was all they were going to talk about, then there wouldn't be a problem, but now that he knew Cathy was infatuated with him, he suspected their conversation would be less about computers and more about getting his hardware into her software.

OK, Fergus knew he was good-looking – a well-built five-ten with a mop of unruly red hair and green eyes set in a chiselled face that shouted his Scottish ancestry – but he wasn't available. What interest in women he had left was reserved for Kelly Stanyard, who roomed in the same apartment building. Besides, Cathy wasn't his type: it wasn't that she was unattractive, it was just that there was so *much* of her.

He thought instead of Kelly and her insistence on no emotional involvement – a truly vital element in their relationship. For his own part he was faithful. (What need he did have of other sexual partners when he could depend on Kelly for great sex?) They'd had sex the night before, in fact. Hard and rough and noisy, the way she liked it, and the way Fergus had no problem performing (though not as noisy as that infamous evening a few weeks back in the closed bookstore, when he'd had to stuff her bra into her mouth to stifle the shrieks).

He still didn't understand how Kelly could bear to live in Dale Cresdee's old apartment, knowing that the poor man had been murdered there. She had moved in a week after Dale had been cremated, apparently unfazed by the place's violent history. True, she had added some extra bolts, but otherwise she seemed remarkably unperturbed. However, as Fergus still felt uneasy there, their trysts took place in his own apartment upstairs (and, on that one memorable occasion, in the history section of the Ryecatcher Bookstore).

Thoughts of Kelly and her lithe body began to make sitting uncomfortable, so he stood up and, switching off the Compaq PC, stared out of the office window at another beautiful, late-September day.

The leaves on the trees were fighting to lose their greens, their palette toning towards yellows and coppers and reds, as nature repainted itself prior to surrendering to winter's greys and whites. Fergus had always considered fall in Vermont the best time of year in the best of locations. Although the seasons were just as obvious in New York – the city to which his parents had moved from Scotland when he was two years old – he had found every day there to be an angry adventure, its frenetic pace draining and dehumanizing. But for those lucky enough – like himself – to appreciate the Green Mountain state and its autumnal eiderdown of flames and rusts, Vermont was, as the phrase had it, 'like no other place'.

The street below was as busy as it ever got in September in Lewisville, with its eclectic mix of tourists and students both equally surprised to find that the town was so bland. Sadly, Lewisville couldn't boast the movie-set good looks of a Middlebury or a Shelburne. Fergus loved it none the less, and the anonymity it afforded him, because these days he was a walking definition of Anything for a Quiet Life.

But old habits die hard, and the spectre of the alcoholism that had driven him to his present dead-end job and his lack of emotional commitment was always there, nudging him towards the nearest bar. That he had resisted the urge for two years – ever since he had woken up one morning to find that his wife and three-year-old daughter had abandoned him – was one of the minor miracles in his life. If only he had realized sooner how far he had gone, he might have been able to salvage his marriage. But that was not to be – and his family had disappeared down the same seventy-proof sinkhole as the latter half of his college years.

What a waste. What a goddamn waste . . .

To take his mind off his misery, Fergus switched on the transistor radio on his desk. The Beach Boys' 'Do It Again' was in full swing, but just as its summery innocence began to lift him, a news bulletin interrupted. President Burridge had been rushed to hospital with suspected appendicitis. While Fergus considered Burridge to be a bag of wind in a tight suit, he had also suffered the same misfortune in his teens and couldn't help feeling sorry for the man.

The news ended, Tommy James and the Shondells came on, and Fergus began singing along. So absorbed was he in singing the praises of 'Mony' that he didn't realize there was anyone else in the bookstore until he heard a knock on the office door behind him. He turned to face its frosted glass and saw a dark figure standing at the top of the narrow steps leading down to the shop below.

'Hello?' he said, thinking it might be Cathy Farrelly.

'Mr Kintrey?' said an unfamiliar voice. 'My name's Anderson, FBI. I wonder if I might have a word.'

'Come in,' said Fergus.

An insignificant-looking man entered, carrying a large brown briefcase. He was average height, average build and forgettable of face and features, apart from an oddly antiquated pencil moustache that clung to his upper lip as if worried about strong breezes. He was dressed in a styleless dark-blue suit, with a white shirt and pale-blue tie. He looked like an accountant trying to impress an auditor –

smart but not too flashy, and with no hint of spending money on anything other than the need to look a credit to his profession. To complete the picture of blandness, he wore round tortoiseshell glasses.

'How did you get in?' asked Fergus, rising from his seat. The Ryecatcher didn't open on Sundays.

'The front door was open.'

'I must have left it unlocked. Bad habit.'

'Safe enough out here, I'd have thought,' said the man. 'Catch anyone doing that back in DC, they wouldn't have a store left to lock up next day. Here's my identification.'

'So, how can I help you?' said Fergus, as he looked at the FBI badge. He had never seen one before, except on TV.

'May I sit?' asked the man.

'Yes. Sorry.' Fergus picked up a pile of Spanish-language books from the room's other chair.

As Special Agent Anderson settled himself, clasping his briefcase on his knees, the light from outside reflected on his spectacles, hiding his eyes from Fergus.

'Thank you. I'll come straight to the point, Mr Kintrey. Have you recently received an e-mail on your computer here – a list of names and addresses?'

'Why?'

'A long story. There's been an administrative foul-up. I shouldn't be telling you this, but the FBI keeps tabs on magazine subscriptions – just to see who buys the more radical publications.'

'I only subscribe to *Time.*'

'No revolutionary you,' said Anderson humourlessly. 'But some subscriptions are basically donations to extremists, cults and radical groups.'

'Is that legal – you checking on them?'

'Well, someone has to keep a watch those who would threaten the democratic freedoms this great nation allows us. It's a trade-off most people accept – except, of course, those with something to hide. As I was saying, there was a mix-up – and some *Time* subscribers with an e-mail facility have accidentally been sent a list of subscribers to a magazine on military history.'

'Not exactly subversive.'

'It is if it contains urban-warfare tactics, or explains how the French Resistance created home-made explosives for use against the Nazis.'

'Ah.'

'Ah, indeed. Well, fortunately, these e-mails were intercepted pretty quickly. However, thirty or so *Time* subscribers from this part of the world will have received the list and, now, we want to erase them to preserve security.' He offered what he might have considered a smile. 'So, Mr Kintrey, were you in receipt of such a list?'

Fergus was pleased to see the mystery cleared up. 'Yes. Last night.'

Agent Anderson's attempt at a smile widened. 'Did you look at it?'

'Yes.'

'Did anyone else see it?'

'No.' He *had* mentioned it to Kelly in bed but, as she hadn't actually seen the list, this didn't seem relevant.

'And where is it now?'

'Gone,' said Fergus. 'Wiped. I glanced quickly through all four pages but, when I tried to reread them, it was blank.'

'Mind if I try?'

'Be my guest.'

Anderson put his briefcase on the floor and, under Fergus's guidance, checked through the PC's files. Five minutes later, he was forced to agree that the e-mail list no longer existed.

'Did you copy it, or print it?'

'No. I didn't have time. It came; it went.'

Anderson sat back in his chair and stared at Fergus for some moments, as if trying to judge whether he was telling the truth. Then, apparently satisfied, he leaned over towards his briefcase. As he delved inside, he said, 'And you're sure no one else saw this list?'

'I was alone in the shop.'

'Can you remember any of it?'

'I have a photographic memory, but – '

'I know you have, Mr Kintrey, and that's the pity,' said Anderson, his demeanour suddenly frosty.

'What do you mean?'

The man sat back up and Fergus saw that he was pointing an automatic pistol. With a silencer attached.

'Had you not read the information, all would be well, Mr Kintrey. And as you haven't printed it or copied it, again, fine. But your photographic memory . . .'

'Look, I don't know what your game is. I *do* have a photographic memory, but it only – '

'Turn away, Mr Kintrey.'

'Pardon?'

'Turn away. I don't like to see a man's eyes when I shoot him.'

'When you *what*?'

'Please, Mr Kintrey, let's make this as painless as possible for both of us.'

'What the fuck are you talking about?'

'Mr Kintrey, a disk, a photocopy, these can be destroyed. A memory, however –' he tapped his forehead with the forefinger of his free hand – 'lives on as long as its owner lives. The solution is therefore simple. Brutal, but simple. Now, take a last look at the world outside.'

'You fucker! Just for a *Time* magazine subscription list!'

'A remarkable memory in a rather dim brain, it seems.'

Fergus watched him raise the gun until it was level with his eyes and about five feet away. His pulse racing, Fergus could think of no action, no words.

'It's nothing personal, Mr Kintrey.'

'It's pretty damn personal to me!'

'One last time: will you look away?'

'No!' Fergus wanted to jump at the intruder, to stomp his face into the floor, but he was frozen to the spot, all his senses focused on the gun about to spit death at him. Then, over Anderson's shoulder, he caught sight of a movement on the stairs behind the glass door.

Anderson noticed Fergus's eyes betraying the newcomer. In an instant, he had spun round in his revolving chair and fired directly through the door. There was a faint cry as a small hole appeared in the middle of the glass, and then the dull clumping of someone falling backwards down the stairs.

Anderson swung round almost immediately, but not quickly enough to counter Fergus's attack.

His paralysis finally ended, Fergus had leaped from his chair and dived for his assailant, his sole aim being to keep the gun pointed away from him. And, while Fergus was no fighter, he did have the advantage of size – and surprise.

Anderson let out a short yelp, firing into the ceiling as both he and his chair were knocked flying. He tumbled to one side, while the chair skidded back and smashed into the glass panel of the door, shards of it showering over the stairs beyond. He still managed to kick out wildly at Fergus, making contact with his stomach and seriously winding him.

As Fergus rolled over, clutching his abdomen, Anderson righted himself sufficiently to stand in the middle of the room and take aim with his pistol. But Fergus charged for the man's knees, throwing him back against the desk.

As the computer dug into his spine, Anderson let out a howl of pain. Fergus then grabbed the man's briefcase, swinging it over his head, before smashing it down on to the agent's gun hand. The weapon exploded a third time, the bullet shredding carpet. As Fergus grabbed desperately for the other man's hand, he found himself clutching the gun barrel instead.

Anderson began to haul himself upright again, forcing his arm round so as to fire into Fergus's midriff. But Fergus grabbed at his attacker's throat and forced his neck back, meanwhile kneeing him in the groin. As the other man deflated, Fergus used his free hand to slam Anderson's wrist on to the table edge. Fergus saw the weapon drop and, wanting to get Anderson away from it, pushed him back over the desk with as much strength as he could muster.

There was a loud crash as Fergus found himself suddenly free of the other man's weight.

Two seconds later there was more smashing of glass and Fergus opened his eyes to see the broken window – and the empty space on his desk where his PC had been standing. Leaning over, he peered down into the street.

The man was lying on the ground fifteen feet below, surrounded by glass and plastic, with his legs and arms extended at odd angles. The pool of blood beneath his head was spreading outwards with dark finality. Two women standing near by screamed in surprise. They stumbled into the road, stared up at Fergus, then began screaming again.

Fergus stepped back, observing the wreckage their struggle had caused, and felt the dead man's automatic in his fist. Then, remembering the victim on the stairs, he rushed over to the shattered glass door and pulled it open. He raced down towards the pile of green and blue clothes which lay at the bottom. But this clothing contained a body: Cathy Farrelly.

He laid the gun to one side, then eased up her body till her eyes were gazing up at him. Her face was completely drained of colour, her bloodied lips trembling.

'Oh, Cathy . . .' he moaned, his words tumbling over each other. 'I don't know . . . this madman . . . FBI . . . he was after some damn list . . . he had a gun . . .'

'It hurts, Fergus. It hurts so bad,' Cathy managed, her voice a mere whisper.

He cradled her in his arms, ignoring the blood seeping from the corner of her mouth and the growing stain on her voluminous lime-green blouse. She felt so heavy, a dead weight in his embrace.

'Help will be coming soon,' he soothed, brushing the

dyed blonde hair out of her eyes. 'Someone'll have called the police.'

'It hurts, Fergus.' She coughed. 'What happened to me?'

'You've been shot – ' he started to explain.

She spasmed again and gripped his upper arm, her nails digging into his shirt sleeve.

'I love you, Fergus . . .'

'I . . . I know. And I'm sorry . . .' Sorry for what? Sorry that she'd been shot? Sorry that they hadn't become lovers? That he couldn't imagine her naked without shuddering? Sorry she was *dying*?

'It hurts, it hurts.' Her grip was weakening and she began to shake.

'Hey, Cathy, hold on. Help is coming . . .'

She ran one of her trembling hands through his hair, her eyes widening. He had never noticed before the greenish tint in her pupils – her eyes were really quite beautiful – but now they were beginning to lose their focus.

'I love your hair,' she murmured, though not seeing it. 'So red and – '

Her grip suddenly became painfully tight, tears now rolling from those same green eyes.

'Oh, God, I'm dying . . . I'm dying . . .'

'No! No, Cathy!' he yelled, as if raising his voice would keep her with him. 'Not yet. Not here . . .'

'Kiss me, Fergus, please . . .'

Fergus lowered his face to hers, pressing it to her bloody lips. God, they were so cold. Her hand clawed at him again, making him cry out in pain as she tugged sharply on his hair. Then, with a little gasp, she fell limp.

Fergus continued to hold her close until the police arrived.

He would never forget that her dying breath had tasted of cappuccino . . . or that the state of Vermont still wasn't far enough from the violence he thought he had left behind in New York City.

TWO@Chapter

At the same time that Fergus Kintrey heard the first police siren approaching the Ryecatcher Bookstore in the leafy Vermont town of Lewisville, Harry Sixsmith awoke from a nap in his bare bedroom to face another boring afternoon.

It was two weeks since he had been grounded and he was really missing the buzz of flying. He was the first to acknowledge that he had been ill-advised to fly beyond the programme's flight plan, but he was growing tired of the same old routine and the stuffy rules. Still, he had overstepped the mark and now he was paying the price – and it was a heavy one.

That price was boredom.

From his empty grey room without any view – other than a tatty poster showing Lake Superior – to the equally windowless Canteen, from the endless artificially lit corridors traversed by their rickety electric railway to the twilight world of the Control Room and Hangar, Harry had nothing to do once off duty, because there was nowhere else to go. He had even been barred from the Education Facility (classwork was a chore, but at least it offered something on which to concentrate). Oh, how he longed for the daily grind of the ground check, the monotony of the pass flights, the predictability of the speed and manoeuvrability tests and the inevitability of his flight's termination when radiation levels were deemed too high. For, despite the tedious routine, this did represent the only freedom he was ever likely to enjoy: the freedom of flight itself.

How many times had he pored over those old aircraft manuals, in awe at the bravery of the men who had pioneered flying, wondering if he would ever be allowed the chance – or find the nerve – to master such rudimentary machines? For it was one of the odd ironies of 'progress' that the more sophisticated a machine became and the easier to operate, the less natural ability was demanded of its pilot. Just consider the mini-railway that rumbled by his door night and day. The original iron horses of all those Westerns he sat glued to regularly in the Movie House, with their confined pressures and hissing pistons and wheels and rods, those were machines that required mastering by a special breed of men with an innate understanding of the dynamics of steam power. But now the electric train outside had just two buttons: GO and STOP – no skill, no expertise, just the press of a finger. And how many of them would know how to fix it in the event of a breakdown?

Harry opened his wardrobe and extracted his alternative set of clothes. They were grey, with a looser fit than his black flying suit. So, what to do meanwhile? He had been asked to report to Commander Ulrich at 16.00, in less than an hour. Were he not so nervous about the outcome, he might have relaxed with a game of pool, or maybe caught a film in the Movie House – which ran for twenty-four hours a day, to cater for all shifts – but he knew he would just sit there with his feet drumming anxiously, annoying everyone else near by.

Donning his customary sunglasses, he left his room and set off down the long grey corridor towards the Recreation Area. Perhaps a short spell on a sunbed might perk him up.

On the way he passed several people he knew, and they smiled or nodded, but none engaged him in conversation. Now, that might have been merely a coincidence, but it did nothing to leaven his pessimism. Perhaps they were privy to the outcome of his imminent meeting with Commander Ulrich, so didn't want to talk to him for fear of letting slip bad news. Blow it, he *would* go to the cinema.

He took a left, waited for the three-carriage electric train to rattle alongside, then hopped on to an empty seat. Its small engine could haul up to six carriages: simple carts with a rows of seats hanging on to either side which could accommodate ten people. Though it never travelled faster than a brisk walking pace, some of his journeys could be a mile long and so it was a more comfortable method of getting about. This train was empty except for a handful of mechanics, each of whom also ignored Harry.

Three minutes later he hopped off outside the Movie House. Admission was free and he strode through the lobby, deciding against buying a drink, and carried on into the welcoming womb of the darkened cinema.

He was pleased to find that it too was almost empty. But as he sought a seat as far away from the other few patrons as possible, he realized why. They were showing a documentary about World War II – how many times had he sat through this one? He then remembered that it was Sunday, and Sunday traditionally remained No Fun Day, so Harry slipped out and headed instead for the Canteen.

Harry Sixsmith had woefully few friends. He had never really felt easy in company, too often finding himself the centre of attention for all the wrong reasons, so he tended to keep himself to himself. But one friend he did have was Douglas Rogerson: two years younger than Harry himself and still learning his trade as a mechanic. He found Douglas sitting on his own, sipping a cola.

'Hi,' said Harry, sitting down opposite him at the bare table.

Douglas glanced up at him, then frowned. 'Thought you had a meeting today?'

Harry sat down. 'I do – but not yet.'

Douglas was blond, tall, gangly and good-looking. Sometimes Harry envied him his looks – but then Douglas didn't get to fly, so it was a fair trade-off. As their conversation stalled, Harry started tapping his feet.

'Stop that,' snapped Douglas.

'Sorry, it's just nerves,' said Harry.

'Well, you're getting on mine.'

'You don't have a session with Commander Ulrich,' said Harry.

Douglas gave him a strange look.

Harry could sense people's moods, but he wasn't very good at interpreting body language. 'What do you mean?' he continued.

'I didn't say anything.'

'It's the way you looked.'

Douglas shook his head. 'It's nothing.'

'You're lying.'

'Harry, I like you, but . . . you piss everyone off! You've got the best job of all, but it's still not enough.'

'Best can get boring.'

'Oh, and like the rest of us don't get bored in this place?' He swept his hand around the Canteen.

Forty grey metal tables, each flanked by six grey metal and canvas chairs, all standing empty until the next grey meal was served at 18.00 hours. Then it would be full of the smell of food, conversation, the clatter of cutlery, but right now it was dolefully empty – and Harry sensed that Douglas wanted to be out of there as well.

'I'm sorry if I've annoyed you,' said Harry.

'You don't know how to be sorry.'

Harry shut up and looked at the clock. Only ten minutes left till his meeting. Punctuality was a cardinal rule for him – except occasionally when flying, of course.

'Gotta go, Harry,' said Douglas, rising.

'I've got to go myself.'

Douglas walked briskly away, but turned at the door. 'Harry, I'm your friend, your best friend. Just do whatever they tell you.'

'I didn't do anything that much wrong.'

'Yes, you did – and you know you did. Just tell them you're sorry. Do that for me.'

'Okey-dokey.'

And with that Douglas was gone, stepping on to the electric train.

Alone now in the Canteen, its serving hatches shuttered as if to protect the food from predators, Harry sensed for the first time just how much trouble he was in. The way

Douglas had reacted towards him, maybe they'd never let him fly again. He wished he didn't possess this streak of curiosity – a dangerous quality in such a high-security environment.

He hurried out of the Canteen to catch the next passing train and, five minutes later, hopped off outside Commander Ulrich's office. The only thing differentiating it from dozens of other doors in the same corridor was its impressive black nameplate, and the inviolable instruction to KNOCK AND WAIT.

Harry dutifully waited for the familiar gruff tones to summon him inside.

Instead, he heard a female voice. 'Come in, Sixsmith,' it said.

Harry opened the door and peered inside. Oh, blow, he thought.

Commander Whitney J. Ulrich was seated behind his grey desk, as always: a large man in a stiff green uniform, his slab of a face hewn with surprisingly small features and topped by white hair cut so short it looked like a punishment. To his right sat two men from Flight Control, identifiable by their dark-green coveralls. To his left was the flight surgeon, Dr Fellinboro, short and fat, but also a woman dressed in a white coat that failed to hide her generous figure, or distract from her handsome face and short-cut hair that was quite the most beautiful red Harry had seen in an age.

'Come in,' she repeated in a kindly voice.

Harry did as instructed and, removing his sunglasses, he stood to attention in front of the Commander's desk. There was clearly no chair for him to sit on.

The Commander's voice was deep and gruff, and to the point as ever. 'Sixsmith, I am not going to waste either your time or ours by going over the whys and wherefores of your latest disobedience. For a period of nine minutes you deviated from your flight plan and disregarded repeated messages ordering you back to base. Only the threat of being shot down by A-Wing forced you to return and then you carelessly damaged your landing gear – repairs to which have taken fourteen days. And this is not the first time you've ignored your orders. To be frank, Sixsmith, I myself was in favour of having you terminated.'

Harry's eyes widened in shock. He had known he was in real trouble but –

'Stop that,' ordered Dr Fellinboro, turning away from Harry's gaze.

'Harry, please,' soothed the woman.

Harry looked towards her, narrowing his gaze. She still seemed calm, while the others, even Commander Ulrich, appeared nervous.

'However,' said Commander Ulrich, indicating the woman, 'Dr Ralston here has persuaded us that there will be no repeat performance.'

'Harry, you and I are going to become friends,' she said.

Harry saw no problem with this. He had few enough friends and now even Commander Ulrich, the man he had considered his staunchest ally, seemed to have suddenly turned against him.

'We'll work together, Harry – sort out your problems, get you back on track,' Dr Ralston continued, her voice warm.

'Thank you,' said Harry, remembering Douglas's advice. 'I'm sorry. Very sorry.'

'Words are fine, Harry,' said Commander Ulrich, his tone noticeably friendlier. 'But it's actions we want to see.'

'And it's actions you'll get, sir.'

'Very well,' said Dr Fellinboro, scribbling a note which he then handed to Dr Ralston. 'You've got one last chance, Harry. Fail us and then, regardless of the amount of time and money we've put into your training, I'm afraid you will have to be terminated.'

'But we'll be all right, won't we, Harry?' said Dr Ralston, walking round the desk to stand in front of him, looking straight into his eyes.

Harry narrowed his gaze further in respect.

'Good,' she said, appreciating this gesture. She took his hand and shook it.

'I'll not let you down,' Harry said, putting his sunglasses back on.

'Well, in that case, you should be able to resume flying tomorrow.'

Harry smiled at them, and everyone took that as a good sign.

He and Dr Ralston walked to the door.

'Last chance, Harry,' reminded Commander Ulrich, his affection for Harry betrayed by the use of his forename. 'And you *know* I mean it.'

Harry did indeed. He knew of five others who had been terminated, and had no wish to join them. He and Dr Ralston left the room together, then waited outside for the corridor train.

'I've gone out on a limb for you,' she said. 'I hope you won't let me down.'

'I won't, Doctor. It's just that when I'm up there, seeing so much, I simply want to see more.'

'We all have to walk before we can run.'

'Then I'll have to learn to walk again.'

'That's the spirit!'

She had a lovely smile, and Harry had to admit she was really rather beautiful.

The train came already loaded with shift workers from the Environmental Section changing shift, but they managed to hop on.

As they travelled back towards his quarters, Harry's feet began tapping again. His impetuosity had nearly cost him his life. Blow it, he was such a fool. He vowed to himself to be more sensible from now on, both for his own sake and out of consideration for this Dr Ralston.

But what twelve-year-old has ever been able to keep to such a promise?

THREE@Chapter

Fergus Kintrey was sitting in the office of Sheriff Eloise Wesley on the first floor of one of the oldest buildings in Lewisville. Its ground floor served as a bank, and the upper storey contained the local police station, entered via a wide wooden staircase leading up from Main Street. It comprised mostly a large open-plan office cluttered with desks and, to one side, the sheriff's office, adjacent to an empty holding cell.

Fergus had been brought in from the bookstore, half an hour after the police arrived to find a double homicide and him there with a gun by his side. Since then he had remained seated in silence across a tidy desk from the sheriff herself. He had forced himself to drink the coffee she had poured him (the smell a bitter reminder of Cathy Farrelly's breath) and it now sat in his stomach like acid.

As word spread of what had happened, and that the victims included Cathy Farrelly and an FBI agent, a curious crowd gathered inside the police station. Sheriff Wesley had barked at everyone to get on with their duties, then she had closed the door to her office. After removing Fergus's handcuffs, she settled herself behind her desk to sip slowly on her cup of Nescafé. Although the blinds were down, she knew the attention of people outside would now be fixed on her office door, imagining the interrogation going on inside.

Sheriff Wesley made an imposing figure – five foot ten, plump rather than fat, with a hard, now somewhat flushed face. But her cropped blonde hair was plastered down with sweat and her hands looked as unsteady as Fergus's own. Lewisville was a small college town with a low crime rate and murders were unusual there. Today's two homicides had exactly doubled the number of murders she'd experienced since being elected sheriff six years before. And she hadn't solved the other two either, including that of the late Dale Cresdee. But for Sheriff Wesley the most worrying aspect of today was the fantastical story Fergus Kintrey had babbled to her in her cruiser, driving over from the scene of the crime.

She thought she knew most of the people in town and certainly Fergus Kintrey. He had been at the Ryecatcher Bookstore for two years now and prior to that had worked at the college, until the pressures of teaching persuaded him to give it up. OK, so he wasn't a hundred per cent stable, but a recurring drink problem and a failed marriage don't a killer make, otherwise half her deputies would be in the slammer. She drained her paper cup and addressed Fergus for the first time in ten minutes. Her voice was a soft contrast to her forceful looks.

'You sure you don't want a lawyer, Fergus?' she asked.

'No. I haven't done anything.' He avoided her gaze.

'I can call Pete Drury. Court'll appoint him if money's a problem for you.'

'Money's not a problem. I'm the *victim* here.'

'Seems to me there're a coupla other people more victims than you.'

Fergus got angry. 'I told you what happened.'

'So tell me again, then. And remember, Fergus, I'm on your side.'

'Yeah, sure.'

'Oh, but I am, son. Seems to me a smart guy like you could work out a better story than this bunch of horse feathers.'

Fergus let out a big sigh, afraid for a moment that it might turn into a sob. 'Like I told you, Eloise, he was asking for that list.'

'Gary's over at your office now. Claims there's no e-mail on the system.'

'I explained it was wiped! I told the FBI guy too it had gone. He checked it was deleted – and that's when he decided to kill me.'

'But if the list was wiped, why did he –'

'He knew about my having a photographic memory. He probably thought I could remember it all.'

'And can you?'

Fergus concentrated hard, but nothing would come. 'Can't remember a thing now. It was a list, that's all I know. Names and addresses in alphabetical order. I remember a Baker, a Baxter. Addresses in Akron, Charlottesville, New Jersey . . . But I wasn't paying real attention. It scrolled up. It went blank. Then that bastard turns up and . . . poor Cathy.'

Again he remembered her breath smelling of coffee.

Sheriff Wesley leaned back, her black leather high-back

chair creaking, and planted her hands on the top of her head. Sweat patches showed at the armpits of her grey uniform. 'She had a thing for you, you know?'

Fergus stared back at the sheriff. Looking younger than her fifty-two years, Eloise Wesley was as good a friend as any to him in town. Prior to being elected sheriff, she had helped her husband, Frank, run his autoshop. The pair of them were solid citizens, both honest and dependable. They had invited Fergus to their home for Thanksgiving and Christmas the year before, knowing that he was lonely.

Fergus saw little point in denying what she had said about Cathy, so instead asked her how she knew.

'Aunty Eloise knows all,' she explained. 'We were down at Weight Watchers a month back; afterwards we celebrated our weight loss with a burger and beer. Cathy got drunk, sobbed a little. She knew it was hopeless – you heartbreaker.'

'Hey, I never encouraged her – '

'I know. Keep cool. Whatever your emotional problems, bedding a woman out of sympathy ain't in your nature.'

'Problems? What do you mean?'

'Kelly Stanyard.'

'How'd you know? . . . Oh, right, Aunty Eloise knows all.'

'And you're sure you *didn't* copy this mysterious list and take it home with you last night?'

'No!' Fergus realized she was using the standard interrogation technique – get good and friendly, then drop a probing question on him.

Sheriff Wesley reached for a red telephone. 'Celia, patch me through to Marcus at the Kintrey apartment.' To

Fergus, she said, 'Hope you don't mind us searching your place.'

'Don't you need a warrant for that?'

'Do I need a warrant, Fergus?'

'No. I've nothing to hide.'

She nodded, then spoke again into the receiver. 'Hi, Marcus, it's Sheriff Wesley. Got your gloves on? OK, check all of Mr Kintrey's computer disks.'

'What?' said Fergus. 'There's dozens of them!'

'Marcus needs the overtime. You got a password for us, Fergus?'

'Is this necessary?'

'As necessary as hell.'

'It's "Cassie".'

'Your daughter's name, right? When was the last time you got to see her?'

'Couple of years.'

'That's where boozing gets you . . . Marcus, the password's "Cassie".' She put the phone down.

'You don't believe me, do you?'

'Doesn't matter what I believe. It's what the law can prove. And right now I can prove you threw an FBI agent out of a window and your fingerprints are on the same gun used to kill Cathy Farrelly.'

Just then there was a rap at the door and a uniformed deputy leaned in. 'FBI are here, Sheriff. Shall I – '

Two men in dark-grey suits pushed past him and into the office, their officious manner immediately making Eloise bristle.

'Thank you, Deputy, that'll be all,' said the taller intruder.

The deputy, as annoyed as his sheriff, looked over at her for guidance.

''S OK, Cedric. A good suit's no guarantee of good manners these days. And these don't look to be good suits anyway.' She leaned sideways to peer between the two agents and out into the main office. 'And tell Frank he might as well go get a donut. Looks like we'll be here some time.'

Cedric looked back at Frank Wesley, a tall, thin man with a head as bald as a cue ball, who nodded his frustrated understanding as he began to gather up his Sunday newspaper. Cedric then closed the door on them.

'Gentlemen,' said Sheriff Wesley, 'I'd appreciate it if you'd show a little more respect to my men. Now, who exactly are you?'

The shorter agent pulled out his ID. 'Special Agent Parker. This is Special Agent Hadfield. We're here from Montpelier.'

'Show your ID to Mr Kintrey.'

Special Agent Parker turned and thrust his ID too close to Fergus's face.

Both men looked much the same – apart from Hadfield's extra six inches. They had short, dark hair, hard faces and eyes as severe as the cut of their clothes. They acted as if being in a small, out-of-the-way burg like Lewisville was akin to standing in dog dirt.

'Look the same to you, Fergus?' said Wesley.

'Yes,' replied the seated Fergus.

'And what exactly is that supposed to prove?' said Hadfield.

'That my suspect is being accorded all his rights.'

'Your suspect? Bought him in a sale, did you?' said Hadfield.

Sheriff Wesley was now furious. 'Just who the hell do you think you're talking to?'

Special Agent Hadfield leaned over her desk. 'Nobody,' he spat.

Wesley was shocked by the implied insult. 'I'll give you two five seconds to—'

She stopped as Hadfield suddenly pulled out a Ruger Mk II automatic pistol complete with suppressor. Before she could react further, he had grabbed her right shoulder and, jerking her towards him, shot her through the heart. Her death was signalled only by a muffled cough from the gun's silencer.

As a horrified Fergus tried to shout for help, Special Agent Parker clapped a hand over his mouth and knelt down to whisper into his ear.

'One peep out of you, fucker, and you get to leak like the lady.'

Hadfield then turned to face Fergus. He smiled as he put his gun away.

'Mad Dog Killer Kintrey,' he said, as Parker pinned Fergus to the chair by his forearms. 'Seems there's no stopping you, is there?'

FOUR@Chapter

Rage coursed through Fergus. His anger wasn't about his own predicament, or his impotence, but about the cold-blooded murder of his friend. They had *executed* Eloise Wesley as casually as if she had been a rabid dog. But why? What had she done? And who were they?

He began to struggle, his arms straining, his legs kicking out at Hadfield. Special Agent Parker jabbed his thumb into Fergus's cheek, at the point where his gums met. The pain was excruciating. Fergus stopped thrashing about immediately, his eyes watering, his attention focused solely on the sharp pain that racked half his face.

Parker spoke to him. 'We're not done yet, Kintrey, so start behaving – and do exactly what we say. You understand?'

Fergus could barely nod, the pain was so intense. He would have agreed to anything.

'Good. Now, you keep quiet. And you keep still.'

Parker removed his thumb and the pain suddenly increased. Fergus kept rubbing his face, unable to remove the cramp from his jaw.

Hadfield, meanwhile, had moved around Sheriff Wesley's desk. There he swung her chair through ninety degrees and carefully eased her body forward. Looking up, Fergus saw him touch at the woman's grey-uniformed back and rub some blood between his fingers.

'Clean exit,' he remarked, then pulled a pair of metal tweezers from his pocket.

Digging into the small hole in her leather chair, he extracted the slug of metal, which he put into his pocket along with the tweezers. Then he carefully propped her back into her chair and turned it round so she was facing Fergus. Her eyes were still open, face frozen in shock.

Using a handkerchief, Hadfield took the Smith & Wesson .38 revolver from her holster, flipped out the barrel and let all the bullets fall into his hand. These he also put into his pocket – except for one, which he slipped back into the gun, closing the chamber and aligning it with the barrel. He then walked over to Fergus and held the gun out to him.

'Take it,' Hadfield ordered.

Fergus shook his head, but Parker pulled out another automatic. 'Do as you're fucking told.'

Fergus took Sheriff Wesley's .38 in his sweating hand.

'Now things get real clever,' said Hadfield. 'Just stand up.'

Fergus rose and Hadfield turned and stood in front of him, facing the sheriff's corpse.

'Try anything and you die immediately. Now, put your arm round my throat, like you're going to choke me.'

'What?'

'Put your goddamn arm round my throat, like I'm your hostage!'

Parker grabbed Fergus's left arm and hooked it around his partner's neck.

'Now we're going out of here, with me as your hostage,' said Hadfield. 'You try anything, Parker here shoots you.'

Parker held up his own Colt .38 and forced his face to register panic. 'Oh, boss, what we gonna do?'

Hadfield smiled. 'Kintrey, you run, he shoots; you speak, he shoots; you lower your arm, he shoots. You do *anything* except walk me out of here, he fucking shoots. Now, aim that revolver at the sheriff.'

Too dazed and shocked to do anything but obey, Fergus lowered his weapon. Parker leaned over and, sighting down its barrel, carefully aimed it at Eloise's chest. Then he pulled back sharply on Fergus's trigger finger.

The report was shockingly loud as the bullet entered her body through the existing bullet wound.

'Put the gun back to my head!' hissed Hadfield.

Parker stepped aside and raised his own gun to Fergus's head. 'Stop there, mister!' he shouted. 'Stop right now!'

The door burst open behind them and Hadfield kicked back at Fergus's shin to make him turn. Two deputies were pointing weapons at the pair of them.

'Don't you move!' shouted Deputy Galligan.

Parker took charge. 'Kintrey grabbed the sheriff's gun! He shot her! Too fast for us!'

'He shot Eloise?' gasped the younger deputy, Cedric McCory.

The crowd outside hushed.

Parker continued. 'I suggest we do as he wants. He's got my partner. He's killed three people already today. Don't want it becoming four.'

Deputy Galligan looked undecided, his eyes darting from Fergus to Hadfield to Parker to Eloise Wesley.

'Oh, Jesus, Jesus . . .' he moaned.

'*He* ain't here right now, Deputy. Let us handle it.'

'You've not done much of a job so far,' said McCory bitterly.

Fergus began to speak, despite the terror consuming him. 'It's not what – '

Hadfield interrupted him. 'I know you're all itching to shoot this motherfucker, but I ain't about to get my head blown off while you get your aim right. Now, just back off and let my partner handle it.'

The crowd outside the door was undecided.

'*Move!*' shouted Parker, his gun aimed at Fergus's head. 'I got him covered. If he does anything, I've got him. Let's just not make a bad situation worse, people.'

Hadfield started moving, pulling Fergus along with him. Fergus glanced at Parker, the black hole of the Colt .38's snout only twelve inches from his face. He clearly had no option. As if joined together, all three edged slowly out of the sheriff's office.

'Lower your guns,' ordered Parker. 'Don't want no accidents here. One shot and you'll all go crazy – and we'll all end up dead.'

The two dozen people in the room slowly backed away, the only sound scraping chairs. Then other people came running up the stairs, the urgency of their clattering feet in stark contrast to the sudden tomb-like quiet inside the station.

'Hold them off!' shouted Parker, never taking his eyes or aim from Fergus's head.

McCory went to open the main door above the stairs leading down to the street. He held up his hands, his nervousness apparent. 'Stop! Get back! No one comes in here. All of you, back off down. Get out of the building.'

There were some shouted questions, but the deputy flashed his gun at the assembled onlookers and they slowly worked their way back down the stairs.

'Just keep moving,' whispered Hadfield.

'There's nowhere you can go, Kintrey,' growled Galligan, an overweight officer working towards his pension.

'Shut up,' said Parker. 'Just do as the man says.'

Everyone was too stunned to notice that Fergus hadn't actually said anything so far, but his gun – and the guns of the FBI agents – spoke volumes. And no one noticed that Hadfield's determination to get out of the main office meant that he was almost dragging Fergus along with him.

For his part, Fergus's mind was in turmoil, completely unable to fathom what was happening. He glanced at Parker and realized that he would be blown apart unless he did exactly as the agents demanded, first by Parker himself and then by every other gun-toter in the room.

They had reached the top of the staircase. Everyone had by now exited to the street, except for Eloise's husband, Frank, who was standing halfway down, gripping the handrail, his face completely pale.

'Where's Eloise?' he croaked up to Deputy McCory.

'Frank, it's all right,' the deputy replied. 'Just step out into the street. It'll be over soon.'

Frank Wesley was not a fool. 'Where's Eloise, McCory? She OK?'

Deputy McCory didn't know how to react. His biggest

problem usually was kids urinating on the war memorial. Now his sheriff was dead and he had a hostage crisis.

'Frank, please, just go outside.'

It was the desperate whine in his voice that triggered action. Frank Wesley dashed straight up the remaining stairs.

Hadfield shouted. 'Stop, you fool! Don't you see he's got a gun.'

Wesley pulled up short as he registered Fergus holding a gun to someone's head. 'Fergus, what you doing? Where's Eloise?'

Parker butted in. 'She's dead, you old fart! Kintrey here topped her. Now get the fuck out of the way!'

Frank and Fergus just stared at each other. Fergus started to shake his head, to open his mouth to speak, but Hadfield pressed sharply down on Fergus's foot with his heel, making pain rocket up his leg.

'Get out of the way, sir,' ordered Hadfield, experience telling him they had a complication. When someone loses a person dear to them, logic tends to get buried along with the corpse.

'You shot Eloise?' Frank Wesley paused there with his shoulders slumping, his eyes wide in disbelief.

Then Fergus began to cry. He didn't give a damn what happened now. He couldn't let these bastards get away with what they'd done. He began to lower his useless gun.

'I surrender – '

Hadfield reached over behind him, grabbed at Fergus's waistband, then lunged for the top of the stairs, bowling the stunned Frank Wesley aside.

Fergus began to stumble on the steps, but Hadfield

steadied them both. Parker then edged past the white-faced Wesley, who suddenly ran for the door of the sheriff's office.

Deputy Galligan failed to intercept him. 'Frank! Don't go in there, please!'

Hadfield and Fergus were halfway down the stairs by the time they heard Frank Wesley's anguished wail. And they were two steps away from escape into the sunshine – and a crowd of anxious onlookers – when they heard Frank Wesley bellowing behind them.

'Get out of the way. Get out of the way!'

Parker turned back to see Wesley looming at the top of the stairs, one shaking hand training a revolver on Fergus.

'Sir, put that gun down,' barked Parker, stepping into his line of sight. 'We're handling this.'

'Bastard killed my Eloise. He killed my Eloise.' The man's eyes were red, his white face streaked with tears, his whole body shaking with emotion. He advanced a couple of steps downwards.

'Please, sir, put down the gun,' said Parker.

As Deputy Galligan appeared, minus his gun, Frank stared at the FBI agent. 'What you gonna do? Shoot me?'

'Oh, God, no,' said Deputy McCory, stepping down in front of Frank Wesley. 'Come on, Frank, this ain't helping.'

'Shut up, Cedric. You didn't help Eloise none.'

'We didn't – '

Frank ignored him. 'Get out of the way!'

Parker raised his own gun, levelled it at Frank's midriff. 'Can't let you do that, sir.'

'Well, you'll get hurt too,' said Frank.

'Mr Wesley!' shouted Parker. 'Put the goddamn gun down now or I'll shoot you! You're interfering with – '

Frank Wesley took two more steps, his eyes never leaving Fergus and Hadfield, who had stopped at the bottom of the staircase by the open front door. 'He killed my Eloise . . .'

Hadfield nudged Fergus. 'Get us out on the street.'

Fergus began to walk again.

There was a shot.

Everyone froze.

Fergus and Hadfield looked back up the stairs.

Parker turned to look down at them. His face showed surprise. Blood suddenly rilled from one side of his mouth and, without a sound, he fell to his knees and rolled down the stairs. Fergus and Hadfield then saw the smoking gun, held by an equally surprised Frank Wesley.

'Drop it, Frank!' shouted McCory. 'Drop it right now!'

Frank looked down at Parker, the FBI agent he had just shot. His lip curled in a sneer of contempt.

'Drop it, Frank, *please*!' said Galligan.

Frank raised his arm, pointing the pistol at Fergus and Hadfield.

'He shot my Eloise.'

Suddenly there was another shot and everyone jumped, except Frank Wesley, who instead stumbled sideways, then fell, mashing his face into the wall, before tumbling down the stairs to land on top of the dead Agent Parker, the two lying like comrades-in-arms at the feet of Fergus and Hadfield.

There was screaming and crying, and Deputy McCory, who had just shot Frank Wesley, fell sobbing to his knees, the gun limp in his hand.

'What a fucking mess,' muttered Hadfield.

Fergus suddenly realized he had an advantage. He tightened his grip around the FBI agent's neck. 'Don't move, you fucker,' he hissed.

'What you gonna do? Choke me? Gun's empty.'

Fergus looked at the crowd around them. Most were frightened bystanders, suddenly regretting their Pavlovian reaction to a crisis, but he could also see two guns drawn.

'Only you know it ain't loaded,' hissed Fergus. 'Someone tries to shoot me, they might just hit you.'

'So where you gonna go? They think you shot the sheriff. You got the fucking gun in your hand. You'll be lucky they don't lynch you.'

Fergus didn't know what to do next. This was worse than any of the blood-filled nightmares that would often wake him up in the night, sweating and shaking. This was real – and it would be his word against someone he was apparently holding hostage. But truth simply wasn't the issue any more – all that mattered was survival. His only hope was to get away, get his head straight.

The crowd was actually beginning to swell, their eyes all fixed on him, their hatred for him now stronger than their fear of his weapon.

'Give it up, killer,' Hadfield called out. 'I'll speak in your defence . . .'

Fergus tightened his arm-hold, cutting off further words. Scanning the crowd, he then edged them both towards another deputy, whom he recognized as Heb Goodrich. Pulling even tighter on Hadfield's throat, Fergus turned his gun on the deputy.

'Give me your weapon.'

Deputy Goodrich shook his head.

'Give me the fucking gun, Goodrich, or I'll shoot both you *and* him!'

The deputy glanced at the choking Hadfield, then slowly eased the hammer of his .38 back into place and turned the gun over until it lay flat in his palm. Fergus dropped his own gun to the floor – bitterly aware that it provided all the proof that forensics experts would need to prove he had fired the fatal shot – and seized the deputy's revolver. Placing it to Hadfield's head, he eased his arm-hold.

'Now, you murdering fucker,' he whispered to Hadfield. 'Looks like I'm really in charge after all.'

Just then several officers ventured down the stairs of the police station, stumbling to a halt on the sidewalk as they saw Hadfield and Fergus still standing ringed by twenty onlookers in the middle of the street. Traffic, unaware of the unfolding tragedy, was stalled and honking in both directions and drivers were shouting their discontent at the sudden assembly blocking their path.

Fergus knew his only hope now was to play out the game that Hadfield had begun. 'This here is an FBI agent!' he shouted. 'And this is a loaded gun. So anyone shoots at me, I shoot the Fed! There's already been enough gunplay today, so me and the Fed are walking over to that car there!' He nodded at Goodrich's white Chrysler Lumina cruiser. 'Now, everyone, get out of the way!'

As they reached the cruiser, Fergus pushed Hadfield through the passenger door and across into the driver's side. Then he climbed in beside him, keeping the gun to his head.

'Now drive,' hissed Fergus. 'Unless you want to end up like your partner . . .'

Hadfield drove them past the crowd, which retreated quickly on to the sidewalk, and then headed on to Main. Fergus checked the rear mirror. Already flashing lights were whipping round the street corner, a pursuit inevitable.

'Right, now lose them,' Fergus growled.

Hadfield glanced at him and saw a wild-eyed man on the very edge of sanity. Kintrey was cornered, and when that happens, people either fight like tigers or curl up like kittens. Fergus was clearly one of the former, which came as a surprise considering the man's history. If ever someone should wear a big red sign marked LOSER, it was Fergus Kintrey – but this made his unpredictability all the more dangerous.

'Lose them,' repeated Fergus.

'Got a magic wand with you?'

Fergus jabbed the gun hard into the man's face. 'No, but if you're FBI, you'll be a skilled driver. So get out of here!'

Hadfield stepped on the gas and wove the Lumina through the light afternoon traffic, taking turns at random, until they fetched up on Eighth Street and, without any sirens near by, Fergus was finally able to think.

There was no way he would get away from Lewisville in a police car, but staying within the city limits was also impossible. He needed another vehicle, something anonymous, to get him out of there long enough to work through his dilemma. He was surprised that he was thinking so logically, but when your world has been narrowed down to the basics – run or die – focus somehow gets a lot easier.

'Give it up, Kintrey,' Hadfield was urging. 'We can work something out for you.'

'Now, why should I believe a man who doesn't even seem too upset by the death of his partner?

'It's all business. Nothing personal.'

'Whose business?'

Hadfield stayed silent.

Fergus jammed the gun into his side. 'You going to explain any of this?'

Hadfield shook his head. 'More than my life's worth.'

'Jesus, slow down!'

They were touching sixty miles an hour while approaching an intersection with the lights at red. Ahead of them a car straddled the middle of the road, waiting to turn left. Fergus suddenly realized the imminent crisis.

'Decision time, Kintrey. Want us to take out this poor sap in the Buick? Toss the gun, I'll obey the light.'

Oh, God ... There was no way they could make it through.

'OK, OK!' yelled Fergus, tossing the weapon into the back seat of the cruiser.

Hadfield laughed, and slowed, but he didn't brake. Instead he punched Fergus hard in the face, enough to daze him, then wove expertly through the traffic, sounding his horn. Once past the intersection, he slowed down to thirty, looking out for somewhere to pull over.

'Never play a man's game if you ain't got the balls, Kintrey.' He said it with a smile.

Fergus knew he was doomed. As soon as the car stopped, this man would be on him. He'd be dead in seconds and Hadfield a hero. He had to do something fast. He grabbed the handbrake and jerked hard.

The cruiser began to spin, its tyres screaming. Hadfield locked up all four wheels as he slammed on the footbrake. The vehicle wove across the two adjacent lanes and ploughed into a parked VW van, toppling it over the high kerb and on to the sidewalk. Both of the Lumina's air bags deployed instantly and for a few disorientating seconds both men were lost in a white, oppressive blur.

Neither of them had belted up, but Fergus had anticipated the collision and had braced himself for the impact. The air bag saved him from the windshield.

Hadfield was less lucky, however, his bulk hurling him forwards and his head smashing on to the upper rim of the steering wheel.

Fergus feverishly pushed open his door, tumbled out and began crawling away, as his lungs tried to fight the sudden pressure of the impact. Rolling over and gasping, he looked back to see Hadfield slipping sideways over the gearshift, knocked unconscious.

People were starting to run towards them and it was also Fergus's first instinct to run. But, remembering the revolver in the back seat, he scrambled over to the car on his hands and knees, pulled open the rear door and retrieved the loaded .38 from the footwell. Then, before a crowd could assemble, Fergus ran off down an alley between two stores.

He heard shouting behind him, but fortunately no running feet. Despite the continuing pain in his chest and the terror that engulfed him, this was his chance to take flight – the first since that FBI agent had come into the Ryecatcher Bookstore for him. So he ran, and ran, his destination unknown – wanting only to put distance between himself and Hadfield. Eventually, however, he had to slow, both his legs and his lungs chorusing their inability to continue.

Fergus staggered over to a nearby wall and leaned against it, bent almost double, his breath seeming not to come fast enough. He eventually looked up to see where he was.

Jesus, he'd run eight blocks. Unfortunately in a straight line, so he would be easy to track. He needed to change his direction – and quick. There was already a siren in the distance, coming nearer.

Moving around the corner of the whitewashed wall, he found himself standing on Carlin Avenue. The wall belonged to a Korean grocery store, with a dark-blue Cadillac Catera parked out front, its black driver tapping his fingers on the steering wheel in time to a booming rap track.

Black people were still rare enough in parts of Vermont to attract some stares, but one in a Cadillac, polluting a quiet Sunday evening with rap music, was more than likely to attract the police. Damn! But he did need a getaway car . . .

So, as if it was second nature – although in fact one instilled in him only within the last half-hour – he walked round to the driver's door of the Catera and pushed the snout of the .38 through the open window. The driver slowly turned his head to look at it.

'Get the gun out of my face, man.' The deep voice was barely audible above Warren G's musical boasting.

'No. You get out of the car,' said Fergus.

The man stared him in the eye, his face expressionless,

his eyes hidden by a pair of Ray-Bans. Gold glinted on his neck, his ears, his fingers – even on his nose.

'Or what, you heated-up piece of chicken meat?' he finally replied.

Fergus was feeling desperate. 'I'll shoot you.'

'Hey, country boy, watch you don't get me wetting my Calvins.'

'Are you stupid?' said Fergus.

'Looks to me stupid is being too yellow to follow through with your whiteboy threat. You want the car, you shoot me. Them's the rules.'

'What?'

'Just blow, before I smacks you for dissing me.'

Fergus stepped back from the car, unsure. It was a scary world some people lived in when a gun in the face didn't seem to worry them. He was almost walking away, but then the distant siren underlined the hell he was currently living through. So, instead, he leaned back into the car, took aim at the tape deck and shot it to bits.

'What?' shouted the driver, wincing at the blast.

'Now that rap shit's shut up, maybe you'll – '

'Rap *shit*?' yelled the man

'Yes, get – '

'Rap *shit*?' snarled the man again.

Suddenly he kicked the door open, forcing Fergus back into the street. The enraged man stepped out of the Catera. Dressed all in black, he was sumo huge: six foot six, 300 pounds.

'Rap *shit*? You blew up the G. Nobody does that, you hear. 'Specially not some strung-out whiteboy junkie motherfucking asshole wimp who goes about dissing with the black man's art!'

Fergus was shocked by the man's lack of fear and realized he would have to do something drastic – or he'd would find himself smeared all over the blacktop.

'Stay back. I'll shoot!'

'Better shoot yourself then, boy, 'cos it'll seem like a pure fucking pleasure compared to what I'm gonna do to your sorry motherfucking ass.'

Near to total panic now, Fergus shot King Kong in the foot.

'My shoe!' the man yelped, and bent over.

Oh, my God, thought Fergus, and slammed the butt down against the man's temple. He went down further, but not all the way. So, rather than prolong their confrontation, Fergus slipped round him and into the Catera. He roared off, leaving the kneeling giant in a cloud of rubber smoke and 'motherfuckers'.

Getting out of Lewisville was surprisingly easy. It wasn't a large town: a population of ten thousand swelled by a student body half that number again. But it was Sunday and traffic was light and the resources of the police were already stretched, with double homicides in two locations. It would be some time before the state troopers could make an effective presence and by that time Fergus hoped to have found a place to hide.

After an hour he was fifty miles away, somewhere west of Interstate 91 and south of Springfield. On his single-minded drive there, he had passed tourist attractions like Quechee Gorge and 25,000 Gifts and Woolens, where in daylight the fast-brightening plumage of maples and cedars seemed to line every road – like a repetitive, multicoloured cyclorama unrolling – but now the dusk and heavy rain made them seem distant and irrelevant. He had been back-roading for a good fifteen minutes now and was thinking of heading for the New York State line. It didn't really matter how far he drove, for there would be a nationwide APB out for him by now: the police and the FBI both out for his blood. What he needed was time to stop and think – but where?

The decision was made for him when he noticed the stolen Cadillac was low on gas. As he had no money on him (having emptied his pockets in Sheriff Wesley's office), it looked like he wasn't going to get much further anyway.

He spotted a motel up ahead and slowed. He rooted around in the glove compartment, but found nothing. Then he brought the car to a halt, stepped out into the rain and checked under his seat. Jesus. A sawn-off shotgun and a plastic bag containing several phials of white crystals and about two thousand dollars in twenties and tens, obviously the proceeds from numerous crack sales. At least he was now solvent.

On the back seat there lay a brown raincoat. This he put on, tightening the belt. He also found a Mets baseball cap and, tucking in his distinctive red hair, he pulled it low over his eyes. He checked himself in the rear-view mirror: he still looked just like a fugitive.

He then drove the Catera into the Eezilay Motel – its main source of income probably advertised in its name – and parked it out of sight round the back. He headed for the office, trying to avoid eye contact with the sleazy, middle-aged owner but muttering something about his goddamn wife throwing him out, and paid for two nights in advance.

The clerk offered him the key to Chalet 8, together with a card announcing the choice of cable porn for that same evening.

Once inside his room – a sparsely furnished riot of russets and greens designed presumably to echo the famous New England fall – he locked the door, drew the shades and collapsed on the bed, shaking like a child.

One day ago, his greatest crime had been parking in the disabled space outside Elvira's Eatings. Now he was top of the FBI's Most Wanted list and in possession of a stolen crack-dealer's Cadillac. He hadn't a prayer.

FIVE@Chapter

Harry Sixsmith was playing chess with his friend Douglas Rogerson in the other boy's bedroom. Douglas's mother had brought them milk and cookies and – after some gentle chiding of Harry about his errant behaviour – she'd left them to get on with their game.

As he often did, Harry was letting his ten-year-old opponent win. It wasn't that Douglas wasn't any good at the game – in fact, he was very good indeed – it was just that Harry's analytical powers were so much greater.

'When's your dad back?' asked Harry.

'Couple of days.'

'At the Scrubbers?'

'Where else?'

One of the most vital operations in the complex they all called Down Town was the air-conditioning. This vast plant not only purified the air circulating within Down Town, but also ensured that there was no contamination from the atmosphere outside. Both of Douglas's parents worked for the Environmental Section and one of their tasks was to help in the manual cleaning of contaminated air-filters – the Scrubbers. To do this they would be locked into the cleaning area for a week, working eight hours on, eight hours off. Workers remained in the plant for the duration of their shifts to cut down any risk of pollution. With everyone's life constantly at stake, it was a small price to pay. So, for one week out of every four, Douglas's father would be absent from home; and then it would be his mother's turn to be away.

'Must be hard work for them,' said Harry. 'I watched a video about it the other day. Didn't recognize your dad, though.'

'Very funny.' Douglas had seen the same video, where everyone wore yellow protective suits and helmets, making them all look like giant jelly babies.

Douglas finally spotted the checkmate Harry had been trying to give to him for the last six moves and declared his triumph by whooping round his bedroom, hands held high.

'Want another game?' asked Harry.

'No,' said Douglas. 'You might let me win again.'

Harry finished putting the game away, then reclined on the bed. He took off his glasses, even though he knew he shouldn't, but the frames were digging into the side of his head.

Douglas perched on top of his grey metal chest of drawers, swinging his legs back and forth. The scuff marks on the middle drawer showed that he did this regularly. Meanwhile, he stared at the pictures on the walls – similar to those in Harry's spartan quarters. They showed skiers on snowcapped mountains, damp Brazilian rainforests and vivid New England autumns, wide lazy river deltas and gushing river rapids. A dozen landscapes cut from *National Geographic* magazines, yet none of them resembling anything Harry or Douglas had experienced first hand. For they had never enjoyed the smells of a spring meadow, the crunch of snow underfoot, the sound of birdsong in a wood, the crash of surf on sand . . . All they knew so far was Down Town – and Down Town didn't amount to much more than a lot of grey walls without any windows.

'So they're letting you fly again?' said Douglas.

'Yes.' The relief was palpable, since they both knew that the alternative would have been termination.

'And you'll obey orders this time?'

'Oh, yes.'

Douglas was plainly relieved at this. Harry was his best friend and he didn't want to lose him. They had even been brought up together, Harry becoming almost a second son to the Rogersons after his own mother had died. That Harry was different from them was obvious: he had started walking and talking at just six months – his progress enhanced by the teaching regime in Down Town. There had been high hopes that more offspring would be born, but there had been many miscarriages, or ones born with incurable defects. Radiation was usually blamed.

Notwithstanding their circumscribed existence, Harry and Douglas were content. Both were keen to learn the tasks allotted to them: Harry as Down Town's only test pilot and Douglas as a mechanic.

However, several events over the last few days had set Harry to thinking about Down Town's isolation. 'Have you ever wondered what it's like outside?' he said, not for the first time.

'You know we're not supposed to think like that.'

'When I'm up there, in the dark, sometimes I swear I can see lights – in the distance.'

'Stars, you mean?'

'In the desert. Moving lights.'

'Do you report it? What does Commander Ulrich say?'

'Says I'm imagining them; that *everything* out there has been dead for at least ten years. Says I should concentrate on mastering the Hubcap, not sightseeing.'

'He should know.'

'Oh, I know he's right, Douglas. But then why do they keep changing my flight programme so that I don't go anywhere near where I saw the lights before? And *why* can't I ever fly higher than 3,500 feet?'

Douglas left the chest of drawers and sat down next to Harry.

'So what do you think those lights were?' asked Douglas in a whisper, his curiosity now getting the better of his caution.

'I've no idea,' admitted Harry. 'Radiation's high out there – even where I fly. The read-out still turns red sometimes, enough to kill anyone who stays there for more than an hour. No one could survive at those radiation readings, never mind the lack of water and extreme temperatures.'

'So you must have been imagining the lights.'

Harry didn't know and should have dismissed it. One did not question Commander Ulrich, after all. Except there had been other things. Small things he had started paying attention to.

'I don't know whether I should tell you this stuff.'

Douglas's own eyes widened. He went over to his record-player and put on his scratchy *Best of the Carpenters* vinyl LP, turning the volume way up.

'Close to You' filled the bedroom as Douglas again sat down close to Harry. 'Come on. Tell me, then.'

'It's little things. I saw a couple of technicians with suntans.'

'They use sun beds.'

'These weren't the flashes we get for our skin tone. They looked like those people we see in movies, who've been lying out in the real sun.'

Everyone in Down Town had been locked inside for nearly thirteen years and in all that time no one new had come in. They couldn't, of course, since everyone outside was dead. And everyone who had since died in Down Town had been cremated in the furnaces. Because there was no way to get out of there, except through the escape hatches now sealed shut by cement and welded girders – or through the protected doors of the Hangar.

Douglas didn't have a solution. 'Anything else?'

'Where did this Dr Ralston come from? She says Biomedics, but I've never seen her before – and I'm in Biomedics more than anyone else.'

'Maybe she worked on different shifts.'

'Maybe, but at different times I've been there on every shift. Besides, if she was being put in charge of me, surely she'd have had contact with me before now?'

'Maybe she'd heard of your bad BO.'

'Hardy-ha-ha,' said Harry. He knew he liked Dr Ralston – but her sudden appearance *was* odd. But then, so much else was odd in their isolated little bunker. 'Well, I should have seen her in the Canteen at some point. *Everyone* goes there.'

Douglas shrugged. 'If you didn't know her then, you wouldn't have looked for her, would you?'

'No, I suppose not. But I still feel they're trying to *hide* something.'

All everyone in Down Town really wanted was to get out into the real world again, so surely anything that would help promote that ambition was worth pursuing? If Harry saw lights, shouldn't he be allowed to seek out their source? And if not, why not?

But he had been saving the weirdest bit till last. 'I found this,' he said, extracting a piece of scrunched-up paper from his pocket. He unfurled it carefully, to reveal a red-and-white Kit-Kat wrapper. 'I found it yesterday in one of the corridors. But chocolate bars ran out *three* years ago.'

'So, someone's been hoarding their ration?'

'Look at the competition on it.'

'*Win a mountain bike.* What's a mountain bike?'

'Don't know, but look at the closing date.'

'Entries must be in by November 28, 1998. It must be a misprint . . .'

'You never misprint competition details. This wrapper was printed *this* year – twelve years after we were all sealed in Down Town.'

'Impossible.'

'So what do you suggest?'

Their puzzled silence was suddenly interrupted by the front-door bell, its innocent twin chimes making them jump.

'Oh, blow!' said Harry.

A wide-eyed Douglas explained, 'Mum's got one of her friends round tonight. For cards.'

They stared down at the Kit-Kat wrapper on the

coverlet between them, as they vaguely heard a muted conversation outside. Both boys' legs were now tapping nervously. Suddenly, Douglas let out a yell.

'It's a test!'

'What?'

'They leave it lying around, see who finds it – and what they do with it. When did you pick it up?'

'Three days ago.'

Suddenly the bedroom door opened. Mrs Rogerson came in with another woman. Harry quickly donned his sunglasses.

'Hi, boys, this is Dr Ralston. She's come to have a word with Harry.'

Douglas and Harry stared at each other, Harry's thigh covering the damning evidence.

'Hello, Harry,' said the doctor. 'I think you and I need to do some talking.'

The speed of Harry's leg-tapping set new records.

SIX@Chapter

By 6.00 p.m., Fergus was a national television celebrity. After all, it's not often that quiet New England towns endure five homicides in the space of one hour, including two FBI agents and the town sheriff.

CBS led with the story: interviewing witnesses, police deputies and – much to Fergus's anger – Special Agent Hadfield. Sporting a bloodied bandage over his right eye, he it was who christened Fergus 'Mad Dog Killer Kintrey', so setting the seal on his public legend. All that remained was for Fergus to be caught, tried and quickly executed; truth and justice were now irrelevant. No matter what he might plead, he was seen as guilty. He might just as well save everyone's time and kill himself here and now in the motel room.

Except Fergus refused to accept his fate.

He knew he hadn't committed any of those murders. He guessed there was some insane conspiracy going on; so the key to it all was included on that list of names, although he couldn't even recall it in any detail now. For his photographic memory to work, he had to compose his mind to retrieve the information – much like a video-recorder being switched on and tuned in. But, however useful people might think such a mental facility would be, it was often pretty impractical. Even for obvious things such as passing his college exams, it meant memorizing pages and pages of information, only to have to wade laboriously through it all to find the piece of data needed to answer the question.

In disbelief, he continued to watch the story unfold, the only comfort hearing a report of his being sighted in Burlington, heading for the Canadian border. Finally, the story finished, moving on to an update on President Burridge's appendicitis. After being rushed into hospital and operated on that afternoon, he was expected to make a full recovery. *Well, bully for you*, thought Fergus; if only his own problems could be solved so easily. He turned to a porno cable channel – anything without news – and watched without interest, or arousal, as a young girl was double penetrated by two men at once. Turning away, he settled back with his fourth mini-bottle of motel spirits. It had been a long struggle to avoid the temptation to blot out this horror with drink.

It wasn't that he had a problem *holding* his liquor; it was that he could hold *so much*. His late adolescence had passed in a beery haze, then in college he had surrendered to the pleasures of bourbon. The result was a period stretching from the end of his sophomore year until a good year after he had failed his exams – embracing some thirty months of which he retained no memories, the excessive alcohol having absorbed all information. He called those his Disappeared Years – because that's exactly what had happened to them.

He had finally kicked the habit after attending his mother's funeral in Queens, NYC. Newly sober, he had then retaken his English degree at night classes while working in a drugstore during the day. Once he had passed his exams, he had secured a job teaching in Lewisville, Vermont, through the aid of a friend of his late father. There he had met Sarah, married her in haste once she realized she was pregnant, then settled down to raise Cassie – now six years old – and had then thrown it all away by succumbing to the bottle again when the college laid him off. All that saved him from repeating his Disappeared Years was Sarah walking out on him and taking their daughter off to New York. There she still lived, the alimony a monthly haemorrhage in his bank account, but her abrupt departure without any kind of contact for over a week had served to sober him up at least. And what few friends he had left had testified to his bad behaviour towards his wife and child. His ranting, unreliability and drunken self-pity had tried their patience once too often.

Since then he had abstained, even attending a handful of AA meetings, but his newly impoverished circumstances – working for a bookstore is not the route to riches – had played a far bigger role in keeping him off the bottle.

But now what better to numb the misery than Absolut and Jim Beam, while he waited for the inevitable knock on the door.

He thought over his life and the waste it had been – and how it seemed to have been blighted by alcohol. Of course, that was the alcoholic's traditional excuse – *problems drove me to drink, rather than drink being the cause of the problems* – but it offered him a little comfort. After all, if he laid all the blame at his own door, what else would there be *except* drink? He was thirty-one years old and who did he have he could turn to? He had lost touch with his college friends, having driven them away with his boorishness. And, after ruining Sarah's life, his friends had sided with her and shunned him. Since then he had been wary of making any real acquaintances. His closest and only confidantes were Cathy Farrelly, his lately murdered boss; and Kelly Stanyard . . .

Kelly?

Drink and desperation suddenly made his sometime lover the focus of what little hope he had left now. If he could just talk to her, convince her of his innocence, at least he would have an ally. He would call her at her apartment. Yes, *she* would understand, be able to help him. So, what was her number?

He emptied a mini-bottle of gin as he tried to remember it. No good: he had rung her only three or four times since they had become intimate, so he didn't recall her number offhand. However, he did have his photographic memory. Just about the only consistent use he had ever found for it was committing to memory all the telephone numbers he required. He looked around the room for the prop he needed and settled on a pillowcase. Despite his drunken state, he knew that if he followed his 'rules', he would soon be able to picture his phone list.

He hung the white pillowcase over the mirror on the dresser to give it a totally flat surface, then seated himself on the edge of the bed and focused on it until all he could see was white. Then he imagined the word 'telephone' in bold capital letters with a Smiley for an 'O', as he had written it on the top of his original list.

TELEPH☺NE

Having brought the list's heading into his mind, that immediately unlocked the remainder of the page, and within a split second he had the printed page in his mind as clear and readable as if hovering right in front of his face. He was able then to run his eyes down the list, while it remained fixed in space, until he found Kelly Stanyard's name towards the bottom. There were three numbers against her name.

The first he recognized as her apartment number, because it had the same area code as his own; the second, the one he had never called, was her work number in Farrar; and the third was for a cellular phone.

He mentally switched off the page, jerking as the real world rushed back into view. The alcohol didn't improve matters any, but he was soon beside the telephone and punching in her home number.

It was only as he heard it ringing that he stabbed at the cradle to close the line. The FBI were bound to know about their relationship by now, so her line would be bugged. Damn them. He grabbed yet another bottle from the mini-bar and slugged back its contents in one go. He didn't even register what it contained. And didn't care. He dialled again, trying Kelly's cellular phone.

It was answered after five rings.

'Hello,' said a familiar voice. Smoky Okie, Fergus had called that voice, Kelly coming from the moneyed side of Tulsa.

Fergus nearly burst into tears. Although their relationship was basically physical – she insisting she was too busy with her career for serious involvement – Kelly had been his only intimate association since his marriage break-up, and maybe the only person in the world he could trust.

'Hi, Kelly, it's Fergus.'

'Oh, Fergus, what have you *done*?'

It came out in a rush. 'Nothing. None of it. This guy attacked me at the bookstore. He shot Cathy. These FBI guys shot Eloise Wesley and forced me . . .' He realized he sounded like a kid trying desperately to excuse the damage one of his pranks had caused. 'Have they spoken to you yet?'

'They were here for an hour. They said it'd be best for you to give yourself up.'

'And for you to tell them if I rang.'

'Yes . . . and to try to find out where you are.'

'*Would* you tell them?'

'I don't know.'

'Thank you for being honest.'

'Did you do *any* of it?'

'I pushed one FBI guy out of the window – after he shot Cathy. That's all, I swear it. Christ, I *waited* there for the police to come. Eloise seemed sympathetic, then these bastards . . . I just don't know what to do.'

'Have you been drinking, Fergus?'

He didn't answer. He feared a lecture.

'Where are you, Fergus?'

'In a motel. I stole a car.'

'You need a lawyer.'

'I need a goddamn miracle!'

He reached for another mini-bottle. It was Beefeater gin. Kelly was his last fragile hope, but it was obvious there was nothing she could do. He shouldn't even be talking to her. He unscrewed the cap with one hand.

'Look, Kelly, I'm sorry. This is *my* problem. I don't want you dragged into it. These guys mean business and anyone who gets in their way . . . God, if they'll blow away a sheriff in her own office, they'll do *anything*. I'd better go now and keep you out of this mess.'

'No! You *do* need a lawyer. If you give yourself up, you must get a fair hearing. Tell me where you are and I'll come and fetch you.'

Fergus so much wanted to say yes, but knew it was pointless. 'I'm sorry.' He put the phone down. Then, in a fit of anger, he tore its flex from the wall socket, downed the gin and hunted for more alcohol.

Half an hour later he had finished all ten bottles from the mini-bar and was seriously considering venturing out in search of more. But fatigue and shock and, of course, the booze finally took their toll. Lying back on the bed, he fell asleep.

How long he lay there he didn't know, but when he awoke, night had long fallen, his head was booming and his mouth was dry. He had been roused by another of his recurrent nightmares, as inexorable and bloody as always. It was terror of it that had forced him from his stupor. Shaking, he staggered to the bathroom, where he peed a torrent of deep-yellow urine, then gulped water direct from the tap and rinsed his face. He stared at his ashen visage in the mirror and tried to control his shaking by gripping the washbasin. *Bad boy, Fergus. Bad boy.* Then he heard a noise outside.

His heart hammering, his mind whirling with violent possibilities, he edged back into the darkened bedroom and stared through the window. A light was moving outside: a flashlight.

Then the sound of feet on planking. Someone on the

veranda. Then whispering – which meant more than one person. Then a metallic click. Two more clicks. Pistols being cocked? Shotguns primed?

He backed into the bathroom, unable to think clearly. Every move of his head made him squint in pain. He peered around the small room. It stank of pine disinfectant. There was a window on one wall, only a small one, but he might just be able to squeeze through it. He moved across.

Then another light flashed outside it. Someone was at the rear of the cabin as well. He was trapped. It was over.

SEVEN@Chapter

Fergus was under the bed when they stormed his Eezilay Motel room. His location wasn't an attempt to hide; it was simply the safest place to be if they started blasting before giving him a chance to surrender. After all, there were few who would care about the niceties of civil rights when it came to bringing down a multiple murderer.

And there *were* shots, three of them, one blasting part of the ceiling.

'For cryin' out loud, Dan, will you stop with the firin'. Kintrey! Kintrey! You here?'

Fergus didn't dare answer, convinced he had only seconds to live.

'Kintrey! We know you're here, boy. Gonna give you five seconds to show, then we torch the place!'

Torch? thought Fergus. Who the hell were these guys?

'Torch it?' echoed another man. 'You din't say nothin' about torchin' the place.'

'Shut up, Vern. Money we get for his sorry ass, you can buy yourself a dozen new cabins.'

'To say nothin' 'bout the movie rights, the TV shows, right, Pa?'

Money? Fergus couldn't concentrate. His terror, their

strange dialogue, his imminent death . . . all were playing tricks on his mind. In fact, so confused was he that he began to shout, 'OK, OK, I'm here! Don't shoot! Don't shoot! I'm coming out!'

'You'd better come out hands first, boy. I so much as smell a gun, you're gonna be taken outta here in pieces.'

Fergus began crawling out from under the bed head-first, but before he was halfway out hands grabbed him under the shoulders and dragged him clear. Then he was slammed back against the wall, two shotguns to his head, a pistol buried in his stomach.

There were three of them. One Fergus recognized as the motel's owner, the second was an older man and the third a teenager. The latter pair looked like they could be the father and son, and it was these two who held the shotguns. The older one spoke first, his face flushed, his corpulent body barely confined within blue-denim work clothes.

'Looks like we got ourselves the killer,' he wheezed.

'Sure don't look much,' said the son, also fat, but dressed for some reason in a red football uniform, shoulder-guards and all.

'They never do, boy,' said the motel owner with all the authority of a seasoned serial-killer hunter. 'But this un's worth fifty grand, and that makes him real special.'

'Fifty grand?' braved Fergus.

He winced, as the gun in his belly tried to worm its way into his duodenum.

'Sheriff you offed, her son's some rich businessman – put up a reward,' explained the motel owner in a haze of onion breath. 'Fifty big ones for whoever brings you in. And it looks like that money's already ours.'

His accomplices laughed and let out celebratory whoops.

'And he din't say nothin' 'bout you bein' dead or alive,' added the father.

More sniggering, then Pa hawked up a wad of phlegm at Fergus, but missed, instead decorating a faded painting of a covered bridge.

'Din't say nothin' about his condition at all,' sniggered the son.

'You wanna rough him up some?' said the father, as if offering to let his boy have a drive of the new lawnmower.

The motel owner sneered. 'I wanna rough him up a lot. He paid me cash and I wanna see what else he's got.'

The boy punched Fergus on the nose, so his world turned spiky and red.

'Hey, son, don't wanna leave too many marks.'

'Get him on the bed,' said the motel owner. 'You two soften him up. I'll go call that number, then we look for his cash.'

Fergus went flying on to the bed, where he was forced face-down by the boy jumping on his legs, then punching him repeatedly in the small of his back.

'Make him hurt, boy. Make the murdering mother *hurt.*'

Fergus could do nothing except oblige them, as his kidneys took a pounding.

But then he heard a fourth voice: a woman's.

'And just what the hell do you morons think you're doing?'

'Who the hell are you, lady?'

'Who the hell are *you*, beating up a suspect?'

'A suspect? He's a stone killer, lady,' growled the father.

'Oh, you were there, were you? Saw it all? Got it on video?'

'The TV said – ' started the boy.

'The TV says Mork comes from Ork and eating bran is fun, but that don't make it so. Now, if you'll – '

'Hey, lady, this guy's wanted and we – '

Since the boy had stopped punching him, Fergus looked across towards the door. There stood Kelly Stanyard, dressed in a long black raincoat over a dark trouser suit. She wore a matching beret, which pulled her hair back tight off her face. She was as tall as any of his three attackers, so she made quite an imposing figure. Her voice also betrayed no fear. She stepped further into the room, face to face with the father, whom she must have assumed was the one in charge.

'Don't you "Hey, lady" me, you fat Green Mountain goat. This man here is wanted by the FBI and now I'm taking him in.'

'But our reward . . .' bleated the son.

'Harm him one bit more and the only reward you three'll get is an assault charge.'

The motel owner remained silent – as did the boy, his face betraying his uncertainty – but the father wasn't convinced.

'Who are you, anyway?'

'Your biggest nightmare: a woman with a badge.' She reached for the medium-sized handbag hanging from her shoulder, but didn't open it. 'You hicks have got two choices:

hand the suspect over to me right now, or try and remember the number of your lawyers – if your brains can stretch to that.'

'But our fifty grand . . .' The father was near to tears, his new Mountaineer pick-up fast disappearing up the road.

'Tell you what,' said Kelly, seeming to take pity on the trio. 'Give me your names and addresses and I'll put you in my report. Being a government employee, I can't accept the reward anyway. So I don't see why you boys shouldn't get it. But I need your co-operation and I need it *now*.'

The three men looked at each other, nodding suddenly.

'OK, hold Mr Kintrey while I handcuff him, and then I'll be on my way. You, son, get to writing down your names and addresses.'

The boy eagerly complied, dollar signs flashing once again.

All this time Fergus had lain silent, almost unable to comprehend what was going on. Kelly was a buyer for a department store: in fashions. She was tall and well built, with a figure any woman her age – she admitted to thirty-four – would pay a surgeon for, and she was as accomplished in bed as any woman Fergus had ever had the pleasure to sleep with. But she was no tough guy – or girl – as far as he could recall. So he was totally unprepared for this V. I. Warshawski transformation.

He was also unprepared for how rough she became with him, pulling him up by his hair, slamming him face-first into the wall, pulling his arms up behind him and slapping his wrists painfully together, then slipping handcuffs on him. Once they were ratcheted tight, she spun him round.

'Start walking. The car's outside.'

The other three men, clearly mightily impressed by this display of control, stood back quietly as she marched Fergus out of the cabin and into the rain.

A red Ford Taurus sat alongside the Cadillac, the driver's door open, its engine still running.

'Get in,' she said, opening the passenger door, then shoving Fergus forward to tumble in and land painfully on his cuffed hands.

'You gonna be OK with him?' said the father, his shotgun cradled in his arms.

As Kelly walked around the front of the car, she pulled out and displayed a small pistol.

'Girl's got to have her protection these days. You got your details written down yet?'

The boy ran over to hand her a scruffy piece of paper covered with barely legible scrawl.

'Fine, fine. You'll be hearing from us soon. Thanks for your help. If there were only more people like you three, America would be a safer place.'

The men visibly swelled with pride.

'Hey,' said the motel owner, 'what about his car?'

'Stolen. The police'll come get it. If it's still here then – do you get my meaning?'

The three looked at each other. It took a while for the light to dawn.

'Hey, thanks, lady.'

'No problem,' she said, reversing out into the parking area, then roaring off through the puddles, towards the highway. 'Assholes.'

It wasn't until they were out of sight – and the

darkness of night had filled the distance between them and the motel – that Kelly let her guard down. 'Whoah, Jesus. I don't want to do that again.'

'That was incredible. You even got *me* believing you,' croaked Fergus.

'That was the point. No way would they let you go if I claimed you were innocent.' She glanced at the paper the boy had given her, then screwed it up and tossed it out of the window. 'As it is, they'll get caught with the stolen car.'

'Any chance of you taking off these cuffs? They hurt like hell.'

She brought the car to a halt, fished a key out of her coat pocket and, turning him away from her, undid the lock.

'Got them from a sex store,' she said as she dropped them on the back seat.

'What for?'

'Sex. What do you think? Had them a while, just never used them. They were the finishing touch, though. It convinced them.'

Fergus nodded as he rubbed his chaffed wrists.

'So why did you come?' he asked, as they set off again.

'You're in trouble – needed help.'

'Trouble is putting it mildly. You've seen all the shit on TV. So what makes you think I didn't do it?'

'Call it pillow talk.'

'Ted Bundy was a whiz with the ladies, Kelly.'

'I never suggested you were a whiz . . . Look, I figure I owe you.'

'What for? So we're friends and we sleep together. This is a high price to pay for good sex a couple of times a week.'

'Good for whom?'

She noticed his surprised expression and laughed. 'Christ, in the middle of all this shit, he worries he might not have been doing it right! Don't worry, Fergus, you're one hot loverman.'

He grinned, acknowledging her sarcasm. 'I must be: you're here. So where are we going?'

'I hadn't thought that far ahead. To be honest, I didn't expect to find you alive after I heard those gunshots back in that fleapit.'

'Neither did I. How did you find me anyway?'

'Callback. Checked the last number that called me on the mobile. Got through to that motel owner.'

'Good thinking. Look, I appreciate your rescuing me, but this isn't going to end good and I don't see why you should get dragged down with me. This is accessory after the fact: aiding and abetting a felon, whatever.'

'What happened to "I am innocent"?'

'I am! But I can't prove it. And neither can you. The only witnesses to Eloise Wesley's murder did it! And they're both FBI, and one of them's dead. The best lawyer in the world isn't going to save me now.'

'Maybe there's forensic evidence to prove they did it.'

'*I* was holding the gun when it fired! She was already shot dead, but they'll only find my bullet because they removed the previous one from her chair. And all that hostage shit, they set that up to make sure the world and his wife knew I'd done it. Parker was probably aiming to shoot me out on the street. He'd be a hero. No need for a trial then. Just their word . . .'

'So why did they shoot Sheriff Wesley?'

'No idea. But the police'll want me dead too, it's

inevitable. So even if I turn myself in, I'm dead. They'll find a way: shot while escaping, or a cell suicide. Lots of ways . . .' Fergus trailed off and stared out at the dark, wet Vermont countryside. Naturally a melancholy man, he could see no hope at all.

They drove on in silence until Kelly pulled off the road and parked up in an empty Public Rest Area, out of sight of the highway behind a swathe of elder.

'We need a strategy,' she said firmly, switching off the engine.

Fergus suddenly grabbed her to him and kissed her hard on the lips, his whole body trembling. 'Oh, God, Kelly, I'm so scared.'

'I know, baby. I know. We'll work something out . . .'

She returned his kiss and soon they were fumbling with each other's clothing . . . he pulling up her sweater and bra to uncover her large breasts, which he devoured like a hungry child . . . she struggling with the belt of his trousers. Once his buckle was undone and the zip lowered, she pulled out his erect penis and stroked its hard length vigorously, all the while holding his mouth to her nipples, urging him to suck hard.

The result was inevitable, and quick, with Fergus sinking his teeth into her breast as he erupted over her hand.

He began to apologize for coming too soon, but Kelly would have none of it – instead clasping him tight and letting him shiver.

'Poor baby, poor baby, it'll be all right. Don't worry, we'll work it out. Don't worry . . .'

It was the first time Kelly had ever been tender in their lovemaking. They usually shared a vigorous physical workout followed by a satisfied silence, and then an excuse from one or the other to slip out of the bed. But here, now, they were like young lovers lost in a world of their own making, the quality of the lovemaking secondary to the simple fact that they were alone with each other, open and honest.

By the time they dressed again, the car windows had steamed up, masking the darkness beyond.

'So what now?' said Fergus.

'We rest up. I reckon those assholes at the motel will cut their losses and try and sell the Caddy. If they're caught, which is highly likely, they'll spill the beans about you being in that motel. Eventually the police'll check for prints and confirm it. And then they'll have a description of me. So . . .'

She popped the trunk and stepped out into the cold evening. It had stopped raining but the air was chilly and damp.

'Come on,' she said. 'Working in a department store does have its advantages.'

When Fergus saw what was in the trunk, he hugged her close all over again, raining kisses on her face.

EIGHT@Chapter

Dr Ralston's quarters also doubled as her office. She had tempered the prevailing greyness with prints or photographs cut out of old magazines. They showed men on horseback, tigers and lions, racing cars in action – all of them scenes Harry had only ever seen in movies or books. Her space was split into two: a smaller, inner area containing a bed and a shower was screened off from the adjacent, larger office area by a grey curtain on which were pinned notes and memos.

'I like to work long hours here,' Dr Ralston explained as she gestured around. 'They'll even bring my food in on request.'

'You must be important.'

Another of Down Town's cardinal rules was that *everyone* went to the Canteen to eat, even those of higher rank. But not Dr Ralston, it seemed – one explanation as to why Harry had never seen her before. She motioned him to take the canvas chair in front of her desk. Despite her other privileges, all her furniture was of standard-issue grey metal.

'Harry, you and I have a lot of work to do. And I don't think I have to emphasize the consequences if you fail Commander Ulrich again.' She sat on the edge of her desk, her white coat open to reveal a yellow dress that reached to just above her knees.

Daringly short, thought Harry, a consideration based on knowledge of the rules rather than any interest in the woman's knees. Dr Ralston saw his glance; she crossed her legs and ran a hand down one of them to the ankle.

'Like them?' she asked.

'They're legs.'

She gave him an odd smile, and he sensed she was pleased, but why?

'Right, Harry. I'm not going to bore you with a sermon about your disobedience – or your previous record of flouting the rules.'

Harry fretted with the Kit-Kat wrapper in his pocket and his leg began tapping. Then, suddenly, he shot up and blurted out his discovery.

'I found *this* three days ago! I didn't hand it in! Sorry.' He passed the wrapper to her, and sat down again.

Dr Ralston looked it over, her face expressionless.

'I know it's some sort of test, and I've failed at it, but please don't tell Commander Ulrich, please,' pleaded Harry.

'A test?' said Dr Ralston, puzzled.

Harry explained how he assumed this must be a test of his observational powers – or even his loyalty.

Dr Ralston nodded slowly. 'And you're quite right . . . I argued with them that putting this year's date was silly; anyone would spot that. After all, there's been no chocolate for over three years now.'

She laid the wrapper to one side, then sat down properly behind the desk. 'Harry, they're planning another flight in about an hour. Are you ready for it?'

So soon? 'Yes!' he said with genuine enthusiasm.

'Good. Well, just remember to do only what you're told – and nothing more. And don't worry about this test.' She scrunched up the Kit-Kat wrapper and dropped it into her empty metal wastepaper bin. 'You passed with flying colours.'

Dr Ralston led him out of her office and down a long drab corridor, past the Infirmary and into the Control Room that overlooked the Hangar.

Harry was happy to be flying again and that he had passed Dr Ralston's observation test. Clearly he was back in their good books.

The Hangar was barely larger than the Hubcap itself. The craft was positioned on a ramp that rose at a forty-five-degree angle for one hundred yards as far as the outer doors. These doors were flanked by giant fans which could be brought up to maximum revolutions in order to exclude the outside atmosphere. Then the outer doors would be opened and the ramp would be shifted fifty yards out into the world beyond. Harry could then take off and land without the worry of grazing the entrance to the Hangar. In the early days it had become quickly apparent that, although his mastery of the controls was good, the aircraft itself wasn't as responsive as they had expected at slow speeds. Like some big, lumbering dog, it would obey commands dutifully, but stopping or turning could prove a little clumsy.

Commander Ulrich was sitting in the crowded control booth and he waved down at Harry through the window. Then his voice came over the loudspeaker.

'Hello, Harry. Good to see you. This is a routine flight again. Only going through the motions. There have been some modifications since you last flew. Response rate should be up twenty per cent, but you'll need to be careful all the same.'

'Okey-dokey,' shouted Harry, and donned the large black flying helmet with FLYBOY stamped across the front. He was glad to be back at work and happy to be the centre of attention again.

In the Control Room were half a dozen other men in uniform, and on the Hangar floor a similar number of flight engineers and maintenance crew. Constantly changing shift patterns meant Harry hardly recognized any of them, but he greeted them none the less. Few responded, however, and Harry decided to ignore the miserable so-and-sos. As for the craft, it looked the same as ever. *Beautiful!*

The Hubcap's official title was 2H-SAV, which stood for Hybrid High Speed Air Vehicle. However, in 1959 some bright spark noticed its striking resemblance to the hubcap of that year's Cadillac Eldorado Biarritz. Since then the nickname had stuck. (The likeness was so startling, in fact, that the General Motors designer was put under brief investigation by the FBI to find out how his design for part of a luxury car could look so startlingly like a captured UFO.)

The craft was totally black and completely circular, thirty feet across, twelve feet deep. Its base was more or less flat; its upper side featured a central raised section where the pilot sat, with fifteen fins running down to the rim. When the pilot was seated, he could see clearly through the gap between any pair of fins, although from the outside it was impossible to tell there was a viewing section. Power was supplied by a central thrust from the base, but it was provided by a source the scientists had failed to discover, even after all these years. Forward momentum and all-direction manoeuvring were provided by a series of vector jets ranged round the rim, each with its own power source. These were used to turn and angle the craft, but also to automatically ensure the pilot was always facing forward when the ship was in motion. The base-drive unit always remained in position, only the top of the ship revolving – much as a tank turret spins independently of its chassis. The top speed was in excess of five thousand miles an hour, its potential rate of ascent two thousand feet per second, the resulting forces impossible for a man to survive. And this, of course, was where Harry came in.

The sealed drive unit was seemingly possessed of limitless power, and apparently invulnerable to intrusion, like an impenetrable egg. Its power had something to do with gravity, its energy producing an effect rather than a reaction – like a helicopter hovering without rotors, or a jet accelerating without fuel or turbines. Numerous crashes during the test flights had done little damage to the ship itself – although crewmen had died – and it remained a thoroughly enigmatic form of transport.

Even attaching clamps to secure the ramp struts had taken four years of trial and error, as its hull steadfastly refused to accept welding. Only the development of super-polymer resins finally provided a solution.

Dr Ralston accompanied Harry to the steps up to the cockpit. She adjusted his throat microphone, then spoke to him like a mother would.

'Just remember the rules, Harry, and everything will be all OK.'

'I always remember the rules, Dr Ralston, otherwise I wouldn't know when I was breaking them.'

She frowned at him.

'That was a joke,' he said.

'Jokes are supposed to be funny, Harry. That's why they're called jokes.'

Harry shut up. He, at least, had thought it funny and, given his growing misgivings about the flight programme, he thought he was putting on a good show. He climbed up into the black cockpit with its two seats, one behind the other, settled into the front one and began tightening his three separate seat belts.

The feet-operated pedals were connected to the base of the seat and there were control columns on either arm. In front of him was a control panel showing very little to distinguish it from the smooth matt-black surfaces that completely surrounded him. He could call up all the information he needed either on the panel itself or in a head-up display on the 'windshield' in front of him. Speed, acceleration, G-forces, descent and ascent rates, direction, trim and so forth, the alien read-outs were now understood and judged by the intensity of their lights rather than by using figures or needles or dials. There were, however, two additions to the panel, both glued on. One showed the temperature read-out for the hull, exterior and interior, and the other was a radiation gauge. The only other unusual feature was the 'windshield' or vision screen itself. Measuring five feet wide by four feet deep, it gave a superb view forward over the rim of the ship. It wasn't made of glass, of course, but was a screen that translated the outside view through a photosensitive variant of the same material that made up the rest of the ship. For want of a better description, it was transparent metal and was the other major feature that had yet to be fully understood.

Progress in analysing both the drive and the vision screen had virtually stalled when it became apparent that in order to study their workings properly they would almost certainly get damaged beyond repair. As Mrs Rogerson had succinctly explained to Harry, 'The operation might be a success, but the patient would die in the process.' In other words, the 2H-SAV would end up about as useful as a real hubcap – pretty to look at, but of no practical value.

'Obey your instructions, Harry,' repeated Dr Ralston.

Harry had tightened his helmet, so further conversation with her was impossible. He was now in direct communication with the flight controller standing next to Commander Ulrich.

'OK, Harry, we'll keep it simple. Once you leave the ramp, follow Flight Plan B. I repeat, Flight Plan B.'

The figure of eight with the central spike, thought Harry. It would test the craft more than it did Harry, but that was the point.

'Hey, Commander Ulrich, I was reading that in the Fifties and Sixties one in four US test pilots got killed,' piped up Harry, as the hatch closed beneath him.

'Yeah, Harry – and most of them while they were actually flying.'

Harry stared at the Commander's face through the vision screen. The man's face finally broke into a smile and Harry laughed along with him. He liked Commander Ulrich and was glad that they were friends again.

'Just do your best, Harry, and everything'll be fine.'

'Okey-dokey, sir.'

The underside hatch was sealed, the control panels came on line and the craft turned and began its tedious trundle up the slope to the Hangar doors, the roar of the huge fans audible even through the hull and his helmet's earphones. He used the four minutes this took to run over his controls, confirming their functionality with the control room. At the Hangar doors, he waited as they were opened and the night sky became visible through his screen. Again he felt the slight vibration as the ramp heaved itself out into the open. Once in position, Control gave him permission to take off and Harry felt the rush of acceleration set his whole being tingling. *It was good to be back.*

Beneath him, the desert stretched away into the darkness. Harry didn't know its true colours because he had never seen it in daylight, and his vision screen, with its night enhancement, rendered his view monochrome anyway. The Hubcap's flights always took him to different sections of the same wide basin surrounded by mountains on all sides. It was nine miles wide, twenty-six miles long and provided an effective if monotonous test area. The desert floor looked inhospitable, its rough surface dotted only with whatever scrub could establish a foothold in such a raw environment. There were no animals out there and Harry had never experienced any rain on his flights. To one end of the valley a dry saltpan offered a flat expanse that in the moonlight looked like a body of smooth water. At the other end were a couple of dry river beds, which joined to produce a substantial gorge.

And on all sides there were the mountains, some rising

as high as seven thousand feet, their sides steep and weather-worn, their bases skirted by scree slopes looking like chippings from a giant sculpture. Blocking out the surrounding desert, they stood like guards around a parade ground: a dead and hostile environment that might as well have been another planet.

Occasionally Harry caught glimpses of abandoned buildings and runways out to the north of the basin. They looked remarkably well preserved for facilities that hadn't been used for so long but, as Commander Ulrich explained, the dry, hot climate was non-erosive – metal wouldn't rust, wood wouldn't rot, stone would remain unscarred – so these buildings could stand untouched for centuries. Today's projected test, however, kept Harry away from the northern end and he concentrated now on his instrumentation.

Fifty-five minutes later, Harry had completed his instructions – no more, no less – and, as usual, had seen no other air traffic, nor detected any movement on the ground. But why should he? During the day the temperatures rose to 130°F, and plummeted to −40°F at night – to say nothing of radiation levels that his monitor warned him were still relatively high, peaking in unexpected pockets. To set foot down there would be like entering a minefield, except the hidden peril wouldn't blow up in your face but would eat up your stomach or lungs some fateful day in the future. Besides, down below there was nowhere to go, nothing to see and nobody to encounter anyway.

Finally, Harry sighted the buried green lights that indicated his landing zone (even when airborne, Down Town was invisible from all directions until the Hangar's landing lights were illuminated). He brought the craft in low and slow, parking it with remarkable precision directly facing the Hangar doors. Then, while waiting for the fans to come up to speed and the doors to slide open, he made his report to Commander Ulrich.

'Everything ran smoothly, sir. Bit of lateral displacement coming out of one of the drops, but that might have been due to wind sheer.'

'Anything else?'

'The speed adjuster's much smoother. Have you been playing with that?'

The Commander laughed. 'Yes, we've eliminated one of the linkages so you'll get a better feel for the response.'

Harry heard the ramp click into position. 'Bring me in,' he instructed.

The ramp began moving, then juddered to a stop, humming loudly. 'Something's up,' said Harry anxiously.

'One of the supports isn't properly in place.'

There was another sudden lurch and Harry, who had already unbuckled his seat belts, found himself flung against the control panel. Shocked and winded, he let out a cry.

'Harry?' said Dr Ralston. 'What happened?'

'Got jerked . . . in my seat. I'm OK now.'

But he wasn't OK. Physically, he was fine, yes – it would take a lot more damage to disable him – but in hitting the control panel – impossible when strapped in as ordered – he had banged into his own radiation read-out. The craft's basic design hadn't changed over the years, but the radiation counter had been the first and most vital addition. Linked to external monitors, its readings ran from *green* lights for safe to *red* lights for danger. If these lights ever showed red for more than ten seconds, Harry was to immediately reverse the craft along its flight path until the green showed again, then hold that position, facing the Hangar, and await further instructions.

Three times that had happened, and three times Harry had dutifully obeyed his orders – terrified of the consequences of radiation poisoning – and each time, thankfully, he and the Hubcap had both checked out OK. But now the read-out box had been sheered from its mounting and was hanging by a single wire. *Oh, blow.*

A mechanic wearing a yellow radiation suit ran out, armed, to Harry's surprise, with a large hammer. After some banging that rang metallically through the ship, the mechanic stood in view of Harry and gave him a thumbs-up. Then he ran back to Decontamination, struggling against the blast from the giant fans.

The Hubcap started moving forward again, this time without any hindrance. However, this allowed Harry less time to deal with his problem. Given the current need for him to exhibit exemplary behaviour, the simple act of detaching his seat belts prematurely constituted a serious breach of discipline.

Risking further wrath by not strapping in again for the jerky descent along the ramp, he leaned over and examined the damaged radiation counter. If he could only get it back in place, he could then plead ignorance until it failed to work during the next pre-flight test.

He took hold of the black box, which was little bigger than his hand, and tried shoving it back into its bracket, but it wouldn't fit properly. He leaned over further, his head touching the vision screen, and tried to pull it through the other way, but this proved equally useless. So he sat back down again, his nerves fraying, his leg tapping loudly in the silence of the cockpit. The rigours of test-flying were nothing to what Commander Ulrich would do to him if he'd let them down again. Perhaps if he extracted the unit completely and tried to adjust its bracket instead? He took hold of the box, its lights still showing green, and pulled hard. It came away almost immediately and he sat back with a jerk. *Oh, blow!*

The wiring had come free, so the unit was disconnected from its sensors. There was no way he could hide this from them. Then he noticed something curious: the lights were still registering fully. He had detached the box from its power source and the wires that connected it to the ship's external sensors, yet it was still giving him a clear reading. Now, how could it do that?

The Hubcap was already halfway down the ramp inside the Hangar and the outer doors had closed behind it, the fans whirring to a halt. Soon the Control Room would be in sight. He laid the box on the floor and studied its mounting. It had buckled slightly at the top and it was just a small task to pull it straight again. He slotted the box back into its bracket, punching it with his fist to force it into position. He had got back in his seat and strapped himself in just as Commander Ulrich came into view. He was standing beside a smiling Dr Ralston.

Harry waited for a mechanic to unstrap him again, then, with a quick glance at the counter, still showing green, he climbed out of the cockpit and headed for debriefing.

Later, back in his quarters, Harry lay on his bunk and considered the anomaly of the radiation counter. What was the point of it registering green for *safe* when it wasn't even connected to its sensors? More to the point, how would it show red for *danger*? Taken in isolation, it would just have been an odd fact, soon forgotten. However, it wasn't the only irregularity Harry had noticed lately. He was beginning to have serious doubts.

NINE@Chapter

The blonde woman was sweet-talking the owner of Ma Casey's Grocery Store, while her dark-haired, mustachioed male friend hovered suspiciously by the cereals. The man was trying his best not to appear nervous, but his eyes kept darting from the Cheerio boxes to the checkout desk to the window that fronted on to the street.

Provisions purchased, the blonde woman signalled to him and he followed her out, his eyes carefully avoiding those of the jolly woman at the checkout.

'Have a nice day, sir,' she said cheerfully nevertheless, and, as was the way in Vermont, she meant it.

They exited into bright sunshine, the woman walking casually towards their Taurus parked on the main street of a small town. The day was warm, traffic sparse, the surrounding countryside ravishing as the forested mountains began changing into their autumn overcoats, the many shades of green now flecked with browns and golds as if God had become a fan of Jackson Pollock.

But the glorious panoramas evident around them meant nothing to the man, who kept bumping into his companion in his anxiety to get to the safety of the car. Finally she stopped and whirled round on him outside an antiques store.

'Will you stop it? You're acting like a damn criminal. No one knows who we are, no one knows we're here, so stay calm, will you?'

'Easy for you to say,' complained Fergus, resisting the urge to adjust his wig.

'Just shut up! I've got you this far, haven't I?'

Far? They were still in the tiny state of Vermont, half an hour from the Massachusetts border. They had been together for less than a day, having slept fitfully in the car overnight, then driven on until Kelly pulled up at a motel just outside Arlington. They could have hitchhiked faster.

They got into the Taurus without further discussion and drove the two miles back to their motel.

The night before, Kelly had explained that she'd rented the car by using a colleague's ID. The woman, who was on vacation in Europe for three weeks and had left Kelly with a key to her house so she could go in and feed her fish, hadn't taken her driving licence with her. The car was thus untraceable to either of them, so they had a relatively safe mode of transport. Kelly had also persuaded Fergus that the more travelling about they did, the greater the risk of being spotted. Besides, what good was running away? Fergus needed to know why he had been landed in this mess and the only clue was that mysterious list of names.

The transformation in their appearances had also begun the night before, once Kelly had revealed the contents of the car trunk. She had appropriated several wigs, assorted make-up and items of clothing from Lecky's, the store where she worked in Farrar. She had forced Fergus to let her cut his hair short, then tailored a dark-brown wig to fit him, fixing it on with adhesive. She had also glued a moustache to his upper lip, and, to complete the ensemble, had used eyeliner to darken his normally red eyebrows. His wardrobe ended up with red jeans, a white shirt and a brown bomber jacket. Studying himself in the rear-view mirror, it was a startling change, true enough: now he looked like a villain from an episode of *Charlie's Angels*. Kelly pointed out that he also looked like a cheapskate tourist stretching his vacation bucks by staying in cheap motels.

Kelly had refrained from cutting her own chestnut hair, but had donned a medium-length blonde wig and changed into an unflattering trouser suit of dark green with a yellow-patterned blouse.

Fergus stared at the two of them. They did indeed look like geeky tourists. It wouldn't fool anyone who knew them, but, as Fergus had reflected bitterly, most people who knew him well were dead.

The Wayward Inn in Arlington was a tired-looking ten-room rustic motel just off the main highway, and run by an elderly couple. Ensconced in their new hide-out – complete with the small kitchen Kelly had been insistent on – Fergus had switched on the TV to catch the news.

One fortunate aspect of Fergus's lonely existence was that there were no decent photographs of him. (His wife had destroyed all she had, he possessed none himself, his family were dead and all the police could find were some blurred snaps taken at a college barbecue three years ago and his six-year-old driver's-licence photograph.) This meant that New England was being terrorized by an artist's impression of Side Show Bob in a downpour. The first time Fergus saw the sketch he laughed out loud, but then paranoia set in again, not least when the reward being offered by Eloise Wesley's son was upped to a hundred thousand dollars. From that moment on he found himself in a state of constant panic, and all decisions or interactions with other people became Kelly's province. He had to admit she did have a way with people.

'You try buying fashion for Lecky's in New York,' was her explanation. 'It's a war. Gotta go in high and fast. Your job depends on it.'

'I've never had that problem,' said Fergus.

It wasn't that he was a coward; it was just that he valued his own even temper, and getting into hassles with people about double-parking or queue-jumping at the post office wasn't worth the risk. He knew he was capable of rage, but it was usually brought on by alcohol, by which time it had developed a life of its own. Kelly also had rage, it was clear, but she had learned to adapt it; to focus it on problems and use it for her benefit. Unfortunately, it was as they returned to the Wayward Inn that Fergus found himself the object of that focus.

'That's the last time you do that to me, Fergus!' she growled. 'I'm doing my best for you, but I may as well loop a collar round your neck and drag you about like a reluctant poodle!'

'Well, tough. Out there people are waiting to shoot me. You get out, fine – but leave me here.'

'So you can hide?'

'Sounds like a pretty good idea to me.'

'Well, if you *are* going to hide away, use your time to remember what was on that damn list.'

'I've told you,' he said, slumping against the kitchen

counter. 'I need a key: the heading. If I knew what was at the top of the page, I'd be able to visualize it. But as it was just a meaningless list, I'd no reason to take it in!'

Kelly lay back on her bed and punched the headboard with her fist. 'We need a lawyer, that's what we need.'

'He'd earn more turning me in! Christ, even a mob lawyer wouldn't help me.'

'I'm trying to help you.'

'Why?'

'Because . . .'

Fergus began pacing the room, rubbing his head, his scalp feeling prickly. 'Because what? We're not exactly bosom buddies, are we? You know more about me than I do about you – and most of that's shitty. We talk some, we sleep together.' He nodded at the TV set: a *Happy Days* episode with the sound turned down. 'We're not exactly Mr and Mrs Cunningham.'

'Suits you. Suits me.'

'I know it suits me. I'm just wondering why it suits *you*.' Fergus was now sitting on the edge of the bed and stroking her leg.

'I like you, but I don't want any commitment,' she said.

'There's a long way from enjoying a lay to risking your life for someone. I'm just not worth it.'

'You're whining again,' Kelly warned.

'Haven't I good reason?'

'If you'd remember that list, then you'd have a chance. Otherwise, you might just as well go whine to the police!'

Annoyed, he picked up a white paper bag from the

grocery store and held it up in front of his face. 'White surface. I picture the keyword at the top. And then it all falls into place for me to read.'

'But you need the keyword?'

'Yes! I've told you a hundred times – '

She slapped him hard. Her face was white, her eyes angry. 'I like you, Fergus. That was why I came. Like you enough to believe you're innocent. But now I'm starting not to like you.'

'Tough.'

She slapped him again. His face stung and he put his hand up to touch it. But she grabbed his hand away and slapped him again, and again . . . until he retreated off the bed and stumbled to the floor, staring up at the harridan glaring down at him, her fists balled, her face ugly.

'You fucking wimp!' she snarled finally, then stalked off to the bathroom.

Great, thought Fergus. *I'm on the lam with Lizzie Borden.* He pulled himself up, making sure both beds were now between himself and Kelly before he massaged his reddened face.

She came out of the bathroom and threw a wet cloth at him. 'Sorry. I just can't stand a guy who whines.'

'You sure you don't get dressed up in leather on your product-buying trips? Christ, some guys'd *pay* you to take dresses off their hands!'

Kelly's temper had mended quickly and she offered him a laugh. 'One last try with the sheet, then we forget it and figure out another strategy.'

Fergus knew better than to point out that there wasn't

another strategy; instead he sat back on the bed. Resting the paper bag on his upraised thighs, he concentrated on the rectangle until all he could see was white. Kelly leaned down to him and whispered in his ear.

'What?' he said, as if in a trance.

She repeated what she had said and suddenly the list appeared: word perfect. From Peter Anzanoy in Wardle, Michigan, through Stevie Favro, Akron; Buzz MacQueen, Philadelphia; Brick Sawney in San Diego; to Hy Zildjyan of Rapid City, South Dakota. As clear as any print-out, he could run his eyes up and down the list. A couple of hundred names, complete with addresses.

'I can see it. I can see it!'

He ran his eye up to the heading, FAIL:SAFE.

'How did you do that?' he gasped.

'Do what? All I said was you have to remember that list for Cathy Farrelly and Eloise Wesley's sake.'

'No, that wasn't it.' He couldn't remember her exact words. 'I needed the keyword.'

'So what's the heading?'

'Failsafe.'

'Well, I certainly wouldn't have said *that* out of the blue. Maybe you just don't know your talent as well as you thought. I'll get a pen and you dictate – '

'No. This doesn't get written down; that way *you're* not involved.'

'But I am, Fergus. We're in this together.'

Mention of Cathy and Eloise conjured an image of Kelly herself being shot dead. Whatever else was going to happen, he would not be responsible for Kelly's death too. 'No! It stays where it is – in my head.'

Kelly took her time, then said, 'So what do you suggest we do about it now?'

Fergus scanned the list in his mind again. 'They're the names of men and women all over the country. No other clues. I suppose we could always talk to one of them, see if *they* know what this is about.'

'OK, give me a name and an address. I'll call enquiries, get a number.'

'No. What would you say? Better to speak to them face to face.'

Again, Kelly took her time agreeing. 'So we go visit some. Any of them live near here? Vermont, Massachusetts, New York?'

He read through the addresses. 'There are four in Vermont.'

Kelly went out to the car and returned with a roadmap of the state. 'Compliments of the hire company. OK, give me some places.'

'Carritown, Trevor, Manchester Top and Halston.'

'OK, we're only ten miles from the Manchesters. Halston's thirty beyond that, Carritown another hundred and Trevor . . . well, trip over in that place and you're in Canada.'

'So we go calling.'

Kelly checked her watch. 'It's only 2.00 p.m. now. No point wasting any time.'

Fergus had to agree with her, however reluctant he was to show his face to the outside world. Had he known what lay ahead, however, he would gladly have dialled 911 right then and taken his chances with the courts.

TEN@Chapter

The rain held off as Kelly drove, the afternoon pleasantly warm. Passing through Manchester, with its old-fashioned charm and refined air of a college town, they arrived mid-afternoon in Manchester Center, with its discount stores and clothing marts. After making enquiries at a 76 station, they were given directions to nearby Manchester Top and so to Bitter Lane, the address of Everald Nolting.

Bitter Lane was approached over one of New England's unique architectural features, a covered bridge. As their car clacked over its short, enclosed length, it seemed as if they were passing through a time tunnel, for once they exited the bridge they were away from the busy highway and into a rural wilderness awash with the flaming lustres of fall. Then, as if to reinforce this feeling, they found that Bitter Lane's blacktop soon petered out into a single rutted track, with the occasional house springing up unannounced amid the trees on either side of the gently winding road. Nolting lived at No. 10, and a study of the postboxes clinging to both sides of the road showed that that would be, literally, the tenth house they encountered.

Sure enough, it came into sight a mile further on – as did the end of the track itself, for any further progress was impeded by a dense swathe of trees that rose in front of them like a multicoloured tsunami.

Kelly parked immediately outside the simple white clapboard farmhouse. An old pick-up truck rusted to one side, a brown dog dozing on its hood like an oversize ornament, seemingly unaware of their approach.

'Let me do the talking,' said Kelly.

Fergus agreed. He was damned if he knew what to say anyway.

They got out, Kelly slamming her door to announce their arrival. The dog looked up at them with sleepy eyes, offered a half-hearted grumble, then thought *what the hell?* and rested his head on his paws again.

'Lively neighbourhood,' said Kelly.

Fergus looked around. It was a natural cul-de-sac, with trees on three sides and, behind them, the road disappearing from sight within a couple of hundred yards. They were at the end of the world here, the only sound the chattering of birds and the breeze rushing through the trees like gentle surf across a warm beach. He thought it was completely wonderful and regretted having to pollute such peacefulness with his bloody troubles.

'I like this,' Fergus said, envious of the owner.

'You would,' said Kelly, leading the way to the open side door. 'Somewhere to hide.' She tapped on the screen door.

A stout, red-faced woman in a blue floral-print dress and sandals appeared, still stirring a bowl of cake mix.

'Lost, huh?' she said, smiling.

'Only if this isn't the Nolting residence,' said Kelly.

'Well, I'm Marjorie Nolting, so it looks like you got the right place, my dear. Come in.'

Fergus never ceased to be amazed by how welcoming people were in Vermont. If this was New York, the chances were Marjorie would by now have a gun trained on them, and the dog would have sicked on them too.

Kelly pulled open the creaking screen door and walked into a cool farmhouse kitchen furnished with worn pine. Bread was baking on a blackened range and the many shelves and open-front cupboards were overloaded with home-made pickles and preserves.

'Come a long way?' asked the woman, gesturing for them to sit at the table.

As they settled, Kelly confessed they had not.

'Thirsty?' asked Mrs Nolting. She looked to be in her sixties, but her weather-beaten face and lack of make-up could have added ten years to her appearance.

She fixed them home-made lemonade and pulled out a plate of steaming blueberry muffins from the oven. 'Prize-winners two years running up to Rutland State Fair,' she said proudly. 'Think I've improved on them already. High hopes next year. High hopes.'

The warm muffins and the iced lemonade made a spectacular combination, the sweetness of one complementing perfectly the tartness of the other.

'I suppose we'd better come to the point,' said Kelly.

This should be interesting, thought Fergus.

'My colleague and I work for a computer-programming company in Boston. We process mailing lists for major companies and – '

'You're not offering us free roofing, are you? Had a fella over here – '

'No, no, nothing like that. One of our computers went a little haywire, began throwing up lists of people with no explanation. Your husband's name was one of them. What we want to know is why?'

'I'm sure I don't know. We don't own a computer.'

'Look, it'll only take a minute,' said Kelly patiently. 'Can we talk to your husband? If we can ascertain why he should be on this list . . .'

'And you've no idea what it's for? We do get a couple of magazines mailed out.'

'It might be that.'

Kelly had obviously been paying proper attention as Fergus had described to her the FBI agent's visit to the Ryecatcher Bookstore. Maybe she really *did* believe him.

The woman got up and walked to a bright-blue box attached to the wall beside a large antique refrigerator festooned with handwritten fruit labels. She pressed a button.

'Ever, you awake?'

They heard mumbling, then a croaky voice over the hiss of static. 'Yeah, I'm here, hon.'

'Got some visitors. Want a word with you.'

There was a pause. 'Who are they?'

Kelly walked over to the intercom.

'We're from a processing house, Mr Nolting. We log data on to computers for companies. We had a glitch. Your name came up and we want to find out why.'

'You ain't selling nuthin'?'

'No, no, I assure you. We want to fix it. Don't want you to find yourself knee-deep in junk mail.'

The man coughed heavily. The woman pressed the button again so her husband couldn't hear.

'Bad chest. Catches up with him every winter. Bed-ridden most days now, poor bee. Sometimes I don't know if he'll – '

The man spoke again. 'What's this list?'

Fergus walked over and joined the women. 'It's just a lot of names and addresses, sir,' he said. 'We don't know who they are, or even why they're on the list, but until we do our system's all fouled up.'

'You contacted anyone else?'

'You're the fourth today,' said Kelly. 'The thirtieth this week. But still no clues.'

'Doubt I can help you then.' The intercom static silenced.

The woman looked embarrassed. 'I'm sorry,' she said. 'He's switched off. When he gets a mood on . . .'

'We understand,' said Kelly, patting the woman's arm. 'Any chance we could ask him one more question?'

'You can ask. Can't say you'll get an answer.' She pressed the intercom again.

'Mr Nolting,' said Kelly. 'About this list, I don't know if it would be any help, but it has a heading. Doesn't mean anything to us, but it might to you.'

Silence.

'The list's headed with the word "Failsafe".'

Still no reply and his wife shrugged again, as if to say 'I told you so'.

'Mr Nolting, did you hear me?'

No response.

'Sorry, young lady,' said Mrs Nolting, 'but it obviously doesn't mean anything. Seems you've had another wasted journey.'

'Not with these muffins,' offered Fergus.

Kelly frowned at him. 'Seems we did.'

She walked out on to the porch, Fergus following.

Mrs Nolting came to the door and offered them another muffin from the plate. Kelly declined but Fergus eagerly accepted. He hadn't eaten in a while and they were quite the best muffins he could remember tasting.

'Sorry for your wasted journey,' said Mrs Nolting.

'Not your fault, just our problem,' replied Kelly, stepping out into the sunshine and looking up at the bedroom windows. 'We get expenses.'

Fergus had a face full of muffin, so he could only nod in agreement.

'Well, bye,' said Mrs Nolting, closing the screen door and disappearing into her aromatic kitchen.

'Well?' managed Fergus as he swallowed.

'Strike one,' said Kelly, pausing at her open car door to look up at the upper-floor windows.

Fergus followed her gaze, but saw nothing untoward. 'Hell, it ain't a crime to be unsociable,' he murmured.

'Good thing too,' said Kelly, 'otherwise you'd be wanted on a few further charges.'

Just then there came a gunshot, shockingly loud in the quiet haven of the small valley.

'What the hell was that?' said Fergus, as the dog set to barking.

But Kelly was already running towards the kitchen. *The woman's mad*, he thought, then forced himself round the back of the car to follow her into the house. Keeping low, he reached the back door, in time to hear Kelly's shoes clattering up the staircase.

'Kelly!'

He pushed open the screen door and entered the kitchen. He knew he had to follow upstairs, but he sure as hell didn't want to go unarmed. Looking round for a weapon, he spotted the knife-block and pulled out the biggest-bladed knife he could find.

Then came a cry, and he recognized Kelly's voice, which galvanized him into action. He charged up the stairs and paused on the bare landing.

He could now smell gunsmoke, but no other clue as to what had happened. Cautiously, his heart racing, Fergus edged towards the first door on his right, directly above the kitchen. His heart hammered faster as he caught sight of Kelly on her knees. Mrs Nolting was collapsed against her, her whole front drenched in blood. Then he noticed the blood pumping between Kelly's fingers. Mrs Nolting's throat had been slashed.

'I can't stop it. I can't stop it!' wailed Kelly. The stricken woman jerked and looked up at Fergus, but he knew her eyes didn't see him. She was trying to speak but could only gurgle.

'What happened?' was all Fergus could manage to say, the knife hanging limp in his hand.

'Don't know,' gasped Kelly. 'But he's dead. Shot.'

Fergus leaned further into the room. Though white and airy, the room was weighed down with dark, solid, wooden furniture. The biggest item was a large four-poster bed without a canopy, in the centre of which lay a small man with sheets drawn up to his throat, his mouth an open toothless circle. Blood fanned out behind his head, like a peacock's tail across the wall. Both of his arms lay motionless on the covers, a revolver still clasped in the spindly fingers of his left hand.

'I can't stop her bleeding . . .' repeated Kelly.

Suddenly Mrs Nolting fell still and went limp. She was clearly dead, but Kelly eased the woman's head off her lap and, keeping her hand over the gash in her windpipe, tried to administer CPR, but only got a bloody face in return.

Finally Kelly sat up with a look of helplessness.

'After the shot I came running upstairs. Ran in. She was already in here, standing where you are and clutching her throat. I thought she was just shocked, but then I saw all this blood . . . Blood everywhere.'

Fergus was stunned. Kelly herself was drenched in blood – as much as on the dead woman or on the bedroom wall behind Everald Nolting. Then the obvious question occurred to him.

'Who did this to her?'

Kelly stared at him and shocked realization stole across her face. They both made for the centre of the room, their eyes fixed on the door.

'Whoever did it must still be here,' she hissed, grabbing at his arm.

'No one came down the stairs . . .' Fergus began, confirming the danger of their predicament.

'Unless . . .' Kelly dashed to the window.

Pulling aside the drapes that shifted in the cool breeze

like uncomfortable bystanders, she leaned out. '*There! There!*' she shouted.

As Fergus joined her, she pointed a bloody finger at the treeline beyond their car. 'I just saw someone running into the woods. Wearing jeans and a dark jacket. And look there, near the car . . .'

Fergus could see a knife on the ground, its scarlet blade plain in the sunlight.

She leaned further out. 'He must have escaped along the porch roof and jumped off at the far end.'

'But who?'

Kelly looked down at the backs of her hands, where Mrs Nolting's blood lay thick enough to form rivulets between the tendons.

'I don't know. And I'm not waiting here to find out.'

She headed for the door, then on an impulse reached down and touched her fingers to the dead woman's bloody lips. 'I'm sorry,' she said, then was hurrying downstairs.

As Fergus reached the kitchen, he found Kelly wiping at her hands with a dishcloth – though failing to remove much of the blood.

'Let's go,' she panted.

'What about them?'

'What about them, the poor bastards? Fergus the Mad Dog Killer comes calling and five minutes later they're both slaughtered.'

'But you know I didn't – '

'Like the *real* killer's gonna confess. We've got to run – and *now*!'

They raced pell-mell for the car, the rushing of the wind in the trees, which so recently had sounded pleasant and relaxing, now like a million accusing whispers. And amongst those same trees lurked a ruthless killer, his eyes maybe even now staring from the shadows at his next two victims.

Fifteen minutes later, they had pulled off the highway into an empty picnic area alongside Route 30. There Kelly stripped off her bloodstained clothes, washed her face and hands thoroughly in a nearby stream and dressed herself in another outfit from the trunk of the car.

'Best bury these,' she said, prodding her previous clothes.

Fergus, still too horrified to speak, began using his hands to dig into the mossy earth.

'So what now?' he began a while later, snaking the Taurus back on to the highway and heading north.

Kelly grabbed his wrist and squeezed it. 'What now is we drive nice and slow and careful and do nothing to attract any attention to ourselves.'

'Easy to say,' mumbled Fergus.

Finally succumbing to his emotions, he slewed the car to the side of the road. There, just in time, he pushed open his door and threw up the late Mrs Nolting's muffins.

ELEVEN@Chapter

Harry was sitting at a computer terminal in Education, searching out as much new information as possible about Down Town that he didn't already know. His friend, Douglas Rogerson, was the only other occupant of the small room, and he too was working one of the six IBMs that lined the long table in the centre of the book-lined room. Douglas was concentrating on his maths homework, trying to ignore Harry's rapidly tapping feet. Harry was so nervous because, unsurprisingly, he'd had little success finding anything new. His password gave him access only to Level Two, which encompassed the approved history of Down Town, the workings of the base and any relevant information needed by a pilot of the Hubcap.

So far he knew that Down Town had once been a part of Groom Lake Air Base, lying some seventy miles from Las Vegas, Nevada. The base itself had been huge – about half the size of South Carolina – and was the place where the government's most secret work had been carried out since 1937. Then, in 1985, when a state of emergency was declared, Down Town had been totally sealed off. Included among the six hundred military and civilian personnel sequestered underground was Harry's mother. She was a research biochemist, then five months pregnant. The emergency outside had suddenly become a conflict, then all-out war as President Reagan had been forced to act against Russia's simultaneous invasions of Poland, Czechoslovakia and East Germany, following a botched NATO appeasement attempt. In the ensuing nuclear exchange, much of the giant air base had been destroyed, but Down Town itself had survived, sealed off and secure in the base of Grumble Mountain.

From then on news from the outside world was virtually non-existent, but it became clear to those in charge of Down Town that the short but devastating conflict had left no real winners, just widespread desolation and dangerous pockets of radioactivity. It was then decided, by the US Department of Naval Intelligence officers in charge of the complex, that in order to ensure their survival, not only would Down Town have to be maintained at peak performance – so as to provide safe air and a continuous supply of food and water – but there would also have to be work for all. Giving six hundred frightened people something to do was undoubtedly the best way to maintain what little morale remained. And this, Harry understood, was why the Hubcap was considered so important.

Originally, Down Town had been designed as a support facility for the 2H-SAV programme, and as such had included maximum-security measures in case of attack or incursion. There were food stocks for four years, hydroponic labs capable of supplying fresh food indefinitely, sophisticated air-conditioning to provide usable air, and fresh water derived from a deep and, as yet, unpolluted artesian well. All the population of Down Town had had to do was accept their fate and get on with living as best they could.

Unsurprisingly, not a few were unable to come to terms with the reality of their new underground isolation and they killed themselves – including Harry's mother, barely a month after his birth. As a result he had been brought up an orphan and subject to special training.

Now, twelve years on, he was sitting speed-reading the eighty-page history of Down Town within a matter of minutes. It was one of several outstanding skills he had either been born with or learned as he grew up. Harry knew that he was, technically, abnormal, no doubt the result of his mother's exposure to radiation. He was short and thin for his age, but gifted mentally. His special upbringing had previously ensured that he was docile and compliant, almost emotionless, ever eager to do as ordered, not least when being trained to pilot the 2H-SAV.

Papoose Lake had been used for the initial tests of the Hubcap, but once that top-secret base had become publicly known as Area 51, even its air-exclusion zone of twenty-six miles and its land-exclusion zone of thirteen miles proved inadequate for security. As a result, Down Town had been constructed well away from the main air base, concealed in a secluded valley surrounded by mountains.

All the wild rumours and fevered speculation about Area 51 had been true, though those who had attempted to prove the fact had failed to provide satisfactory evidence – not least because the government was so adept at disseminating disinformation. What better way to confuse the gullible than to offer three versions of the same story, each of which might contain a kernel of truth but couched in such absurd terms, and with such sensational details, that the sceptic is forced to dismiss *all* of it? Twenty-five per cent of the US population might have believed in UFOs when the war broke out, but no one had ever produced the evidence that would stand up to serious scientific scrutiny.

The Hubcap, however, most certainly would.

Having finished with the history file, Harry turned to the Hubcap data, starting with all the cover-ups. Common UFO mythology had it that an alien craft crashed in New Mexico in 1947, when its remains – and its pilots – were taken to the Roswell Army Air Field, home of the 509th Bomb Group of the 8th Army Air Force, where they had been experimented on ever since as scientists sought to understand alien technology.

Harry knew that something *did* crash at Roswell, but it wasn't a flying saucer, nor was it the weather balloon that Major Jesse Marcel, the Bomb Group's Intelligence Officer had been humiliatingly forced to offer as evidence. What did crash was a USAF B-29 that had been downed by a UFO, its metal chemistry having been altered by some unknown force. The perpetrators of the crash were unknown, but in the paranoid post-war era it was thought better to encourage rumours as preposterous as aliens in flying saucers than to allow the possibility of Russian air supremacy.

A concerted programme of aerial surveillance eventually led to a confrontation over Montana in July 1949. Here an alien ship did crash, and aliens were found, albeit dead from the impact. It was another four years before any attempt was made to fly the landed saucer, and in every case the G-forces involved disabled or killed its test pilots. The ship, to all intents and purposes, remained unflyable. Worse still, its technology was also indecipherable. So the craft was mothballed at Groom Lake, waiting for human science to catch up with it.

In 1980, it finally did.

All this Harry knew, and he also knew that the Hubcap offered him the only chance of ever leaving Down Town. It was resistant to radiation, capable of high speeds and would ensure Down Town control of the skies, and thereby of anyone left alive outside.

But first it had to be mastered – and that was Harry's job.

While the Hubcap's controls were simple, it had nevertheless been designed to fly at high speeds, with rapid acceleration and startling manoeuvrability. In ordinary aircraft, high G-forces occur when an aircraft turns sharply or climbs rapidly. At 4.5G, normal pilots will start to lose their vision, as their bodies become four and a half times their normal weight. At 7G, most pilots will black out, as gravity forces the blood from the head down to the lower body, thus starving the brain of oxygen. This is called G-lock. Occasionally, aircraft will hit 9G and the pilot still stay alert long enough to survive, but at this force a 160lb man will weigh over half a ton, so such pressure cannot be sustained for more than a few seconds. Harry, however, was able to survive and function at up to 15G or 16G, and maintain completely normal reactions for sustained periods at 12G.

This ability arose from a combination of factors. First, his lack of height: the closer the head to the heart, the less distance the blood has to travel. Second, his low body weight, just 83lb. Third, the width of his arteries: the thinner the blood vessels, the less power needed to pump blood through them. And last, his physiology: his muscles, though not particularly strong, were able to function under extreme conditions for far longer than pilots pumped up by aerobic exercise. Harry was thus able to zip the Hubcap up and down and from side to side, accelerating and stopping in split seconds, while enjoying a responsiveness that was truly astonishing – a facility impossible for even the best pilots to imitate.

Harry scrolled through all the data on the ship, including his own test flights, the successes and the failures. Nothing new there. He then looked up his own personal file. Again, nothing he didn't already know. He tried to access his medical file, unsuccessfully, but that was only to be expected. So what else? Nothing at all, it seemed. He was allowed to know all he wanted about the outside world up until the moment Down Town was isolated – but after that only what Commander Ulrich permitted.

Harry was not by nature a suspicious individual; he trusted Commander Ulrich and his staff. Their continuing research on the Hubcap, even if it proceeded at a snail's pace, did make sense. It gave everyone a purpose and, since it was unlikely that they would be able to leave Down Town for decades, even this thoroughness seemed logical. Their ultimate goal being set, it was important that it wasn't reached too soon, for what would there be for them to concentrate on *then*? So Commander Ulrich's insistence that Harry's flights be kept short and limited in altitude and range was sensible. It was frustrating for him, obviously, but Harry was part of the team; his job was to obey. But now doubts kept occurring – and such doubts would spread like a cancer unless checked.

He leaned back and stretched, jumping when he noticed Dr Ralston sitting two seats along the table from him, staring in his direction.

'Homework?' she asked, smiling.

Douglas lowered his head behind his VDU, aware of what Harry had been doing.

'Sort of.'

'What were you looking at?'

'Everything. History, technicals, personal.'

'Why?'

Think of something, Harry. He was tempted to use his eyes on her, but realized she would guess then that he had something to hide. 'I . . . I wanted to know more about *me*.'

Dr Ralston nodded.

What did I just say? thought Harry.

'Good. That's perfectly natural, Harry. At your age, everyone wants to know more. And you being an orphan . . . Sorry, is that painful?'

'No,' said Harry truthfully. 'It's a fact.'

'You want to establish your identity, prove you're an adult.'

'You approve?'

She walked over and clamped her hands on both of his shoulders. Her nails were long and they dug into him. 'Of course I approve, Harry. But if you want answers, why not ask *me* the questions.' She reached over and switched off his terminal. He could smell her perfume.

'But I don't *know* the questions.'

'Again, perfectly natural. You've seen the movies, the rebellious teenagers, the exasperated parents? It's what happens. However, you are unique, Harry. Your skills are vital to the future of Down Town – so we can't afford for you to stray. I saved your ass recently because I believed it was worth saving, but *no one* is bigger than the programme. So, no more computers now. You want to know something, just ask me, OK?'

'Yes, Dr Ralston,' he said.

She offered him another smile and walked off.

Harry sensed he had been reprimanded but couldn't be sure. As soon as the doctor was out of sight, a very jumpy Douglas got up to leave, switching off his own terminal.

Harry said, 'You wouldn't lend me your password, would you?'

Douglas kept moving to the door.

'Douglas?'

'Harry, weren't you listening to what Dr Ralston said?' The boy had stopped by Harry's chair. He looked frightened.

'I know, but . . .'

Douglas kicked Harry's chair. 'You *promised* you'd follow the rules!'

'I know. It's just that things are . . . different now.'

The two boys stared at each other, neither of them understanding this recent change in Harry.

'You're going to get yourself terminated, Harry. You're becoming *dangerous.* Just don't talk to me again.' And Douglas ran out of the room.

Harry stared after him; now he had driven his best friend away.

TWELVE@Chapter

Kelly stood glaring at Fergus, hands on hips. 'We won't get through this if you give up now.'

Fergus rubbed his face in despair. 'When they find the Noltings murdered, my name will be head of the list automatically.'

'But they still need proof,' said Kelly, heading back to their car. They had pulled off US7, for a brief rest-stop.

'Oh, Christ, they have got proof!' he blurted out. He was picturing the kitchen knife he had taken up to the bedroom and all the other things he must have touched in the Noltings' house.

Kelly took the wheel and they drove back on to 7, heading now for Halston, another small town that looked perfect enough to be an off-cut from Disneyworld.

It was after five o'clock by the time they pulled up outside a house in Sandal Street. The sky had darkened and it looked like rain again. Such was the way of the region – 'Vermont don't have a climate, it has weather.'

Caryl Lowry lived in a large neo-Federalist house: square, low-roofed and free of any ornamentation except the wide porch. The rest of the street was scattered with similar generously sized residences, their driveways boasting Lincolns,

BMWs and Volvos. Brick barbecues could be glimpsed through neatly coiffured garden hedges and it was quiet, except for children laughing somewhere and an electric mower buzz-cutting a lawn. It was hard to believe that he and Kelly had so recently witnessed murder.

'I'm not sure I'm up to this,' said Fergus, tasting bile.

'You *are* up to it, but I'll do the talking. We'll use the same story.'

'As long as it doesn't have the same punch line,' Fergus muttered.

'Shut up.'

'Yes, boss.'

They walked up the path to the house, finding a child's red tricycle abandoned by the front steps. A hand-painted wooden sign hung from the low porch roof, flanked by hanging baskets of flowers. EASIGO, it read. Kelly reached the front door and pressed the bell. A pleasant chime rang inside, answered a moment later by a blonde woman holding a young child dressed in red dungarees to match her own.

'Hello – Mrs Lowry?' said Kelly.

'Yes.' Both mother and child regarded Kelly with curiosity rather than suspicion.

'We're from an accounting company in Boston. Our computer's thrown a tantrum and we're getting some data printed out that, frankly, baffles us.'

'I don't understand.' The woman, quite short and slight, shifted the child from one arm to the other.

'We have a list with your husband's name on it, but we don't know why. We were wondering if we could have a word with him, to see if he can shed some light on it.'

The woman seemed in two minds, but finally stood aside and let them enter the house.

The interior was airy and it was clear that the woman herself had chosen the decor: plenty of lace, blue and white china, fresh flowers, most of them yellow, set off by rich blue-striped wallpaper. It looked fit for a magazine spread.

'Lovely home,' said Kelly. Fergus mumbled his agreement.

'Why, thank you, Miss . . .'

'Lesky. Is your husband home?'

'He's out back fixing a puncture on his dirt bike. I'll call him. Would you like a drink?'

'No, we're OK,' Kelly said, before Fergus could speak.

The young woman left them to take a seat in the lounge. Here again, blue was the predominant colour, with white wood acting as a contrast. It wasn't so much expensive, as tasteful and well thought through. Fergus sat down in a high-back armchair, his body tired. But Kelly chose to walk around the room, until she was facing into the backyard, where she saw the woman calling to her husband.

'Oh, shit . . .' Fergus heard Kelly say. 'Get out, Fergus! Go back to the car. Wait there. I'll make something up.'

'What's wrong?'

'Lowry's a cop! And he's coming in now.'

Fergus dashed out into the hall and briefly noticed, for the first time, a framed certificate honouring Caryl Lowry as Deputy of the Year.

As he snuck out on to the porch, he heard Kelly launching into her spiel again. She had some balls, that woman. He climbed quickly into the passenger seat of the car and hunkered down, pretending to be engrossed in a map.

Several minutes passed, then the rain arrived. Fergus began fretting over whether Kelly had been rumbled and the deputy had called his colleagues. Deputy of the Year or not, he would be foolish to attempt arresting Mad Dog Kintrey without back-up. After a couple more minutes of mounting paranoia, watching the house through the heavy raindrops lacing the car window, Fergus decided she needed his help, whatever the risk to himself.

He had actually stepped out of the car, with no idea how to tackle an armed cop, when Kelly finally appeared at the door.

'Thanks. No, no, I'll be fine,' he heard her say, over the rain hammering on the porch roof. 'Sorry to have bothered you.'

Kelly shut the front door and hurried down the path.

'Well?' said Fergus, eyeing the house over her shoulder.

'Nothing, really. Nice couple, cute kid, but he clearly didn't know anything about it.'

'You mentioned "Failsafe"?'

Kelly gave him a hard look and ducked into the car. 'So what now?' he asked, as she drove them away.

'Too late to get to Carritown. Best rest up now and call there first thing in the morning.'

That was fine by Fergus. All he wanted was sleep. At least in his dreams he could feel safe – unless it turned into one of his nightmares.

He had been plagued by bad dreams most of his adult life and understood that tension often sowed the seeds of those bad nights – and if today didn't qualify as stressful . . .

The dreams always revolved around blood, but since the murder of Dale Cresdee they had taken on a new and repetitive twist.

He would find himself on his own in the Ryecatcher Bookstore at night, looking through books on a shelf, irresistibly drawn to taking down volume after volume, only to find their pages dripping with blood, which was steadily accumulating at his feet. Yet he was unable to stop opening book after book after book . . . He would always awaken sweating and shaking – and after their experiences at the Noltings' house, he was virtually guaranteed a further recurrence tonight.

Half an hour later, Kelly was registering them into a small hotel outside the town of Danby. Comprising several bland brick blocks huddled around a parking area forlornly patterned with puddles and shadbush, the Tabor Tempo Inn did not look inviting. However, it did provide the anonymity they needed. Their room was painted dark green with gloomy lighting, but neither had the inclination to complain. As Kelly took a shower, Fergus checked out the mini-bar: it contained just six miniature bottles of spirits and a couple of cans of Pepsi, but was very tempting none the less. He was wondering about sneaking a couple of vodkas before Kelly returned when he felt a sudden thwack on the back of his head and a bar of soap bounced off the wall.

He turned to see Kelly standing naked and dripping wet. 'Touch one drop, Fergus, and I walk out. You need a clear head now, so act your damn age.' She glared at him for a moment, then returned to the bathroom.

He reluctantly closed the fridge door. Running over the events of that terrible day, another thought suddenly occurred to him: why had the mystery killer chosen that precise moment to murder the Noltings, unless to frame Kelly and himself deliberately? And, if that was the case, he must have followed them there.

Kelly emerged from the bathroom wrapped in a bath sheet. She found Fergus kneeling by the window, peeking out through a crack in the blinds as if looking for someone. On explaining why, he immediately condemned them both to a night spent wide awake, with the television off, jumping at every sound.

THIRTEEN@Chapter

Harry Sixsmith was fifteen minutes into his next test flight when on impulse he deviated from his flight path and, rising to five thousand feet, began flying steadily south. It was night-time, as always, and the Hubcap was invisible, black against the black night sky. The vast emptiness beneath was visible only as a monotonous grey, its minimal detail enhanced by the vision screen.

He had spent the previous day pondering on the cracks that had begun to appear in his concept of the world called Down Town. Worse than his deepening suspicions was the fact that he had no one he could talk to.

Douglas was avoiding him completely and self-preservation prevented him from approaching Commander Ulrich. For if anything strange *was* happening, Ulrich was sure to be privy to it. Nor did Harry trust Dr Ralston sufficiently yet. No, he *had* to find out for himself, and what he was doing now appeared to be the only course of action – while ensuring that he wasn't terminated for his initiative. It was a couple of minutes before he spotted what he had been looking for and by then he was able to ignore the hysterical yellings in his helmet from the Control Room. But his elation at seeing moving lights came with the realization that this might also be the last he ever saw of the outside world.

He could see seven narrow white beams travelling from left to right. They then seemed to stop, a couple now pointing his way. What could they be? Nothing had lived out here for thirteen years.

'Sixsmith, return to base at once!' screamed Ulrich. 'Abort your flight plan! Return to Hangar, stat!'

'But I can see some . . .' And it was at that same moment that Harry understood something was *really* wrong.

When he had mentioned anomalies previously to Commander Ulrich, they had been brushed aside, the Commander insisting that Harry was mistaken or that they didn't matter. But without investigating, how was anyone to judge their significance? Perhaps others had survived outside and adapted to the new environment. Could there actually be people living away from Down Town?

'The lights have stopped. I'm going to check,' said Harry doggedly.

'No, Harry! Return at once, or else,' yelled Dr Ralston.

Or else what? Harry thought. What was that phrase Mrs Rogerson sometimes used? 'In for a penny, in for a pound'? He had been given his final warning, and had already done enough tonight to justify instant termination, so what did he have to lose? Harry switched the radio off and concentrated on the mystery lights ahead.

He dropped to three thousand feet and approached cautiously, his speed little over fifty miles per hour. He had no way of judging their distance because he didn't know how big these lights were, nor had he ever ventured this far east. The Hubcap did not possess radar, the sheer sophistication of its drive and its controls being strangely at odds with its reliance on radio and visual markers. That meant he was now flying blind, since he couldn't see either the Hangar or its lights, or hear his controllers. This was exciting.

But his bravado quickly turned to trepidation as he approached the now stationary lights. They were strung along a dark ribbon of highway. He realized they must be automobiles, but how could they function in such adverse conditions? The temperature outside read at −9°F and the radiation level was . . .

But he already knew the radiation level was a lie, so why should the temperature gauge be any more reliable? In fact, why should he rely on anything except his own ability to fly this craft? Deciding to play safe, he zipped his ship up to four thousand feet, then tilted the craft to look directly down.

He could see the vehicles more clearly now and slowly eased the craft down until he could make out more details. There were seven of them, four cars and three pick-up trucks – as he recognized from the videos he had seen. They were parked up against a fence, along the edge of a two-lane highway. And there were people too.

Harry felt his feet starting to drum uncontrollably as he lowered the craft to five hundred feet. Yes, they *were* people, and none of them was wearing a protective suit. Just ordinary jeans and sweaters. There were even some smaller figures: children? And then they spotted him.

Heads lifted to look at him; flashlights lanced upwards. The Hubcap was hovering too high for their beams to reach, but they were ensuring his presence was recorded, with camera flashbulbs exploding.

He whipped the craft back half a mile and soared up to seven thousand feet, the momentary 10G pressure barely registering on him. Relieved that his audience had lost sight of him, he circled to approach them from the rear, silently gliding down to one thousand feet, and observed them for a while once again.

Then there was another commotion as the flashlights whipped round. He zoomed back up to six thousand feet in three seconds, then scorched five miles west until their headlights became an indistinct white speck on the horizon.

This was fun, but it was also scary. Not because he believed these people were radioactive mutants, but because clearly Commander Ulrich and his team had lied to him. Just how much else of Down Town was a lie?

Harry scanned the horizon. There were more lights, moving rapidly – and in the sky. Blow it, A-Wing!

A-Wing comprised two fighter planes – Harrier AV-8As – which were used in emergencies to locate the Hubcap if it became disabled or landed short. They had to be hauled out of the Hangar by tractors, but their vertical take-off and landing capabilities were admirably suited to operating without an airstrip. They were also armed with machine-guns and Sidewinder missiles.

Harry anxiously watched them circle, then wheel round to face him, waiting to see what they would do next. They approached suddenly at high speed, only rolling to either side at the last moment, passing him at more than five hundred miles an hour. As their jet wake buffeted his craft, Harry revolved to wait for them to loop upwards and commence a return run. Just as they reached him, he plummeted to a mere hundred feet off the desert floor.

The two Harriers circled above him, high and wide, their exhausts flaring across the night sky. Then, lining up side by side, they flew straight down towards him. This time, however, their approach was signalled by the rapid flashing of machines-guns from under their wings.

Harry shot the Hubcap up to ten thousand feet – hitting 14G and losing sight of his attackers, as they would of him. He revolved until he could get a bearing on the automobile lights, then zoomed silently down towards them.

He was suddenly privy to an insight that made him smile. If Commander Ulrich had been keeping the real world away from Harry, then he must also have been keeping the Hubcap secret too. So, for fighter aircraft to attack it in front of witnesses would be unthinkable. As long as Harry could keep himself near to his new audience, the fighters wouldn't open fire on him.

He dropped back to a hundred feet from the ground, hovering less than a hundred yards from the parked automobiles and directly over the nearby highway. The onlookers' attention had meanwhile been drawn by the Harriers, but as Harry's craft reappeared, they went berserk, running out into the middle of the road, cameras raised, arms waving. Satisfied that he was now safe, Harry slowly revolved to scan the skies for the hostile fighters. Now he understood why no radar had ever been added to the Hubcap: so he wouldn't be able to detect any movement out of his visual range.

When Harry spotted the Harriers, they were flying down towards him on his left. It would be only a matter of moments before the pilots realized they too had an audience and would no doubt break away, asking the furious Commander for further instructions. Curious as to the reaction of those below, Harry revolved the Hubcap yet again to watch.

Every face was upraised, cameras aimed at Harry, but then they spotted the approaching fighter planes. Some started back in alarm, others redirected their cameras. Harry estimated the Harriers would overfly within seconds. But as they did so he saw the highway explode with sparks and shrapnel. He watched his audience below begin to jump and dance as both they and their vehicles were torn apart by 30mm cannon fire.

As he steadied the Hubcap, still rocking in the wake of the passing aircraft, he saw – through the rising smoke and flames from two burning pick-ups – that everyone lay unmoving on the ground.

Unable to believe what he had seen – in missing him, the jets had obviously hit the innocent bystanders by accident – he lowered the Hubcap even further. He saw twisted limbs, severed torsos, headless bodies: men, women and children torn apart by giant-calibre bullets designed to puncture metal not human flesh.

As the Harriers screamed overhead, Harry suddenly realized what had *really* happened: A-Wing had killed the people on purpose – to eliminate any witnesses of the Hubcap's flight.

Something like anger coursed through him – it was a completely new experience – and he grabbed the controls and pulled back as hard as he could. The craft shot up vertically at a speed in excess of a thousand miles an hour. Even Harry reacted to the 20+ G-force, and he vented a scream of pain until, ten seconds later, he let go of the controls and found himself hovering at twelve thousand feet.

Harry wanted to cry. He knew tears signified remorse or just plain unhappiness, and he felt both. But he couldn't cry. Not yet – if ever. All his life he had believed the lies they had fed him about Down Town being all that was left of the world. Now he knew that wasn't so. Even if they had been trying to hide the Hubcap from prying eyes, why all the *other* lies? What was the point of Down Town at all? His best course of action now seemed to be to let whatever lay beyond the desert know of his presence, and maybe save himself. But in which direction should he fly?

He revolved the Hubcap, estimated the position of Down Town and began to fly in the opposite direction, dropping down to six thousand feet so as to see the landscape in more detail. Then he remembered A-Wing!

Slowly turning, he scanned the skies, looking for lights or the glow of jets. He spotted one of them quite a way off. He could easily outrun and outmanoeuvre the Harriers; all he needed to know was where both of them were . . .

He accelerated to 150 miles an hour, spinning so he could keep the same fighter in view, but suddenly his view was scarred by traces of light across his bow. Immediately whirling the craft through ninety degrees, Harry spotted the other Harrier flying head-on towards him, its under-wing cannons blazing.

He tried to drop out of the way, but even the Hubcap's responsiveness could not evade the 700 miles an hour closing speed of the two aircraft. The Harrier's left wing clipped the Hubcap, the fighter instantly exploding. As Harry lost control, the Hubcap dropped like a stone, its main drive out of action.

With only six thousand feet to the desert floor, Harry

had little enough time to react anyway, but now, without power, he was a lump of alien metal at the mercy of gravity. He struggled to get the drive refired, to give himself lift and retro-braking, but it would take some minutes to bring it back on line.

Five thousand feet.

The only power left to him was through the vector jets on the Hubcap's rim, which were powered independently of the main drive. But even if he could bring their auxiliary power on line, all they could do for him was spin the craft round.

Four thousand feet.

He had no means of braking, no means of lifting. Still, he hit the general vector button to give him rotation.

Three thousand feet.

There was a jolt as all the nozzles aligned. He hit the button again.

Two and a half thousand feet.

The Hubcap juddered, then began to revolve. Harry was forced against his seat belts as centrifugal force took hold of him. Adaptable though he was, even Harry could not survive anything above five revolutions per second. He quickly cut the power to minimum: enough to keep the craft level at least, though not to reduce his speed of descent.

Two thousand feet.

He studied the vector controls. There were thirty vector jets around the ship, each capable of being fired independently, of being raised or lowered five degrees to allow small height variations during level flight. If he were to fire the five vectors to his rear, and angle their nozzles downward, he should have some semblance of forward thrust – even though these rim jets offered vastly less power than the main drive.

Eleven hundred feet.

He could see the desert floor clearly now, lit by flaming debris falling about him like a meteor shower. It was coming up towards him very quickly. He chose his five vectors, touched the lights that would obey his command and stroked the angle control.

Eight hundred feet.

He felt a kick at his back and the rate of descent decreased, but the craft would still disintegrate on hitting the ground. Judging his new angle of descent at seventy degrees, rather than vertical, it would still mean slamming into Nevada.

He spotted a wide empty river bed, its edges sharply defined by steep banks at least a hundred feet deep. Lowering five front nozzles this time, he gave them too a split-second burst.

Three hundred feet.

The nose of the Hubcap lifted as his angle of descent reduced to fifty degrees.

Two hundred feet.

He then hit his outer vector nozzles, forcing the ship forward so that, as it impacted, it would clip the rim of the river bank.

As the craft bounced into the air, then began to plummet down into the canyon, he angled all vector jets at maximum down-angle, firing them now together. The Hubcap immediately began to rotate with increasing speed.

Harry's wild gamble was that the Hubcap would skim across the valley floor, the power of its down-pointing nozzles giving it enough lift to come in like a flat pebble skipping across a lake. But it had to happen soon, otherwise this rotation would spin Harry's mind into oblivion.

The Hubcap made its first contact with the valley floor just as Harry himself blacked out – the ensuing jolt fortunately shaking him conscious again. He could see nothing beyond the vision screen except a dark blur, as the world spun round in a circle. He knew that once he lost consciousness to G-lock, the ship would become uncontrollable, so he took the risk of cutting off all rotation.

The Hubcap started to slow its spin rate, but Harry's mind was still shutting down. There came another impact, and another, and then the Hubcap was sliding on sand.

Finally, once the ship stopped, Harry switched off all the power. He tried unbuckling his seat belts, but found he couldn't co-ordinate his dazed mind or oxygen-starved muscles. He sat back with an anguished cry of frustration, aware that it would be some time before he could rescue himself – or prevent his executioners from coming on board.

FOURTEEN@Chapter

Traffic was snarled up for as far as both Fergus and Kelly could see. More worrying than the jam was that neither of them could think of a reason for such a delay this early on a Tuesday morning. However, with no alternative, they had to sit and wait. The rain of the previous evening had passed and it was promising to be a warm and sunny day, but this did nothing to lift Fergus's spirits. After the previous night's desperate vigil in their motel room, they had crept out at dawn and driven most of the way to Carritown before pulling off at a Public Rest Area and grabbing a few hours' fitful sleep.

Following their uncomfortable rest in the Taurus, they had stopped at a crowded Travel Information Plaza just west of Carritown, where Kelly had found out how to get to the next person on their list. (She had also picked up a *Burlington Free Press* newspaper, but as Fergus was the front-page news, she had hastily thrown it away.)

Now this goddamn traffic jam ... Cars and pick-ups stretched ahead for a good half-mile, chrome, glass and polished paintwork flaring in the sunlight. Yet there were surprisingly few signs of impatience: no beeping horns, no drivers leaning fuming and frustrated out of their cars. The queue continued to edge forward slowly.

'Must be roadworks,' offered Kelly.

'Or an accident,' said Fergus.

Suddenly a police car rushed past them on the opposite carriageway, heading straight for the top of the queue. Fergus gripped the steering wheel and ducked.

'It's a roadblock!' he hissed.

'We don't know that.'

'It must be. They're obviously checking all the vehicles. I'm turning round!'

He began to edge the Taurus out of the queue, till Kelly grabbed his wrist.

'Do that and you'll attract attention. Remember, they're looking for a red-haired man on his own, not a dark-haired guy out with his wife. Safer to bluff it out than draw attention. The traffic's moving now, so just keep your nerve.'

Fergus soon spotted a couple of police cars pulled up on the verge; a cop was standing next to one, with a radio microphone to his mouth. He was staring their way, eyeing the cars.

'Oh, Christ,' muttered Fergus.

'Don't lose it now! Just remember we're from Boston, on vacation.'

'Boston, right. Where the Strangler came from . . .'

As the queue moved forward some more, Fergus caught sight of a line of cars ahead of them leaving the road.

'They're pulling everyone off the highway!' he hissed. 'We're fucked.'

Again he began to edge out of the line, hoping to do a U-turn back towards Carritown.

Then Kelly began to laugh. 'Stop panicking. It's not a roadblock.'

The cars ahead of them edged forward again and Fergus straightened up to look.

'It's a State Fair,' she explained. 'Look, the police are simply directing traffic. Most of them are turning left and parking up.'

Twenty yards further on, a sign came into view which had previously been hidden by the autumn trees:

THE 87TH

CARRITOWN GREEN MOUNTAIN STATE FAIR.

TURN FIRST LEFT.

When, ten minutes later, they reached the fair entrance, they found a burly cop directing traffic. With a shaky hand, Fergus signalled that he wanted to drive on, so the cop held up another stream of oncoming traffic heading for the fair and waved him through.

Across the fields they could now see the Ferris wheel and the mini-roller-coaster, the hot-air balloons, the carousels and a huge parking lot rapidly filling. It all looked so innocent and wholesome.

The remainder of their journey proved uneventful and within a mile they found the turn-off to Antony Crudduck's house.

The track led to a single large farmhouse set on a hillside. A blue-painted, Dutch-style barn two storeys high, with small white-framed windows peering out at the green and brown hills all around. The only oddity was a parking lot out front with spaces marked for at least a dozen cars. As they pulled in between an old BMW 316 and a brand-new Lexus GS400, Fergus checked the building itself in his side mirror.

It may have been a farmhouse once but plainly it had another function now.

The near side of the long building faced over a sweeping valley lush in fall colours. The occupants could enjoy the view to the full thanks to a wide panoramic window above the entrance.

'Any ideas what this place is?' said Fergus.

Kelly shook her head. 'All we have is your list.'

They got out and stretched. The valley was quiet, except for what sounded like a radio playing faintly in the distance, as if coming from one of the other five vehicles parked along with their own. It was only while crunching over the white gravel towards the entrance that Fergus realized the music must be coming from the State Fair, some distance behind them.

At the door they found a discreet bronze plaque, but it only added to the mystery:

PTD INSTITUTE
DR A CRUDDUCK, DIRECTOR
'CELEBRATING THE INEVITABLE'

'What the hell *is* this place?'

Kelly pushed the main door open and they walked inside – to find themselves in another world.

The reception area boasted a cool grey marble floor and mirrored walls. One corner of the large square room contained a single lemon tree heavy with fruit, sprouting from the floor itself. In the opposite corner was a high marble-surfaced desk manned by an attractive middle-aged woman with grey hair so rigid it could have been a helmet. In the centre were four low powder-blue chairs positioned evenly around a low black marble coffee table, on which lay a selection of nature magazines. Set into the wall behind the receptionist was a blank TV screen. Muzak was playing, its melody drowned by a simpering beat and strings. Whatever the intentions of the designer, the whole room resembled nothing so much as a giant hotel elevator.

'Good morning,' said the receptionist. 'How can I help you?'

She was smiling, but the look in her eyes did not reflect the polite tone of her voice.

'I was wondering if we could see Dr Crudduck?' said Kelly, taking the lead as ever.

'Do you have an appointment?'

'No.'

'Well, that might be difficult. Does it concern our programme?'

'Not entirely,' said Fergus, not having a clue what programme she was talking about.

'Not entirely?' echoed the woman. The smile remained, but the eyes now showed puzzlement.

'Yes, yes, it does,' butted in Kelly, waving a pamphlet she had taken from the coffee table, which she now handed to Fergus. 'My husband's not entirely convinced yet. It's his mother . . . Cancer.'

Fergus stared at her. What the hell was she talking about?

The receptionist, whose badge announced her name as Molly, smiled indulgently. 'We often get that. There's nothing to worry about, sir, and a lot to be grateful for, as I'm sure your momma will agree.'

Yeah, right, thought Fergus.

Molly kept smiling. 'I'll check if Dr Crudduck is available. We always try to oblige.'

Kelly nudged Fergus. 'Yes. Thank you.'

'If you'll just take a seat,' said perpetually smiling Molly.

They sat down next to each other, facing the receptionist. Fergus studied the pamphlet in his hand.

The Prepare to Die Institute Welcomes You, proclaimed the laminated sky-blue cover.

The Prepare to Die Institute ... What was this place? He flicked through the glossy pages, took in an array of pleasant photographs, the testimonials from half a dozen smiling faces, then he started on the text.

The only certainty in life, whether we be rich or poor, is that sometime, somewhere we will die. Death comes to us all eventually. The poet called it the great leveller and this is indeed true. But he also encouraged us to be brave, to remain happy, to celebrate the inevitable. Fine in theory but, faced with our own deaths, our natural reaction will be despair, anger, denial, even panic. At the PTD Institute, we believe we can help you make the inevitable more agreeable; and ensure that you not only accept your fate with good grace but also welcome it, and that you embrace the ultimate trip ...

The ultimate trip? What are these people on?

... in the bosom of your family, amid your favourite, familiar surroundings.

Ah, maybe they're into real estate.

PTD is a simple programme combining audio-visual stimulation, light drug therapy, counselling and hypnosis controlled by qualified experts . . .

Qualified?

. . . to allow you to continue to enjoy all that has been good about your own life, and that is good about life in general. And, as you begin to accept that your allotted span is soon to be reached, then the inevitable will become not only acceptable but even welcome. Far from dying in fear, you will die with dignity and grace, accepting the future as a beautiful mystery. PTD therapy operates effectively alongside all major religious and humanist beliefs. We also accept all major credit cards.

'Is this for real?' Fergus whispered to Kelly.

'Who the hell cares? The guy's on your list, so we gotta see him.'

Just then Smiling Molly coughed politely. 'Dr Cruddduck will see you now.'

They both started to rise, but Kelly pressed Fergus's knee.

'I'll go see him. I'll say you're reluctant. That way we can get two bites at the cherry.'

'What?'

'If I screw up you've still got a chance with him.'

That seemed logical, so Fergus remained seated,

watching as Kelly passed through a door that had opened silently in the mirrored wall beside the reception desk.

Fergus put down the pamphlet – the guff saps will buy: the ludicrous concept of sweet-talking people into accepting their terminal illness as a friend.

'How much would a course of this PTD cost?' he asked Smiling Molly.

'It varies. For cancer? I'm guessing she's in her sixties . . . so five thousand dollars.'

'And how long does it take?'

'One day.'

'One *day*?'

Molly's smile began to slip as she took in his clothes and general dishevelment. Glancing at himself in the mirror, Fergus would agree with her: he didn't look like he possessed fifty dollars, let alone five grand.

'Does that thing work?' he said, nodding at the TV screen over her shoulder. Anything to change the subject.

'Yes. Would you like me to switch it on?' Her smile was swiftly back into place.

It was running a chat show, but with the sound turned down.

'Is there – '

'The earphones are beside you.'

He picked up a small set of earphones from the coffee table and plugged them into a socket set into the table top.

For a couple of minutes he tried hard to become involved in *Women Who Date Men Who Look Like Their Pets.* But he was fast losing interest in the doings of an accountant who looked like a schnauzer, when the programme was interrupted by a newsflash.

'A brutal double murder has shaken to its core another quiet Vermont town. Over now to Mike Praxis for an on-the-spot report.'

Fergus braced himself for a story on the Noltings' murder. But the picture that flashed up of a house surrounded by police, state troopers and paramedics wasn't the one at the end of Bitter Lane. Instead it showed an equally familiar residence in Halston.

The male reporter stared into the camera, all gravitas in an Armani suit. 'Early yesterday evening, Deputy Caryl Lowry and his wife, Andrea, were shot dead, execution style, in their home here on Sandal Street in Halston. Their three-year-old daughter, Elaine, apparently the only witness, was found by neighbours sobbing over the dead body of her mother. Both her parents had been shot in the head at short range in their own kitchen. So far there are no leads as to who was responsible, or as to why such a brutal slaying should take place. Deputy Lowry was a well-respected member of the local Sheriff's Department, and his wife was active on community projects for the poor. Detective Gaines is in charge of the investigation . . .'

The camera pulled back to reveal a short, fat man in a too-tight grey suit.

'Deputy Lowry and Mrs Lowry were shot last evening at exactly 5.35 p.m. We can be precise about the time because Deputy Lowry had called in to the Police Department to run a check on someone when suddenly the phone went dead. Calls back from the department failed to arouse any response, so a unit was dispatched and arrived on the scene within four minutes.'

Fergus couldn't take any more. Of all the horrors that had happened over the last couple of days, this was undoubtedly the worst. At 5.35 precisely, Kelly herself had still been inside the Lowry house.

'I'm sorry you had to see that,' said a voice beside him.

Fergus looked up to see Kelly standing there. Next to her was a tall man in his fifties, with white hair, white moustache and white lab coat, making him look a bit like an angel.

'*You* shot them?' Fergus gasped.

'You're such a slow fucker, Fergus,' sneered Kelly.

'But why?'

'Not your problem. Now get up.'

Fergus shook his head, unable to comprehend.

Kelly grabbed his nose between her thumb and forefinger and dragged him upright. As she let go, she continued, 'Just do as we say and things'll be a lot easier on you.'

'And what if I refuse?' Tears of pain had sprung to his eyes.

The white-haired man slammed a blackjack to Fergus's head, and he crumpled to his knees. As he looked up, he could see Smiling Molly behind her desk, still smiling down at him. Then he was clubbed a second time.

'Not very scientific, but effective,' he heard Kelly say before he blacked out.

FIFTEEN@Chapter

Harry came round to find himself naked and strapped to a cold metal table in an unfamiliar room with white tiled walls.

On one wall were shelves full of surgical instruments, on another dozens of glass jars containing specimens. Tilting his head, Harry could see there were two doors, one of them with a large handle and a temperature dial. Beyond it obviously lay a freezer. On another table, similar to his own, lay the charred remains of a corpse, the smell of burned flesh fighting with the disinfectant enough to make Harry's eyes water behind his sunglasses. This was clearly an autopsy room and Harry was pinioned immobile on an examination table. Now he knew he was to be terminated.

While he couldn't summon up fear about death, he could certainly terrorize himself with thoughts of what they might do to him prior to that. Glancing over at the other body, he could see a tray of surgical instruments glinting in the neon lights. It didn't take much imagination to picture himself at the working end of a scalpel. He struggled against his restraints to no avail. All he could do was wait.

The room door opened and a uniformed Commander

Ulrich walked in. He came over to Harry and stared down at him with a look of sadness.

'I'm sorry about the restraints, Harry. Doctor's orders. I realize all this has come as a bit of a shock to you,' he said.

'A bit of a shock?' croaked Harry. 'I've lived my entire life here underground, believing the outside world was obliterated by a nuclear war, and that to stray outside for more than a few minutes meant painful death by radiation. Now I see people walking about totally casually – before A-Wing blasts them to pieces. A bit of a shock?'

The Commander rubbed tired eyes. 'Harry, there were reasons. Let me explain.'

'If everything I believed in so far has been a lie, why should I listen to you now?' reasoned Harry.

'I'll ask you to remember who you're talking to!' For a moment the Commander struggled to control himself. 'OK, Harry, I'll take your shades off and you look at me while I talk. I'll tell you the truth now. You have my word.'

The Commander removed Harry's sunglasses and allowed him to stare into his eyes. Apart from his exceptionally high IQ and his unique capacity to cope with G-forces, Harry also possessed a hypnotic ability in his eyes. If someone stared into the darkness at the centre of his pupils, they quite soon became his to command. This was first discovered when he was an infant and he had been able to persuade his nurses to give him whatever he wanted. It was why he had been forced to wear sunglasses from an early age and why people still tended to avoid his gaze.

Commander Ulrich continued staring at him, maintaining eye contact. 'You see, Harry, I trust you, so I'll tell you the truth.

'The Russians did win, but the war was halted before all-out Armageddon. The US military had been left in disarray by the initial attack and subsequently were no match for the Russian forces that landed. Fearing the worst, we in Down Town were in lock-down. Only the occasional sighting of your flights ever gave our presence away and, this being the Nevada Desert, there was little of interest here to the Russians once they had plundered what they could from the rest of Groom Lake Air Base. Those flights were necessary because the Hubcap holds the potential of becoming a weapon of unmatchable ability.'

'I know all this, but who were those people on the ground?' said Harry, continuing to stare into the man's eyes.

Commander Ulrich took a deep breath. 'Americans,' he replied quietly.

'Not Russians?'

'No. The Russian presence proved impossible to sustain, so they left four years ago, leaving the USA much as it had been prior to World War II, without a nuclear capability and struggling to find its feet again.'

'So why are we still here? And why did your pilot kill those people?'

'When you destroy authority, you leave a vacuum, and this is inevitably filled by those who are the most ruthless. Once the Russian forces found themselves recalled to deal with unrest at home, the instruments of government were left open for those who could grab them. So religious fanatics took control and they are still running the country at large. Were we to emerge, we wouldn't stand a chance against them. And if they got hold of the Hubcap and its technology, they would turn it first against their ideological enemies within the USA, then use it against the Russians. What peace there is would be shattered irrevocably. And remember, the Russians are still armed with nuclear weapons, so the USA might quickly cease to exist.'

'But they must realize such conflict would mean their own destruction?'

'Harry, you're still so young and you know so little . . . If you're a fanatic and believe you alone are right, and that the righteous enjoy eternal life with God in heaven, do you care if the whole of the world becomes toast? Hell, boy, you'd maybe *welcome* it!'

Commander Ulrich stepped back, brushing imaginary creases from his immaculate uniform, a gesture that plainly said 'Mission Accomplished'.

'And that's the honest truth, Harry. Knowing that for us to come out into the light would mean dying at the hands of other Americans . . . well, I *couldn't* sanction that.'

Harry stared up at the ceiling, confused. 'But how can we stay secret after blowing those people apart? And there's the wrecked plane as well.'

'Since every single military aircraft in the USA has either been destroyed or taken abroad, they'll assume it was Russian.'

'But how do *you* know what they think out there?'

'Good old-fashioned radio. We have some secret antennae high up in the mountains.'

Harry felt physically sick. Commander Ulrich took Harry's cold, thin hand in his own and squeezed it.

'I'm sorry you had to find out like you did. Luckily, the Hubcap is still flyable, but now I have a real dilemma.'

'Me and my mouth, you mean?' sighed Harry.

Commander Ulrich nodded, unable to smile. 'I need everything to continue just as it was. If you talk now, *everyone* is at risk. All it needs is for one confused or angry individual to get out of Down Town and then we're *all* doomed.'

'You're saying I could get everyone killed?'

'Yes. But if we master the technology of the Hubcap, it may well be the ticket for us all to get out of here. So, what I need to know, Harry, is are you still part of the team?'

Harry stared up at his mentor. Never had the Commander been so frank. There was a tone in his voice, perhaps regret, maybe even pleading, that Harry had never heard before.

'Yes,' he said finally. 'On one condition: I see the evidence of your explanation.'

Commander Ulrich's expression was hard to fathom as the light was now behind him and casting his face in shadow.

'If I'm part of your team, sir, I should know what *they* know.'

'Harry, you're a twelve-year-old pilot. A *disobedient* pilot who nearly cost us our survival. You should not be making demands.'

Harry thought over his past life. All the times he had been forced to listen to propaganda lectures; taught to regard the day Down Town sealed itself off as the first day of Year One. How the best any of them could hope for was simply to keep living. *How his entire life had been a lie.* And even though the Commander had now told him the truth – with

Harry's eyes unshaded, he wouldn't have been able to lie to him – he felt he was owed a lot more than a handshake and an apology.

'I want to be part of the team, sir – and I want to know what *they* know.'

Commander Ulrich leaned down in exasperation. 'Harry, *please*. Do as I ask. It's for everyone's good.'

Harry shook his head. 'Proof, sir.'

Suddenly the door burst open and Dr Ralston came in, face white with fury.

'I told you it was a waste of time, Ulrich,' she announced, before putting a silenced automatic pistol to the back of the Commander's head.

Blood and brains splattered across Harry's face as the man's nose and mouth disintegrated.

As the Commander slumped to the floor, Dr Ralston turned the gun on Harry.

'Fucking kids,' she hissed. 'You're all the same.'

It was to be ten seconds before she lowered the gun and regained her composure. Dressed as always in a white lab coat, she idly hefted the Sig Sauer P-230 before running its stubby barrel along Harry's leg, over his crotch, then along his stomach until it came to rest on his chest. His leg began to drum.

'Nervous, are we?' She held his knee steady with her other hand. She leaned down over him. 'Get used to it, kid. *I* don't need to tell you anything, Harry, except what to do, but I will explain why your brains aren't being wiped up off the floor. Unlike Ulrich, you still have your uses.'

'And what he was telling me?'

She sighed, running a finger over his brow. 'That was

a last desperate attempt to keep you on the straight and narrow. I told him it was a waste of time. Can't fight puberty. But now, no more bullshit. You do exactly what you're told or you'll end like him.' She nodded down at the corpse by her feet.

Harry stared at her. He wasn't wearing his shades, but she didn't seem bothered. Maybe she was *too* confident.

'What do you want from me?'

Dr Ralston squatted down beside him. 'That's what I've always liked about you: you're so pragmatic. You may be an awkward little fuck at times, but you do take things on the chin and get on with it.'

'I'm so glad,' said Harry, widening his eyes.

She smiled unconvincingly. 'Sarcasm – who'd have thought it?'

Harry continued to fix his stare on her.

'Oh, I get it now,' she chuckled. 'You're trying to work your old voodoo eyeball magic on me, aren't you? Give me a blast of the hypnoshit and get me obeying your orders.' She leaned in close. 'Little secret, Harry. It won't work any more while we're protected.'

'Protected?'

She walked back to the desk and placed the automatic in the drawer, then turned to face him. 'Now, I think I'll call one of the Paragons in here.'

'*The Paragons?*'

She laughed. 'And while you're pondering that one, ask yourself the jackpot question. Why do you think you were the only one of us who was able to fly the Hubcap?'

'Were?'

'Yes, past tense. We do have other pilots.'

Harry was genuinely surprised by this. 'Other pilots? But they always said no one else could fly it. How often did it crash before I started flying?'

'Every time. Harry, I think it's time you learned a few truths about this place.'

'I think I know all there is to know. Before you murdered Commander Ulrich, he told me the truth.'

Dr Ralston laughed coldly. 'Harry, if you only knew . . . Now, look at me. Stare into my eyes. *Prove* to me you know everything.'

Harry did as she asked, no longer having any feeling for the woman. 'I know everything because Commander Ulrich couldn't hide it from me,' he insisted. 'And neither can you.'

'How can someone so advanced be so fucking naïve?'

'Naïve?'

'About your eyes, Harry. Do you honestly think after all this time we haven't figured out a way to control your power?'

'Yes, it doesn't work when I wear the sunglasses.'

'Five years ago we figured out how to cope with you. So when you were having your chat with Commander Ulrich, he was lying to you.'

'No!'

'Yes.' She leaned over to him, her eyes filling his own. 'Look closely, Harry. What do you see?'

Harry studied them. They were the same brown he remembered. Beautiful really, he had thought, yet they now seemed as ugly as the laser sights on a gun. Then she tilted her head aside slightly and he noticed a crescent of reflected light.

'Contact lenses?'

'Yes, Harry. They block you out. We discovered that the source of your hypnotic power was a pattern hidden inside your retina. All normal people have unique patterns of blood vessels in their eyes; they can even be used as fingerprints. But yours have a pattern that is totally geometrical, ensuring a regular and precise blood supply to all parts of the eyeball. When your heartbeat touches sixty per minute, the capillaries in your eyes pulse at one hundred and twenty. These same capillaries also absorb ultraviolet light and, if you catch your subject at the right angle, the UV is bounced back, flashing at two beats per second. And that's what's hypnotic – not unlike the way flashing lights can give an epileptic a fit of *petit mal.* That's the way you influence susceptible targets, enabling you to direct their actions, forcing them to reveal whatever you want to know, or even to erase their memories. But if we wear UV sunglasses or contact lenses, they stop the pulse getting through. And everyone you'll encounter from now on will be wearing either shades or lenses.'

She sighed and sounded genuinely regretful. 'Oh, Harry, we could have had such an exciting time together. But you're unstable, and intrinsically unstable experiments aren't worth pursuing – the outcome is too unpredictable. The Paragons, however, have proven themselves utterly reliable.'

Harry struggled vainly against his restraints. 'So I'm just an experiment to you?'

'You've no idea, Harry ... but enough chitchat. It's time you met one of your successors.' She moved back to the desk and pressed the intercom. 'Philip, would you come in, please?'

The door opened and in stepped a short, thin, black-haired boy dressed in a red tunic. He walked over towards her, paying no regard to the body on the floor.

'Yes, Dr Ralston.' His voice was quiet and accentless.

'Philip, would you explain to Harry who you are?'

The boy turned to Harry and their eyes locked. He looked very much like Harry, but his skin was healthier and his eyes weren't quite so dark.

'Hello, Harry, my name is Philip. There are eight of us Paragons and all our names begin with P. We're ten years old and we've been designed for the sole purpose of furthering experiments in Down Town. We will obey implicitly any order given to us, regardless of any cost to ourselves. Our job is to learn how to fly the Hubcap and advance the programme. Your job is to teach us how to master its controls.'

'So what's better about you than me?' Harry sounded indignant.

'Dr Ralston, should I demonstrate?' asked Philip.

'Go ahead,' she said.

But Harry could sense that she was uneasy.

Philip leaned over the tray of autopsy instruments and selected a scalpel. He then turned quickly to Harry and stabbed its sharp point into his restrained upper arm. Harry gave a cry of pain. When Philip shifted the blade to within an inch of Harry's eye, Harry was suddenly terrified.

'You see, Harry, *you* are frightened,' explained Philip impassively.

Harry *was* frightened and angry, his leg drumming furiously, his gaze never leaving the sharp point of the scalpel. 'So what? Being blinded *is* frightening. It would frighten anyone.'

'Dr Ralston?' said Philip. 'Shall I proceed?'

The doctor took a deep breath. 'Yes.'

Philip turned the scalpel around and jabbed the blade into his own wide-open eye, then sliced it downwards.

Harry stared, appalled and astonished, as Philip pulled the scalpel from his eye and laid it calmly back on the desk. A slick of blood was running down his face.

Dr Ralston again smacked the intercom.

Two guards entered, took the now weeping Philip under the arms and dragged him away.

'Take him to the Infirmary. They'll know what to do.'

Harry's heart was racing. He couldn't speak.

Dr Ralston walked over to her chair and sat down, her face drained of colour.

'*That's* the difference between you and the Paragons. They do what they're told without question.'

'What will happen to him now?'

'Well, he's half-blind, so he's useless for flying. And as that was what he was bred for . . .'

'Terminated?'

'Eventually.'

'And he knew that when he stabbed himself?'

'Yes.'

'Oh, blow. Oh, blow . . .' Harry chanted, feeling his bladder relax, emptying onto the table.

'Not so confident now, are we, Harry?' said the doctor, as the smell of urine pervaded the room.

'Why? Why create these Paragons?'

'Harry, you're now twelve years old. For a long time you've simply believed you're a bit unusual. Some people are tall, some are thin, some have special talents. You thought you were just a weird-looking kid with a natural talent for flying. Then you started to misbehave. Like any boy your age, you began to want your own way. We tolerated it because we had no alternative. Now we have the Paragons. But you still have your uses – for a while.'

'So all that stuff the Commander told me?'

'To be honest, it doesn't matter *what* the truth is. You will do what I tell you or you will die.'

She got up, wrinkling her nose at the stench, and picked up an item from the autopsy instrument tray. 'I'll let you rest now. Big day tomorrow.'

'I don't need to rest.'

But she had already stabbed the syringe into his thigh. He was unconscious before she left the room.

SIXTEEN@Chapter

'What's this all about?' demanded Fergus in shock.

Kelly leaned in close to him. He could smell coffee on her breath, which reminded him of Cathy Farrelly. 'This isn't a movie, Fergus. You know, the one where the hero's about to die so the bad guys explain the plot and then he escapes to save the day. Because you sure as hell ain't no hero, and you're not escaping either. You're just going to die.'

'But why?'

She stared at him for several seconds. 'Don't you understand fucking English?' She stood back and slapped him across the face. 'You've no idea how hard it was for me not to beat you senseless all those times you wimped out on me. God, if there's one thing I can't stand it's weak and whining men.'

'So why did you offer to help me? And why did you sleep with me all those times?'

'A woman's got to justify her salary.'

'What do you mean?'

She ignored him and walked over to Dr Crudduck. It was only then that Fergus appreciated she had lost her blonde wig and was sporting her own brown hair again.

Fergus glanced around the room to find he was strapped to something resembling a dentist's chair and facing a low, black control panel that extended the width of the room. Here Dr Crudduck was playing with a whole recording studio's worth of knobs, switches, slide controls and buttons. Arrayed along the wall were several video monitors showing silent images of flowers and children and waterfalls and kittens at play. It could have been the control room of *Sesame Street.* To the right was an exit and filling the remainder of the wall were shelves containing sculptures, ornaments and potted plants flowering in a variety of colours. To his left was that same panoramic window looking down the valley. Fergus could not see behind him because he was restrained by straps on his wrists and ankles and across his forehead.

Dr Crudduck then came over to him. 'Mr Kintrey,' he said, his voice sounding Texan and as laid-back as an airline pilot's, right at home with his Southern-gentleman appearance, 'I trust that you're reasonably comfortable.'

'Fuck off.'

The doctor ignored him. 'I don't know what you may know about us here at Prepare to Die and frankly I don't care. The process is simple enough: some drugs, some films, some hypnotherapy, all designed to induce a state of *acceptance* – nothing more. Everyone who gets to sit in that chair is going to die, and you apparently – ' he glanced over at Kelly – 'are no exception. But whereas those others get some time to live out the rest of their foreshortened existence in a state of calm resignation, appreciating to the full all that is good with the world, you unfortunately will die in that chair.'

'So why don't you just shoot me, instead of giving me the fucking pseudoscientific babble?'

'Pseudoscientific? I'll have you know – '

'Shut up, Crudduck,' interrupted Kelly. 'Kintrey, we're going to use a drug on you. But instead of the normal sedative used here, it'll be a truth drug. Instead of pussy cats and kiddies, it'll be all your very worst nightmares – till you tell us what we need to know.'

'What the hell do you want?'

'The list.'

'The same list that brought us here?'

'Is there any other?'

'If *he's* on the list, you must know who else is.'

'Ah, but I don't, Fergus.' She crouched down and slid her fingers under his chin to hold his head up. 'I think I know why Crudduck's on that list, but I don't know why the Noltings were, or why that police deputy was included. And I need to know *all* the others. So, you tell me their names and addresses, then all your worries will be over.'

Fergus was all for blurting it out. Christ, he'd etch it in the marble flooring with a nailfile if they wanted him to. Now he knew the list's heading, he could call it up any time he wanted. But then he wondered about the consequences. Two out of the first three names he had revealed had been instantly murdered and the list contained *a couple of hundred* others. If he recited the names, would *they* all die too? And once he'd told them, he'd be dead.

So, instead, he spat in Kelly's face.

She laughed and licked the spittle off her lips. 'I've tasted far worse from you, Fergus. So now you want it the hard way?'

He didn't answer.

'Doctor, I suggest you do your worst.'

She walked across to the control desk, leaning back on it with her arms folded.

Dr Crudduck extracted a syringe from his pocket. He uncapped it and injected one of Fergus's exposed arms.

'Just one thing, Doctor,' said Fergus.

'Yes, Mr Kintrey?'

'How do you know she isn't going to pop you as soon as I've spilled the beans?'

Dr Crudduck frowned.

'He doesn't,' said Kelly. 'That's why he's being so co-operative.'

The doctor walked over beside her and began working his control panel.

Suddenly, Fergus's chair began to swivel until he found himself facing the panoramic window. Then, as the seat travelled forward several feet, a large projection screen was lowered from the ceiling and his entire field of vision was filled with white. He glanced to his left just before the chair reached its destination and, at the previously unseen end of the room, caught sight of another bank of monitors, all frozen on various numbers or telecine cue clocks. There must have been thirty of them at least.

'Last chance,' said Kelly behind him. 'Otherwise, your nightmares will look like Disney.'

Fergus ignored her, trying to figure a way out of his predicament. There was no getting his body away from here, but perhaps there was a way to get his mind out of the place.

He stared at the white screen in front of him, then he imagined the word 'Failsafe' – but that didn't trigger the list.

Perhaps the drugs were already working. Think, Fergus, think.

Failsafe.

Failsafe.

Failsafe.

Nothing, just the white expanses in front of him. He sensed the rest of the room darkening. He had only seconds now.

Failsafe.

Failsafe.

Fail . . . No, it didn't read that way. There was a gap between *Fail* and *Safe*. What was in that gap? A blank space? No, punctuation: a colon. And it was all upper-case.

FAIL:SAFE

Instantly the list formed in front of him, complete with names, addresses, states; close-set type, mysterious. Now, if he could only continue to concentrate . . .

Lights began to flash and he knew the films had started running. His mind was becoming lazy, his desire to focus on the list lessening. No, concentrate. *Concentrate!*

Images flared. Some he could make out – explosions, mutilations, car wrecks, plane crashes – others seemed just colours and shapes. *Concentrate.* He began to run through the list, scanning it for common links. First the surnames. Four Johnsons, three Schulzes, two each of Jacobs, Morales and Paige. Next forenames. Here he found several Davids and Franks and Sarahs. Then he counted through the names slowly and methodically to reach a total. Then he began checking out how many there were per state.

The list rolled up and down in front of him, the appalling images a vague backdrop to the words in his mind.

Then he heard a voice, threatening and hateful, promising pain if he didn't co-operate; threats to his wife and child, to anyone else who knew him. But Fergus was able to ignore the voice, to tune it out. He had to protect those people on the list at all costs – people who could get murdered if he so much as whispered their names. So, for all the wasted time and opportunities in his life, he was now to make amends. He was at last to make good on his talent. For here, before him, was an opportunity no one else possessed – and no one was going to take it from him.

Next he tried adding up the house numbers, then seeing how many 'avenues' and 'roads' and 'streets' there were. Then he tried to see how many names were alliterative: like Dave Denby, Michael Malcolm, Margret Mannano.

His mind remained focused on the list, so soon he was able to close his eyes and still see it hovering there like a white light guiding him through the darkness, trying to devour him. But then Kelly's voice intruded shrilly, again demanding the names.

'Tell me the list, Fergus. Tell me the list.'

Fergus smiled, even though he couldn't sense if his face muscles still worked. 'Everald Nolting, 10 Bitter Lane, Manchester Top. Caryl Lowry, 26 Sandal Street, Halston.' He paused.

'The others, Fergus. The others.'

He repeated those two names over and over, like a mantra, each syllable compounding his determination to resist – to save all the others from the murderous bitch.

Finally her voice stopped and silence fell, and he found himself slipping into blackness, the list shredding and vanishing.

Fergus wasn't sure if he had actually blacked out, but the next thing he knew the room was flooded with light, the projection screen was rising and he could feel the chair running back to its original position. And as it swung to face the control panel, he saw Kelly waiting for him with a large knife. He decided to play dumb.

'Either you're smart or Crudduck's stupid,' she snarled. 'All that Operation Bluebird and Chatter mind-control stuff always seemed a crock to me. Either way, I think it's time we resorted to the tried and tested methods.'

Fergus stared at her without changing expression, or even looking at the knife.

'Just how out of it is he?' she hissed at Crudduck.

The doctor, looking flustered, pushed past her and began to check Fergus over, opening his eyelids wide, checking his pulse.

'I'm not sure. At that level of dosage he should be totally responsive.'

'We'll see.'

Fergus guessed what was coming and, focusing quickly on Crudduck's white coat, he called up FAIL:SAFE again. As the list appeared in front of him, it blotted out the image of Kelly lunging towards him with her knife. The blade stopped just three inches from his face, but Fergus didn't flinch, kept staring into space.

She stared back, trying to read the face of the man she had lain next to all those times in bed, and with whom she had recently pretended to share the depths of despair and panic. The threat of imminent violence obviously didn't work either.

'What'll cut through that?' she finally said to the doctor.

'No drug will reverse the process. You'll have to wait for it to – '

'There's no time. How about pain?'

Fergus saw his list quaver.

'Unlikely.'

'Well, let's find out, shall we? And let's not mess about. Let's get right to it. Fergus, your cock, it's about to come off.'

Fergus felt his belt being unbuckled, his zip moving down. He remembered the last time that had happened, in the Taurus after she had rescued him from the motel. *Rescued for what? Why?*

'Why?' he heard himself repeat. Oh, shit.

'He speaks,' said Kelly. 'The old ways may be crude, but they're proven. Tell me, lover, how'd you get through all *that* crap?'

'I pictured the list.' There was no point in lying if he was to manoeuvre her where he wanted. 'Blotted it out. Then I played around with the names, kept my mind off the sounds.'

'So are you going to tell me now?'

'Yes.'

'Why the change of heart?'

'Like you said, I'm a coward. I just wish I could have had a proper dose of this Prepare to Die shit, then I wouldn't be so scared.'

Kelly snorted with laughter and stood back up. Despite his attempt at humour, Fergus suddenly realized with total horror that he was now actually telling the truth because he *had* to. Lying was futile, the truth so much easier. It was the damn drug. Oh, Christ . . . he had to stop Kelly from asking the right question, otherwise he would tell her exactly what she wanted. He had to get himself some kind of advantage.

'Can I get up? I'm hurting,' he said honestly.

'No. Now tell me about the list.'

Fergus was incapable of fiction. 'The list's got two hundred and forty-three names on it. It will take a lot of time to dictate it to you. I'm thirsty and tired and uncomfortable. I've said I'll tell it to you.'

Kelly tapped the blade of the knife against her full lips as she considered his request. 'If I let you up out of that chair, will you try to escape?'

Oh, shit. *Of course he would!* He gritted his teeth as if he could keep the words of truth from spilling out.

'Well?' insisted Kelly.

Dr Crudduck was now standing beside her, as curious as Kelly as to Fergus's response.

'Answer, Mr Kintrey,' said Crudduck. 'If I loosen the straps, will you try to escape?'

Fergus realized the doctor knew the drug had taken effect and now saw a way for him to redeem himself in Kelly's eyes. He also knew what he wanted to say. A single word: *Yes.* Of course he wanted to escape. It was such a stupid question, anyone would answer it in the affirmative. But then he had another idea. And a moment later, he replied.

'No.'

'You won't try to escape?'

'No. You let me up, I will not try to escape.'

'We've broken him,' said Crudduck with satisfaction.

'All right, release him. I'll get a tape-recorder.'

Dr Crudduck unbuckled the straps holding Fergus's wrists and ankles, then untied the one restraining his head. He was about to help Fergus out of the seat when Kelly intervened.

'Leave him in the damn chair!' She came over carrying a mini-tape-recorder, which she held out to Fergus's mouth.

'The list, now.'

Fergus felt blood pounding through the previously constricted areas of his arms, wrists and temples, the pain of it adding to his determination to resolve this situation one way or another.

'The list,' she repeated, brandishing the knife so its blade caught the overhead light. 'Or I'll make sure we won't need straps in future to stop you walking.'

Fergus had only one chance and he took it then, hurling himself from the chair and bowling her over, the knife skittering across the floor. Landing on top of her, he grabbed her hair and slammed her head back on to the marble floor. Her eyes fast lost their focus.

'You should have asked me if I intended to try to kill you, you bitch! Then you'd have got the right answer!'

He slammed her head a couple more times till she went slack, then smashed her head down once more.

'Fucking bitch!'

As he staggered up he saw Crudduck reaching for Kelly's knife. 'Touch that and I'll fucking kill you too!'

Crudduck paused, then slowly rose.

'And *you* know I'm telling the truth.'

'Believe me,' the doctor began, 'I know as little about all this as you do.'

'Maybe, but that didn't stop you assisting this cunt, did it?' Fergus made his way over to him, his legs barely responding as he wanted. 'How long's this drug gonna last?'

'Not long. Your system's up and running again. But fighting the after-effects will tire you.'

'You mean if I try telling an untruth?'

'Yes.'

'OK, so since you know I really would kill you, tell me what you know about her?'

The doctor moved back to the wall of monitors, plainly scared, despite his superior size. 'Nothing at all. I've never seen her before.'

'So how did she coerce you? Threaten you? Bribe you?'

The man gave Fergus a look of disdain.

Fergus glanced back at the unconscious woman, spread-eagled on the floor.

'Just tell me within the next two seconds or you get to see the inside of one of those monitor screens behind you.'

'She said a word.'

'*A word?*'

'Failsafe.'

'What does that mean?'

The doctor shook his head, which Fergus initially took as a denial. But then he noticed movement reflected in the glass screens lined up behind the doctor. Throwing himself to one side, he heard Crudduck gasp as the knife speared his throat and he fell to his knees.

Rolling over, Fergus saw Kelly standing up on the other side of the dentist's chair, swaying slightly and clutching the back of her head. Then, examining the same hand, she saw the blood.

'Fuck the list,' she growled, drawing herself upright.

Fergus squirmed back against the wall, looking round for a way to escape. But instead of coming straight towards him, she lurched over to Dr Crudduck and grabbed the knife handle sticking out of the choking man.

Blood showered across the floor at her feet as she pulled it out. The doctor gasped and slumped on to his front, hitting his head on the floor with a resounding crack.

Fergus forced himself to his feet, but soon realized he couldn't get past her to the exit. Nor did he have any weapon to hand.

'Gonna gut you like a fish, Kintrey.'

'Got to catch me first,' he said, the drug apparently still guiding his answers.

'Better get going, then, wimp.'

Her eyes were fixed on him, her teeth bared.

'You really are one ugly bitch, ain't you?' he said.

As she screamed and charged at him, he had to escape, but unfortunately found himself confronted by the giant window. The projection screen having raised itself, the valley was again visible outside. Below the window were several parked cars, all so close and yet so far. He skidded on the marble, realizing he was trapped.

Kelly then began to rant.

'All those times you fucked me, all those times I gave you head, all those times I listened to you whining on about your fucking wife and kid . . .'

He worked his way along the window, the glass cold against his back, his sweating palms sticking to it with each sideways step.

'So you're a whore as well as an assassin.'

She laughed again. 'I'm whatever it takes.'

He stepped away from the window at last, trying to get a free run to the exit door.

He reached a spare chair, placed his hands on its back. It was a metal-framed, white plastic stacking chair.

Kelly nodded at the chair. 'Give it your best shot,' she sneered.

He gripped the backrest, judging its weight. 'I will,' he said truthfully, then picked it up and swung it.

Kelly stepped back, ready to dodge it. But Fergus continued turning and then hurled it at the window.

The massive glass pane shattered on impact, and even before the thousands of crystal shards had reached the floor, Fergus was leaping through it and out into the parking lot. He landed on the roof of the BMW, bounced on to its hood, then crashed face-down in the gravel.

A sparkling shower of glass danced around him as he tried to decide what to do next. Galvanized into action despite the pain in his legs and ankles, he began dragging himself across the gravel. Then he heard a clatter by his feet and saw the bloody knife bounce past.

'Luck's run out, Kintrey!' he heard Kelly yelling.

He looked up to see her standing by the ragged oval where he had punched through the panoramic window. For a terrifying second he thought she was holding a gun, but then he realized she was speaking into a radio. She was calling up reinforcements!

He hadn't even got the keys to Kelly's Taurus, or the knowledge of how to hot-wire another car.

Just then the main door opened and Smiling Molly came out.

The sight of Fergus, the broken glass and the dented automobile stopped her in her tracks – and finally wiped the smile off her face.

'My car!' she gasped, staring at the damaged BMW.

Fergus limped over, pointing at her handbag.

'Keys!' he demanded.

She stared at him, unmoving. 'You did this to my car?'

It gave him immense satisfaction to smash his fist into her mouth and feel those ever-smiling teeth break under the impact. As she fell back, pole-axed, on to the ground, he grabbed her handbag, ripped it open and emptied its contents over the gravel. Finding the keys, he jumped into the BMW, getting it started just as Kelly and a man burst through the entrance.

Spraying all three with gravel, he aimed the vehicle towards the exit lane. Then he saw a 4×4 coming straight towards him, so instead he yomped over the kerb that divided the parking lot from adjoining grassland, then drove down the long, grassy hillside of the valley as fast as he could manage.

His vision was limited by the frosted windshield he himself had created, but what he could see in the mirrors were two cars charging down the hill after him.

The field was relatively flat, his progress good, but he knew that those pursuing him would be able to make equally good use of the terrain, so that the chase would soon just be about speed. And good make or not, Smiling Molly's BMW was in bad shape compared to Kelly's Taurus and the black Shogun pursuing him.

Two minutes later, his progress down the gently sloping field still unimpeded by anything other than knee-high grass, he spotted the hedge. With no way of escaping the inevitable impact, he fumbled frantically for the seat-belt buckle that was slapping against the door to his left.

Grabbing the buckle, he hauled it across his chest and succeeded in locating the retainer beside the handbrake just as the hedge loomed closer, extending the full width of the narrow valley. With no alternative now, he didn't brake, but instead clicked the belt home and braced himself.

The BMW smashed through the hedge with no problem, but unfortunately there was a fifteen-foot drop on the other side. Fergus could only stare in horror as the hood plunged downwards and the entire windshield filled with green.

The car dug its nose into earth, the air bag exploded in his face, then the car began to roll.

How long the car tumbled and bounced he didn't know, but he *did* know he felt every impact in every bone in his body. His lungs were slammed empty of air, his abdomen pummelled time and again, his head thumped continuously against the headrest, the door frame, the roof lining, the air bag. Finally all motion stopped, the engine died and, by some miracle, the BMW was upright.

Fergus opened his eyes to see that the Shogun had followed his lead and ploughed through the hedge, but had slammed nose-first into the earth and remained there, its occupants unmoving.

Kelly's red Taurus had stuck halfway through the hedge itself. Kelly and the man were already trying to kick their doors open, to continue the chase on foot, but were hindered by the encroaching hedgerow that held the front of their car suspended over the bank.

Gasping for breath, Fergus undid his seat belt – he refused to contemplate what could have happened without it – and scrambled through the open windshield, then across the smoking hood, before tumbling over one side.

A door in the black Shogun opened and a bloodied man fell out and began to crawl away. Meanwhile, Kelly had managed to free herself from the stranded Taurus and start looking for a safe way down the embankment.

Fergus spun round desperately and saw, a short distance away, a wire fence. Beyond that were the backs of several carnival stands. The Green Mountain State Fair – and *crowds* of people. Suddenly he became aware of the piped music.

Forcing his reluctant legs, he hurried as fast as he could across the open field, each painful step accompanied by the terror that a bullet would slice into his already wounded flesh at any second.

As he reached the fence, there was shouting behind him. Clawing his way over the wire, he fell head-first over the other side. Then, hauling himself upright, he continued stumbling towards the welcome noise and anonymity of the bustling carnival. Now all he had to do was lose himself in the merry crowds. Lose himself and *live.*

But even as he reached the first stand, and the sound of a throbbing diesel engine began to drown out all other sounds, he heard Kelly shouting behind him.

'*Kill him! Kill the cocksucker! I want him dead!*'

SEVENTEEN@Chapter

The 87th Carritown Green Mountain State Fair was in full swing. Fergus, pushing his way between two close-set stalls, soon found himself on a midway. The wide avenue running between the sideshows, food stands, games stalls and video-game tents was already packed with eager punters seeking fun or hoping to win something. Most knew they were set to be conned, but that was half the fun.

Fergus forced his way into the colourful throng, intending to put as many people as possible between himself and his pursuers. All around him were laughter and shouting, screams from the rides and from a dozen different sources, rock and pop music fighting with country and western. It was a happy, noisy time for everyone else – for the crowd enjoying a day out, for the stall-holders hoping to rook as many punters as time would allow – but for Fergus there was no such gaiety. He was living proof that one can be alone in a crowd, and was oblivious to everything but his own survival.

Peering anxiously over the heads of those milling around him, he could see no sign yet of anyone chasing him, but knew they were bound to spot him eventually. He just needed time to think and to catch his breath.

His feet sinking in the muddy grass, he edged across the crowded midway and joined a queue that was forming. Country fiddlers played raggedly near by, and he could see pairs of heads bobbing rhythmically back and forth as contra dancers stomped on a makeshift dance floor. His respiration was beginning to recover as he moved with those ahead of him towards their goal.

Suddenly, a voice cut through the racket. 'Hello, Kintrey. So there you are.'

Fergus turned round as the queue moved forward. He backed up against a fast-food counter as he spotted the man in an inappropriate dark suit standing a few feet behind him.

'Let's not make a scene. Just come with me.'

Fergus stared at the muscular build, piercing eyes, hard-set mouth, close-cropped hair – and noticed the hand buried in the side pocket of his jacket.

'Gonna shoot me here?' said Fergus.

'If I have to,' the man said blandly, his face showing no change in expression.

'What you want, buddy?' said a voice behind, and Fergus turned, startled.

A fat man wearing a chef's hat and a red, stained DWIGHT'S DOGS apron was staring at him, greasy tongs in hand. 'Come on, buddy, what you want to eat? Other people's waiting.'

The queue he had joined was for a hot-dog stand and it was now his turn to be served.

The man in the suit moved closer, whispering, 'Move your ass, motherfucker.'

Fergus raised his arms, as if in surrender, then grabbed

the mustard bottle from the counter and squeezed its contents into his pursuer's eyes. Shrieking, the man staggered back, frantically rubbing at his face.

Fergus pushed his way past his yowling adversary and slipped up the midway towards the carnival rides. Here the crowds were even denser, the good weather having enticed them out. Rock and roll was blaring out – Jerry Lee Lewis's 'Great Balls of Fire' – and even Fergus began to relax, happy for the anonymity offered by the crush about him. He smiled as a group of giggling schoolgirls passed by perched on a hayride, natural modesty fighting high spirits as their red gingham uniform dresses rose up to expose white teenage thighs. God, it was all so *normal.*

But then came the gunshots and he dropped to his knees, his new-found composure quickly shattered. He lay still for several seconds, as more shots sounded, then realized the crowd wasn't reacting at all. In fact, most were giving him a wide berth, thinking he was either crazy or drunk.

Fergus slowly righted himself and was ashamed to identify the source of the firing as a rifle range. He almost laughed with sheer relief as he rejoined the flow of the passing crowd.

Suddenly a punch in his back sent him flying and he fetched up against the rifle range, ruining the aim of a fat farmer clad in a jarring combination of green Hawaiian shirt and red dungarees.

'Hey, what's your game, son?'

Fergus began to haul himself up, but felt another blow from behind that mashed his face into the counter.

'You been drinking?' growled the angry marksman.

'No!' shouted Fergus, grabbing the farmer's BB gun. He spun round and took aim at another dark suit. 'One move and I'll shoot!'

This one, unlike his stony-faced colleague, actually affected something approaching a smile. Perhaps more like a crack in cement.

'Whoah, scary. I've had bug bites worse than what that pissant pellet'll do.'

'So you don't mind losing an eye?' snarled Fergus, aiming straight for the bridge of his nose.

The man's smile cooled a few degrees. 'Take your best shot, fucker. Then I'll take mine.'

Fergus saw the man's hand move into his jacket pocket and, aware that this was his only chance, he fired. The rifle spat. There came a cry. From someone else in the crowd.

'My ass!' shrieked a middle-aged man, clasping his rear. Fergus lowered the gun and stared at it. 'Always knew these damn things were fixed,' he muttered.

His assailant in the dark suit stepped towards him, the smile widening dramatically. Fergus juggled the rifle, grabbed it by the barrel, then slammed the butt into his pursuer's face. The man staggered back and Fergus pressed home the advantage, raining blows on the man's head – watching with satisfaction as he slumped to his knees, amid the legs of the suddenly panicking crowd about them.

Sensing that he might have gone too far in front of so many witnesses, Fergus dropped the rifle and plunged through the throng. He leaped over some railings . . . ducked under the rotating Ferris wheel . . . on through a maze of generators and cables . . . until he found himself on another, less crowded alley which was flanked by rows of white canvas tents, offering country crafts or home cooking.

Here the smells were sweeter, more homely, and the crowd was slower and more appreciative. At several stalls, rustic costumes were in evidence, with elaborate, hand-painted, carved wooden signs, each proclaiming the specialities on offer. Aunt Bessie's Maple Syrup Delights, Mrs Winthrop's Pickles and Preserves, Perfectly Pretty Pot-Pourri, Nancy & Carlotta's Aromatherapy, Frank Taubler's Candle Cascade – these were just a few that he could see and smell.

But friendlier though the atmosphere might be, this ambience also made Fergus more vulnerable and visible. He needed somewhere to hole up quickly.

He ducked in and out of half a dozen tents – 4-Kidz Wooden Toys, Mother Lang's Quilts, Evermont Cheeses, Green Mountain Cakes, Very Vermont Pottery, Dale's Dough Sculptures – until he settled on Bob and Bill Holdings' Country Cane & Woodcraft, since the layout inside allowed him to hide at the rear, out of sight of the passing thoroughfare.

And there he paused for several minutes, ignoring the patient explanation by Bob to a customer of how to fashion a traditional chair leg from cedar, before Bill filled the tent with the high-pitched whine of his lathe, followed by the tickly smell of fresh sawdust.

Fergus had almost convinced himself that he might be safe when he spotted a head of familiar chestnut-coloured hair outside. It swivelled to face the tent he was standing in and begin to move towards it. Inside here he was now a sitting duck.

He looked around him, checking vainly for exit flaps, then noticed a lighter-coloured panel secured by loose threading. Pushing his fingers between two layers of coarse fabric, he pulled hard and there was a loud but satisfying ripping sound, though it was drowned by the whine of the lathe. As the flap came loose, he pushed an arm through, followed by one leg, his head and body and other leg. Then, straightening up, he turned to flee, but collided with a passer-by.

'Sorry,' he offered, ducking his head.

'Not so fast,' said the shirt-sleeved cop. 'What you doing, son?' The officer was middle-aged, overweight and sweating, so probably not in the best of moods.

Fergus could have thrown a punch, but that wasn't guaranteed to do more than piss the man off. Alternatively, he could have tried to run, but then he would just have another pursuer to evade. There was only one solution.

He glanced back towards the gap in the tent.

'I surrender!' he suddenly announced to the cop.

'What?'

'I'm Mad Dog Kintrey.'

'Stop talking shit – '

'I killed Sheriff Wesley up in Lewisville – an FBI agent too. I'm giving myself up. Arrest me!'

The cop stared at him, then his small eyes widened and he reached for his gun. But suddenly his expression changed and his hand stilled. He looked for a moment like he had forgotten where his gun was – but, as blood leaked from the side of his mouth, Fergus realized with horror that he'd actually forgotten how to live. It was then that Kelly moved over to withdraw a long-bladed throwing knife from the policeman's side.

'Your turn, Fergus,' she said, slashing it towards him.

Fergus grabbed the collapsing cop's arm and pulled the bulky man in front of him. The blade sliced into the dying man's face, entering his cheek and exiting via his chin, the blood obscuring his green Carritown Police Department epaulets.

Fergus didn't waste any time. Instead he charged for the crowd ahead. Worming his way through the tightly packed throng, he could hear Kelly giving orders to 'circle and corner him'.

Christ, where was he to go?

Reaching through to the front of the crowd, he found a falconry demonstration in progress.

The falconer was explaining to his audience how he would swing a rope with a weighted leather decoy attached to attract the attention of the bird when in flight.

'The bird you see circling above is a redtail hawk. Note the red tail with the white tip. Beautiful colouring . . . She's used to catching her prey on the wing, after hovering until ready to strike. When diving, she can reach speeds in excess of a hundred and fifty miles an hour . . .'

Fergus edged his way around the inner rim, annoying almost everyone he stepped in front of. He stopped dead when he recognized the man he had bludgeoned with the air rifle pushing his own way through the crowd towards him. His bloodied face drew occasional gasps, but his eyes were focused on Fergus.

Fergus looked back to see Kelly close behind him. He had nowhere left to run . . .

'Now,' continued the falconer, 'who would like to try landing Cassie?'

Fergus's head jerked up at the mention of his daughter's name.

He eyed the falconer dangling his lure: a bait composed of a black leather weight with a piece of raw chicken and a pair of pigeon wings attached.

'Any volunteers?' he repeated.

A dozen people were looking interested, but Fergus stepped forward quickly. 'I'll do it,' he said.

As he walked into the open space, he caught sight of the brown bird flying in a high, tight circle above them. It gave a long shrill whistle, as if impatient. The falconer seemed disappointed at such a dishevelled volunteer, but removed his leather gauntlet and helped Fergus to put it on.

'OK, what you do is swing this rope round and round, but keep your eye on the bird. When I say "Now", you let go. As it lands on the ground, you call the bird's name. She'll dive on to the meat, then I take over. OK?'

Fergus turned his eyes towards Kelly. She was standing at the front of the crowd, her eyes boring into him, a handbag clutched in front of her, obviously concealing the knife.

All the other faces were also fixed on Fergus. At least with so many witnesses he was safe. He began swinging the ten-foot length of the lure round and round.

'Watch the bird. Watch the bird!' the falconer was urging. 'OK, she's coming closer. Get ready.'

Fergus looked up to see the brown silhouette hovering against the clear blue sky – then he glanced back towards Kelly. Suddenly a woman screamed and all heads turned towards the rear of Bob and Bill's woodcraft tent. Someone had just discovered the corpse of the Carritown policeman.

'What the hell . . .' said the falconer. 'Call her in. Watch her. *Watch her!*'

Fergus was now watching her all right, swinging the lure rapidly around his head. But in his mind he was watching Kelly, remembering the people she had murdered: Mrs Nolting with her throat slit; the bullet in the head of Deputy Lowry; the local cop just recently knifed. To say nothing of the deaths of Cathy and the Wesleys.

'Get ready to call Cassie in,' urged the falconer, worried about the crowd's sudden dispersal – and the effect it might have on his temperamental redtail hawk.

Mention of the name Cassie hit Fergus once more. He feared he would never see her again, would never be able to explain or apologize, to make up for all the mess he had caused. His own daughter would go through life convinced her father was a psychokiller. And all because of that cold-hearted, conniving, duplicitous, murdering bitch standing barely thirty feet away from him.

She was on her own now, as the crowd dispersed to other more immediate attractions. She was smiling at him.

'Now!' said the falconer.

'What?'

'Throw it. Throw it!'

Fergus let loose the weighted lure and watched it fly across the emptying circle.

'*Cassie!*' he shouted at the top of his lungs, watching as the lure reached its target – striking Kelly square in the face. Even as she stumbled back from the impact, three pounds of hungry redtail hawk slammed into her, descending at a hundred miles an hour, the razor-sharp talons extended, hooked bill open, ready to grab and pull and tear.

Kelly dropped to the ground, screaming as the bird continued to rip at her face. The remnants of the crowd witnessed this horror, but their own screaming only infuriated the bird more as it flapped furiously about Kelly's head, gouging and slashing.

EIGHTEEN@Chapter

The falconer cursed and bounded across to the writhing woman. Meanwhile, Fergus dropped the glove and turned away, joining the rest of the mob as it left the scene.

A loudspeaker to his side suddenly blared out, 'Hey up, folks, it's Monster Time. The grand parade first, then these growling monsters be going head-to-head – and that's when the fun really starts. But, for now, get ready to gasp as the state's finest monster trucks show themselves in all their mean, mother-loving glory!'

Then there came the roar of a motor, a matching roar from the crowd, and above the heads of the crowd Fergus saw a blue pick-up truck slowly approaching. When they said monster, they meant monster. He pushed through till he could see them clearly.

There were six of the beasts, all sporting absurdly huge tyres with treads the depth of kerbstones. Their cabs were vaguely recognizable as normal pick-ups – a couple of Chevrolets, a GMC and a Ford among them – but the wheels, the axles, their chromed engines, the exhaust stacks, the lurid paint jobs, to say nothing of the dinosaur roaring of their engines, made them sound and look like nothing else on earth.

This first monster was a cherry-red GMC, the name HELLACONIA emblazoned in black and yellow flame on its flanks. As it rumbled past, the ground vibrated. It was like watching a building on the move.

A second truck lumbered by – a canary-yellow Ford called MY LITTLE CHICKADEE. Suddenly there was the sound of sirens behind him and Fergus turned to see flashing blue lights through the crowd. A bit too close for comfort. Soon the cops would fan out to search. Christ, what was he going to do? His clothes ripped and dirty, his face bloody – he actually looked like someone who had recently jumped through a window, crashed a car and been chased since then by killers.

A third monster drove past, the size of a tugboat, this one a livid purple with the words BEETLEJUICE glittering on its side. The loudspeaker gave a run-down of its mind-boggling statistics that did nothing to help Fergus with thinking clearly.

As the fourth truck approached, a mutated Ford F series, he stepped under the restraining rope. The monster black creation was named NO ESCAPE. The irony of its name was not lost on Fergus. As it growled above him, he felt overwhelmed. Its wheels alone stood eight feet in diameter, its cab higher off the ground than an upper-storey window. He glanced back at the crowd, most of whom were in awe of the truck, but he saw one curious pair of eyes fixed upon him. It was a young boy dressed in combat gear.

Fergus walked over. The boy was about nine years old, with short blond hair, and held a water-pistol in his hand. It was black and slick and looked like an automatic pistol.

'Can I borrow your gun?' Fergus asked him.

'No!'

'How much if I buy it, then?'

The boy considered the toy gun. 'Twenty dollars.'

'Fine. I owe you twenty bucks, kid.' Fergus grabbed it from him.

He walked away, ignoring the yells behind him. The thing was heavy, obviously fully loaded, and still felt warm from the boy's tight grip. As Fergus trotted alongside NO ESCAPE, he kept the toy in his left hand so no one could see it.

At the first opportunity he grabbed a handhold and hauled himself up the side of the truck until he could look into the driver's cab.

'Hey, buddy.' The driver's voice was muffled by his crash helmet. 'Get the fuck offa my rig!'

Fergus brandished the toy gun through the open window. 'My rig now, buddy,' he explained.

Pulling open the door, he slid into the passenger seat, pressing the gun close to the driver's side.

The man's helmet declared him to be HI-TIME HAL and otherwise he was dressed entirely in black.

'What the fuck you doing, boy?' He slammed on the brakes.

'Hijacking your truck – what's it look like? Now you can jump down or be shot down. What's it to be?'

The man eyed the gun carefully. 'What you gonna do with that water-pistol? Clean the windshield?'

Fergus raised the toy to the man's face and in frustration repeatedly squeezed the trigger. The driver shrieked and scrabbled at his eyes, then kicked open his door and tumbled out on to the ground.

Fergus could hear him still shouting as he eased into the driving seat. The man must have a phobia about water.

Curious, Fergus fired the pistol into his hand, then raised his hand to his nose and sniffed. The sharp stench of ammonia made him blink. That little asshole kid had filled his water-pistol with urine – and pretty potent piss at that.

Putting the truck back in gear, he slowly continued his way round the arena. Most of the nearby crowd seemed unaware of his hijack. Maybe they thought this was part of the fun.

From his newly elevated position he could discern police cars, with lights flashing, arriving from several directions at once. He could also see cops and security men running towards the arena. Time for him to find an exit.

Unfortunately, his recent escapade had been observed by the driver of the fifth monster truck, immediately behind, who was now blaring his horn and flashing his lights. This in turn attracted the attention of someone in the crowd, who dashed across to the following white GMC Safari-based truck called ROAD DEMON and scrambled up the side to talk to the driver.

Seconds later he was inside the cab, while the driver emerged from the other side – landing in a heap beside the driver of Fergus's NO ESCAPE.

It was his suit that gave the game away. This was one of Kelly's men. And already his truck, ROAD DEMON, was accelerating towards NO ESCAPE. Fergus punched the gas and felt his vehicle lurch and bounce, then find traction and start chewing up the grass as it coursed towards the crowd.

At first the spectators ringing the arena had thought it was all part of the show, but then excitement turned to horror. As they saw two of the mechanical dinosaurs cut loose and head straight for them, they began to scatter. Fathers and mothers, couples young and old, pensioners, children, all were falling over each other to get out of the way. Fergus wanted to slow down or swerve, but knew either action would compound the threat, as his truck would become uncontrollable. He could now only pray they would get safely out of his way.

The truck chewed through the rope containing the crowd and headed on over ground that had been six deep in spectators only seconds before. Thankfully everyone had got out of his path, so he was able to manoeuvre through the empty gap and out into the field beyond. Some fifty yards ahead of him he could see the wire fence that marked the state fairground perimeter.

Behind him roared ROAD DEMON, gaining ground, its driver obviously intending to ram him. What would happen then, Fergus dreaded to think – and he doubted if the bastard behind had thought it through either. He had seen film footage of monster trucks once they lost control. As unwieldy as rabid elephants, and equally unpredictable, they could stall or turn; they could even flip over. Luckily there were fewer people here, and all of them running for safety. But he himself being fifteen feet up in the air, on top of twenty-four litres of highly volatile Chrysler engine, he might as well be strapped to a bomb.

Suddenly he saw cattle running in every direction, their terrified bellowing audible even over the roar of his engine. He was now traversing a cattle show, causing a stampede. Praying he wouldn't hit any of them, he powered on to the opposite side.

The perimeter fence came all too quickly, but the truck crashed through as if it didn't exist, the ROAD DEMON following him seconds later. The rough, undulating terrain ahead demanded caution, but Kelly's associate revealed no such qualms. His increasing speed already had the ROAD DEMON lurching up and down alarmingly.

Fergus shifted down a gear, stabbed the accelerator and accepted the inevitable: this was going to end only with one or both of the giant trucks crashing. For anyone watching, this chase must have been an exciting and awe-inspiring spectacle; but to Fergus it was the most terrifying ride of his life. The truck was so unwieldy that any adjustment of the steering wheel had no effect for several seconds, and as often as not was countermanded by the uneven ground under the giant tyres. He was bucked and thrown and juddered about, his foot often losing contact with the gas pedal, his hands dancing on the steering wheel as he fought to keep hold. His only consolation – as occasional glances in the rear-view mirror confirmed – was that ROAD DEMON was experiencing just as much difficulty.

The field ahead was long, its slope gentle, but the numerous hummocks ruthless, bouncing both vehicles about so much that it became less a chase and more two individual struggles for survival. Fergus knew that he would have to get back on to level ground. He wasn't sure of his direction, but guessed that the highway swung round in an arc, so that the banking ahead must signal the edge of it.

He felt a sudden thump and looked right to see a flash of white as ROAD DEMON bounced away from him. Their wheel-to-wheel contact would have done neither truck any favours.

Fergus accelerated, but again ROAD DEMON slammed into him and again he only just won his battle to retain control. Looking over, he could see the big white truck staying level with him, its door open and the driver trying to aim a gun but having to keep grabbing at his own wild steering wheel.

The embankment was getting closer and Fergus was tempted to floor the gas pedal and use the subsequent surge to give him some ground on the other truck, but at the last moment he instead slammed on his brakes, feeling the vehicle fight to grip the grassy soil before sliding to a halt and teetering on the top of the steep bank that loomed over the highway.

ROAD DEMON's driver, however, had taken his cue from Fergus's initial burst of speed and so mounted the embankment at thirty miles an hour. Too late he realized his mistake, but by then ROAD DEMON was airborne.

Fergus stared down the steep slope in front of him, and at the line of cars queueing to enter the fairground. He felt as if he was about to plunge off the top of a building and into a street. The opposite lane of the highway was almost empty, which was just as well, since this is where ROAD DEMON slammed into the blacktop, barely missing a Ford Galaxy full of gawping kids.

The monster truck bounced just once, then its front axle shattered; its wheels splayed out sideways as the driver's cab nose-dived into the ground. But the truck ploughed on, its momentum unstoppable, rather like a crash-landing aircraft. Then through a low hedge, into a row of trees, where finally it was brought to a jarring halt and its driver catapulted through the windshield. The engine exploded and within seconds the surrounding foliage was alight, flames shooting thirty feet into the air.

Fergus realized how lucky he was, but also that if he stayed here he was vulnerable. So he eased his truck down towards the highway, intending to clear a way through the traffic lining his path. However, his frantic honking and flashing of lights failed to distract attention from the burning wreckage beyond, even among the automobiles directly in front of Fergus's sliding monster. For the angle of the slope now ensured there would be no stopping the moving truck's progress.

He saw people leaping out of their threatened vehicles and running, but one lone driver in a Honda Accord resolutely refused to budge, staring defiantly up at the great black truck as Fergus bore down on him like a mountain bear on a sleeping dog.

Too late, the Honda driver realized his mistake, but now he had no option but to sit and watch – bug-eyed and loose of bowel – as the hood was compacted by two giant Goodyear tyres and the monster truck crawled over both his own car and the roof of the empty Malibu sitting in front of him.

Leaving both cars wrecked, their owners dumbfounded, Fergus wheeled the monster round to the right, through a growing bank of smoke from the demolished ROAD DEMON, and set off down the highway.

With a clear lane ahead, his progress was quick, any vehicles coming towards him immediately finding a route off the road to let him pass.

Fergus soon got NO ESCAPE up to thirty miles an hour, zipping past the tail-back traffic queueing for the State Fair, but his dramatic escape from the showground was bound to have attracted attention. Sure enough, a couple of minutes later, he caught sight of the familiar blue flashing of a Troop C State Police car. Before he could decide whether to leave the highway, a police cruiser came roaring round the corner – but immediately chose to drive over the verge and nose-dive into the ditch, allowing NO ESCAPE to storm past unimpeded.

This was more like it.

Fergus checked the fuel gauge, suspecting such trucks were fuelled for short bursts of activity rather than overland hauls. It read very low and, considering the amount of fuel these beasts must consume, there would be barely enough left to take him another couple of miles. He had to work out some way to use its size and relative invulnerability to advantage before he was forced to abandon NO ESCAPE. Otherwise the damn thing would live up to its name.

Another bend, another police car destined for another exploration of the nearest ditch. And it was that same ditch to his right and the cars still queueing on his left that ensured he would have to keep driving ahead, with no hope of turning off.

Another long, lazy bend, then suddenly the whole road in front was knee-deep in police cars. He was able to count half a dozen at least, with lights whirling and parked right across the full width of the highway. Officers on foot were dotted about, with guns drawn. Unfortunately for them, and also for Fergus, his speed was such that he didn't have time to react and he was on top of the roadblock before his foot could even find the brake pedal.

NO ESCAPE hit the first cruiser at thirty-five miles an

hour, launching itself into the air so as to land, one front wheel on a second patrol car and a rear wheel on a third. Bouncing clear of them, it hit the ground at an awkward angle, sheering off the right front wheel and sending itself to the left, almost toppling over. There it slammed into another police cruiser, spinning it around furiously like a child's toy. Meanwhile, the monster truck, still relatively stable on its three good wheels, hit a low wall and lurched over the top of it, slamming down into a field, where it began to topple sideways.

Fergus, who had been bounced about the cabin like a dried pea in a tin can, still retained enough of his senses to guess the outcome. Reaching for the door, he pushed it open with his shoulder. Then, just as his world began to roll over, he hurled himself out of the cabin, convinced he was about to die.

Landing on grass, he bounced for what seemed an age, his eyes catching glimpses of whirling metal and sunlight and grass and huge rubber tyres pounding into the earth, before he came to a halt against a hedge. The truck was disassembling as it bounced away down the steep hill. Within seconds there was shouting, and several cops poured over the damaged wall and began to run after the truck.

Fergus grabbed at tufts of grass to pull himself out of sight, finally rolling away behind a tree. Trying desperately to regain his breath, he watched in amazement as more than a dozen police continued down the hill in pursuit of the shattered truck – and ignored him completely. But now there was nowhere obvious for him to run – if he moved, he'd come into plain sight – and once they found there was no one in the truck, they would mount a ground search that was bound to locate him. Successful escape was therefore going to be determined by what he could achieve in the next few short minutes, before they found the truck was empty.

Despite the pain in his shoulder, he struggled to his feet and worked his way back towards the highway through a thin cover of trees. It was just as he reached the wall itself that he heard the first shouts behind him.

'He ain't in the cab!'

'Musta been thrown clear!'

He crouched behind the wall to survey the road. His progress had wrecked four of the police cars – axles broken, wheels splayed sideways, windows smashed – but three others were standing undamaged. There were several onlookers out on the road, having left their own vehicles to see what had happened, but their attention was completely focused on the gap in the wall and the activity further down the hill.

Fergus pulled himself over the wall, almost crying out at the pain in his arm. Keeping low, he worked his way along the side of the road, his eye on the spectators gathered by the wall. No one looked his way, so he was able to slip across to the huddle of cop cars without being seen. There wasn't a single police officer near by, so the obvious thing would be to steal a squad car. He already had his hand on the door of a Carritown PD Breeze, observing it still had its keys in the ignition, when he heard an ominous sound that rendered his plan pointless. A helicopter was hovering into view.

It was approaching from the Green Mountain State Fair and was likely to have been called out to look for him specifically. Once its occupants had him in their sights, with or without a stolen patrol car, he'd be lost. *Damn, damn, damn!* For the same reason, there was no point running for the fields; the helicopter would spot him anyway. Even taking a hostage was futile. He might as well just wait here to be picked up.

And then he had another idea.

NINETEEN@Chapter

Harry was sitting in Commander Ulrich's old seat, in the Hangar Control Room. Dr Ralston was seated to his left, talking on the radio to Peter the Paragon, who was in the cockpit of the Hubcap.

'Now, Peter, you will do precisely what Harry tells you, unless it conflicts with the parameters of the test programme as you've already been briefed. Today's task is simply an exercise in accessing controls, understand?'

'Perfectly, Doctor.'

'Right, Harry, he's all yours. Tell Peter what to do.'

Harry stared at the set of panels in front of him. Although designed to record and process the same information relayed to him when on board the Hubcap, its layout here was completely different. Instead of the Hubcap's lux displays – read-outs based on the intensity of a light rather than on figures or scales – here they were presented as conventional dials. Part of the reason why the retro-engineering of the Hubcap had taken them so long was the need to achieve replicable results, and that could come only through effective recording. Which, in turn, relied on understanding alien technology. After forty years they had mastered the electronics – based entirely on fibre optics – and also the few mechanical controls, but they were still no nearer to understanding the drive system. Speed and acceleration figures were therefore relayed via gauges fixed to the ship's hull.

'Tell Peter what to do,' repeated Dr Ralston.

'I don't think so,' replied Harry. He had no idea what the *truth* was any longer. The only sure fact in his life now was that he was being used for some ill-purpose. A conspiracy this large couldn't be explained away so simply to him. And at the very heart of it all was the Hubcap itself.

No one had ever disguised the fact that it was alien technology. This was, after all, why they didn't know how it worked – and why Harry had been brought up and trained from birth to pilot it. And now they had found someone else to do his job; someone who would obey them. All these Paragons had to do was learn the craft's ins and outs, then Dr Ralston could carry on her work without needing Harry. His imminent termination was so inevitable that it was no longer a major part of Harry's thinking; what is inevitable can be discounted. What did matter was what happened between now and then – and how Harry could manage to thwart Dr Ralston's plans.

'Tell Peter what to do,' repeated Dr Ralston firmly.

Harry sat back and smiled up at her. 'Nope.'

To his surprise, Dr Ralston gave him a smile back. She pecked him on the cheek, leaving a red lipstick mark.

She too leaned back in her chair and stared at the ceiling. 'I know you're not an emotional creature, Harry. We bred most of it out of you – which is why your recent errant behaviour has proven so galling. However, even though you have somehow been able to discern that Down Town is a falsehood and your entire existence apparently a lie, I don't believe the same can be said of your friend Douglas Rogerson. I doubt he will be able to apply such clinical reasoning to being told that he was brought into this world simply to provide a suitable companion for you.'

'What?'

She punched up a monitor in front of them which showed a room in the Education Facility. Douglas was sitting at a VDU, comparing what he was reading on screen with something in a notebook on the desk beside him.

'What, no smile of recognition, Harry?' Dr Ralston jerked forward and prodded the lipstick on his cheek. 'Douglas exists because *you* exist. Since bringing animals up in isolation produces psychological problems, it was thought better that we provide you with a playmate.'

'Do the Rogersons know this?'

'Hell, it was their idea!'

Oddly, this news affected Harry more deeply than his own hollow circumstances. As Dr Ralston kept saying, his genetic make-up was such that he could remain coldly analytical about himself, but Douglas was just a boy, a ten-year-old child on the brink of all the confusion of puberty. And what boy could endure with the knowledge that not only was his entire existence merely some experiment but his parents had fully connived and colluded in this deception; that their own son had been created as a plaything for Harry.

He knew Douglas, knew how the boy would react and how it would destroy him. Douglas was such a trusting soul and now all that *faith* would be smashed as effectively as if they had taken a hammer to his blond head while he was sleeping. That was evil, pure and simple – and Harry couldn't let it happen.

Dr Ralston ran one finger round in a tight ring on the video screen, encircling the boy's head. 'Fail to co-operate with us again, Harry, and I *will* tell Douglas the truth. Yes, and I'll make you watch the poor boy's universe crumble.' Her finger then shifted to the intercom button. 'I'll call Douglas in here now, shall I?'

Oh, blow. Oh, blow . . . Harry had no choice. He knew she would do it, and probably enjoy it. He had only to remember Commander Ulrich's chilling fate. So all he could salvage now from the disaster that had befallen him was to preserve the sanity of his only true friend.

Without taking his eyes off the smirking doctor, he began, 'Right, Peter. Here's what you do.'

But even as he led Peter through his pre-flight checks, helped him guide the Hubcap up its ramp, then, out in the open, put the craft through its gentle paces, Harry was planning his revenge.

For Dr Ralston and her associates had made one miscalculation creating Harry's psyche. By breeding out most of his emotions, yes, he might have become compliant, but the inevitable rebelliousness that adolescence brings was about to bear bitter fruit. The all-too-familiar pattern of stubbornness and self-righteousness in a child struggling to establish its own adult identity, that was to provide the fuel Harry needed in his contest with Dr Ralston. She had indeed cultivated in him a mind capable of viewing his options without emotion.

As a result, his first new conclusion was that he was right and they were wrong.

His second conclusion was that this discovery gave him licence to do whatever was necessary to escape from Down Town.

And his third conclusion? Given the fate of Commander Ulrich – and no doubt himself soon – if blood needed to be spilled, it *would* be spilled.

TWENTY@Chapter

His watch had been smashed when he jumped out of the crashing monster truck, so Fergus didn't know the exact time. However, he reckoned that he had remained hidden for at least four hours now so it must be dark outside. And it had been an hour since he had heard any voices, so now was as good a time as any to emerge from his cramped hiding place. He slipped his hand into the catch, ignoring the pain that shot through his fingers, and worked the mechanism back and forth until the trunk lid of the police car swung up with a loud snap.

Cool night air fell on him and Fergus greedily sucked it in, luxuriating in its tingle as it explored his sweat-sodden body. Such was his relief that it took several minutes before he could summon up the strength to push himself upright and take stock of his new surroundings.

When the helicopter had arrived, he knew he must get under cover instantly, but with so many cops around, never mind members of the public, his options were seriously limited.

The wrecked patrol cars had presented his only option. Three of them were so badly damaged by his rampaging monster truck that they could be removed only by towing away. This had provided a possible escape route in a desperate situation. He had tried two of the trunks – one failing to open, the second full of weapons – before he found the third empty except for a smelly blanket. So he had rolled inside, pulled the lid shut and covered himself with the dusty tartan rug as if it might hide him.

It proved a very nervous two hours before he heard the wrecking truck pull up alongside, and another hour before his own Plymouth Breeze was hauled up on to a flatbed truck. All through this time, he had to listen to myriad conversations, some on radios, some shouted uncomfortably near, and one actually in the cop car itself as its driver had cleared his personal belongings from the glovebox. It was the menacing vehemence with which the officers had referred to him that had been the most frightening aspect of his wait. More than one cop was threatening to 'plug the bastard' even if Kintrey decided to surrender. Fergus couldn't begin to imagine his fate if they had opened the trunk of the car and found him there.

It had then been another long, hot, terrifying hour before the truck arrived at its destination and the remains of the police car were lowered to the ground. More voices then, but they had eventually receded and he was left alone, sweating and semi-delirious, in the hot confines of the Breeze's trunk. He had forced himself to keep still for yet another hour, before braving a look at his new whereabouts.

He found himself in an automobile junkyard, his vehicle lined up alongside the wreckage of a second cop car. Both had wheels missing and their hoods were squashed. They were plainly unsalvageable, and would now await an insurance assessment before being stripped down and rendered into metal cubes. Everyone seemed to have gone home for the night, so he was able to move freely about the yard. At first he feared there might be guard dogs, but none came to threaten him. Eventually locating a hut with an unlocked door, he found himself a haven in which to recover.

Inside he switched on a low-wattage bulb to reveal a cold tap, washbasin, kettle, coffee, sugar, powdered milk and a cupboard containing working clothes and a picture gallery of naked girls showing everything they had except their dignity. He first turned on the tap and leaned down to let it gush cold water into his parched throat. Then, for the first time in hours, he allowed himself to relax, while he enjoyed a dark mug of Maxwell House instant. Its aroma was a reminder, as bitter as the coffee itself, of how things in normal life should be. Coffee meant breakfasts and vending machines and after-dinner espresso – not *The Fugitive* meets *The Blues Brothers*. Christ, how much damage had he caused? Two monster trucks, half a dozen police cars . . . to say nothing of Kelly's ruined face.

He thought he might feel sick at the memory of the hawk's talons digging into those beautiful features, but instead he received an odd satisfaction. That woman had been responsible for too many deaths – she deserved to have her face ripped off, the bitch.

He finished his coffee and stretched, deciding to strip off and wash himself. The water was icy cold but he didn't care. He hadn't felt clean for days, so the freezing liquid was like a baptism, washing away his sins and filling him with a new resolve. Up until now he had just kept running, with no serious thought to his actions, but through all the atrocities one simple fact remained: Fergus Kintrey was innocent.

Fergus had never been really committed to anything in his life; even screwing up his marriage had been a haphazard exercise. But now he had a definite purpose, other than merely paying the rent. *He had to clear his name.* Not just in order to live the rest of his life in freedom, but also because he wanted to avenge those who had died. That meant the guilty must be punished – and, given the alternatives, he was prepared to die in the process. It was as good a commitment as he was likely ever to find.

But, despite his new-found dedication, he was also dog-tired. Too tired even to think straight. Nonetheless, he forced himself to keep awake, studying his face in the mirror. Using washing-up liquid in cold water and a large pair of blunt scissors he found in the table drawer, he began to pare away Kelly's theatrical disguise and the adhesive from his scalp and upper lip. It was long, painful, tearful work – like pulling out nose hairs with a pair of tweezers – but within half an hour his task was complete, the moustache removed and his own red hair on show.

He next selected a change of clothes from the locker – red check shirt, black denim jeans – and some aftershave, which he sprinkled liberally. Finally satisfied that all he needed was a good shave, he made himself comfortable at the table and, resting his head in his arms, fell quickly asleep.

It was soon after dawn when he awoke, feeling surprisingly alert and refreshed. Time to begin putting the next stage of his plan into operation.

Searching out a blank piece of cardboard, he sat down

and stared at it, calling up the FAIL:SAFE list. First the next Vermont name: Elizabeth Pea, Respect Street, Trevor. Maybe she would know why she was included. But how to get to see her?

There was a route map of Vermont pinned to the wall, the location of the junkyard marked in red. It wasn't far off the main highway, some sixteen miles east of Rutland. He concentrated on the map, focusing on the heading, STATE OF VERMONT, and then let it fill his mind. Two minutes later, he had its entirety locked in his head, able to call it up at will – as easily as if he had slipped the map itself into his pocket. So, the easiest way to travel upstate? Hitch a ride, he supposed.

He studied himself in the cracked mirror. He didn't resemble the FBI's sketch of himself, or look like he had done at the State Fair, from where no doubt they had issued another description. And if he hitched rides only from vehicles with out-of-state licence plates, there was a possibility that they wouldn't know so much about Mad Dog Kintrey. Grabbing a piece of card and a pen, he scrawled CANADA on it for added authenticity, then made his way out of the hut. He slipped through the yard, over the front fence and out into the access road to Highway 100.

An hour later found him in the cab of a frozen-meat truck. Its driver was an ageing bear of a black man, his white hair looking like snow on treacle, who was anxious for some company after the long overnight haul from Kansas.

Their conversation ranged from sports to politics and back again. He even suggested Fergus use his electric razor 'so's you look civilized'. And, all the time, Fergus was silently thanking God that the driver was tuned to his CB rather than the radio. Occasionally, the man would grab the microphone to indulge in coded conversation with other rig drivers, but none of their exchanges related to the police. It was noon by the time the driver pulled into the Hot Bird Truck Stop just outside Eden, where he bade Fergus goodbye.

'I gots to bed down now,' he explained. 'It's the laws and all. Be a good six hours before I can haul ass again. You're welcome to hang around if you want, but I guess you'll be anxious to get on home to your sick little girl.'

Fergus had spun him a yarn about being out of work and trying to get back to his ex-wife's house to see his daughter, who had broken her leg in a car crash. Fergus offered his thanks, and forced himself to enter the Hot Bird.

Inside was all red plastic, faded chrome and fried junk food, this tired combination signally failing to cheer up a small number of equally tired-looking customers. Fergus took a stool at the counter and, checking his change, found he could afford only a coffee, but with free refills he decided to make the best of that.

Fergus eyed the TV as he waited for the only waitress to finish serving a trayload of cholesterol to a couple of truckers, both of whom patted their stomachs as if they were faithful pets. The biggest stories nationally were a fighter-jet crash in Nevada that had killed a group of tourists on the highway – eight of them dead and a USAF spokesman promising a full inquiry – and President Burridge's successful appendectomy. The local news, however, was all about yesterday's chaos at the Green Mountain State Fair.

There was mention of a killing at a local clinic, a murdered deputy, a monster truck chase, several wrecked police cars, and the additional comment that there was still no sign of Kintrey, the Mad Dog Killer. On screen appeared another artist's impression, looking not unlike the late Frank Zappa. As the next story continued, Fergus's attention wandered. There was something missing from that report about yesterday's turmoil at the fair, but he couldn't figure out what it was.

The waitress was a bonny seventeen-year-old blonde with a pleasant, puppy-fat face marred by a rash of zits. She filled his cup for him, then moved off to serve a couple of newly arrived bikers at the other end of the counter.

He took his cup and retreated to a booth. Bryan Adams was playing on the jukebox, the music so loud that his world was filled with the 'Summer of '69'. It was then that he began to think back over his times with Kelly.

She had moved in a week after Dale had been cremated, and they had begun sleeping together about two weeks after that. It had all seemed so natural at the time: a random meeting, a couple of dates, then bed, and then bed regularly. It allowed him innocent fun without commitment, but now he wasn't so sure. The way she had been around right from the moment he had called her from the motel, after his escape from the FBI agent in Lewisville, and had come running to his rescue, all eager to help and equipped with disguises. Had their positions been reversed, would he have dropped everything for Kelly, especially after all the media coverage of the murders? He doubted it, but then again he was a coward. Now it was clear she had come along with him for the sole purpose of finding out who was on his list. And then she had set about killing them.

So who the hell had sent him that list? Then a horrible realization stole over him. Maybe Kelly had moved into the house with the express purpose of seducing him. So that when the list arrived, he would trust her. But they had been sleeping together for a couple of months, so how in hell would she know it was coming? And if she did, why wouldn't she know who was on it? He felt himself suddenly shivering and forced himself to concentrate on other thoughts.

As he drained his coffee, he stared out at the traffic driving past in the sunshine. The view beyond the highway was one of beautiful, lazy green and yellow hills. Under the blue sky, it was the kind of view to inspire travel posters – but it might as well have been just a poster for all the relevance it had to his life now.

The waitress returned. Her name was Donna. She refilled his cup and they chatted for a minute.

'So where're you heading?' she asked casually.

'Going north to Trevor. Got this cousin might have a job for me in his garage.'

'No wheels?'

'No wheels,' he admitted. Then turned over his hand and dropped eighty-seven cents on the table. 'And no money either.'

'I'll see if anyone wants to give you a ride.' And she was off again before he could protest.

A minute later a tall scarecrow of a man came up to him dressed in ill-fitting stonewashed denim.

'Donna says you're needin' a lift.'

'Yes. Just to Trevor.'

'I can git you within two miles, that OK?'

'Fine, thanks.'

As he walked after him, Fergus waved at Donna, who waved back to him, maybe disappointed that he was leaving.

'If'n it don't work out, you come back, y'hear?' she shouted after him.

'That I'll do, Donna,' he replied, and wished to God he meant it. For in the girl's eyes he had seen simple trust and kindness, things he thought the world had long run out of.

He climbed into the scarecrow's battered pick-up and reflected warmly that he had just encountered three decent human beings in a row. Perhaps not everyone in the world was out to do him down.

An hour later he said his thanks and began walking the remaining two miles into Trevor. He noted the place lay just twenty-five miles from the Canadian border. Stopping at the post office for directions – forgetting that his poster might well be on show – he headed on until he came to a short side road almost at the other end of the nondescript town.

Only six houses occupied Respect Street, four on one side, two on the other, the two empty lots taken up by a darkened patch of rubble. He guessed there must have been a fire and that a couple of houses had been razed. Elizabeth Pea lived in the first house beyond. All the other five houses were modest white-painted, two-storey, blue-collar affairs with smart blue- or red-framed windows, neat cars in driveways, their gardens small and tidy. Elizabeth Pea's house, however, looked a wreck. In need of a good coat of paint, the window-frames were yellow and peeling, their panes grimy; the yard was untended and overgrown. It was also plain to see that no automobile had parked in the untidy drive for a while. If it hadn't been for the high-pitched warbling of Michael Jackson drifting through the open front door, the place would have seemed abandoned.

Wading through uncut grass and waist-high weeds, Fergus stepped on to the veranda, which creaked ominously. A fat white cat rolled on to its back and offered its belly for tickling. Fergus obliged and was still squatting down over the purring animal when a girl came to the door with a knife in her hand.

He rose slowly, not wanting to startle her. She was an attractive young woman in her early twenties, with short black hair, no make-up but perfect skin. Her dark eyes were almost black too and, set in a pale oval face, lent her a haunted look. She was slim and barely five feet tall, wearing a short yellow halter-top over her full breasts, and black denim cut-off shorts. Her feet were dirty and bare. Despite the recent summer sun, she looked as if she hadn't stepped out of the house for months. But he found himself staring at her right foot, on which the two smallest toes were missing.

'Hello,' he said, forcing himself to look into her face, and pleased the knife was being held so limply. 'Are you Elizabeth Pea?'

She nodded.

'I was wondering if I could ask you a couple of questions. It won't take long.'

'Sure. Wanna come inside?' Her voice was husky with an unusual, almost Southern accent.

Fergus followed her into the house, which was sparsely furnished with old furniture, much of it obviously hand-medowns or bought cheaply in garage sales. The air inside was hot and musty, and the whole place smelled like an old attic. Yet there were no odours of food or coffee, or even air-freshener. It just smelled *unused.*

She led him into the kitchen. 'Wanna drink?' she asked.

'Sure. So long as it's cold.'

Putting the knife on the table, she opened an ancient refrigerator and handed him a can of Coke.

'So what's your questions?' she asked.

'Can I sit down?' he said, taking in the drapeless windows and cluttered worktops, the pans congregated on the stove, the profusion of handwritten notes fixed to the fridge and the cooker doors. 'I've been walking a while in the sun,' he added.

'Sure. Kick back, relax. S'what the day's made for.'

He sat down on one of the four unmatching wooden chairs, opened the Coke and took a long, satisfying sip. It seemed probably the best thing he had ever tasted in his life.

'I know what I'm going to say will sound odd,' he began.

She watched him silently as she sipped on her own can.

'Look, my name's Paul Burrows. I'm with a – '

Fergus was about to spin her that Computing Firm in Boston nonsense, when she snatched up the knife and pointed it at him.

'No, you're not. You're Fergus Kintrey, the Mad Dog Killer. Have you come to kill me too?'

TWENTY-ONE@Chapter

Harry was in lock-down. Confined naked to his room, he had been left to contemplate the error of his ways – and also his limited future. Not only had he been forbidden access to the Education Facility, but his network password had also been rescinded. He couldn't even access his own computer terminal.

The primary testing of the Paragons had gone well, four flights now completed, each with a different Paragon in the cockpit. The Hubcap's flight programme had remained virtually the same as his own test flights, but the speeds had been reduced to keep the G-forces within reasonable parameters initially. Read-outs had revealed a maximum of 5G, at which point none of the four Paragons had even shown an increase in heart rate. They were altogether scary creations. Philip, the one who had punctured his own eye, had offered only a glimpse of how well programmed and disciplined these boys were.

When one of them, Paul, had tripped descending from the Hubcap, he had gashed his knee on a support strut. Though his leg was sutured on the spot – even as the Paragon continued debriefing – his face had not even registered a wince.

But it was clear to Harry that, just as the earliest space programmes had depended on the use of anonymous chimps and dogs to take the risks, the Paragons were equally expendable. For the first time, he felt sorry for them; after all, he wasn't too much different himself.

But now, sat helpless on his bed, both legs drumming feverishly, he was trying – and failing – to formulate an escape plan. However he juggled his thoughts, he knew that there was only *one* way to get out. He had to use the Hubcap. He stood up and hammered on the door of his room.

'I want to see Dr Ralston.'

'Shut up,' replied a bored voice outside. 'Just be a good little boy and keep quiet.'

Having decided that arguing was pointless, Harry chose another tack: he started to smash things up. First to go was his chair, then the desk, then the chest of drawers and its contents . . .

'Do what you like,' sneered the voice from outside. 'It's only your own room, after all.'

Harry stopped in mid-smash. *Oh, blow!* The man was right. All he was doing was wrecking his own property. So what else would make them take notice? Harry looked at his PC on its stand.

'Okey-dokey, I'm going to break my computer!' he shouted.

'Be my guest!' came the mocking reply.

Harry smashed the screen and wrenched out some cables. 'Now I'm going to grab hold of the electric wires.'

There was a long pause, then, 'But you'll electrocute yourself.'

'That's right. And only you can stop me.'

Panic entered the guard's voice. 'OK, OK. What do you want?'

'Take me to Dr Ralston.'

'I'll need to – '

'Now!'

The lock rattled and the guard entered.

Harry was holding up some bare wires, which led down into the floor socket. 'Take me to her now,' he demanded.

As the guard led the way out again, Harry paused to retrieve a large splinter of glass from the shattered screen, then they set off down the long corridor.

Those they passed came to an abrupt halt as they observed the nervous guard walking three paces ahead of a naked boy who was holding a piece of glass to his own throat. Harry offered each of these passers-by a smile, but it did nothing to assuage their sense of puzzlement.

Minutes later, the guard was rapping at Dr Ralston's office door.

She was sitting in front of her VDU, scanning carefully a document on the screen. On seeing the strange pair enter, she pressed ESCAPE and swivelled her chair round to confront her visitors. The guard began to stutter an explanation, but she held up her hand and shook her head in dismay.

'Leave us,' she ordered.

The guard hurried out, grateful to have momentarily escaped the doctor's wrath.

'So, what can I do for you now, Harry?'

He moved over towards her, holding up the glass splinter, its jagged edge catching the light.

Dr Ralston ripped open her blouse, exposing generous breasts confined in a black bra. 'Get it over with,' she offered.

'I haven't come to kill you,' he protested.

'I know,' she replied, pushing her blouse back into place, 'but I thought one piece of melodrama deserved another. No doubt you're here with more tiresome questions?'

'Something like that.'

'Be precise, Harry. It's what you were bred to be.'

'There's that word again.'

She held his gaze, shrugged her shoulders, then turned back to her keyboard and punched in a string of commands.

'Look here.' She leaned back so Harry could see the screen: a photograph of four men holding champagne flutes.

'Who are *they*?'

'Daddy.'

'What?'

'They were the four scientists who ran the original breeding programme here. Doctors Clarence Smith, Valeri Kolygin, Simster Allward and Professor Stanton Fellinboro. Each donated samples for DNA experimentation, and you are the result of Clarence Smith's sixth experiment. Sixsmith, you see?'

'But my mother's name was Sixsmith.'

'No, it wasn't. Look, Harry, I'll make it plain to you. You were *created* to fly the Hubcap. But because of your subsequent recalcitrance, your job now is to train the Paragons to fly the ship. Once they are proficient enough, your work here is over. The Paragons have proved themselves utterly reliable – unlike their prototype. And who needs a prototype any more, when you've got the improved model?'

'So I'm just an experiment to all of you?'

'Yes, you always were. Conceived in a test tube, implanted in a surrogate mother, brought to term, raised from birth by a team of scientists, and all no different than if you'd been a laboratory animal.'

'Like a monkey or a rat?'

'No, more of a mutation. You see, we hit lucky with you, Harry. There were twenty-nine before you who didn't make it – or who failed to come up to our expectations.'

Harry was finding it hard to grasp the meaning of her words. '"Come up to expectations"?' he repeated. 'You mean, when they didn't turn out the way you wanted, they were . . . terminated?'

'Yes.' She said it as if it was the most obvious solution.

'And the Paragons?'

'For someone so bright, you can be awfully slow. *You* were a fluke, Harry. We weren't sure why you had made it and the others didn't, but we decided to capitalize on our success. We used *your* DNA to develop them.'

'Cloning?'

'Of sorts, yes. But with modifications.'

She stood up and stretched, plainly bored.

Harry mulled over her last few words. *My DNA. New techniques. Cloning of sorts. Oh, blow! Oh, blow!*

As he started to hyperventilate, the doctor pushed his head down between his knees.

'Just breathe in deep, Harry. Take your time. Must be a bit of a shock learning you're a father.'

She pushed down harder, then let go and walked away to the door. He heard her summon the guards from outside and then he was being escorted to his own room.

As he was dragged away down the corridor, for the first time he could remember Harry experienced anger. It wasn't a pleasant emotion, but he let it engulf him. So much so that, as he shrieked and thrashed, he soon had to be forced to the ground by four guards.

As he gradually calmed, he saw Dr Ralston near by.

'Get him back to his room,' she snarled with contempt. 'We wouldn't get any of this shit from a Paragon.'

TWENTY-TWO@Chapter

Fergus was astonished by Elizabeth Pea's reaction. Even though she recognized him, she wasn't running screaming out the door.

'I'm not a killer,' was all he could manage in reply.

But she stood her ground, the food-stained knife glinting in the sunlight. 'Yes, you are. And I knew some of those you killed.'

Again Fergus was astonished. 'Who? Everald Nolting? Deputy Lowry?'

'Yes. Dr Crudduck too.'

Oh, Jesus, this was all too much, too fast.

'I didn't kill them, you must believe me,' he insisted. 'That's why I'm here. I need to find out *why* they died.'

'But you know who *did* kill them?'

'Yes. A woman called Kelly Stanyard.'

'Don't know her.'

'Look,' he said, 'maybe if you put the knife down, we could talk.'

'OK.' She laid it down on the table – just like that – then sat opposite him, swigging from her Coke can. Either she was incredibly trusting or incredibly stupid. Either way, her easy compliance was unsettling.

'My real name *is* Fergus Kintrey,' he explained, then began to run through his story so far, keeping it as brief as possible.

When he had finished, Elizabeth Pea merely nodded, as if he had confirmed some of her suspicions.

'And you said you knew three of these victims?' he said.

'Yes, we were all at the Lab together.'

'The Lab?'

'It does have some other high-falutin' name, but everyone there called it the Lab.'

'Where is this place?'

'I don't know. None of us did. They kept it well under wraps – took us there and brought us back in sealed trucks.'

'What went on there?'

'All sorts of stuff. Experiments, research – lots of things.'

'Why were *you* there?'

'For research. I have a condition and they wanted to see if they could cure it. They couldn't, though.'

'So they let you go?'

She nodded. 'Gave me a pension. Made me promise not to tell anyone.'

'And have you?'

'Nobody's ever asked.'

'Do you know what the other people were in for?'

'Everald Nolting was a diviner. You know, he could find water with a stick. I watched him do it a few times. They'd put dozens of upended boxes on the floor and he'd have to find the one with the glass of water underneath. Just using a hazel rod – he was good. But they let him go. All he could find was water in the ground and they wanted more than that.'

'Like what?'

'Don't know. Oil was mentioned.'

'And the others?'

'Dr Crudduck was into hypnosis. He could get people barking like dogs, or eating onions like they were apples. It was funny to watch.'

'But they let him go too?'

'Yes. Apparently they couldn't get him to control people who didn't want to be; only the ones who were willing anyway. They cancelled all his work, and he'd been there a long while. He'd been working on some projects called MK operations – whatever that means.'

It looked like Crudduck had subsequently put what talents he had to profitable use at his Prepare to Die Institute, Fergus reflected. Not that the money was much use to him now.

'And Deputy Lowry?'

'I only met him once, but I remember he was a really good-looking guy. Really sexy. But he was married – and faithful. He could do something strange with Polaroids. He'd hold an unexposed film in his hand, concentrate hard, then a picture would develop there. He did one for me once: a butterfly. Leastways, that's what he said it was, but it didn't look much more'n a blob as far as I was concerned.'

'And they let him go as well?'

'Must have done.'

Fergus sat back and drained his can. The crucial list was headed FAIL:SAFE. All four people, including Elizabeth Pea in front of him, had failed to shine at this place called the Lab and been sent away to live normal lives. *Safe* lives. But why was he himself on the list when he had never even been to the Lab?

'This list I saw, there's a couple of hundred names on it,' he said. 'Was it big enough for that many?'

'Oh, yes. I was there six months, saw maybe a hundred people over that time, but we were only located in one part of the place. Must have been lots of others too.'

'And you've no idea where it was?'

'No. I was referred to them by my psychiatrist – '

Psychiatrist?

' – but they interviewed me here, then made me an offer. Well, I didn't have much luck holding down a job, my mom and dad were finding it difficult to cope, and the money was good. They paid me two hundred dollars a week while I was there, and I still get two hundred dollars, so long as I don't tell. Doesn't seem to matter now. They came for me at night, blindfolded me first, then put me in a truck with no windows. I fell asleep, so I've no idea how long I travelled. Woke up in my room inside the Lab and stayed indoors the whole time.'

'You never went outside at all?'

'Only once. They had a fire alarm, so they let us out into this compound. It was night and really cold, and all I could see was this empty parking area and a lot of trees. Could have been anywhere.'

'And when they let you go, it was the same type of journey? Sealed truck, no windows?'

'S'right. How'd you know?'

'Good guess.' He walked over to the sink and ran the tap, splashing his face with cold water.

'Do you remember the names of anyone else you met there?'

She thought for a while, then offered him five names: four men and one woman. Two he recognized from his list, but he couldn't check the others without calling it up – and he wasn't about to do that until he felt sure he could trust this woman.

'I'm not so good with names really,' she explained. 'It was only when I recognized their faces on the news that I remembered all those people you killed.'

'I *didn't* kill them.'

'OK.'

'Have you got a pen?'

She gave him a ballpoint and he wrote down the five names as she repeated them. Then, finally deciding he had to take the risk, he cleared a patch of table and, staring down at the white-pine surface, called up his FAIL:SAFE list. Four of her names matched, one of them didn't. Maybe they were still there at the Lab. Or maybe they weren't subsequent failures. Or, worse, they weren't safe either.

He looked up to find her staring at him, her vaguely simple expression unchanged. He had to admit that she was very attractive – in a Jennifer Tilly sort of way. He now realized he was staring back, but she seemed unperturbed by his attention.

He cleared his throat. 'I'm on this list too, Elizabeth.'

'Call me Izzy. So what did you do at the Lab?'

'That's the point: I've never been there! I don't have any special abilities either, except my photographic memory. But that's no use to anyone but me, and then not very much either.'

They fell into a long silence.

'Hungry?' Izzy asked eventually.

'Starving.'

'I'll fix us something.'

A bag of Doritos with Kraft cheese slices on stale crackers didn't constitute 'fixing' in Fergus's book, but he was hungry enough not to complain. And looking around at the unwashed crockery and cutlery scattered all over the room, he was pleased that the chips and cheese slices had come out of packets at least. He idly scanned some of the yellow stick-on notes attached to the refrigerator.

WATCH DATES!
DO WHAT THE LABEL SAYS!
IF IT SMELLS BAD, DON'T EAT IT!
CLEAN TEETH BEFORE BED

What was it with this girl? Was she a moron?

He finished his plate, the crackers barely palatable. 'Any idea why they'd want to go around killing people on that list?' he asked, as he upended the chip bag and savoured its remains.

'No,' Izzy replied, popping open another can of Coke and passing it to him. 'I haven't spoken to anyone about my time there – until now.'

'These other people you knew, what did they do?'

Izzy explained that Winston Hibbert was a black man from New Jersey who could identify playing cards without seeing them; Mary-Anne Mero was from Tallahassee and could predict the future, except she couldn't; Cory Plover could supposedly move things, but the only thing she ever saw him manage was switching off the TV without using the remote control; and then there was Dr Dorling Hindman.

'Except he wasn't one of us,' she explained. 'He was one of the doctors.'

'In charge, you mean?'

Izzy pondered this, her face scrunched up. Fergus might have called her expression cute if he wasn't so unsure about her mental stability.

'He was a remote viewer, but his job was to look after the other remote viewers. There were usually three or four of them.'

This was getting weirder by the minute. 'What on earth is a remote viewer?'

'They can see things at a distance. Hundreds of miles away sometimes. You show them a map and point out a place, and they can picture what it looks like, even when they've never seen it before.'

'Hogwash!'

'It ain't. Seen it done myself. They'd show Dr Hindman and the others a map with some place ringed on it and ask them to describe it or sketch it. Dr Hindman's problem was that he couldn't draw accurately; he could only do scribbles that *represented* what he saw. But some of the others, when their drawings were compared to photographs, they were recognizable as the real places.'

'But not this Dr Hindman's?'

'No. The one I remember involved a field of cows next to an airport. Dr Hindman drew a lot of milk cartons and an elephant with wings.'

'I don't follow . . .'

'Cryptic clues: milk cartons for cows and a jumbo jet. Get it now?'

'Yes . . . but what's the point?'

'Spies and stuff, I suppose. If you can see what the enemy's place looks like, you can plan operations more easily. It's like taking reconnaissance photographs without a camera. Dr Hindman and the others could do it from the air too, so you could even peek behind enemy lines.'

Spies and stuff? Enemy lines? Reconnaissance? This was more like it. The way overkill had descended on him after receiving that list, there had to be some logical explanation. And here were inklings of national security, an activity with the reputation for employing extreme measures.

'Was the Lab run by the military?'

'Not that I know. There were soldiers about, some sailors too I think, but no one *we* dealt with was with the army.'

'Did they ever explain why they had you all together like that?'

'The X-Men,' she said.

Fergus spluttered into his Coke. 'Pardon?'

'You know, the comic book? This doctor came to talk to us one time and claimed we were all different in some way. But instead of feeling oddballs or outcasts, we should realize we had "the potential to be of great use to our country, if only these differences could be utilized".' She plainly took pleasure in quoting this verbatim.

'So they were trying to stop you feeling like, what, freaks?'

She seemed to ignore his unintentional insult. 'Yes, they used that word too, but they said we shouldn't think of it as a *bad* word, especially when we could put our special talents to good use. Except most I knew couldn't really – me included.'

Fergus finished his second Coke and wondered what he should be doing next. The kitchen was very warm and he was sweating heavily. He got up, went back to the sink again and ran the tap.

'Elizabeth – sorry, Izzy, what *was* your, er, talent?'

'It wasn't so much what I have, but what's missing. Ever since I was a kid – '

'Oh, shit,' Fergus hissed.

Izzy came and stood beside him. 'What?'

Fergus nodded through the window and on to the street. 'You know him?'

Izzy studied the man outside. 'No. Do you?'

'No, but who wears a suit on a day like today in a town like this?'

The man glanced their way and Fergus ducked back out of sight. Izzy, however, didn't react at all.

'What's he doing?' whispered Fergus, suddenly realizing that one of the windowpanes was missing.

'He's waving at someone down the street,' said Izzy. 'There's a car coming along.'

'Have *you* got a car?'

'It's at Hank's on the common.'

'Does it go?'

'Last time I drove it, yeah.'

'Is there a back way out of here, Izzy?'

'Yeah, out the back.'

Fergus stared at her. Was she taking the mickey? 'You'd better come with me,' he suggested.

'Why?'

'Because those guys are coming to kill you.'

She looked at Fergus as if he hadn't even spoken. The loopy bitch.

He grabbed her hand. 'Get us out the back, now!'

She led him out of the kitchen, down a hallway and into an empty room at the rear of the house, with a space in the wall where a door should be. How did she live in this dump, wondered Fergus.

'Those guys mustn't see either of us, or we're dead, understand?' he whispered.

Izzy nodded.

He noticed her bare feet, with the two missing toes. 'You got shoes?'

She looked at him blankly. 'Yes.'

'Put them on.'

'OK.' She retrieved a pair of trainers from the hallway and slipped them on.

'Any money?'

She pulled a few bills from her shorts' pocket.

'OK, let's go,' said Fergus.

The backyard was a tumble of weeds and scrub, with no fence to divide it from the overgrown field beyond. Keeping a firm grip on the girl's hand – after all, he felt responsible for her now – he led her in as straight a line as possible towards a screen of trees beyond, whose leaves formed a patchwork of scarlets and ochres – all the time keeping the bulk of the house between themselves and the men out front.

Once under cover of some half-dead apple trees, Fergus paused, forcing them both down. This girl didn't seem to have an ounce of sense about her.

'How far to Hank's now?'

She rose up to point and he grabbed frantically at her waist, bringing her crashing down to the ground.

'Hey, why did you – '

He slapped a hand over her mouth. 'Will you shut the fuck up, you dizzy bint! They're here to *kill* us! You know what I mean? Bullets in the head, knives in the ribs!'

'Sorry, sorry . . .' She now looked puzzled rather than startled, definitely lacking a few million brain cells. 'It's over there, about half a mile. I can get to it easy.'

'OK,' said Fergus, trying to stay calm. 'I want you to go collect your car and meet me somewhere out of town. They shouldn't know what you look like, so you'll be OK. Now, turn round.'

Izzy did as asked, unconcerned to be turning her back on a supposed mass murderer. Fergus stared at the white skin of her shoulders until he could summon up the map of northern Vermont he had memorized.

'I'll meet you at the north end of town, on the road leading out to Troy. What kind of car have you got?'

'Yellow Pinto.'

'Right. So I'll meet you on 100 in half an hour. I'll flag you down, OK?'

'OK.'

'And keep low till you get out of here.'

She did as she was told and he soon lost sight of her. He somehow doubted she would ever turn up, but he was satisfied he had done his best to ensure she didn't become embroiled in this dangerous mess. Keeping her house well in sight, he crouched low and ran across the field. Then, cutting across another field and a couple of backyards, he used the church steeple by the town common as a reference point and began trotting along a dusty backroad that seemed to run parallel to 100.

Fergus made good time, reaching the main highway within fifteen minutes, keeping himself out of sight of any traffic. Fear helped him to make rapid progress, but just as the half-hour was up, he spotted another car, driven by a man in a suit, heading into town from the north. He could only hope they hadn't caught Izzy. Barking mad as she was, she didn't deserve to be mixed up in this shit.

He hid behind an abandoned roadside fruit-stand and waited. Three cars passed before he spotted the yellow Pinto. Checking there was no other vehicle in sight, he stepped out into the road and held his hands up. The girl veered across the highway towards him, but didn't show any sign of braking. Only when a matter of feet from him did she lock the wheels – by which time he'd had to throw himself out of her way, landing heavily and scraping his hands on the gravel at the roadside.

Cursing, he forced himself up to run to the now stationary Pinto. He pulled open the passenger door and climbed in.

'Didn't you see me standing there?' he yelled, as the car slithered off the hard shoulder and back on to the highway.

'Sorry, misjudged it. Haven't driven for a while,' she said, as if she had just merely nudged the kerb, instead of almost mowing him down.

'Jesus, you can't have driven in years.'

'Five years, six months.'

'What?'

She began to weave across the road.

'Hey, keep it on this side, will you?' he demanded. *The girl's insane.*

'OK.' She swerved the car back on to the right.

Jesus, how fast were they going? *Seventy?* What was she playing at now?

'Slow down!' he yelled.

Izzy immediately slammed on the brakes and Fergus came close to eating the dashboard. The car slithered to a shrieking halt.

'What is it with you?' he burbled, hastily buckling up.

'Told you, I'm out of practice. It'll come back to me.'

'OK. Just keep it at forty, will you?'

As they set off again, he noticed she wasn't even belted in. He reached over, grabbed the buckle and slipped it over her substantial bosom, then rammed it home. When he looked up, they were approaching an intersection blocked by a slow-turning Ford U-Haul truck. Fergus checked the speedometer: they were doing exactly forty.

'Are you going to slow down?' he asked nervously.

'Why?' she asked.

Oh, mercy! He grabbed at the steering wheel and heaved it half a turn. As the Pinto barely missed the U-Haul, its driver revealed his extreme displeasure with a lengthy blast of the horn.

Once out of sight of the truck, a sweating Fergus ordered her to stop the car. Again she slammed on the brakes and they slid sideways up on to the verge, coming to rest, facing the wrong way, in a cloud of dust that filled the vehicle through its open windows.

'Are you mad?' he gasped, once he had cleared his lungs. 'Is that your special "talent", then, killing anyone who hitches a ride with you? Or were you meant to give the Russians driving lessons, so they'd smash all their vehicles up before they got to the fucking battlefield?'

He looked over to find her staring at him quizzically, as if she had no idea what he was talking about.

'Out!' he ordered in exasperation, aware still of the urgency of escaping. 'I'll drive now.'

'OK,' she said levelly.

Places swapped, he turned the car north.

After a mile or so, he relaxed a little. 'I'm sorry about snapping at you.'

''S OK.'

'Will you stop with the . . . I'm sorry. Look, Izzy, we're in serious shit now and I need you with me. It's the two of us now, fifty-fifty, and I can't afford to have any passengers.'

'OK.'

Her expression hadn't changed a whit. God, her IQ must be smaller than her bra size!

'Izzy, tell me something. Just why did they have *you* up at the Lab?'

'I've got this condition.'

'I know that, but what the hell is it?' The words 'premature senility' sprang to mind.

'I don't know what fear is.'

TWENTY-THREE@Chapter

'You mean *nothing* scares you?' said Fergus.

'Nothing.'

'So that's why you weren't worried about that truck back there?'

'No.'

'Or being seen by that man I said would kill you?'

She shook her head.

'And even when you knew Mad Dog Kintrey was in your kitchen, you weren't scared at all?'

'No.'

'You mean you really have no concept of danger? No fear of being hurt or killed?'

'That's right. The doctors explained it to me. It seems I don't understand *consequences.* I don't see a link from what I'm doing now to what happens next, so I can't conceive that something might hurt me.'

He glanced across at her. Once again she hadn't fastened her seat belt.

'Buckle up, Izzy.'

'OK.'

As she did so, he noticed the scars on her hands.

'What are those marks?'

'Burns. Cuts. I don't seem to realize that hot things can burn me. How sharp knives can be.'

'But surely you get to know?'

'*Now* I know, so I never touch hot things. I don't drink coffee any more, because I don't anticipate it might burn my mouth. Same goes with food.'

He looked over at the passenger door. Sure enough, it wasn't closed tight. He reached across her and tugged it shut.

'So that's why there are all those notes about the house – to remind you?'

'Yes. But I'm not stupid. In fact, my IQ's been tested at 157, but I just don't appreciate consequences. At home, I know what I'm eating and drinking is safe, but if you handed me a cup of hot coffee, I'd drink it straight down without checking first.'

'Even though you know – '

'But I *don't* know. Without realizing the consequences, I always trust everyone and everything.'

'So when you nearly ran me over . . .'

'I did brake too late, but it never occurred to me you might get hurt.'

Fergus was amazed. 'How in hell have you lasted this long?'

'By reading all my notes carefully. Every time I have a bath, it's one part hot, four parts cold, and never more than six inches deep. I always check the labels on food. I always eat it cold. Always drink from cans.'

'That's why the Doritos and cheese slices and Cokes?'

'Right. And I don't have a job and they took the car

away. When I go out walking, I stay off the roads and away from high places – *if* I've remembered to read my notes . . .'

'What else do you do with your time?'

'Puzzles, crosswords, competitions. Lots of them. I'm good. And I read; it keeps me busy. And there's TV: the Shopping Channel. Most other stuff I don't follow.'

'Don't follow?'

'You know, thrillers and stuff.'

Then Fergus understood: if she couldn't even appreciate threat, then there would be no such thing as suspense or mystery for her. And horror would be a big nothing. Whether it was Hitchcock or Hammer or *Homicide*, it would seem just so much wallpaper.

'But don't you think you're, well, just wasting your life away?'

'No – because I don't understand the consequences of wasting time. I live in the now.'

Fergus tried to understand how her life must be: how every action had the potential to be lethal. Drop a glass and she'd walk on it without thinking it might cut her; she would change a light bulb without switching off the power first; and she would never lock doors because she wouldn't be worried about intruders – which would explain the broken windows and the missing doors at her house. Good grief, even a hole in the roof wouldn't get fixed, because she wouldn't anticipate the rain coming in. But it got worse, didn't it? Outside, she would talk to all and anyone – even a recognized Mad Dog Killer like himself – because of not understanding the danger an attractive girl could put herself in by talking to complete strangers. It was a wonder she didn't get raped or worse.

They were driving through Newport, heading for the turn-off to 91. Lake Memphremagog glistened smoothly to their left, the majority of its twenty-five-mile length actually lying in Canada. There was no sign of any pursuit yet, so Fergus had a breathing space to formulate their next move.

'You got a boyfriend?' he asked, curious.

'No. I did have one once. Clark Gunson. A nice boy. He got killed.'

'I'm sorry.'

''S OK, it was a while back.'

'What happened? We're you giving him a lift home?' He smiled at her.

'How did you know?'

Oh, shit! Now it was *his* turn to slam on the brakes.

'Izzy, I'm sorry. That was a terrible thing to say. I'm a complete pig.'

''S OK, you weren't to know. Don't worry, I say stupid stuff all the time. It's one reason people stay away from me.'

'How come?'

'Because I tell the truth. I don't realize that it may hurt people's feelings. Consequences, you see. And even when it does, I'm not embarrassed by it.'

'Because embarrassment's a kind of fear – a fear of looking foolish in front of others?'

'Yes. Old Mrs Magintee, she explained that to me the time I told her her hair was falling out and she had funny-looking tits. Right down to her waist, they were, and she never wearing a bra.'

'I can see she might take offence at that.'

'Oh, she did. And so did everyone else.'

'Everyone else?'

'In her grocery store.'

Fergus burst out laughing and Izzy soon joined him. Now he realized that she wasn't the kook he had assumed, he was warming to the girl.

'How old are you?'

'Twenty-three next month.'

'And when did your parents die?'

'About nine months ago. Lived on my own ever since.'

'How did they die?'

'Propane-gas explosion. There was a barbecue next door blew up. They got killed, and the people next door. Their house was destroyed, the one beyond it burned down too. Lucky mine didn't go up.'

'Where were you at the time?' asked Fergus, fearing the worst – and knowing that, whatever, she would tell him the truth.

'Away at the Lab. That was when they let me go home – for the funeral – but they decided they wouldn't have me back.'

'So they hadn't cured you?'

'No – and I don't think they wanted to. They were trying to find out if I was born this way or if I'd developed it later. They wanted to see if they could adapt fighting troops so they'd become fearless like me.'

'Makes sense,' muttered Fergus before he could stop himself. 'Sorry, I didn't . . . but once you eliminate fear, you've got soldiers who'll do *anything*.'

'Yes, so they did blood tests on me and checked my DNA. Then did loads of psychological tests too. Hypnotherapy, regression . . . they kept me busy. For a while they had designs on my amygdalae.'

Don't we all, thought Fergus, catching sight of the curve of her breast. 'What's your amygda . . . thingie?'

'Amygdalae. They're two small M&M-shaped structures up here – ' she tapped her forehead ' – in the temporal lobe. If they're damaged, you can lose your sense of danger.'

'What did they do to you?'

'X-rays, CAT scans. But those didn't show up anything unusual, so they left off trying.'

'Then they let you go?'

'No, they tested my fearlessness physically, to see if anything ever scared me.'

'Tested how?'

'Hung me off the ceiling, set fire to me, made me handle snakes and scorpions. Thrown in with a lion once, roaring his head off. They dunked me in water a lot – nearly drowned me a couple of times. Electric shocks. They even had me raped once.'

'*What?*'

'Well, almost raped. Middle of the night, they sent a couple of guys in who pulled me out of bed, stripped me and started messing with me. They stopped just when it got interesting.'

'Interesting?' Fergus was appalled.

'I hadn't been laid in months and here's two well-hung guys ready to give me a good fucking.'

He was astonished at her honesty, but, then again, hadn't she admitted she didn't think of other people's reactions when she spoke her mind.

'But they must have been hurting you. Rape's about control, not about sex.'

'Well, yes, they were a bit rough, but I live in the now,

remember. Every time they hit me, I didn't consider they'd do it again; all I noticed was their cocks. If you leaned over and hit me now, I wouldn't assume that was the start of a beating.'

Fergus shook his head. 'I sure don't envy you. It's a scary way to live.'

'Except to me,' Izzy added.

As they were approaching the I91 intersection, Fergus slowed.

'I don't know how they discovered where you live, Izzy, but they're sure to find out you'd a car stashed at Hank's, so they'll be able to trail us. Given where we are now, the obvious thing would be to head straight for Canada – and really screw up their jurisdiction. I'm hoping they'll assume that. But, truth is, we're heading for Auburn in Maine.'

'What's in Auburn?'

'The Connor Hospital, and Dr Hindman works there now. You said he was on staff at the Lab, so he should be able to give us some answers.' He drove on to the Interstate, looking for a roadside diner. 'Now, I think it's time you had some real food. So we'll kill two birds with one stone: we'll grab a quick meal and at the same time make sure we're noticed heading towards the border. But how do we make sure we *do* get noticed?'

Fergus glanced at her: all legs and cleavage. Only a blind man would fail to remember her. No, that bit would be fine; it was the getting to Auburn afterwards that might prove tricky, if Kelly's men had a make on their Pinto. But, then again, it wasn't the local cops who had turned up at her house earlier . . . Perhaps, for some reason, they were forgoing co-operation from local police forces. That was a very big 'perhaps', but it was just about all he could hang his hopes on.

Five minutes later they pulled into the Buzzsaw 24-Hour Diner, where Fergus sat Izzy down as close to the door as possible. That way, everyone coming in or out would see her, and he felt confident that she would make an indelible impression, while no one would pay him much attention.

Izzy got to enjoy her first cup of hot coffee in six months, but only after Fergus had tested it for her. Likewise, a quarter-pounder with chili. Then, check paid and a map of Canada bought at the counter (with considerable debate about which was the most accurate), he made Izzy sashay all the way through the restaurant to the restroom. Finally, satisfied that every man in the joint had got an eyeful, they went out and burned rubber conspicuously in the parking lot before heading north.

Five miles further on, he turned off the highway and, by way of backroads, drove them back down to I91. Their next stop was Dr Hindman and, please God, Fergus begged, at last some answers.

TWENTY-FOUR@Chapter

How long Harry wept for he didn't know, and didn't care. He had been carefully trained to suppress his emotions (and to avoid 'turning on the waterworks', as Mrs Rogerson put it). So he had learned to always contain his distress, having been convinced it was a sign of weakness – particularly in someone who was supposed to be special. But now, with no hope left, he let it all out.

And Harry wasn't crying only about his imminent destruction, but for all those times before when he had silently endured his scrapes and bruises, his illnesses and scoldings, his failures and humiliations all bottled up.

And he hadn't cried only for himself. He had also wept for Douglas . . . and even for the Paragons, who would never know the simple pleasures of losing oneself in a fantasy world of cowboys and pirates, or allowing your best pal to beat you at a game purely for the smile it would bring to his face.

Harry had even cried for Mrs Rogerson. Not for the apparently calculating woman who had sold her own child to the service of science in Down Town, but for the warm-hearted foster mother who spent so much time with him. For she had been as good to him as if she were his mother, and he couldn't believe such kindness was *all* an act. Not considering all those little things: the carefully wrapped presents on his birthday, the hot milk when he was feeling sickly, the bedtime stories shared with Douglas when they were very young . . .

So Harry had hugged the pillow round his ears and sobbed his heart out. This experience was new and frightening for him, but also cathartic. By the time he paused to catch his breath and wipe his face, his pillow was soaked and he himself felt empty – empty of tears and empty of emotion.

And then they had come for him, again.

Four guards, each equipped with wrap-around sunglasses, steroid-enhanced muscles and a bad attitude, without warning burst through the door. Harry tried to struggle, of course, but as two held him down, a third one sprayed his face with a small aerosol. He was temporarily blinded, coughing and sneezing uncontrollably, while the fourth guard rolled in a two-wheeled trolley, to the metal surface of which had been welded a lengthy T-shaped upright.

Hoisted up on to this, his wrists snagged to the handcuffs hanging from the cross-bar above him, Harry was forced to remain standing with arms stretched above his head. The bizarre trolley was then wheeled backwards out of the room and pushed down the corridor.

The entire journey took at least five minutes, by which time Harry had recovered from the spray. But his throat was sore and his eyes watered profusely, giving his guards cause for mockery.

'Iddy biddy baby cry-byes?'

'Ain't so smart now, are we, freak?'

'Make the most of it, you fucking mute. No one gives a shit for you now.'

As they approached Dr Ralston's office, their taunting ceased. While they at last felt free to vent their long-held dislike for Harry to his face, they didn't want to antagonize their boss. As the trolley approached, Dr Ralston emerged in person and stood there, hands on hips.

'Hello, my little monkey,' she cooed, producing a hypodermic syringe.

Harry managed at last to speak. 'Please don't terminate me. I'll be good.'

She tilted her head. '*Now* the little monkey wants to play ball. Well, it's too late. I've just called time,' she hissed.

She jabbed the needle into his arm, smiling with satisfaction as its contents polluted his bloodstream.

'Please,' said Harry, as his world began slipping sideways. '*Please . . .*'

TWENTY-FIVE@Chapter

Fergus and Izzy made good time to Auburn, shunpiking the one hundred and fifty miles in a little over three and a half hours. They had met no hold-ups, the Pinto running like a dream. It had registered only 3,500 miles when put in storage by Izzy's parents (after she had crashed her then boyfriend's Charger and narrowly escaped injury).

'How come Hank let you have your car back, since you're known to be such a menace on the roads?'

'Hank wasn't there, so I helped myself to the keys.'

They reached Connor Hospital a little after 4.00 p.m. Fergus was surprised to find from the sign that it was a mental institution. Set in large, well-tended grounds, the hospital was designed in Southern antebellum style. The approach led through an unusual gateway, the arch cut through a large, stone-built circular edifice at least fifteen feet in diameter. Its upper level was adorned by a row of vases, so the gateway resembled a giant eternity ring. Fergus suspected the architect of this monstrosity may have ended up as one of its first patients.

They drew up and parked at the hospital entrance. Apart from two small brass plates on the columns flanking either side of the portico, and the discreet wire mesh visible in many of the tall windows, the building barely reflected its purpose. It could just as well be a rich man's country mansion.

'Let me do the talking,' said Fergus, combing his unwashed hair in the driver's mirror. 'How do you think Dr Hindman will react to you?'

Izzy considered this. 'He only spoke to me a couple of times. You see, I wasn't one of his remote viewers. I do remember he kept looking at my tits.'

Understandable, reflected Fergus, but not really a basis for a conversation. He led the way across the gravel, up through imposing double doors into a wide, marbled hall-way. A small reception desk was almost hiding itself under the wide, sweeping staircase and a pleasant scent permeated the air. The reason was the large vases containing pink and red roses set in numerous small circular alcoves around the hall and up the staircase. Music played quietly in the dis-tance, but otherwise it was silent, almost like a hotel lobby. This illusion was immediately spoiled by a large red-faced woman in a seriously starched white nurse's uniform who appeared suddenly from a door behind the desk.

'Good afternoon,' she said in a bass voice. 'How can I be of assistance?' Her hair was pulled back so severely, it looked like an attempt to stop her face falling apart.

'We wondered if we might have a word with a member of your staff, Dr Hindman?'

'I'm afraid we have no one here of that name.'

'Dr Hindman? Are you sure?'

'I'm certain.'

'Perhaps he's left. How long have you worked here?'

'Eighteen years, and I fail to see – '

'Maybe he's a patient,' whispered Izzy.

'Have you a patient called Hindman?' Fergus continued.

The nurse glared at him. 'Yes, we have a Dorling Hindman, but – '

'Can we see him?'

'Are you relatives?'

'Obviously not.'

'Then I'm afraid – '

'Can we see your superior, please?'

'Dr Van Deusen is a very busy man.'

'Let Dr Van Deusen decide about that.'

Huffily, she picked up a phone and, after a short discussion, she pointed to a door on one side of the hall. 'He'll see you now.'

As they reached the door, they were greeted by a short, balding man with a black moustache. He wore an immaculate pin-stripe suit, a crisp pink tie and a matching rose in his buttonhole. He smelled strongly of aftershave, with a vaguely effeminate air reinforced by his manicured nails and soft handshake.

'Good afternoon, Mr, er . . .' he began. His accent was possibly Canadian.

'Pea. Frank Pea,' said Fergus. 'This is my sister, Elizabeth.'

'Hello, my dear.' He obviously liked the look of Izzy. 'Come in. Come in.'

They entered a dignified wood-panelled study that smelled strongly of furniture polish. Two of the walls were lined with medical journals; a third displayed a large oil painting of Dr Van Deusen himself in scholarly robes, with one hand resting on a phrenology bust. The fourth wall boasted a tall window overlooking the grounds; on the sill was a glass tank containing, of all things, a tarantula.

Dr Van Deusen sat down behind his polished desk. 'I understand you want to speak to Dorling Hindman?'

'My sister used to be a patient of his.'

'Oh, I see. Unfortunately Dr Hindman is confined in the secure wing.'

'He's dangerous?'

'Only to himself. He's very unbalanced. Seeing him is out of the question. Excuse me, Mr Pea, but have we met before?'

'No,' said Fergus, turning his gaze to the bookshelves. One entire section was devoted to the works of Dr Van Deusen himself. He was either extremely prolific or an egomaniac.

'It's just that your face looks familiar.'

Uh-oh, thought Fergus, *let's change the subject.* He nodded through the window towards the circular gateway. 'Interesting piece of architecture.'

Van Deusen nodded. 'Yes, indeed. It belonged to Johnson Marriott. You know, Marriott the Jewellers?'

Fergus didn't, but nodded that he did.

The doctor continued, 'The Depression broke them and this house was sold off. There are ring-shaped motifs all around the house.'

Fergus remembered the circular alcoves. 'You've written a lot,' he said, turning to the bookshelves.

'Yes, I do like to keep my hand in,' said Van Deusen.

There were rows of photographs on the desk, all including the doctor in the company of others – even one shaking hands with President Bush. Significantly, all were facing outwards, unavoidable to any visitor. This was one vain bastard, thought Fergus.

'So there's no way we can see him? That's a pity. My sister was hoping for some kind of closure on her treatment.'

'I'm sorry to hear that.'

From the corner of his eye, Fergus was watching Izzy. She was staring into the glass vivarium, clearly fascinated by the giant spider.

'Interesting room-mate,' said Fergus, mentally urging Izzy to indulge her curiosity.

'Yes. Timothy is a remarkable specimen. And larger than average, as you can see. You're not phobic, I trust?'

'No, no.' *Go on, Izzy. Go on. Do it. Do it – Yes! Good girl!*

'About this treatment closure, Doctor, I was wondering if you might care – '

'Sorry, I don't do private practice.'

'There might be a medical paper in it.'

'Oh, I doubt your sister is so remarkable that any one of a hundred competent psychiatrists couldn't provide satisfaction.'

Dr Van Deusen was now staring at Izzy.

She had just taken Timothy the tarantula out of his glass tank, and was watching in fascination as he crawled over her breasts.

'It tickles,' she giggled.

Fergus gulped. That was one fucking *huge* spider. She really didn't show any fear – as he now explained to the doctor.

'As you can see, nothing frightens her. Dr Hindman was studying her, then seemed to lose interest . . .'

But Dr Van Deusen was no longer listening. He walked over beside Izzy and stood staring as his eight-legged friend climbed over her. Whether he was more interested in Timothy or where he was wandering wasn't very clear.

'If you'll just let us consult Dr Hindman, maybe Elizabeth could apply to be your patient. She does have a rather unique problem.'

The doctor looked almost totally entranced. Finally, he removed Timothy from her shoulder and slipped him back inside his tank.

'Very well, half an hour. But I do think you'll be disappointed. And when you've finished, come back here. I'll arrange some coffee and we'll take it from there. Is that OK with you, my dear?' He spoke to Izzy as if she were a child.

'Fine,' she said, smiling.

The doctor led them out into the hall, where he instructed the grumpy nurse to take them to Dr Hindman's room. The nurse smiled for the first time, as if she knew something they did not. She preceded them silently into a single-storey annexe, restless with the sounds of numerous patients fighting their inner demons.

Hindman himself was patently insane, his room almost totally covered in sketches. The walls, the ceiling, the doors, his pillowcases and sheets, the parquet flooring, the window-panes, even his own forearms, all were festooned in drawings. Additionally, seemingly any material he could use, from wrapping paper, old envelopes, newspapers and magazines to cardboard, pages from books, wallpaper, even his own body, were also used as canvases for his artistic mill. The majority of these sketches were done in black – pencil, charcoal, wax crayon, felt-tip, ballpoint – but occasionally there were little bursts of colour, predominantly orange. And, when Fergus studied the latter more closely, these orange scribbles invariably looked like lollipops – orange circles on the tops of black sticks. Very strange indeed.

Hindman sat on his bed, stripped to the waist, his head completely shaven. He was scribbling furiously on a pad. As Fergus leaned over to look, he could see a crude, childlike sketch – two triangles with what looked like a sun overhead.

And all the while Hindman was muttering the same phrase: 'I can see you, I can see you, I can see you.'

'Dr Hindman,' began Fergus, 'I'm sorry to disturb you.'

The man whipped round. He was middle-aged but haggard, an athletic build now wasting away. His chest, stomach and most of his face were covered in scribbles: immature visions of everyday objects that would have been an embarrassment on *Sesame Street* but here, on the human frame, looked pure madness. Out of the plethora of childish tattooing, Hindman's most noticeable features were his eyes. Steel-grey, wide-fixed, as he moved his head, they would remain focused at the same point, moving only a second later, as if body and mind were disconnected. First his head tilted towards Fergus, then the eyes followed up to fix on him, that determined expression remaining unchanged.

'I can see you,' he said. 'I can see you.'

'I know you can. But do you recognize my friend here?' Fergus pointed to Izzy on his left.

Hindman's head turned towards her, his gaze still on Fergus, then his eyes latched on to Izzy. But if he did recognize her, he gave no indication.

'I can see you, I can see you,' was all he said.

Izzy leaned over to him, oblivious to the possibility of him turning violent.

'Dr Hindman, do you remember me? From the Lab?'

He stared at her. 'I can see you, I can see you.'

She reached out to touch his hand, but he jerked it back. Then, returning to his pad, he ripped out the page he had previously been scribbling on and began to dash out another sketch.

'We're not going to get anything here,' Fergus whispered.

Izzy picked up the discarded sketch and studied it. 'What do you see?'

'Pyramids? The sun? Bad art?' Fergus suggested.

'It's cryptic clues, Fergus. Crude pictures. That's Timothy the tarantula – and my breasts.'

'What?' Fergus stared at the childish drawing. 'No, it can't be.'

'Yes, it is.' Izzy edged towards the bed and sat down next to Hindman. 'At the Lab, remember? All those tests? You were in charge of remote viewing?'

The scribbling continued.

This is a waste of time, thought Fergus. Their last chance had evaporated. The scribbling suddenly stopped and Hindman froze, just as if someone had switched him off. Izzy leaned forward and stared at what he had drawn.

'Fergus, look at this,' she whispered, carefully ripping out the sheet of paper and holding it up so he could see it.

It seemed to be a crude drawing of a car, except with wheels out of all proportion to the body. A tiny stick-figure man sat in the driver's seat. In the background a spiky squiggle and a line of tight loops, which Fergus guessed represented fire and smoke.

'The monster truck?' said Izzy. 'And that must be the one that crashed?'

Fergus was convinced. 'Pity he's mad. He might have been able to help us . . .' He leaned towards him. 'The Lab, Dr Hindman, the Lab – do you remember where it is?'

The man turned his head towards him, the eyes following a moment later, as if driven by a different power source.

'The Lab? I need to know about the Lab,' said Fergus.

Suddenly, Hindman leaped up, bowling Fergus over, and rushed past Izzy to the corner near the door.

Fergus stood up quickly, intent of protecting Izzy should the man turn violent. But all Hindman did was pull one of the sheets of paper from the wall and hand it carefully to Izzy, almost like a religious offering. Taking it, she thanked him, while Fergus examined it. It was one of the few colour sketches he had done: made up of two elements, both drawn in orange. Another stick figure and what looked like a face.

'I can see you,' said Hindman, before returning to the bed. 'I can see you.'

'Doesn't mean anything to me,' murmured Fergus.

'Me neither,' said Izzy. 'But it obviously does to him.'

Fergus took the sheet of paper from her and shoved it under Hindman's downcast gaze. 'The Lab?' he pressed.

Hindman batted it out of the way. 'I can see you. I can see you.'

Fergus stood up. 'Looks like this is all we'll be getting from him.'

Just then Van Deusen pushed open the door.

'He's given you that drawing? That's about all he gives away these days. A sad, sad case. Are you all right, Dr Hindman?'

'I can see you. I can see you.'

Dr Van Deusen smiled and shook his head at Fergus. 'As you can see, he's too far gone. Now, if you'll come with me . . .'

Fergus folded up Hindman's gift and pocketed it. He followed the doctor, too disappointed to argue.

Hindman picked up his pencil as they headed into the corridor, his mantra rising in pitch and intensity. Fergus stepped back and glanced inside. The man was scribbling furiously. 'I can see you. I can see you!' Was there a note of fear in his voice?

'Something's bothering him,' suggested Fergus.

Dr Van Deusen dismissed his concern. 'He's *always* troubled.'

Suddenly Hindman shot up from the bed, thrusting his pad out towards the three of them. '*I can see you. I can see you!*'

'All right, Dr Hindman,' said Van Deusen soothingly. 'I know you can see us. Now, if you'll let – '

Hindman ripped off the newest sheet and forced it

into Izzy's hand, his face suddenly betraying terror. Then, satisfied that she had taken possession of it, he slunk back to his bed where he began to shiver.

'What's wrong with him now?' asked Fergus.

'Nothing.' Van Deusen closed the door and locked it. 'Seeing visitors has disrupted his routine. As you can see, your visit was futile.'

Izzy was studying Hindman's latest sketch. 'What do you think this represents?'

'Just his usual nonsense,' said Dr Van Deusen, giving it a cursory glance, then leading them back along the corridor.

Fergus examined it more intently, aware that Hindman's outburst must have some significance, if only for the man himself. This sketch depicted a large circle containing two box-like shapes with wheels attached. Automobiles? Next to these were several stick people, one of whom seemed to be carrying a flag. On it was a large cross, above which was a ragged face with stitches for a smile. The figure carrying the flag also had a black blob on its face. What the hell did that mean? And why was Hindman suddenly so frightened?

'I can see you. I can see you,' continued the terrified wail from his room.

'What is this?' Fergus asked Izzy, unnerved by the man's cry.

'Two cars here,' she said. 'Some people. A circle. What's the flag, though? A Smiley and a cross?'

'The Smiley's got teeth.'

'Shall we move on?' said Van Deusen impatiently.

'Just coming,' said Fergus. A face with teeth? 'It's a

skull and crossbones! And that black mark there could be an eye-patch. Look, it's a pirate!'

'With two automobiles?'

True. So what could the pirate mean? Why the cars? And why so alarmed? Then Fergus understood. He looked up the corridor for the green EXIT sign. 'Come on. We've got to move!'

He grabbed Izzy's hand and began to run, ignoring the protests of Dr Van Deusen. As Fergus burst through the swing doors out into the gardens, Hindman's hysterical cries pursued them.

'*I can see you! I can see you! I can see you!*'

Suddenly Fergus gasped.

'What is it?' said Izzy.

'This circle must be the gateway we came through, remember. The pirates are bad guys arriving in cars. And, judging by his panic, they're already here – '

He skidded to a halt as they rounded the corner of the main house. A black Cutlass saloon and a black Dodge Ram pick-up were drawing to a halt. Men in suits started climbing out. He ducked back out of sight. Shit!

'Hindman was warning us: he saw them coming! We need to get out of here fast.'

He peered round the corner. Meanwhile, Dr Van Deusen was emerging from the corridor thirty yards behind them, calling for them to wait for him. Fergus ignored the pompous prig and braved another glance towards the front of the house. All of the visitors had now gone inside, except one man hovering by their Pinto.

Fergus sagged back against the wall. A man carrying a

paint-splattered decorator's ladder was disappearing through another door of the annexe, a Walkman precluding his hearing anything. His Toyota pick-up sat not twenty yards away, the driver's door still open.

'Time to go,' muttered Fergus.

They raced for the pick-up and Fergus jumped into the driving seat. The Toyota was old, its fan-belt slipping – as Fergus discovered when he swung out round the front of the hospital. The pick-up seemed to be almost squealing for attention.

Fergus missed third gear, the lever jumping in his hand. 'Jesus, the decorating business must be in a bad way if he's stuck with this heap!'

As they exited through the peculiar gateway, Izzy peeked back through the cab's rear window. The solitary man who had been studying their Pinto was now climbing into the mean-looking Ram, while another ran out from the front door towards him.

Fergus cursed, then turned on to the main road, heading for the 136 intersection. As they gathered speed down the hill, he caught sight of the Ram pick-up through the boundary hedge. It was kicking up dust as it snaked down the driveway.

'Shit! They'll probably catch us before we even reach the damn highway!'

He wondered if he should pull off the road, so they could try running into the woods. But once they realized he was moving on foot, he and Izzy probably wouldn't get a hundred yards. Their only chance now was to outrun them, but even that forlorn hope was soon dashed. As he barrelled on to the State Highway, he saw the pick-up turn out behind them.

'Maybe they'll run out of gas,' commented Izzy.

Fergus shot her a glance, but her calm face simply baffled him. They were maybe half a minute from being run off the road, yet Izzy couldn't comprehend their danger, merely commenting on events as if watching TV!

He had managed to wind the Toyota up to sixty-five, but it wasn't allowing him any more. The Ram behind probably wasn't out of third gear yet – and it was *big*: it began to fill his mirrors, a great black hulk behind grinning chrome bull-bars, the six lamps on its roof like predators' eyes. Then its darkened windshield lurched closer as it rammed into the rear of the Toyota.

Fergus began to weave frantically, but the Ram was almost twice as wide and his evasive actions merely reduced his own speed. Other traffic was particularly light, so there wasn't much chance of witnesses calling the police.

'We're not going to make it,' he muttered, wondering if Izzy would be spared if they surrendered. He realized that was futile: they were after *everyone* on that list, so Izzy was as much dead meat as himself.

Izzy suddenly opened her door.

'*What are you doing?*' Fergus screamed.

'I've got a plan.'

'Suicide won't help us!'

But she was already reaching up on to the roof. Grabbing for the small rail that ran round its rim, she pulled herself upright in her seat.

Fergus was tempted to slow down for her, but decided

any change of speed might simply throw her off balance. Christ, only a madwoman would attempt climbing out of a vehicle at this speed – but then, *she* wouldn't know that, would she? Now she looked set to fall to her death.

God, what a mess!

They were fast approaching a bend and Fergus eased up on the gas, so the truck wouldn't lean too far over. Izzy had grabbed the edge of the flatbed and was trying to find somewhere to put her left foot inside it. She glanced down at the speeding blacktop. My, they were going fast.

She hitched her leg high, enough to clear the side of the flatbed, then let it slide over the rim.

As a car horn screamed past, the Toyota wobbled dangerously, but satisfied now that her foot was in place, she pulled herself further up until her breasts were digging into the cab roof and she could edge herself sideways and throw herself into the rear of the pick-up. She heard a whoop from Fergus as she did so, and turned to survey her new armoury. It was not inspiring.

Suddenly she was hurled toward the tail of the Toyota as the Ram crashed into them again. Fetching up against the tailgate, she found a bundle of paint rags and threw them at the Ram's windshield. It swerved, with tyres shrieking, then resumed its assault.

There was another judder as it collided with the Toyota, but this time she kept her balance, hurling a bucket. A large plastic bottle of turpentine followed; a selection of brushes proved equally unintimidating. It looked like all her effort was to be in vain.

Fergus, meanwhile, was driving at the max, the Toyota's speedometer wavering around seventy. Izzy was fast running out of ammunition. All that remained was a step-ladder, fastened to one side, and a five-gallon can of white paint. Suddenly she had an idea. So, unfortunately, did the Ram's passenger and he leaned out to take aim with his pistol. The first shot missed her.

Fergus heard the report, then a second shot rang out, shattering the cab window behind him. *Damn! Get down, girl!* But Izzy didn't understand the danger; and instead continued to wrestle with the paint can.

Fergus swung the Toyota into the centre of the road, then he dabbed his brakes, enough to turn his tail-lights red. The Ram's driver reacted instantly and soon there was some distance between them. Fergus used this short respite to steer off the highway on to a back road, hoping the Ram would overshoot the turning. When it didn't, he fisted the steering wheel in frustration. Their only hope now lay with Izzy and the can of paint she was struggling with.

Izzy finally got its lid off, but found the can was only half full. She lifted it up on to the tailboard and waited till the Ram charged at them another time. As it collided, she let go of the can and it flew towards the pursuer's windshield.

Though not heavy enough to shatter the glass, its contents spewed out to cover three-quarters of the windshield in a viscous white.

Suddenly blinded, the Ram's driver veered first to the left, then to the right. He pulled out into the left-hand side of the road as his windshield wipers battled impotently with the paint. As hands appeared from each side window to rub desperately at the paint, a single-lane covered bridge loomed ahead. Fergus aimed for the dead centre, but the Ram driver realized the danger too late and was unable to pull across behind the Toyota in time.

Going from sixty miles an hour to zero in the space of eight inches, both occupants of the Ram exited through their windshield, one on either side of the bridge's roof support. The passenger flew into the stream below, while the driver slammed into the slatted wooden road that ran through the bridge.

Fergus instinctively stepped on his brakes and the Toyota slid to a halt beyond the far exit, Izzy tumbling against the rear of the cab.

'You all right?' Fergus yelled, leaping out of the cab.

Izzy looked shaken but otherwise unhurt.

Fergus took her hand and helped her down, placing her in the passenger seat of the pick-up. He then walked back through the covered bridge.

The Ram's driver was definitely dead, face mangled, head all but ripped off. The Ram itself was hissing its last.

Looking over the wooden parapet, Fergus could see the twisted manikin of the passenger, broken on the boulders in the rapid-flowing stream twenty feet below.

Fergus then searched the driver's bloodstained jacket for his wallet. It held no identification, just twelve hundred dollars in hundred-dollar bills. He pocketed the cash, wiped the wallet on his trousers, then tossed it back at the corpse.

Fergus climbed into the pick-up and squealed away. As the Toyota snaked up the hill, there was a dull *whumph* down in the valley as the Ram caught fire, smoke billowing through both ends of the bridge.

Carefully driving within the speed limit, Fergus turned off I95 at Exit 19 and made his way through the town of

Freeport until he could pull into the big parking lots off the main street. There they abandoned the Toyota truck and headed for the restrooms of the giant LL Bean store.

Half an hour later they were seated in the coffee shop. Fergus had forced down a red dog and Sprite, while Izzy relished a lobster roll and a Moxie. With their stolen cash they next headed out to buy some new clothes, visiting J Crew, Patagonia, Levi's, Boston Traders and Timberland. They then set off in search of a motel.

The fall tourist season had started, so most of the motels were already full, and it was only with some luck they managed to find a vacant room at the Bailey Motor Court. Izzy paid cash for three nights in advance and then, grateful for a hiding place at last, they collapsed on to the double bed.

TWENTY-SIX@Chapter

Fergus and Izzy dozed in their motel room for half an hour. Exhausted, they lay on the bed recovering, listening to the sounds of holidaymakers in adjacent rooms returning from their day's outing. Normal everyday sounds that Fergus found welcome.

Finally, he found the strength to rise, and pulled out the two sketches Dr Hindman had given him. He unfolded first the one portraying the arrival of the pirates and their cars.

'Why pirates?' he mused.

'A cryptic clue,' said Izzy, as she munched a packet of salted pretzels. 'He draws in a hurry, so needs some kind of shorthand. A pirate just means bad people.'

But Fergus wasn't totally convinced. If it simply represented bad, why not show a swastika? No one could misinterpret that. 'What about this other one? Figure that out.'

Izzy studied it. 'OK. What have we got? It seems to be drawn on a piece of a map – so he probably ran out of paper. Two images here: a stick figure in orange crayon and a face also in orange.'

'The figure? I'd say it was meant to be a man,'

surmised Fergus. 'That thing at the top of the legs looks like an erection. An orange man? But look at the other one: the face . . . His faces are usually a circle with two eyes and a mouth. Here it isn't even a shape. All you've got are two eyes, a nose and a pointed chin.'

'So he likes to change his style?'

'No. The orange stick man is the same as his others,' said Fergus. 'This is *more* than just a face. None of its components touch. If these *are* cryptic clues, that must mean something. Let's write each element down separately.' He used the back of a tourist brochure as a pad. 'Now, are those zeroes, or circles, or represent the letter O? A "7" here, and what? A "V"? O-7-O-V. It's meaningless.'

'Who says they're meant to be in that order? If he was trying to hide his message, he might have mixed it up so no one would find it.'

'No one else?'

'He gave this picture specially to *you*,' explained Izzy. 'And it was hanging on his wall. And he knew where I lived and about your monster truck. Who knows what else that poor man's seen? Maybe he even knew we were coming . . . So, it could be 700-V. Or V-700, V-007, OO7?'

'Doesn't make sense, unless you mean James Bond. Anyway, what the hell's that got to do with Hindman?'

'But it has to be important. Remember, of all the pictures around the room, he gave you this one specifically. *After* you'd been asking him about the Lab. Who was 007 – some sort of secret agent?'

'James Bond. Sean Connery, Roger Moore, Pierce – '

'A spy? A V? *Spy*-V?'

'What?'

'Spivey. I've seen that name somewhere,' said Izzy. 'Spivey . . . And then an orange man.'

'The orange man comes first. So we have Orange Man Spivey?' Fergus picked up the phonebook and flipped through it. 'Well, well, well. Orangeman and Spivey Inc., Lumber.'

'Those little orange lollipops he had drawn everywhere,' said Izzy, 'they're meant to be trees!'

Fergus looked at her. 'OK, so what?'

'He must have drawn them for a reason, and he must have given you the picture for a reason.'

Suddenly it hit Fergus! That scrap of paper Hindman had drawn on was an area of map almost void of names. However, closer examination revealed three names in blue italics buried amid his scribblings: Richard, Kemberscuit, Mooseshin Str. Fergus retrieved a tourist map of Maine from the bedside drawer.

It showed the northern end of the state as almost bare of roads, what few routes there were being minor ones and marked PRIVATE ROAD. But he was able to discern the same three names from Hindman's map: they applied to rivers in the North Woods region. And on his tourist map, he also found the fateful words: MANY ROADS IN NORTHERN MAINE ARE PRIVATE. FOR PERMIT INFORMATION AND FEES CONTACT: NORTH MAINE WOODS, BOX 362, ASHLAND, MAINE 04732.

It was the word PRIVATE that leaped off the page, because PRIVATE and SECRET were surely two sides of the same coin.

Using his thumb and index finger, he made a rough estimate of the area of northern Maine that contained these PRIVATE ROADS. Apart from Baxter State Park to the south and the thin ribbon of the Allagash Wilderness Waterway to its centre, most of the country lying west of State Highway 11, from Millinocket to the Canadian border in the north and west, seemed to be privately owned. *An area of roughly 8,000 square miles.* Bigger than the states of Connecticut and Delaware combined, and approaching the same size as Vermont or Massachusetts.

Fergus explained his theory to Izzy. He had been handed a reference to the logging company called Orangeman and Spivey, which operated in the vast and privately owned expanse of the North Woods. It was as good a place as any in which to hide something as clandestine as the Lab.

Izzy headed into the bathroom as Fergus turned on the television. Flipping through channels, he picked up items about the jet crash in Nevada; the President recovering after his operation; and the continuing search for Mad Dog Kintrey. The police claimed to be pursuing new leads, but as of this time his whereabouts remained a mystery. Depressed, Fergus searched for some entertainment, but somehow *I Love Lucy* and *Deep Space Nine* failed to cheer him. Instead he settled for MTV. Yes were playing an Unplugged concert. Well, what the hell, it was music.

Izzy returned from the bathroom with her face glowing, her blouse unbuttoned. She sat down next to him to view the screen. Steve Howe was now playing the acoustic intro to 'Onward'. The love song reminded Fergus of his time at college . . . before the Disappeared Years. Why did he think of them as his Disappeared Years? Could something strange have happened to him then?

He was distracted from these thoughts by the sight beside him. Izzy began unselfconsciously pulling off her blouse, unhooking her plain white bra . . . letting it drop on to her lap. Then, under his astounded gaze, she ran both hands under her breasts, over the thin red lines left by the cups' underwiring. Her large nipples were pink and erect, the aureoles small, like a little girl's.

Fergus couldn't take his eyes away and blurted out, 'They're beautiful.'

'Yes, aren't they?' said Izzy matter-of-factly, staring down as she stroked them. 'And they're real.'

Fergus found himself reaching out a hand to touch them. They felt cool, soft and wonderful. As she turned to face him, he cupped them both and squeezed. Izzy closed her eyes and stretched her arms above her head. Fergus swung his thumbs downwards and felt the subtle resistance of her nipples. As he rubbed his thumbs back and forth, teasingly, Izzy sighed and moaned.

Suddenly she was lying on her back, Fergus's tongue deep in her mouth. Her hand was delving inside his shirt and pinching his own nipples hard. He drew his tongue across her chin, her cheek, down on to her neck, where he teased with his teeth, faking bites from one ear to the next. Then he trailed down on to her breasts, licking at the flawless white skin. Listening to the soft whimpers as he devoured each nipple in turn, the growing growls of pleasure.

Everything after that became a frenzied blur, clothing torn off and discarded, as erect flesh sought a moist berth. And soon he was on top and entering her, her momentary cry of surprise soon forgotten as she dug her nails into his back. And then they were rutting furiously, each seeking their own peak, he lunging into her, she hefting her backside off the bed, opening her thighs wide, wider, as if desperate to have as much of him inside as possible. And then, too soon, he was coming, pistoning furiously and biting hard into her shoulder, his grunts filling her ear. His loss of control triggered her own orgasm and she arched under him, almost throwing him off as he emptied himself inside her.

A minute later a breathless Fergus was apologizing for taking her, for being so rough, for being so selfish . . . Izzy simply told him to hush up and to finish the job, pushing him down towards her open thighs.

Fergus jerked awake some time during the night, his mind still filled with terrible images of books exploding from shelves and drenching him in blood. So shaken was he by this nightmare that it took several moments to remember where he was.

'What is it?' he heard Izzy say in the dark, stroking his stomach under the sheet.

'Nothing. Just a dream I keep getting.' He forced himself to calm down again, wiping the sweat from his face.

As he felt the thudding in his ears recede, with the slowing of his hammering heart, he felt Izzy's hand wander down to his crotch.

In the morning, despite their continued intimacy, Fergus realized they were still virtual strangers. Izzy was the first to mention it, startling Fergus as he stood naked at the washbasin.

'Thanks for last night,' she said. 'I haven't had a jump in ages.'

'I thought it counted for a bit more than that,' he suggested.

He stared with confusion into the steamed-up mirror, wiping it clear to look at his blushing face. Izzy was stepping out of the shower, her beautiful body slick with water. He turned to face her.

'I think I love you,' he said, knowing it sounded crass.

She glanced down at his hardening cock.

He shook his head. 'Last night was truly the best,' he continued. 'But it wasn't just what we did. It was *you*. I know we haven't known each other long and things probably will never work out . . . But I *want* you, more than anything in the world. I want to clear my name and look after you.'

She stared at him, her eyes wide, looking almost like a high-school girl – her face so innocent, even if her body was not.

'You know I can't worry about anything, Fergus,' she said quietly. 'And I hate being what I am. Being like this makes everything potentially dangerous, yet I don't even know what that means. Someone once said love was awful because it meant living in fear that it would come to an end. Well, love isn't awful to me, Fergus, because I can never see that bad side. All I see is the good and the *now*. So you can love me as much as you want, because I won't be leaving, because – '

'Because you'll never see the bad side coming.'

'That's right.' She walked over to him. 'And I'm trusting you to make sure it lasts. Just promise me that you'll do that. Make it last.'

'I'm wanted for a dozen murders. I haven't got a chance of proving my innocence. And when they find me they're likely to shoot me on sight. And if you're there with me – '

'But I don't care about that. Just promise you'll make it last.'

He took her in his arms, pressed his face to her wet hair. 'I promise, Izzy. I promise to make it last as long as I can.'

And Fergus knew that whoever had said love was awful was right, because he knew that what they had now *would* end sooner rather than later, and that he had no right to endanger her. But, then, hadn't someone else also said love was selfish?

He tilted her head up to his. 'I promise,' he repeated.

TWENTY-SEVEN@Chapter

Fergus was determined to find out as much as he could about what Orangeman and Spivey were up to in the North Woods. But the only way he could do that would be to go there, and in order to do that he needed an accurate map of the area.

They had been so tired after their narrow escapes of the day before – and their far more pleasurable activities during the night – that they had both overslept. So it was just after noon when they located the owner of the Bailey Motor Court and made enquiries about the woods.

He reluctantly referred them to an environmental pressure group called the Nanabozhos, whose aim was to return the North Woods of Maine to public ownership.

'But they're a bunch of hippie bums, those Nanny Bozos,' said the owner bitterly, leaning on his counter, still running his eye over the sports page. 'More concerned with savin' goddamn trees than keepin' people here in jobs. Timber means real dollars and real work. What good's a tree if it don't get cut up? Christ, it ain't as if the area's *natural* woodland. Most of those trees been felled and replanted several times. 'Bout as natural as freakin' furniture. But that don't bother those nature-lovin' mothers. Anyhows, they've got these maps'll show you all the roads, and that's more'n the lumber companies'll tell you. Let those goddamn tree-huggers open up all that land and all you'll get is tourists with tents, and what good are they to any of us?'

Leaving the man to his economic prejudices, they followed his directions to the Nanabozhos store. It was a cramped boutique at the tail-end of a shopping mall, next to the disabled toilets. Its walls were covered with hectoring posters: EXPLORATION NOT EXPLOITATION. A selection of cheap-looking Native American artefacts filled the shelves, together with bumper stickers, mugs and badges.

Nanabozhos didn't exactly reek of professionalism and only the sign on the facing wall prevented Fergus from leaving:

NORTH WOODS TRAIL MAPS.

MOST UP TO DATE AVAILABLE. WHERE YOU CAN AND CAN'T GO. WHAT THE LAW SAYS. WHO TO CALL FOR LICENCES. LEGAL ADVICE. CLAIM BACK OUR LAND.

$20 plus tax.

Two girls in tight shorts, both wide of hip and bountiful in cellulite, waddled away from the chipped wooden counter, allowing Fergus and Izzy access to a twenty-something long-hair whose name badge announced him as Kirk.

'Look at that . . . Damn shame . . .' muttered Kirk, turning to the TV at one end of the counter. It had broken off for a news bulletin, which included an item on the burned-out bridge.

'Did you know there's only ten covered bridges in the

whole of Maine?' Kirk continued. 'Looks like only nine now. That was a Paddleford Modified Long Truss too.'

Kirk seemed more upset about the bridge itself than the two men who had died there. Interestingly, the news report didn't mention *how* the bridge came to be destroyed, which seemed very odd.

Fergus pointed up to the sign. 'Those maps? They accurate?'

Kirk blinked at him, then reached under the counter. He pulled out a map, unfolded it and turned it round so Fergus could examine it.

'I know they're expensive, man, but no one else gives you as much information. See those tints? Different colour for each company. See the patterns? Dots mean no way you gonna get across their land without encountering some *serious* public-relations problems. Diagonal lines, it depends what they're doing: some days they ignore you, others they give you the bum's rush. No marking: it's Disneywood! All you do is watch out for the warning signs – "*Swamp*" means swamp; "*Rockfalls*" means rockfalls – and you'll be OK.'

Fergus ran his eye down to the key at the bottom. Unsurprisingly, Orangeman and Spivey's land was marked out in orange – and it was as spotty as a kid with chickenpox.

'So if we tried walking through, say, this area, we'd be – '

Kirk shook his head. 'That there's a *real* no-go area, man. Never known anyone get more'n half a mile before they were thrown out. Heavy-duty security, man . . . and I've heard stories.'

Izzy spoke up. 'What kind of stories?'

'Oh, nothing definite but – well, they ain't protecting

trees, if you know what I mean? It ain't like you're gonna steal their lumber or take a sneak peek at some revolutionary chainsaw.'

'So why, then?'

'Some take it personal, man.' Kirk pointed a nail-bitten finger at a small pink square. 'This patch here, that's owned by Isaiah Seton. Doubt he's had a tree felled in twenty years. Just wants people off his land 'cos it's *his* land. But Orangeman . . . well, they *are* up to something. Get quite a bit of traffic going in, and it doesn't come out for days.'

'Secret stuff?' said Izzy.

Kirk, clearly taken by the depth of Izzy's cleavage, leaned forward conspiratorially. 'Could be anything. But whatever it is, you can't see it from the air – that I do know. These maps are based on aerial surveys – they can't stop you flying *over* their property – though Orangeman have tried injunctions against our pilots. That's why it gets a bit vague in the dotted areas.'

'So how accurate is it?'

Kirk caught sight of Fergus watching him look down Izzy's blouse and he stepped back. 'Accurate to within 200 yards when you get really off track, otherwise it's up to government standard. But remember, you got to pay the tolls at the North Maine Woods, Inc. roadblocks, where they let you in. It's *all* private property, except for the two parks.'

'We'll take it,' said Fergus.

Kirk folded the map and handed it over. Fergus gave him the cash.

'Why are you called Nanabozhos?' asked Izzy.

'Nanabozho was the Great Rabbit grandson of

Nokomis, the Mother of Earth. When her sworn enemies the Underwater Panthers sent a flood – '

It was time for Fergus to drag Izzy away. As they left, they could hear Kirk calling after them, 'Keep off those dotted areas, man! Some of their people can be real unwelcoming – and you'll be a long ways from any help.'

They left the mall and headed along the street. The day was warm, the sidewalks were beginning to crowd with lunchtime shoppers.

'So what now?' said Izzy.

'We go hiking.'

'OK,' she said enthusiastically.

Fergus hugged her, kissed the top of her head. Kirk had just given them a clear warning of danger, yet Izzy was totally unaffected.

He realized the next part of their journey would be doubly difficult because he was taking with him a woman who, to all intents and purposes, was a simpleton. He'd have his work cut out just keeping her safe. Still, he was determined she would get out of this alive, even if it cost him his own life.

Jesus, did I just think that? That I'd die to make sure Izzy survived? In the middle of the bustling sidewalk, he gave her a bone-crushing hug, then a fierce kiss.

Some passers-by applauded and whooped, but he ignored them. He was trembling with excitement. He really had fallen in love.

TWENTY-EIGHT@Chapter

Harry came round in a small room that contained only a bed and a low table. He was alone.

On the table sat a tray holding a bowl of soup and a bread roll, a second bowl half filled with melted chocolate ice-cream and a glass of water. The room was lit by a single bare light bulb. The only door had no handle on the inside. The floor was grey cement, the unadorned walls whitewashed brick. If there was anywhere in the bleakness of Down Town that particularly approximated a jail cell, Harry was locked in it now.

He sat up, head throbbing. Someone had dressed him, and he was wearing his sunglasses. He took them off, but the light was so bright and harsh he had to put them back on. As he lay down on the bed, he thought through everything that had recently happened. Why wasn't he already dead? Perhaps his skills with the Hubcap could not yet be replicated by the Paragons. But, even so, the hatred he'd seen in Dr Ralston's eyes was a sign that his usefulness was now at the absolute limit of her tolerance. This train of thought was suddenly disrupted when the door was unlocked.

A burly guard wearing sunglasses came in. 'Face the wall!' he barked.

Harry did as ordered. 'How long have I been in here?' he croaked.

'A while now. Took them a day to move you here.'

And with that surprising fact, the guard went out, locking the door behind him. A *day* to move him from one room to another? What the hell had been going on?

Dr Ralston had so far tried everything to gain his co-operation – friendship, logic, a pretence at honesty, the appeal to patriotism, threats, drugs, violence – but he sensed that there would be no more chances. She would now want him eliminated whatever the consequences to their flight programme. For he realized her actions had become tainted by personal animosity stronger than logic.

As he nibbled on the dry bread roll, Harry looked the room over, desperate to escape. It was ten minutes later when he realized the glass of water and the melted ice-cream were all he needed to achieve his purpose.

Standing on the table, he flicked cold water from the glass at the hot light bulb until it finally exploded, showering the room with fragments of glass. The room was plunged into total darkness: part one of his plan was now complete.

TWENTY-NINE@Chapter

Under the panoply of Douglas firs and Douglas spruce, pines, birches, balsams, and red and white cedars that made up the forests of the North Woods region, the seasons seemed often as distant as the sky.

The days were dull, the nights black, and only the longest stretches of drought or snowfall would impinge on the springy earth and prevailing damp that gave parts of the forest their distinctive otherworldliness. With the tall trees crowding in from above, and encroaching in ranks on all sides, the narrow tracks and paths seemed to be there only on sufferance, liable to be sacrificed at a moment's notice. Despite decades of exploitation for its natural timber, much of this landscape of green-swathed hills and mountainsides resembled God's own wild garden gone to seed. And, indeed, millions of tourists walked, canoed and climbed these twenty million acres to pay their awed respect – after, of course, they had paid their road tolls to North Maine Woods, Inc.

For amid the natural sounds of the forest – the cathedral-quiet rustle of wind in upper branches, the tinkling of streams and the gush of falls, the whooping of loons, the quark of ravens and the occasional braying of a moose – there was, most everywhere one could travel, the distant rasp of a chainsaw. Despite its primeval appearance and bounteous beauty, the area was little more than a factory floor: every tree in every acre sat awaiting assault by professional rapists with their saws, cranes, draglines and multi-axle rigs. In an effort to cope with their burdensome debts, many logging companies were doing their maximum to blaspheme this awesome landscape, pockmarking it with unplanted tracts as ugly as cigarette burns on emerald velvet. And wherever they *had* replanted, the new trees were often arranged in rows as formal as production lines, all the easier to cull once they attained maturity. But new or old, wild or tamed, Fergus hated it all. Unlike the riotous warmth of Vermont's vermilion-and-gold fall make-over, this expanse was as severe and humourless as the cosmetics applied by a mortician to a corpse. Most of his adult life he had wanted to hide away from the world and its myriad responsibilities, and for the most part he had succeeded. But here, in the midst of the vast forest, he truly was lost, because he had no sense of scale – everywhere he looked just continued on and on – and he had no sense of time. And despite the map he had bought, he also had no sense of direction. In truth, he found his new surroundings every bit as intimidating as the reasons for his being there. Trees and more trees were every-damn-where.

Naturally, Izzy had no such misgivings. She *loved* it all and could hardly be restrained from leaping out of the car to skip through the mossy undergrowth.

'It's wonderful,' she breathed, time and again.

Fergus resisted the urge to disagree; just a glance at her smile was enough to still his tongue. But for him it was simply a long and tedious drive to an uncertain future – and the last desperate hope that he might find some salvation.

The map he had bought turned out to be accurate, and there were road markers at every mile to ensure that loggers and hikers alike would find it extremely difficult to get lost, despite the vast size of the forested area. He had dutifully paid the tolls as they worked their way deeper into the forest, but had noticed a lot of roads were blocked off, denying them access to large areas. It was one of these trails that Fergus turned on to when his map confirmed that it eventually led to Orangeman and Spivey's land.

Together, he and Izzy had struggled to lift the wooden barriers aside, allowing just enough space to scrape their car through. In the half-hour since, they hadn't spotted another soul or another vehicle, not even a logging truck. As he pulled the car over to check their progress, Izzy was out of it before he had even set the handbrake.

'Don't go too far,' he shouted, like a concerned father.

'I won't,' she replied, like an excited daughter.

Fergus began to check his maps. He had already used his photographic memory to imprint the Nanabozhos' map on his mind while waiting in a Taco Bell next to Burka's Car Bargains in Freeport. It was there he had given all their cash to Izzy and instructed her to go and buy them a used car. Half an hour later she returned with an '84 blue Chevette held together by rust and state-unenforceable guarantees. She had only scraped it against two parked cars on the way. After assuring himself that the vehicle possessed an engine and four wheels, Fergus had settled himself behind the steering wheel, then set off northwards. Their journey took longer than anticipated, however, as he had to avoid fourth gear – a ratio the engine seemed to have grown tired of using.

Now calling up his memorized map and comparing it to the real one on his lap, Fergus found that he was already a good third of the way into Orangeman and Spivey's domain. If the terrain carried on like this, however, they could well be wasting their time on some wild-goose chase. He stepped out of the car to stretch his legs.

'Izzy!' he shouted. 'Where are you?'

'Over here!' he heard faintly, and turned to see her kneeling by the side of small creek a hundred yards away.

She was running her hands through the water and, as he reached her, she scooped up a handful and splashed him with it. Her playfulness broke his morbid mood and he began to splash her in return. Such was their preoccupation with this that at first neither of them noticed the orange truck slowing to a halt in front of their car. Nor the two men who clambered out, dressed in military camouflage uniforms and carrying sub-machine-guns.

When Fergus finally spotted the newcomers, he grabbed Izzy by the arm and pulled her down beside him.

The two armed men had entered the trees, about half-way towards them, then stopped as if unsure of their target.

'Who are they?' hissed Izzy.

'Sssh,' Fergus cautioned. 'Let me think.'

When he dared another look, one of the pair had moved off to the right; the other was now closer by a good ten paces. Since when had lumber companies employed guards with sub-machine-guns? Fergus took Izzy's hand and pulled her in further beneath the overhanging branches. There was no point in attempting to run, so they would have to wait it out where they were.

Five minutes passed without a sound, then came four shots, each making him jump. After another long pause, the truck drove off. Fearful that one of them might have stayed behind, Fergus forced himself to remain lying still. Izzy, however, began to rise.

'Don't move,' he hissed. 'Just wait here until I tell you and stay out of sight.'

He eased his arms away from her and carefully poked his head through the branches.

The truck had indeed gone, but he now realized what the gunfire had signified. They had shot out the car's tyres. Their best course of action was to get away from the immobile Chevette as soon as possible, despite its containing their clothes and the map. There could still be someone near by waiting to ambush them; or they might sweep the road regularly in both directions, knowing that the car's occupants would have to get out on foot. Luckily, Fergus had memorized the map, so could identify the stream they were huddled beside. It ran further into Orangeman and Spivey land, before branching to the south – and on into another company's land, which was accessible to the public. Once there, they would be able to hike out on foot, but there was a long trek ahead of them.

He whispered to Izzy, 'Come on. We're getting out of here.'

Izzy nodded and took hold of his hand. Even under the gloom of the trees, Fergus could tell the sky was darkening – and they certainly weren't prepared for a night in the open. It would turn damn cold and they were wearing only T-shirts and light jackets.

Twenty minutes later he halted their progress. The stream had disappeared into the ground. Whatever the cause for this, it meant they no longer had a route to follow. Calling up his photographic memory, he let the map spring into view. Running his eyes over the route he had planned in his mind, he found that the stream should have continued here. But looking around, he could see nothing but trees, and they were still only halfway to the safe road. And now, without the sun, he couldn't even tell which direction they were heading, so they could end up going round in circles. They didn't have any choice: they had to follow the stream all the way back to their car and risk taking the road again.

'If we go any further this way, we'll get lost. So we have to go back.'

'OK.'

He studied her, trying to judge her mood. She seemed content to agree with anything.

Then, 'What are you going to do when we get out of here?'

He loved that 'when'. There were no 'ifs' with Izzy. As to her question, he hadn't a clue. He hadn't really worked out a plan, just entertained a forlorn hope that answers would magically appear. But he was certain that Orangeman and Spivey were hiding something and that it involved Izzy as well as himself.

After retracing their steps for ten minutes, Fergus became increasingly alarmed at just how fast the light was disappearing. Before long they would be in pitch darkness, then their only hope of progress would be wading along the stream itself. The thought of that icy water was not appealing, but then neither was getting totally lost. He gripped Izzy's hand tighter. He hated to admit it, but he was scared. To distract himself, he decided they should tell each other more of their pasts. Unfortunately, his past alcoholism and failed marriage, and her accident-prone childhood and overly cosseted adolescence did nothing to lift his spirits.

She concluded her own story by withdrawing her hand and linking her arm through his. 'As long as I've got you, Fergus, things'll work out.'

He looked at her trusting face through the gloom. The chances were they wouldn't live through the night – if they weren't caught, they'd probably freeze to death – and so he couldn't help wishing that, however much he loved her now, he hadn't involved her. That way she would now be free to carry on with her solitary but safe existence. Then Izzy asked him an odd question. 'Your nightmares, Fergus – how long have you had them?'

'Ever since college . . . since my Disappeared Years,' he recalled. He had never been bothered by blood-sodden dreams in his childhood or at high school. He had always supposed they were first inspired by alcohol, something like the DTs, but they were now so ingrained in his brain that they just sat there waiting to be triggered. Fergus suddenly felt a shiver run through him and just then he sensed a presence.

Up ahead, behind that bush, did he see a movement, hear a rustling?

'Izzy!' he hissed, grabbing for her hand. 'There's someone there.'

But too late. The girl's curiosity took her straight to the spot. Fergus dashed after her, then faltered as he saw her raise her hand. He slowly moved forwards. The hand remained raised. Was someone pointing a gun at her? But why only one hand, he wondered.

Three more careful steps and he was right behind her. Maybe it was an ambush and there were others behind him. He whipped around, peering into the twilight – but saw only a hundred menacing trees.

'OK, OK,' Fergus said, his voice breaking. 'We give up. Just don't shoot, OK?'

But as he drew level with her, he saw why Izzy's hand was raised. Oh, sweet Jesus, he didn't believe it . . .

She was stroking a moose on the nose!

Fully eight feet high, dark brown and hairy, its antlers like a rack of coat hangers, it was staring at Izzy, their eyes locked. Although usually timid, the ugly animal plainly could not detect fear in her, so therefore she was no threat. Fergus couldn't help laughing out loud in relief.

But his outburst startled the moose's reverie. With a shake of its head, it turned and trotted off, soon swallowed up by the undergrowth and the dusk.

'Oh . . .' was all Izzy said as the spell was broken. 'Nice moose.'

As they walked on, Fergus considered that Izzy might well have an equal rapport with *all* animals, just because they would never smell fear on her. But then again, if they met an enraged bear, she would probably go up to the damn thing and call it Teddy!

They were only a couple of hundred yards further on when they saw a huge flash of light to their left. Fergus's heart began hammering again. At first he assumed it was a flashlight, so he dived to the ground, dragging Izzy with him.

But the light continued to grow, filling the horizon, then the sound of an explosion rolling through the trees like a wave. Soon there were more explosions, till the night flared yellow.

Once over his initial shock, Fergus estimated the time lapse between the initial flash and the explosion as a good twenty seconds, which would put the source of it four miles away. He couldn't even begin to guess what caused it but, with armed men all around, his mind ran riot.

Fortunately, the yellow light helped to show them the way and he dragged Izzy hurriedly after him, the stream now a sparkling highway.

The explosions gradually died away, but the light continued to flare in the distance, throwing the forest into a weird form of life as the shadows of the trees bobbed and wavered.

Then they heard the helicopters.

Fergus was terrified, just wanting to run. Whatever was happening, it was now all around them, the helicopters zooming above the trees. And then there came the chatter of machine-gun fire: the choppers overhead were firing at something. As they stumbled on, there was another huge explosion.

It was like a war – and they were right in the middle of it.

THIRTY@Chapter

Harry's guard arrived right on time – more than five and half hours after Harry had broken the light bulb. And again the man entered without knocking.

'The light's busted,' announced Harry as the door opened. 'Watch your step.'

Even as he spoke, broken glass crunched under the guard's boot.

'Damn,' the man hissed. He took a step sideways, but crunched more glass.

'It's everywhere,' explained Harry. 'Bulb just blew up.'

The guard looked towards the bed, thinking he saw Harry there, but the room was dark and the light from outside was blotted out by his own bulk in the doorway. Satisfied that the distance between them made him secure, the guard balanced the food tray and removed his sunglasses. Now he could see Harry sitting watching him.

'Look away,' the guard ordered.

'Oh, sure,' said Harry, turning his head to the wall. The man walked over and placed his new tray on the floor, then reached for the old one. But Harry had smeared the bottom with ice-cream, so it had acted like glue. As the guard tried to lift the tray, it refused to budge, then suddenly came free, scattering its contents on to the floor. Cursing, the guard knelt down to pick up the broken crockery. And it was then that Harry dashed to his side.

'Hey!' he said.

The startled guard looked up – and found himself staring into Harry's eyes, which reflected the light from the corridor behind.

'Leave the plate,' said Harry firmly.

The guard did exactly as he was ordered.

'OK, let's keep it simple. What's your name?' said Harry.

'Matthew Bonito.'

'Okey-dokey, Matthew. For the next hour you will do whatever I say. Only *I* will tell you what to do. You understand?'

The guard nodded slowly.

'Right. First, is this Down Town?'

'Yes.'

'So why did it take a day to get me here?'

'I don't know.'

'Do you know where the wounded Paragon is?'

'Yes.'

The walk to the Infirmary took them a couple of minutes. Harry's new-found confidence was quickly shaken by the corridor. The walls seemed a lighter tone of grey. But if they had been redecorated why couldn't he smell fresh paint?

There was no guard on duty outside the Infirmary but, on entering it, Harry found the outer room manned by a male nurse. Since he wasn't wearing sunglasses, he too was soon a willing member of Harry's new crew.

There were only three patients currently in the Infirmary: two in the main dormitory, the third in one of the side wards.

Like all the others in Down Town, the room was grey. Even the sheets on the metal-framed bed seemed grey with overuse. The room's occupant was Philip the Paragon. His eye was still bandaged, both thin arms strapped down and stabbed with intravenous needles, one in each, their tubes running up to two sets of drip bags. The patient's one good eye stared up at Harry, but offered no sign of recognition.

'Philip, do you remember me?'

Philip scrutinized him as Harry sat down on the edge of the bed. 'Harry Sixsmith, pilot,' he answered. The voice was barely a whisper.

'What are they doing to you?'

'Experiment.'

'What kind?'

'Food and water deprivation. To see how long I can live without them.'

'They're *starving* you?'

'They're feeding me nutrients.' Philip nodded weakly at the drips. 'And every four hours I undertake intelligence tests.'

'Why?'

'For long space flights. Trying to minimize water and food intake while maintaining the viability of the astronaut.'

'Meaning see how far you can pilot a spacecraft without food?' said Harry.

'There are nutrients.'

'And they look like they're doing you the world of

good.' Harry noticed that Philip was looking very pale, even for a Paragon. 'You're going to die,' he added flatly.

'Yes,' said Philip, equally bereft of emotion. He stared at Harry. 'So tired,' he said. 'All this, and the travelling.'

There it was again. 'What travelling? We're still in Down Town.'

'I know, but I remember being in some kind of vehicle. And drugged. But I just can't remember . . .'

'OK, don't worry about it now.'

Harry glanced around the room, then went out to grab some fruit and a pitcher of water from the bedside of a patient who was sleeping. Returning to Philip's side ward, he poured him a drink.

At first he was reluctant to accept, as if being watched – Harry checked to see if there were any video cameras – but finally Philip succumbed to temptation, and he gulped two glasses straight down. He then greedily devoured some grapes and a banana.

'The eye thing was a punishment, wasn't it?' Harry resumed.

'Yes. Because I wasn't perfect.' Philip's voice had improved.

'Nobody is perfect,' said Harry. 'One day they'll learn that. So, what did *you* do that was so wrong?'

'I was misusing the computers. Supposed to be flash-studying . . .'

Harry nodded. He had been taught to study that way too: text and images flashed on to a screen and were memorized as a unit for recall later.

'But?' Harry prompted.

Philip continued, seeming pleased to have a confidant. 'I didn't pay attention as closely as I should. Sometimes I finished early – and had time to play with the computer.'

'So you looked at things you shouldn't have?'

Philip went very quiet. Evidently this boy had looked at *lots* of things he shouldn't have – and probably more than those in charge knew of.

'Do they know what else you saw?' said Harry, pouring out a third glass of water, which he sipped himself.

'I called up our own files – for the Paragons. Saw our progress charts, how they evaluated us.'

'And?'

'I realized I was . . . expendable.'

Philip touched his hand, a gesture Harry appreciated. The boy then tried to sit up, but found the effort difficult, so Harry eased him up gently, doubling over his pillow.

'My test scores weren't high enough and my obedience factor was under question,' continued Philip. 'Somehow they found out I had also read my files and that's why they picked on me. We're not supposed to be curious, just obedient.'

'Join the club,' Harry said bitterly.

It was Harry's turn to pat the boy's hand. 'So what did you find on the computer?'

'I followed my file through all the subsections, until I found a program called FAIL:UNSAFE. It listed names and coded experiments, each ending in a date. A termination date.'

'And you were on it?' Harry guessed.

'Yes. My termination date is in two weeks' time.' He

raised his arms gingerly to show the attached tubes. 'This was my destiny all along.'

Harry looked at the IVs and at Philip's colour. The boy would have to endure an enormous amount of suffering before he expired, naturally or otherwise. Harry checked the watch he had taken from the guard. It was only thirty minutes until he was due to supervise the next test flight.

Philip groaned, pain showing on his face.

'The tubes?'

Philip nodded. 'Take them out. Please.'

Harry did as he was asked, finding, to his disgust, that each tube was connected to a three-inch needle. Small dribbles of blood and cries accompanied each extraction, until both tubes were hanging to the floor, dripping liquid. Philip rubbed his puncture wounds, tears running down his face. He's *ten* years old, thought Harry. What kind of people would do this?

'These other experiments, did you find out anything more about them?'

'There was another file, without so many names – and instead of termination dates it gave addresses. That one was called FAIL:SAFE. I thought it was funny to have all those *addresses* in a file when we all knew the world outside was dead.'

Harry refrained from commenting on that. The more he heard, the less inclined he was now to believe anything he had previously accepted as history. 'What did you do next?'

'I had to assume everyone mentioned on the UNSAFE

list was already terminated, but these others were still alive. Yet every one of them had failed *something* – just as I had. I wanted to know if these others were Paragons too. I wanted to warn them. I wanted to . . .' He began to sob. 'I wanted someone to *help* me. To *save* me.'

He broke off and carefully wiped his eyes. 'Sorry. We're not supposed to cry . . . I tried to find their names on other directories, but nothing showed. Then I noticed that some of the names – just a few – had been flagged. When I checked what this symbol meant, I found a subdirectory containing all these same names with a code number. When I punched in the code it gave an e-mail address.'

'Did you investigate it?'

'No. I didn't know what to say to them. But what I did do was download the list of FAIL:SAFE names, and send it out to everyone with an e-mail. I was about to send the FAIL:UNSAFE list too, as a warning – if those in the SAFE file understood what it meant to them, then they might do something that could also help *me*. But the guards caught me – though I switched off before they could find out what I'd done. And when I wouldn't tell them, well . . .' He pointed at his bandaged eye.

'When was this?'

'Four days ago – maybe five. I don't know time too well any more. I've been sleeping a lot.'

Harry let out a big sigh, his foot tapping urgently. He knew now that he had to help Philip; the boy was set to die an agonizing death. Harry couldn't let that happen, but what could he do to prevent it?

Just then there was a commotion outside. He hopped off the bed and peered round the cubicle door.

A male nurse had entered the dormitory and was arguing with the two still-hypnotized guards, demanding that he should be allowed access to Philip. He appeared to be carrying a tray of plasma bags, and Harry remembered that the two attached to Philip had been near to empty.

'Let him in,' said Harry, quietly but firmly.

The two guards immediately acquiesced. The nurse spotted Harry as soon as he entered the room – but fortunately he wasn't wearing sunglasses.

'Put the tray down,' said Harry, staring into his eyes.

The man then stood transfixed.

'How did you do that?' said Philip.

'Come on, we're going.' Harry started to help the boy out of his bed.

Three minutes later a strange entourage made its way along the grey corridor towards the Hubcap's Control Room. Harry took the lead, flanked by the hypnotized guard from his own room. The two men from the Infirmary were helping Philip along by supporting him under his shoulders.

Harry was expecting the Control Room to be relatively busy now – since the next flight was only twenty minutes away – but as he nudged open the unguarded door, he was surprised to see only one occupant: a technician working on a maze of wires sprouting from an open panel.

Harry turned to his companion. 'Knock him out,' he whispered.

The guard walked briskly forward and thumped the technician on the back of the head. The man was unconscious in an instant.

'Right, everyone inside. And I don't want anyone else to get in here.'

Once the main doors were locked, the three men stood guard while Harry and Philip surveyed the controls.

'What are you going to do?' gasped Philip, the short journey to the Control Room having exhausted him.

'The Hubcap. What else? I don't know for sure who or what is out there any more, but at least once we're in the air we have options.'

Philip let out a weak cough. 'I'm not strong enough. The G-forces. The way I am . . .'

'I'll watch out for them, don't worry. Neither of us has anything to lose.'

'Thank you.' Philip grabbed his arm and squeezed. 'Thank you.'

Harry set about his work of prepping the Hubcap. But he soon realized he had a problem. Although he knew how to fly the Hubcap, he didn't know how to launch it.

In panic he surveyed the array of buttons, lights, switches and slide controls. Given time he could work out some of their purposes, but now his timescale was severely limited. At any second the *whoop-whoop* of the alarm would sound – and then the bullets would start flying.

'Do *you* know how to operate any of this?' Harry asked in vain hope.

'Unfortunately, yes,' said Philip.

'Why unfortunately?'

Philip sat wheezing in a chair and stared up at Harry.

'Oh, no,' said Harry.

'Oh, yes . . . friend.'

Harry leaned back against the control panel and held his head in his hands. 'There must be some other way.'

'Not now, not here,' said Philip, and coughed.

'But I can't leave you here.'

'You can't sacrifice yourself for me. Remember, I'm already terminated. *You* have a chance, so take it. For both of us.'

Harry surveyed the control desk. 'You sure you can't set this up to run without you?'

'Only if you wait outside and I climb up the ramp.'

'Do that!'

'Harry, I couldn't get myself up out of this seat, let alone up the ramp. Besides, you'd have to shut off the drive in order to get the hatch open – and that would leave you exposed to them.'

'It's worth the risk.'

'And then what? Neither of us knows what's out there. You've been lied to all along – and we Paragons have never even been told. I'm just not up to it.'

Harry's foot was drumming on the floor. Philip reached over and pressed his knee.

'There's no point worrying about what *won't* happen. Just concentrate on getting yourself out.'

'But how can *you* know so much about the exit routine?'

'We were here observing during your last dozen flights.'

The deviousness of Dr Ralston really knew no limits, thought Harry. He looked out into the darkened Hangar. Chance of escape sat there, two seats just waiting to be filled.

'Are you sure, Philip?'

'Yes,' said Philip. 'Get going now.'

As they stared into each other's eyes, both knew that, for once, they were seeing the truth.

'I could take Douglas,' suggested Harry desperately.

'You've no idea where he is.'

'But if I could save *him* – '

'You haven't got time,' insisted Philip.

As if to prove the point, an alarm erupted suddenly in the Hangar, its braying filling the air, red lights spinning.

'Oh, blow!' Harry took Philip's hand. 'Thank you. And I'm sorry.'

'It's not your fault,' said Philip. 'And at last I can do something for myself. Now *go*.'

THIRTY-ONE@Chapter

Harry was strapped into the Hubcap. He initiated the main drive and announced that he was ready.

'Roger that,' said Philip, efficiency epitomized. His voice was barely audible over the shrieking alarms.

Harry stared out of the Hubcap at his compatriot. Even in the face of imminent death, Philip was doing everything meticulously, as he had been trained.

'Float me,' said Harry.

The Hubcap juddered as its platform set off, the craft slowly revolving until it faced the outer wall. Then, once the ramp was reached, the Hubcap rose until angled up at thirty degrees and the giant fans roared into life. The Hangar doors filled Harry's view – and slowly opened to reveal starry darkness. But then he heard gunshots over his earphones.

'Philip, what's that?'

'They're trying to get into the Hangar and they don't sound happy.'

Oh, blow! thought Harry. But then he felt the Hubcap begin its slow journey up the ramp.

There came several bursts of machine-gun fire and a dull explosion. Then a strange cry from the doomed Paragon.

'Philip! Philip!'

Utterly powerless, Harry could only sit and listen to the attack on the Control Room, while he himself stared out towards the night sky. There was nothing more he could do to help his new friend. But now the Hubcap was on the ramp, he was able to take control – and he did so.

There was a louder explosion and light flared somewhere behind him, bright enough to make its mark on the night outside.

A familiar voice came on the speaker, loud and outraged. Dr Ralston. 'Abort your take-off. Abort it now!'

Harry could ignore her: there were only feet to go. The Hubcap reached the top of the ramp as Dr Ralston continued to rant at him.

'Come back *now*, Harry! You can't escape. There's no way we're going to let you fly out of here!'

Harry was only seconds from the top of the ramp. But just as the craft settled level and he was about to punch the separation control, the cockpit was flooded with blinding light. Harry cried out in surprise.

It was to be several seconds before he could make out the source – a helicopter's searchlight.

A McDonnell Douglas Apache was hovering about fifty feet up and only a hundred feet from the exit of the Hangar. However low he kept the Hubcap, he would not be able to fly past it. Then Harry noticed its armaments: a 30mm automatic cannon machine-gun and sixteen Hellfire anti-tank missiles in under-wing hard points, hanging from either side of the fuselage like talons on a bird of prey.

'As you can see, there's nowhere for you to go. Don't

make them shoot you down, Harry,' urged Dr Ralston. 'Just bring the ship back in and then we'll talk.'

Instead Harry gently eased the Hubcap off the ramp, hovering inches above the platform.

'Harry, I know you've separated,' shrieked Dr Ralston. 'Just set her down and we'll bring you back in.'

'If you shoot me down, you lose the Hubcap. So it looks like this is a stand-off.' Harry was scanning the scene in front of him, desperately searching for some hope of escape. But all he could see was helicopter.

Philip's breathless voice then came over the speaker. 'Go, Harry . . . Go!'

'Land it, Harry,' threatened Dr Ralston, 'or I'll shoot him – '

'Blow it out your ear,' Harry said calmly, for once allowing himself to be vulgar.

There was a single shot.

Sorry, Philip, thought Harry sadly, but he knew Philip would have done the same if their positions had been reversed. Dr Ralston had trained both of them too well.

'You've got ten seconds before they fire,' warned Dr Ralston.

Harry ignored her threat. He knew the Hubcap intimately, certainly better than anyone in Down Town. He knew that the craft was fantastically strong, able to withstand extremes of heat and cold, and incredibly fast changes in speed. For all their external controls and read-outs, *he* was the heart of the Hubcap now and he knew full well that almost all the damage that had been inflicted on the ship over the years had been to their subsequent additions, not to the basic structure itself. Landing struts, antennae, instruments – these had been destroyed, but never the ship itself. The Hubcap was extremely strong, fast and supremely responsive.

Everything, in fact, that a helicopter wasn't.

'... eight, seven ...'

And a helicopter, however well armed or piloted, was totally dependent for flight on its rotors.

'... six, five ...'

Dr Ralston's voice was harsh and guttural. He could imagine her now with her eyes wide, her teeth bared in a snarl, anger pumping through her heart.

'... four ...'

He only had one option.

'... three ...'

'Sorry, Philip,' Harry said one last time, then, angling the Hubcap up at seventy degrees, he pulled hard on the controls and went for maximum thrust.

The Hubcap sliced off all four of the helicopter's whirring rotors with surgical precision, the chopper's thin blades no match for the power of the Hubcap's acceleration and its super-strong hull.

The Hubcap was already at a thousand feet before the stricken helicopter had plummeted a mere hundred feet to the ground. Harry rotated his ship in time to see his opponent explode, its wreckage flying into the air as its flaming bulk slid down the ramp into the Hangar. A lone missile scarred the night and bullets zapped about in every direction.

Almost as soon as the helicopter dropped out of sight, there came a second, larger explosion as a fireball spewed into the night from the mountainside, like a dragon spitting fire. Other sporadic explosions followed, as flames began to consume the Hangar's innards.

Harry felt as happy as he ever could be, seeing the cause of all his recent suffering being destroyed so violently. But then regret began to gnaw at him – because every explosion meant death for those inside. Even if everyone in Down Town had been part of the conspiracy, this was a dreadful price to pay for obeying orders. Dr Ralston could fry for sure – Harry felt no guilt about her fate – but there were so many others, almost as innocent as Harry himself. Even as he was coming to accept himself as a mass murderer, something else caught Harry's eye.

In a long sweeping arc, he brought the Hubcap down to two hundred feet, until he was level with the giant flame-thrower that was now the mouth of the Hangar, four hundred yards away. From here he could see the world immediately outside it lit up by bright yellow flames. And of all the things he might have expected, he was not prepared for what he saw now – stretching into the darkness in all directions.

Trees . . .?

THIRTY-TWO@Chapter

The Hubcap did not have an autopilot as such, but if Harry removed his hands and his feet from the controls simultaneously, the ship would remain in stasis – maintaining the exact same altitude, speed, angle and flight direction until the controls were touched again.

Rising gently to two thousand feet, two miles to the south of the now-flaming Hangar entrance, he brought the Hubcap to a halt, then released the hand controls and pulled his feet off the pedals. Satisfied that the craft was successfully locked into position, Harry settled back in his seat to plan his next action.

But no sooner had he regained his breath than he saw a flashing light approaching from the west. A McDonnell Douglas Nightfox helicopter. Oh, blow!

He spun the Hubcap through 360 degrees, careful to keep its centrifugal force to a minimum. Oh, no, there were two *more* helicopters: this time a black Sikorsky Eagle, with ominous tubes hanging from its short wings, and a second Nightfox. Harry was surrounded. As one of the Nightfoxes started firing, tracer bullets cut through the darkness like exclamation marks.

Harry surged up a hundred feet and tilted to watch

the bullets slicing the air beneath him. Then the Eagle rose with him and it too began firing. The Hubcap's armour was extremely tough, but a concentrated barrage by the helicopter's 7.62mm-calibre machine-gun bullets might eventually cripple it. And Harry had no way of fighting back.

He first zipped the ship a mile to the east within a matter of seconds. Then he revolved the Hubcap once more to observe the three helicopters circling in on him. He had to eliminate them soon, but how?

He edged over towards one of the Nightfoxes, and was rewarded with another machine-gun blast. By bobbing the Hubcap up and down, he was able to dodge the bullets, and infuriate the pilot in the process. Slowly he edged closer and the Nightfox rose level with him. Its next burst came within feet of his port side. Harry revolved the Hubcap, knowing the pilot couldn't be sure that he was doing so, to check again on the location of the other two helicopters.

Spinning back to face the Nightfox, which was now hovering barely a hundred yards in front of him, Harry waited until it began firing again, then he dipped the Hubcap and made a sudden lunge towards the enemy.

Fearing an imminent collision, the Nightfox pilot panicked and pulled up sharply, though continuing to fire.

The other Nightfox then caught several seconds of its twin's machine-gun blast full into its cockpit. The dead pilot instantly relaxed the controls, allowing the helicopter to rotate slowly to the ground like a dying bird.

Harry watched this death dive briefly, then spun back to face the surviving Nightfox, guessing that the pilot would still be in shock. He eased the Hubcap forward until directly under the Sikorsky Eagle, whose pilot remained ignorant of his new position. Harry glanced up at the helicopter's underside, its landing lights winking brightly. Then, slanting the Hubcap at an angle of forty-five degrees, he jerked his craft up so that its outer edge caught the missile-launchers and gun-pods on the chopper's starboard wing. The Eagle flipped over suddenly and, like the Nightfox, plummeted earthwards.

Seconds later a huge explosion lit up the forest beneath as one of the machines impacted. He felt sorry that men had died, but Harry's resolve was unswerving.

He revolved the Hubcap again and scanned the sky for the remaining Nightfox, but couldn't spot it now. Oh, blow!

Then a flash of light caught his eye and he spun round to see a missile approaching, only a second away from striking him head-on. Instinct took over and Harry pulled back on both sets of controls. The Hubcap rose instantly, but not fast enough. There was an immediate explosion as the Stinger missile grazed its underside.

Though the Hubcap continued rising, it also began to roll alarmingly and even Harry began to feel the G-forces squeezing his skull.

Keep control. Got to keep control.

He slammed the main drive controls to the neutral position and took stock of the ship's behaviour. It was now flipping over like a ball being kicked along the ground. To regain stability, he fired the vector jets on one side and was pleased to find the rolling of the ship begin to slow, until he was able to hold it steady at 3,000 feet. Checking the controls, he found there was no serious damage to affect the ship's performance. The Hubcap was designed to survive.

Flashing lights caught his attention and he stared out

at the single helicopter hovering outside like an armour-plated vulture.

He grabbed the controls again and whipped the ship in a wide arc around his opponent.

As the helicopter revolved to keep track of him, Harry dipped the Hubcap. The Nightfox did not possess a rear rotor, but instead directed blasts from its jet engine through its tail to maintain stability. Harry pulled up the Hubcap's nose and launched it at the helicopter's stubby tail and rudder fins, slicing them off as effectively as if using a laser.

Raising the Hubcap to a halt some 300 feet above the Nightfox, Harry looked down to watch it spin out of control. Its tormented shape was soon lost to the darkness below – until the flash and flames erupted thirty seconds later.

So what now? Harry wondered. He revolved the ship to examine the horizon, hoping to spot something that would give him somewhere to aim for. Some place where he could find out the truth. But all he could see were trees, and more trees.

Then lights caught his attention. He eased the Hubcap towards them hopefully. Headlights from a car? Even a building?

Too late, Harry realized they were the tail jets following a couple of Stinger missiles, fired from the McDonnell Douglas Eagle he had earlier rammed and sent out of control, but which had somehow managed to keep flying. There was only time to do one thing: Harry flipped the Hubcap over on its side.

Without a heat signature to target, the Stingers passed by him on either side, exploding to fill the Hubcap's cockpit with light and noise.

Despite his safety belts, Harry was thrown from his seat and dashed across the control panel. As the ship's main drive shut off, the Hubcap began to fall through the sky.

In a daze he struggled to get back to his seat, but the ship was tipped at too steep an angle and gravity was not with him. The ship was now in free fall, weaving from side to side, the only sound being the rush of wind outside. Inch by inch, Harry pulled himself up the cabin floor until he could hook a hand around one of the pedals, but he knew that impact was only a matter of moments off.

Three seconds later they hit the trees, smashing a swathe through the density of firs and evergreens.

Harry was flung backwards across the cabin as the ship crashed through the foliage towards the ground. There it began to cartwheel down a slope, mashing conifers and undergrowth alike under its momentum. Harry was tossed about like a dice in a cup.

Finally the Hubcap slammed into an impenetrable thicket and shuddered to a halt. Then slowly, almost defiantly, it toppled backwards, falling on to its roof. Harry crashed on to his head in the darkness.

Soon all was quiet in the cockpit again – except for the pounding of Harry's heart as he lay stunned on the Hubcap's ceiling.

And then the clattering of a triumphant helicopter began to grow louder and louder.

THIRTY-THREE@Chapter

The sound of the hovering rotors was deafening even inside the hull of the Hubcap. Harry could see a light flickering through the vision screen and guessed the chopper was surveying the wreckage of the Hubcap with its searchlight.

He forced himself to sit up, his head throbbing. He could take more punishment than most men, but even he could not land straight on his head and remain unscathed.

He felt something wet on his crown and, pulling his hand away, saw a black slickness reflected in the light that flashed sporadically in the cabin. Oh blow, oh blow. Harry knew he wasn't a very quick healer; he could be seeping blood for quite a while if the cut was deep. He looked around him.

Despite the crash, the interior of the Hubcap looked fairly untouched – as he would have expected, since resilience was part of its make-up. The control panel seemed to be still functioning, but its lights were dimmer, as when the main drive was switched off. But even if the main drive itself could be re-engaged, the ship was upside down. He edged his way back to his control seat. Although the vision screen was now upside down, the ship had come to rest on a slope, so the screen was tilted uphill, letting some light in.

The constant clattering of the helicopter would provide a marker for others seeking out the Hubcap. Despite the loss of three helicopters, no doubt there would be jubilation that the ship remained intact. As for Harry, he was dead meat – unless he got away quickly.

The main hatch was positioned in the Hubcap's base, which was facing towards the hovering Eagle. If Harry tried that route, he would be spotted instantly. There was, however, an emergency hatch, though he had never used it. While this was located on the upper half of the overturned ship and therefore hidden from the helicopter crew, unfortunately it was more than likely buried in the forest floor. But what was the alternative?

He knelt down and fumbled for the control to open it. It was some moments before he found the recessed square and pressed it. There was a short sigh as the small wall section opened and cold air filtered inside.

Head-first, Harry squirmed through the narrow opening, surprised to find himself dropping through space before he landed on a bed of broken branches.

Rolling over, he gazed up to see the Hubcap some fifteen feet above him, wedged up against several broken tree trunks and hanging over the edge of a gully, where he lay.

Searchlights circled overhead and the roaring of the helicopters was deafening out in the open, but the beams couldn't reach down to Harry because of the ship immediately above him.

The first thing he noticed was the icy cold. It ate into him as effectively as if he were naked. The next was the pervasive damp. The foliage was wet, the air was fuggy. He had never before experienced rain and he felt momentarily swamped by the experience. He had no idea where to go next, and this cold, forbidding environment marched off endlessly in every direction. In fact it might just as well be the Nevada Desert, for all its inhospitable nature.

Shivering, Harry edged out from under the bushes and peered upwards. A Sikorsky Black Hawk troop carrier had recently arrived and now hovered one hundred feet above the tree, whipping spray from furiously shaking branches. Harry could see uniformed men abseiling down on ropes. Oh, blow, blow, *blow*!

He scuttled back out of sight, then eased himself down through the carpet of broken branches until finally his feet touched solid rock. From there he began walking cautiously along the bottom of the gully, hoping to get far away from the crashed Hubcap.

His first priority being just to get away, he paid little heed to his direction. Once they discovered no body in the ship, they would have to assume he had either been thrown clear or, more likely, managed to make his escape on foot. And once they decided to pursue him, they would definitely have the advantage of knowing the terrain.

Fifteen minutes of stumbling panic and enveloping coldness brought him to water, and he waded into the knee-deep stream. Looking back, he could now see all the helicopters. The Eagle and a Black Hawk were still hovering over the crash site. A second Black Hawk, having disgorged its troops, was circling the area slowly, its searchlight probing the trees that pressed in on the stream from every direction. Then a fourth chopper suddenly screamed overhead, an enormous machine sporting two sets of rotors, one at each end of its elongated body. Harry recognized it as a Chinook capable of transporting payloads up to 30,000lbs. Plainly they were going to lift the stranded Hubcap and take it back with them.

Back where? He had destroyed the Hangar. But it didn't really matter to him now, did it?

He kept trudging along the stream, occasionally gasping at its iciness. All his time in Down Town he had enjoyed ambient temperatures, so cold like this was an alien concept. But now he could feel his legs turning numb and his movements were becoming increasingly slow. He would have to climb out of the water soon. As he looked up at the banks of the gulley, all he could see were the countless trees, rising up near-vertical slopes towards a small patch of starlit night. He felt as if trapped at the bottom of a huge pit with no way out. He was scared and totally at a loss for what to do. Then, looking back, he saw wavering flashlights; there were men following the stream, coming after him.

That made his mind up. He started to run, new determination galvanizing his weary limbs. Blundering on, he sometimes tripped into the water, but always re-emerged, gasping and shocked, and still with enough wits to keep him moving.

Suddenly, up ahead, something glinted high above the water. After several cautious steps, he recognized it as the underside of a bridge across the stream. A bridge meant a road and a road could mean an escape route. Besides, what other option did he have? If he stayed in the water, he would freeze to death. And if he headed into the trees, he would be lost for ever. No, the road would have to be his salvation.

He waded to one side of the stream and pulled himself

up on to the bank. Then, grasping and clinging to bushes and branches, he struggled his way up to the bridge itself.

At one end was a parked truck. He assumed it must have transported men to hunt for him.

Dropping on to his stomach, he wormed his way to the edge of the road and peeked both ways along the single-lane track. Keeping low and out of sight, he dashed across to the tailboard.

Then he heard voices.

He had no choice now but to duck underneath, crawling further in until he was shielded by the large twin wheels at the rear. It seemed there were two voices, but he could not make out what they were saying. Curiosity eventually got the better of him.

Ignoring the pain from sharp gravel, he wriggled forward, still on his stomach and elbows, until he was directly under the cab itself. Now he could hear clearly.

'Base, Base, this is Four. I've got ten men out on range, headed south-south-west on intercept with the site of the crash. Please advise further action.'

'Are they reporting directly to you?'

'Negative. They're tuned to One-four-eight – command frequency.'

'One-four-eight, Roger that, Four. Please hold.'

'Like I'm going some place,' the driver grumbled.

'Four, Four, this is Base. Be advised, search and destroy is prime, repeat prime.'

'Copy that, but what am I supposed to *do*?'

Another voice came on to the radio. An angry voice that Harry was startled to recognize.

'Four, stop your goddamn whining and get back here to pick up more men! I want this mission completed by sun-up. Understand? You return to Base now!'

'Roger, ma'am.'

Ma'am? It could only be Dr Ralston! But how had she survived the explosions in the Hangar?

The truck suddenly started up.

Oh, blow . . . What to do, what to do?

Harry did not know where he was. He was alone, exposed, doomed to be discovered – or to die of hypothermia. The truck above him had been recalled to Base. Even if that meant Down Town, it might improve his chances.

He rolled out from underneath just as the driver scraped into first.

Harry waited until he was level with the tailgate, then he sprinted after it, grabbed the upper edge and pulled himself over and in.

The floor of the truck was hard and unyielding, but he smiled even at the pain of hitting it. But as he rolled on to his back to catch his breath, a foot planted itself on his chest and a flashlight was shone directly into his eyes.

'Who are you?' gabbled a startled Harry.

'More to the point,' said the flashlight's owner, '*what* the fuck are you?'

THIRTY-FOUR@Chapter

Fergus hunkered down behind a tree and held Izzy close. He felt a trembling that first he thought was Izzy, then realized was himself. More heavy-calibre gunfire, further explosions.

He could feel Izzy pulling away from him, curiosity getting the better of her. Just then, another helicopter zoomed overhead and Fergus's frayed nerves snapped. He leaped up and ran, hauling Izzy along with him.

There was an enormous mid-air explosion to the right of them and he dropped for cover again, fearing shrapnel. Then something huge crashed into the trees. It had to be one of the helicopters. But instead of the expected fiery explosion, there was only the sound of trees toppling. Something was crashing through the forest like an angry giant.

Fergus had endured enough now. He got them both to their feet again and, without consideration for their destination, he charged headlong away from those crashing noises – away from whatever was devouring the forest.

Izzy felt no such sense of panic, of course, but she wanted to stick with Fergus so kept pace with him. Indeed, she was soon several paces ahead.

'Izzy!' he yelled at her, pulling up short as his foot got snagged in a tangle of tree roots. He stepped back to avoid the obstruction but, when he looked up again, Izzy had vanished.

'Izzy! Izzy! Where the hell are you?'

Stumbling forward half a dozen steps, then pausing, he continued calling but still there was no response. Perhaps she'd tripped and knocked herself out? And then he noticed: there was no further noise. The monstrous crashing had ceased, the explosions had stopped, and if there were still helicopters, they were very far off. So if Izzy was within earshot, she was bound to hear him.

Oh, God . . . They've got her!

He ducked behind a tree and dragged in desperate breaths. *OK, keep calm. Think it through.* But all he could think of was Izzy at risk. And whatever might be happening to her, it was all his fault for dragging her out on this stupid, no-brain expedition. *God, let her be all right. If only I can get us out of here, I'll turn myself in and take my chances.*

'Fergus?' came her voice, and he spun around.

She was standing there right in front of him.

'Izzy, I was – '

Then he noticed the man in camouflage gear aiming a rifle over her shoulder.

'Hold it right there, nature boy,' he snarled.

Fergus sensed they had to act immediately or it was over for them. Izzy would do exactly what he said, without hesitation, simply because she couldn't realize it was dangerous.

'Run, Izzy. Run!' he shouted.

Immediately Izzy broke to her left, knocking the gunman's aim sideways. Fergus threw himself forward, slamming the man to the ground. Then two hard whacks to the head with a handy branch left him unconscious.

Fergus sat back on his haunches. *Jesus, that was lucky* . . . But Izzy was still darting away!

'Izzy, stop! Come back here!'

She returned quickly. 'Is he dead?' she asked.

Fergus felt the man's neck for a pulse. 'No, but he'll have one hell of a headache when he wakes up.'

Fergus grabbed the rifle and unhooked the man's flashlight. It took him a minute to find their bearings again. Then, still following the course of the stream, they headed for the road.

Ten minutes later they caught sight of their abandoned car. However, the truck had returned, although this time it was parked a good hundred yards away on the curve of a bend with its rear towards them.

'I think we've found ourselves some new wheels,' whispered Fergus.

Crouching low, they skirted the road itself and slipped across to the back of the truck. Fergus pulled himself up to peer over the tailgate. It was empty. He then made his way along the side of the vehicle to the passenger door. Just as he was about to reach up for the handle, he heard male voices near by and froze. Ahead, previously hidden by the truck, stood nine or ten men in combat gear. They seemed to be receiving instructions. Fergus did not wait to hear what was said. Instead he edged his way back to the rear. Oh, God, they were right in the middle of the bastards. He squatted down low to watch the men's boots from under the chassis. Quite soon they dispersed into three groups of three, heading off in different directions, while another one returned to the driver's cab. He and Izzy hadn't a hope.

'They're combing the woods on all sides. And walking along the road is pointless. I don't know – '

'Unless we hide in the truck.'

'What do we do when they come back?'

But then he heard more shouting in the woods and Fergus was suddenly too petrified to think about it further.

'OK, let's get in. Maybe it'll drive off empty.'

He helped her up over the tailgate and under the canvas, and, after handing her the flashlight and machine-gun, he clambered in himself. As they lay together in silence on the wooden floorboards, Fergus realized they had probably made one big mistake.

They had been lying there for at least five minutes, Fergus straining to overhear the driver talking on his radio, when he decided that soon they might need to get out of the truck and find somewhere else to hide. But just then it set off, and someone heaved themselves up over the rear and into the truck-bed.

THIRTY-FIVE@Chapter

'Who are you?' gabbled the startled invader.

'More to the point,' said an astonished Fergus, '*what* the fuck are you?'

Fergus's flashlight revealed not the armed adult he had expected but a strange-looking boy. He had large black eyes in an oddly flat face that tapered to a high, wide forehead, and he was completely bald, with no discernible eyebrows. There was a small cut on his smooth skull and he was dressed in a soaking-wet black coverall without any labels. He regarded Fergus and Izzy with a startled expression that was all the more unsettling because his eyes were *huge*.

So unnerved was he by the boy's appearance that Fergus instinctively took his boot off his chest.

Izzy, however, was merely intrigued. 'Are you all right, kid?' she asked, as Fergus stepped back.

Harry stared at the smiling young woman. She was certainly attractive, but more importantly she wasn't afraid. He took the hand she offered and pulled himself upright.

If Fergus did not know better, he would have sworn an alien had just joined them in the truck. Even the kid's skin was a weird colour: very pale to the point of grey.

'I'm OK,' said Harry, edging sideways so as to position

the woman between himself and the man. His voice was soft. 'They're chasing me . . . . But who are you? You're not from Down Town?'

'Downtown?' said Fergus. 'What's he talking about?'

'I came from Down Town. Where are *you* from?'

'We're from Vermont,' Izzy intervened. 'We came here to Maine to find out why some people have been killed. Somewhere out here there's a place called the Lab.'

'Never heard of it,' confessed Harry. 'But this truck we're in is heading back to Down Town.' He looked confused. 'You just said Maine. So how did I get here from Nevada.'

'Nevada?' The mention of that name and the boy's appearance suddenly locked together in Fergus's mind. 'Your flying saucer lose its way, then?' He laughed nervously.

'Apparently. Or maybe it was moved to a new base.'

Fergus finally overcame his repulsion and reached out to touch the boy's slender arm. He was pleased to find it was smooth and warm, like *real* skin should be.

Suddenly the truck slid to a halt.

'Who's in there?' They heard the voice of the driver. Then a door opened and they could hear him running back alongside the truck.

'Izzy,' Fergus hissed, 'get out of sight.'

The flap fell open, the driver peered in. On seeing Harry and Fergus, he reached for his side holster.

'Kick him!' urged Fergus.

Izzy rose up to one side of the tailgate. She immediately kicked him full in the face. They watched in awe as he dropped to the ground.

Without hesitation, Fergus leaped off the tailgate.

Grabbing hold of the unconscious driver, he dragged him over and, with Izzy's help, hauled him into the truck. He pulled the flap closed with satisfaction.

'These people are looking for you too?' Fergus turned to Harry, who was standing now at the front of the truck-bed. The boy was barely five foot tall.

'Yes,' said Harry. 'I brought down some helicopters. You must have heard the explosions.'

'What the hell with? You're not even armed.'

'With the Hubcap.'

'The what?'

'It's an experimental craft I've been flying. You'd probably call it a flying saucer.'

'Are you an alien?' asked Izzy, as if enquiring whether he came from Boston.

'No, I'm not,' said Harry defensively.

'Could have fooled me,' muttered Fergus. 'So, where *do* you come from?'

Harry gave them a quick explanation of Down Town – and his role there – and how he still could not understand how he had managed to crash-land in Maine.

'This is unreal,' said Fergus, feeling queasy. He sat and stared at Harry in the beam of his flashlight.

The newcomer had the build of a boy of twelve, but his wrists were thin, his fingers long, his head top-heavy. A head that was notably smooth and symmetrical. OK, some kids lose their hair, or have big heads, or particularly small noses or mouths. But no one Fergus had ever seen outside of a science-fiction movie had the eyes this boy possessed. They were perfect ovals, widely set, the pupils taking up far more of the surface than normal. In fact, it almost looked as if the entire eye was pupil. At best this kid was a freak; at worst . . . Fergus didn't want to go on thinking about it.

Harry and Izzy had been swapping information, and now Harry began to concentrate on what to do next.

'Looks like your Lab must be part of Down Town, but I wouldn't advise you to go there. They're out on full alert for me, and now you've seen me, they'll probably kill you too.'

This gave Fergus pause for thought. In his desperation to clear himself, he had somehow got them into the middle of a war zone. But Izzy, to his dismay, was having ideas.

'How well do you know your way around this Down Town?' she asked.

'I only really know the one in Nevada. Though from what I've seen here, the layout is similar.'

Just then there was shouting from near by. Fergus switched off the flashlight and edged open the canvas flap. Men on foot with flashlights were visible among the trees.

'Looks like we haven't got a choice now,' he said. 'Is there any way you can get us to this Down Town pronto?'

Harry shook his head, then eyed the recumbent driver. 'If you can wake him up, maybe yes.'

Fergus pulled the man up a bit and slapped his face. With a groan, the driver blinked his eyes.

'Is he wearing contact lenses?' asked Harry.

'How the hell would I know?' said Fergus, exasperated.

Izzy ran a thumb over the driver's eye. The man cried out. 'No,' she said.

Harry knelt forward and grabbed the man's face in both hands. 'Shine the flashlight right on me.'

Fergus turned the beam on to the boy's face. *God, he*

was freaky-looking. The driver struggled for a moment in Harry's grip, but once they made eye contact he went limp, his face blank.

Harry issued instructions, his thin lips barely moving. The man nodded dumbly. He understood.

'Okey-dokey. So, get out and start driving.'

The driver heaved himself over the tailgate. A minute later the engine started. The truck set off.

'What the fuck was that?' said Fergus to himself.

As the truck lurched away down the uneven track, they were forced to cling to the benches running along its sides.

A couple of minutes later the truck came to a sudden stop, brakes squealing. Then it began to reverse and stopped again. The driver came round and pulled up the flap.

'This way,' he said to them mechanically.

All three clambered out and stared about them.

The truck had reversed up to a loading bay, the last one of six bays, all the others empty. They were standing on a platform raised four feet above a parking lot. High brick walls at either end shielded them from view. But even as Fergus took in this reassuring detail, Izzy jumped off the platform and wandered into the open.

'Jesus Christ,' hissed Fergus, as he dashed out after her. He snagged her arm. 'For fuck's sake, Izzy, keep out of sight!'

She was looking around in awe. 'I've been here before. That night of the fire alarm. This is where they brought us all.'

Fergus looked around at an empty compound about the size of a football field. It was surrounded on all sides by high brick walls that were bordered beyond by overhanging trees. At the far end of one side was a tunnel entrance, which must have been the route in for their truck – and their only route out.

Fergus led Izzy back to the loading bay. They followed Harry and the driver through a pair of black-rubber panel doors, emerging in a short corridor leading straight to another set of similar doors.

Harry turned to the blank-faced driver.

'How big is this place?'

'It's on four levels, each a half-mile square.'

'What?' exclaimed Fergus. 'That's two square miles! We'll get lost as soon as we walk through those doors.'

'Have you computer access?' Harry turned back to the driver.

'Yes.'

'Get us to a computer, then call us up a map.'

The driver preceded them through the second set of doors.

Beyond was a grey corridor so long that they were unable to see either end of it. Every fifty yards a red light was flashing, clearly indicating a current state of alert. The lengthy corridor seemed deserted, its only occupant a lone electric golfcart parked near by. Harry could smell smoke, presumably from the Hangar fire.

'Christ, and there's another three levels of this?' grumbled Fergus.

'The computer,' prompted Harry.

The driver led them past a series of side doors, all of them numbered in the 300s. He finally halted outside Room 334. The sign on the door read JANITORIAL SUPPLIES. He reached inside to switch on the light. The others followed him, Fergus closing the door behind them.

The long storeroom stank of disinfectant, its shelves crammed with cans and bottles of cleaners and polishes, together with innumerable sealed cardboard cartons. To the right of the door stood a desk and on this sat a battered computer terminal. On the wall were fixed pictures of naked women, displaying more than their gynaecologists might ever see.

Harry sat down on the grey metal chair. As he switched on the ancient IBM, he was pleased to recognize a familiar start-up procedure as the hard drive came on line and connected itself to a network. Finally it presented him with a green screen, asking for a password.

'What's your password?' Harry turned to the driver.

Like an automaton, the man leaned over to key in several letters and numbers. There was a brief pause, and the screen cleared, then spelled out a message:

HELLO, DONALD KELP. WHAT DO YOU WANT?

Harry began typing in his questions. A minute later he had access to a map. It covered all of the complex, separated into each of the four levels, but the top level was only partially available.

'Okey-dokey,' said Harry, his foot tapping furiously. 'This man's clearance won't gain him access to the Hangar or its associated facilities – that's the blank portions there – but he's free to roam anywhere else. Pity we can't print this out.'

'Move. I can help you,' said Fergus.

Harry stood up and Fergus sat down, staring at the screen. 'OK, fix it so I get each level in sequence. Keep it on screen for about five seconds, then give me the next one.'

'Photographic memory?' Harry surmised.

As Harry ran the plans on screen, Fergus memorized each section as it appeared. Although all the rooms were identified by number, quite a few were identified also by function. Though the speed at which he was memorizing the pages prevented Fergus from appreciating all the minutiae, certain words did make an impression.

FIRE ROOM. BLACK ROOM. ICE ROOM. BLADES. DEPRIVATION. WHITE NOISE. DISSECTION. CREMATORIUM. It looked like a map of hell.

He had barely finished when there was a rapping on the door.

'Open up now!' a male voice barked.

'Who the hell?' muttered Fergus.

Harry said, 'They've probably got a security watch on the computer.'

'Oh, *now* you tell us.' Fergus glanced vainly around the room for an escape route. God knew how many of them were waiting outside.

'Open up!' the voice repeated.

Harry went over to the truck driver. 'Open it slowly, one hand behind your back. Then signal with your fingers how many are out there.'

Fergus rummaged along the shelves for a suitable weapon, but nothing practical came to hand. Grabbing what he could, he took up position between the computer and the door. He glanced back to find Izzy in plain view – *stupid bloody woman.* But it was too late now, the driver had opened the door.

Fergus waited for the agreed signal. Shit! *Three fingers.* And he himself armed with . . . two cans of Glade air-freshener.

THIRTY-SIX@Chapter

'Kelp,' said a voice outside the janitor's room, 'what are you doing in there? This is Chief Petty Officer Rathbone.'

The door was shoved fully open, hiding Fergus from the man outside, but also trapping him against the desk.

'Who the hell are you?' the stranger asked Izzy.

Unruffled, she answered, 'Izzy Pea.'

Harry too was as yet unseen. Fergus handed him a can of Glade. Harry nodded and eased in behind him.

The truck driver was pushed out of the way and a man in US Navy uniform entered, followed by another, both with automatic pistols.

Too late to worry now, thought Fergus. He tapped the second arrival on the shoulder and sprayed him, as he turned, full in the face with Thai Orchid. Harry, meanwhile, gave the first man the same treatment.

As both men began to claw at their eyes, Fergus sprayed wildly through the open doorway.

'Nice try, asshole,' said a voice to one side. Then he was clubbed on the shoulders and fell to his knees, his vision blurring.

He heard a yell as Harry leaped over him, slamming into his assailant, the two falling to the floor.

Harry sat on the man's chest, fighting to keep his balance, as he tried to prise the fallen man's eyes open. The sailor's arms were waving around wildly, one of them clutching an automatic pistol, which he was trying to train on the mad boy on his chest.

Groggy as he was, Fergus managed to grab the man's arm. He banged it on the cement floor, the gun skittering away.

And then the sailor stopped his struggling. Harry had finally made eye contact.

'Listen to me,' he said carefully. 'I want you to go in there and shut those men up.'

Harry stood up and Fergus watched in fascination as the Chief Petty Officer entered the storeroom. Seconds later, both of the blinded men fell silent.

Fergus stood up, accepting Harry's hand. 'That's some talent you've got there, kid.'

'Thank you. You can call me Harry.'

For the first time, Fergus smiled. 'OK, what now?'

'You've got the map, I've got the men. Together they should help us get where we're going – as long as no one comes to investigate the ruckus . . .'

They both glanced up and down the corridor.

'Where the hell *is* everyone?' muttered Fergus.

Harry shrugged, then re-entered the storeroom.

'And where exactly *are* we going?'

Harry paused inside the door. Izzy and the truck driver were standing by the desk. The hypnotized Rathbone was standing over the two unconscious men. He had found the best way to keep the men quiet.

'Fergus, what do *you* want from this place?' asked Harry at last.

'Izzy, we know, was here before; I want to discover if I was too. I have these vague memories . . . And if so, I want to know why. Izzy and I are both included on something called the FAIL:SAFE list and we – '

'FAIL:SAFE.'

'Yes. Do you know something about it?'

Harry turned to the Chief Petty Officer. 'Where is the nearest computer terminal you use? Can you get us there safely?'

'Level Two. Recreation. This way,' said the CPO.

He led them back out into the corridor. They followed at a fast pace to a door marked E2-44. Pushing it open, they found a stairwell. Then up a flight of steps to another door, which opened on to another seemingly endless corridor. Rathbone pointed to the right.

'Eight doors along that way.'

There were a few other people visible in this corridor, though they were some distance away. Fergus noticed they were all wearing uniforms, so their own civilian clothes would attract interest sooner rather than later.

Harry handed the CPO his pistol. 'Take us there like you have us under arrest.'

Instantly the man had organized a chain: the truck driver at the front, followed by Harry and Izzy, himself bringing up the rear with the gun planted squarely in Fergus's back.

'Move,' he ordered.

They all obeyed.

They passed two black soldiers, who eyed them curiously.

'Hey, Rathbone, what's the party?'

'Caught them sneaking in. Time for interrogation.'

'Need some help?' asked the other soldier.

'No, I'm taking them along to 244.'

The two men fell into step alongside, then one moved ahead to open the door. As he did so, he made eye contact with Harry – and he too was Harry's to command.

The second soldier noticed the change in his colleague, but before he could speak, Rathbone had him in a choke-hold and dragged him into the room.

Harry then ordered the two soldiers to sit on the couch. They meekly obeyed, both now hypnotized. He then placed himself down in front of the computer terminal.

'Your password, Chief Petty Officer.'

'CPO-11–24–3.'

Harry soon had access to all the personnel directories, hunting through the posted files – until he located Elizabeth Pea from 1997.

Although each experiment was coded by a single name and a number, their titles were enough to send shivers down one's spine. RAZOR. ICE. SPEED. HEIGHT. NAUSEA. SPIDERS. RAPE. ASPHYXIA.

'Not exactly scientific, is it?' said Fergus angrily.

There was a last file called APPLICATION, which he asked Harry to open for them. It seemed they had run an identical series of tests on eight volunteers. Only one had come through all the tests successfully, but he had subsequently been classified unstable and the experiments were discontinued. Fergus noticed one unlucky soul had not survived the ICE test.

'What was that one about?'

'Bath full of ice-cubes, pitch dark and no sound. I was

stuck in there for two hours before I passed out. I nearly lost *all* my toes.'

Fergus remembered the two missing on her right foot. 'Fucking bastards,' he said. Then he saw at the end her date of leaving the experiment. The phrase FAIL:SAFE had been added.

'OK, what about me?' he asked.

'Year?'

'Last year at college is the one I don't remember. So try 1990.'

They gathered round to read Fergus's file.

It seemed he had been approached while still at college with an offer to spend time on a government-sponsored course. The attraction had obviously been a $150 salary per week, and free board, for the three months during his summer vacation.

'*Subject showed considerable enthusiasm, probably motivated by a $3,385 Visa overdraft.*'

'That's sounds about right,' muttered Fergus. God, but he had been an asshole in those days.

He had then been admitted to Facility 2 on 7.28.90. A ten-day period of detoxification had rendered him completely sober and fit for experimentation. There followed an assessment of his impressive capabilities at photographic memory, with the conclusion: '*While this subject's ability is within top one percentile of tested subjects, it has no practical application. Ref to PROGRAMMING for re-evaluation prior to discharge.*'

'What's "Programming"?' wondered Fergus.

A woman's voice answered him. 'Your dark secret, Fergus.'

The three of them spun round to find the truck driver

on his knees, clutching the side of his neck, his head twitching. Standing over him was a woman with a badly scarred face, wearing a large, black eye-patch.

It was Kelly Stanyard.

Hindman's pirate!

'Grab her!' Harry shouted to the soldiers on the couch. As they both rose, she fired a silenced Beretta 87 Cheetah. They slumped back on to the couch.

'No one move,' she ordered the survivors.

As Kelly stepped further into the room, another armed woman entered behind her.

'The prodigal son returns,' said Dr Ralston.

Harry flew at her, but she clipped him across the head with her own Beretta. He slumped to the floor at her feet.

'And as impetuous as ever,' she sneered.

THIRTY-SEVEN@Chapter

Dr Ralston first closed the door, then she picked up Harry and sat him in a chair, slapping him across the face until he began to come round.

'Didn't expect to see *you* here again so soon. Tell me, why have you popped back to Down Town?'

'This . . . isn't . . . Down Town.' Harry quickly realized that Fergus and Izzy and the other woman had disappeared.

'Oh, but it is, Harry. It's Down Town *Two*. We shipped you up here while you were unconscious. Brought the Hubcap with us too. Let's just hope for your sake that you haven't destroyed it. There are those still willing to forgive you, but I'm in charge and *I'm* not the forgiving kind.'

'What have you done with Fergus and Izzy?'

'They'll be interrogated by my sister – to discover what they know. Then . . . well, it'll all be settled.'

'They were trying to find out why their names appeared on some list.'

'They told you about it? Yes, all the names on that list were failed experiments here. Except Fergus, apparently, wasn't the failure everyone thought.'

'So, your sister wants to know who sent that list to Fergus?'

'Yes, but I think she'll just be happy to wrap it all up now.'

'*I* know who sent out the list. So if I tell you, will you let them go?'

This news obviously intrigued the doctor. Then she smiled. 'What do *you* think?'

He sighed. 'I think you enjoy hurting people too much.'

She stepped towards him, raising her hand. Harry shrank back, but she merely patted him on the head. 'We are all, in our own ways, the victims of our upbringing. Kelly and I are twins, raised from birth to work for 51. Neither of us ever knew our parents, only the strictest codes of discipline.'

'Which turned you both into psychopaths.'

'And proud of it too! We get the job done. No sentimentality, no fear, no doubts – just do whatever's necessary. You can't conceive what I'm capable of.'

'So why aren't I dead already?'

'Arrangements need to be made.'

'For what?'

'Your autopsy. In a spirit of interdepartmental co-operation, a team of doctors is being flown here to examine your corpse. To see just what is what on a microscopic level. And for that they need the meat to be still fresh.'

'See *what* is what?'

'You've still no idea, have you? I've already explained how Clarence Smith's DNA was used to help create you. But we added to that a little something special: someone else's DNA, just to see what would happen. Actually a dead person's, but DNA can be gathered from anything well enough preserved. Fortunately, in 1949, while relatively ignorant, they were *very* careful.'

'1949? But I was born in – '

'Created, Harry. You were *created* – implanted, brought to term, evacuated, secluded, programmed. Now, 1949 – doesn't that year ring a bell?'

As Harry sat frowning, she suddenly grabbed his head and slammed it into the computer screen, stabbing a key so the screen went black. 'Look at that! Any clues?'

Harry focused on his reflected image. Large, dark, almond-shaped eyes set in a pale triangular face.

'Montana, 1949?' he breathed.

'Bingo! Give the boy an A! We mixed Smith's DNA with a little cultured sample taken from one of the corpses found in that flying-saucer wreck, injected the combination into a human ovum – and here you are. Ever wonder why they named you Harry?'

'It's just a name.'

'No, Harry, it's an acronym – derived from the initials HARI. Do you want to know what they stand for?' She leaned close enough for him to detect her contact lenses. With each word, she jabbed his nose with the pistol. 'H for *Human*, A for *Alien*, R for *Regressive*, I for *Integrand*. Therefore *Human Alien Regressive Integrand*. You're a quarter alien, three-quarters human. In other words, a mutant. We contrived that whole "Down Town Survives World War III" scenario to concentrate your mind on what was most important: learning mastery of the Hubcap. Everyone there had to keep up the pretence – to ignore the way you really looked. If they treated you like a normal human being, theoretically you should act like one. Normal? Jeez!'

She seemed suddenly excited by the look of horror passing over Harry's face.

'Remember Douglas's parents doing their weekly stints at the Scrubbers? They were really out in the real world, at home in Fresno. Commander Ulrich unavailable for days on end? Enjoying the sunshine at Lake Tahoe. Myself hidden away in Biomedics all those years? If only. I've got a delightful condo in Phoenix, overlooking a golf course.

'As technology advanced, we used what we'd made of you to develop the Paragons. But you know what's the best part, Harry? Where we got each ovum later implanted in the surrogates. You see, all those eggs for you and the Paragons came from the same source.'

Harry couldn't think, let alone answer.

'Say hello to Momma, Harry.'

Kelly shoved Fergus into her sister's office, with sufficient force to send him sprawling on to the floor. She then kicked the door shut behind her, grabbed Izzy by the arm and threw her into a chair.

Fergus tried to rise, but Kelly kicked him in the face.

'Stay down, boy,' she barked. 'Be a good little puppy.'

Izzy stood up again, undaunted by this violence. Kelly punched her square on the chin and Izzy collapsed as if pole-axed.

'You really are one dim bimbo,' snarled Kelly. 'You're both going to die, but not before I've had some fun. Pay him back for messing up my face.'

Fergus coughed through a mouthful of blood.

She leaned down over him, tapping her eye-patch.

'Thanks to you, I've got a new look, and a new appearance, and a mean new temperament.' She kicked him in the stomach.

Fergus groaned and curled up into a ball. 'How did you find us here?'

'A waitress in a diner dropped a dime on you, mentioned you'd hitched a ride to Trevor. We just missed you there, but on the way back from Rutland we got a call from a nurse at the hospital. She said someone was visiting Hindman. After that, it was easy tracing you. We found that stolen pick-up in Freeport. We checked every surveillance camera within half a mile. Got a bead on you in LL Bean's, and local cops traced you to that tree-hugger shop. From then it was easy. We've got a saying in the 51: "All you need is badges and money." Almost everyone works for a salary, and some would like to earn more than they get, so they do freelance work for us. No one questions a badge, even if they're just pieces of laminated paper. Offer some of these badge-holders enough and they'll do whatever you want – and once they've been turned, there's no going back. We've got people *everywhere* ready to help us, no questions asked. Badges and money, Fergus. *Badges and money.*'

'Why was I sent that damn list anyway?'

'I still don't know. You had a computer, someone sent it out – and you got to read it. Everyone on that list was considered reliable, including you. Me, I'd have killed them all just to make certain a fuck-up like this never happened. But other wimps had their way. We were in bed together, remember, when you first told me about that list. Once you'd gone, my sister phoned. She told me what had been e-mailed to you – and to some others on the same list. That was a serious security breach, but she didn't know *who* had sent it – or why. There was always the chance that somehow *you* might know, and lead us to them. Obviously I couldn't ask you too much without blowing my own cover and compromising our relationship. So I sent in Anderson, the FBI agent, with orders to make sure you didn't have a record of it, even in your head. But *you* decided to act the hero.' She kicked him in the thigh for good measure.

Fergus thrashed about on the floor, struggling to comprehend her answers. He caught sight of Izzy, blood leaking down her cheek. She was still unconscious, but was starting to moan. Anger at her fate concentrated his mind: as long as Kelly was talking, they were still alive.

'So I then had to set up Sheriff Wesley's killing, in order that our people in the FBI would be able to take charge and cover up all the loose ends. And you fucked *that* up.'

Fergus forced himself on to his side. Kelly turned to look towards Izzy.

'Please, just leave her,' whispered Fergus. 'Why *was* I on the list?'

She kneeled down, grabbed his hair and pulled back his head. Her single good eye blazed at him.

'You were *programmed*, little puppy. A key phrase can set you off – and then there's no stopping you until what you must do is done.'

'*What* must I do?'

She banged his head back on the floor. 'Kill.'

'*What?*'

She leaned close to stare into his face. 'Who do you

think it was sneaked down from his apartment that afternoon and killed poor old Dale Cresdee?'

Harry's legs were beating like snare drums, his mind unable to assimilate these terrible revelations. What appalled him the most was not the discovery of being a mutant, but that this homicidal maniac holding him at gunpoint was somehow his mother.

'You're lying,' he gasped at last.

'Oh no, I'm not. I was harvested regularly. That way we didn't have to involve anyone else, or need to worry about the ethics. Not that 51 has ever worried much about ethics . . . They cut compassion out of me as effectively as if they'd used a scalpel – just like we fucked with your emotions, turning you into the obedient little camper you used to be. It was just that we didn't know quite what the balance would be between the human and the alien. At first we thought your rebellious behaviour was evidence of a swing to the alien side of your nature. But it was actually your *human* side taking control, producing the hormonal pain in the ass that constitutes your typical teenager. There were others who were still hoping to curb your excesses – but a mother knows her son. *I* knew there was no turning you; and that's why we accelerated the Paragon programme. We had big plans for you, Harry, and people found you fun to be with – unlike those automata Patrick and Peter and Perry and Pierce, and the rest. As Ulrich once said, they're as obedient as coffee percolators but with none of the personality. Alas, even favourite pets can get put down, once they've outlived their usefulness.'

Harry tried to compose himself, but his emotions were churning. His legs would not be stopped, his head was buzzing, his stomach was in turmoil.

'No, *you're* the real mutation,' he managed at last, surprised at his own vehemence. 'Whatever the differences between *my* two sides, I know compassion and intelligence are the common ground between them. But you, Dr Ralston, have no compassion, no feelings – and you use your intelligence only for destructive purposes. So *you* are more alien than I am!'

She merely laughed contemptuously.

'So what were you doing with the Hubcap anyway?' he continued. 'Adapting their alien technology to develop a cure for cancer? To discover some cheaper source of energy? To explore the universe? No, what you were after was to produce a deadlier weapon! Aiming to understand the Hubcap's drive systems so they could be used in future fighter aircraft. You were even specially breeding pilots to fly them. But once I showed signs of having a mind of my own, you tried to create pilots who would be even more obedient. And what would you use that obedience for? With advanced technology, mechanical and biological – all you want is military superiority.'

'Wrong! You – and all those other morons out there who would shut 51 down tomorrow – you don't *understand* the world order.'

'And what *is* the world order? I've not been privileged to see it, remember?'

She smiled again. It wasn't a pleasant sight. 'Everyone wants what the other guy has – *that's* the world fucking order! So, anyone who backs off and says, "Hey, let's have a little common sense here," he'll just get his ass kicked. And I'm not about to let this country get its ass kicked by *anyone.* I'll try anything to ensure we keep what's ours. And if that means breeding mutants to fly fucking alien aircraft, then I'll do it.' She raised her gun menacingly. 'And if that also means terminating those who fail to perform to expectations, then I'll gladly pull the trigger.'

Kelly had grabbed the dazed Fergus by his collar and sat him upright against the wall. She stared at his bruised and bloody face with disdain, then slipped the automatic pistol into her waistband.

'You *are* a messy puppy, aren't you? So you still don't realize it was *you* who killed Cresdee?'

She pulled a piece of paper out of her pocket. It was an official form with a signature and date, the latter being 8.8.90. It was headed: *Oath Upon Inadvertent Exposure to Classified Security Data or Information.*

'Signed by you when we started the tests. It's proof that you were here too.'

The form she was waving threatened life imprisonment if he divulged any information about his time in Down Town Two.

'Everyone signed this,' Kelly continued. 'Even the bimbo there.'

'So?' he gasped.

'So it gives me the right to make you disappear. And, furthermore, no one would give a shit. But maybe that would be far too easy.' She scrunched up the paper and tossed it into a metal bin. 'You see, you were the last of the

Scarlet experiments. The last of a long line of failures that started in the 1950s with the MK – Mind Kontrol – programmes. Delta, Naomi, Search . . . Operation Pandora was the parent, with Bluebird, Artichoke, Chatter and Scarlet the children. Crudduck was involved in Chatter, but nothing worked very well for him – though that clinic of his seems to use what he *did* learn. To be honest, we assumed your programming had failed as well. We studied your photographic memory and tried to find out how it worked, but after nine months we'd still got nowhere.

'But the technique your photographic memory uses – the call-up and the recall – there were some who thought this technique might be adapted for use during brainwashing. Using imprint instructions that would get acted upon when a key phrase was either heard or seen. So when you hear the key phrase, you kill. Except we could never get it to work for us while you were here. So we let you go – and, like so many others, you were deemed a failure.'

She now seemed totally engrossed in her explanation.

'Plainly, you were on the wrong list. You weren't a *fail*, and you certainly weren't *safe* – just ask the late Mr Cresdee. But then when we learned your landlord had been murdered, the coincidence seemed too great. So I moved in, seduced you, got on your case.'

She laughed. 'You were always just a *file* to me, Fergus. All that sex was just part of the job.' She ran the toe of her shoe over his zip. 'Though it could be fun sometimes.'

He coughed blood on to his already stained shirt. 'And everything else you said . . .'

'Words, Fergus, just words. Amazing the power they have. Gee you up in bed, string you along . . . get you killing.

I needed to know who else on the list had been miscategorized. How many of them were about to implode and take out their neighbours. If they were caught, we could be implicated.'

'But if you already knew who was on the list, why weren't you checking on them all?'

'Oh, we were.'

'You mean eliminating them?'

'Yes.'

'So why didn't you simply kill me? Why the charade?'

'To see if Dale Cresdee's murder wasn't just a fluke. It was another experiment, little puppy. I had to wing it, of course, which was half the fun. Lab work can be so sterile at times . . . Fieldwork, however, gets the blood pumping.'

'Fieldwork? Killing innocent people? People who have *helped* you in the past with your work?'

She sighed. 'They were just experiments. Data to be scrutinized and discarded. But once you found out how the Lowrys died, your experiment was over. Your time at Cruddock's clinic was the final test: to see if you could be broken. But again I misjudged you.'

'This is all bullshit.'

She placed her heel on his crotch and slowly ground it. 'I understand your disbelief. I thought so too. How could six deliberately chosen random words chance to occur in the right order? The odds are incalculable, but it did happen. It was that time we stayed late in the bookstore and you fucked me over the history section. What I saw then showed me it was true.'

She sat down behind the desk, placing the pistol next to the keyboard.

Fergus remembered the occasion. It had been a Sunday.

'It was there, plain as day, on the shelves behind. Six books with their titles lining up. The key phrase was there too, made up of separate words from titles and authors.' She flicked a stray staple at him from the desktop. 'You must have seen those six words line up in the correct order and that triggered you . . . and Dale Cresdee died.'

Fergus did not want to believe what he was hearing but, in the present situation, she had no reason to lie. 'Why him?' he managed finally.

'The last word in a phrase of six is your target. So think about your stock at the Ryecatcher. I do believe there's a book on Teddy Roosevelt called *The Man and the Myth* by Ian Cresdee.'

This information gave Fergus pause for thought. There *was* such a book, ordered by a history student who had disappeared before collecting it – after a date-rape allegation by a fellow student.

The one-eyed woman smiled at him, an unsettling sight. The large eye-patch was like a black hole, leading into the malevolent depths of her mind. 'So all I need to do now is repeat those six words, but substitute our little Miss Pea's name at the end. Then tragically your girly friend is dead. And when it's all over, you'll ask me what happened.'

Fergus forced a laugh that came out as a bloody gurgle. 'But if I don't remember killing Dale, how can you be sure it was me who did it?'

She threw the stapler, hitting him in the chest. 'Because, little puppy, I tested you.'

'When?'

'At the Noltings' house, of course.'

'But *you* did that! You slit Mrs Nolting's throat, threw the knife out the window, and claimed you'd seen someone running off.'

'No, Fergus. We were standing in the kitchen. I said the key phrase. *You* picked up a knife and followed her upstairs.'

'No!'

'You found Everald Nolting had already shot himself, but you completed your new mission by cutting his wife's throat.'

'No, no, no . . .' he protested.

'Yes, yes, yes,' she insisted. 'Your mind had to find an explanation. I provided it, talking you through it while you buried our bloodstained clothing. But let's prove it works now, shall we?' She leaned over the desk and jerked a thumb towards Izzy. 'All it takes is just six little words in the correct order. A sentence of death for your bimbo here. Let's see what happens . . .'

'You're crazy,' croaked Harry, eyeing the weapon. His stomach was heaving, bile welling up.

Dr Ralston raised the gun.

'One last question, before you die. Who sent out that list, Harry? Was it you?'

Although utterly terrified, he could see no point in hiding the truth.

'It was Philip,' he gasped, fighting nausea. 'But he didn't realize what it was, or what the consequences would be. It was just a desperate attempt at an SOS by a frightened kid.'

'My heart bleeds . . . OK, strike one mystery.' Her face betrayed no emotion as she levelled the gun. 'Let's end this, shall we?'

Before she could pull the trigger, Harry vomited straight into her face.

As she cried out, he clubbed her pistol to the floor. She scrabbled at her eyes, and at the vile fluid that had blinded her. But in ridding her eyes of his vomit, she had instinctively removed the contact lenses.

At last she was able to focus again – straight into the black pits of Harry's pupils.

Dr Ralston was his.

Kelly recited the words slowly and precisely. 'Serendipity. Secession. Samurai . . .'

'This is just bullshit,' said Fergus helplessly.

'. . . Scholar . . .'

'Bullshit!'

'. . . Sherman . . .'

Izzy suddenly appeared at the woman's shoulder, blood smearing her upper lip. 'Kelly,' she added.

The sixth word.

Izzy stared at Fergus, his face suddenly expressionless, as if a switch had just been thrown. Then she turned to look at Kelly. The woman's wrecked face had drained of colour, her single eye wide in horror.

Izzy smiled at her. 'Oh dear,' she said. 'Looks like you *were* telling the truth.'

Her breathing suddenly very rapid, Kelly fumbled for the automatic pistol. But just as her questing fingers touched the handgrip, Fergus launched himself over the table, slamming her to the floor, her chair flying into the corner. Her scream of pain was cut short by the impact of her skull on cement.

It didn't last long after that. Fergus grabbed some of her hair and smashed her head repeatedly on the floor. Eventually she stopped struggling, her hands left his throat, her good eye stared blankly at the strip light above them. Blood was oozing from the back of her skull, staining her hair an even more vivid shade of red. He sat back on her belly, then stepped back dazedly off her corpse.

'Fergus?' said Izzy tentatively. Even she was stunned at the ferocity of his attack.

'What happened?' Fergus stared down at his bloodied hands.

'She used the key words.'

'Jesus Christ!' It was *true.*

Deadly pale, he gaped at Kelly.

'Do you remember the exact words she used?' He was frantically wiping his hands on his shirt.

'Yes. Do you want me to say them?'

'No! Never again!'

'OK, Fergus.'

Suddenly he grabbed Izzy and hugged her tight. 'If she'd said your name,' he gasped. 'If she'd said your name . . .'

And then the door began to open.

*

Now he was sure he had her under his control, Harry ordered Dr Ralston to sit down on the couch. 'Okey-dokey. Let's talk. Where's the Hubcap?'

'The Chinook is salvaging it.'

'Where will it be taken?'

'Into the compound. The Hangar's destroyed. They'll need to hide it before daylight. Helicopters will be here soon to investigate the fire.'

'How long has this place existed?'

'It's been here ten years. We've needed somewhere secret. However much we try to keep people away from Groom Lake Air Base, everyone now knows it as Area 51. So that's not very secret. So 51 eventually built Down Town Two. We can afford to keep open secrets like Cheyenne Mountain and Langley, so long as the *real* secret places remain unknown.'

'What's the difference in what they do here?'

'At Groom it's technical and weapons, including the Hubcap and the breeding programmes. Here it's mind control, ESP, paranormal.'

'That's why Fergus and Izzy were once here?'

'Yes, the Mind Kontrol programmes were run from here and from Fort Meade, as were the Stargate remote-viewing programmes. They were both included on that list: failed experiments they thought they could now trust.'

'And what of the failures they couldn't trust?'

'Fail Unsafes, you mean? Of course, we had some. Screw with people's heads and you're going to screw with people's heads. Those ones all disappeared.'

'How long has this been going on?'

'Since World War II. It started with Paperclip. Nazi

and Japanese scientists received pardons in return for providing the data they had gained from experiments on prisoners. It all stems from that, you see. It's *all* about control, my work.'

'Control of whom?'

'Everybody.'

'Even Americans citizens?'

'Of course. If 51 can prove that it delivers effective results, it'll continue to receive limitless funding. Unfortunately only the hardware side has delivered so far. That's the main reason I have been given Down Town Two – and why Kelly's so worked up about this security breach. Out at Groom we've worked on the U2 and SR-71 spy planes, the F-117A Nighthawk, the B-2A Spirit Stealth, the Predator Unmanned Air Vehicle . . . and then you, of course. While here, after decades of research, there are still no usable results to show. So the leak of that list seemed too big a coincidence. Kelly suspected a plot against her. She's a paranoid bitch.'

'And was there one?'

'There always is! It's the nature of our business. Only this time it was sheer coincidence. But when your entire life is spent lying to other liars, who eventually can you trust? Too much of Kelly's work was run by witches.'

'Witches?'

'People who believe all that Psych Ops shit; who want to prove they're right, rather than be objective. 51 needs facts, not fantasies. *You* are a fact, Harry. So is the Hubcap. Ergo it's me who gets the funding.'

'You keep mentioning 51 – but it's not the same as Area 51?'

'No, 51 is the 51st State. It's everything the people don't know about. The CIA, DNI, ACA, NSA, OCI, USAF, Secret Service – all black ops that need to be funded on the quiet are a part of it. We help each other out, while protecting our own secrets. Kelly doesn't know all my work, I don't know all hers, but we both work for the 51st State.'

'Why call it that?'

'Sheer size. Add all our operation budgets together and jointly they qualify as the twenty-eighth highest annual budget in the Union.'

'What do you mean?'

'We have more money to spend on our projects than the annual budgets of twenty-three US states.'

She fell silent, her face blank.

Harry sat back on the desk, his legs still swinging. What was he to do now? He could control her only for about an hour, then she would either come out of it or fall asleep. One way or the other, he must find a way out. And, just now, escape from Down Town Two was what he wanted most. By getting to the outside world he could let the world know just what this 51st State was up to. But what about his two new friends?

'Where is your sister?' He turned to Dr Ralston.

'In my office, with Kintrey and Pea. Now she has them, they are going to die.' She appeared to smile.

'Pay attention,' Harry snapped. 'You will take me there. Will anyone try to stop us?'

'No. I am in total command here.'

The elevator was empty, and the corridor too.

'Where is everyone?' he asked nervously.

'Out looking for you. I ordered a search.'

They reached her office within thirty seconds. She walked straight in and came to an abrupt halt.

Harry stared at the corpse of Kelly, at the stunned Fergus standing over her.

Fergus watched Dr Ralston, as the woman studied her dead sister.

'Sloppy,' was all she said.

'We need to get out of here,' said Harry.

'My very thoughts,' agreed Fergus.

'What happened here?'

'We'll tell you later.'

'What do we do when we get out?' asked Izzy.

'We haven't got out yet,' said Harry.

'No, she's right,' argued Fergus. 'If we don't have a plan, we're just running again. We need something that'll save our asses.'

'And we haven't got long,' Harry said urgently.

He looked across at Dr Ralston. She was still staring down at Kelly, her foot idly toeing the bloody pool about her sister's shattered skull.

'When's the Chinook due?' Harry asked.

'I'll check the computer,' said Dr Ralston.

She headed over to the keyboard. After a few seconds of key-tapping, she announced that it was just landing.

'And what is the status of the Hubcap?'

'I'll need to talk to someone.'

She picked up a cellular phone on her desk and used it to call a man called Stevens.

'How's the Hubcap look?'

A voice replied, 'As far as we can tell, there's no

disintegrity to the main structure. Struts have gone, but the drive is still on line. We had to be careful with the slings.'

Harry whispered in her ear.

'Once you've landed it, get everyone clear.'

'Roger. But surely the ship will need guarding?'

Again, Harry relayed instructions.

'There might still be serious damage to the drive. I don't know what any leakage will do to your people.'

'Roger that. We'll stay clear,' said Stevens with relief.

'OK,' said Harry, switching off the phone. 'That's our route out of here.'

'The flying saucer?' said Izzy in awe.

'It'll carry all three of us. And nothing will catch us. The only problem is . . . with you two on board, I won't be able to accelerate quickly.'

'Well, we need it as evidence,' Izzy decided.

'But who do we give it to? The 51st State . . . It's so big, involves so much money.' Harry began to appreciate another human emotion called despair.

Fergus did not need persuading that they were up against something big. 'How high up does this 51st State go?' he said to Ralston.

She didn't answer, just stared at his bloody hands.

'So who *can* we trust?' Fergus turned to Harry.

'Not the military anyway – with all the uniforms we've seen round here.'

'Not the FBI either.'

'The police?' offered Izzy.

Fergus shook his head. '"Badges and money," Kelly said. And forget politicians too. The money for all this shit didn't fall off a tree. And the media can be bought or intimidated.'

He was increasingly worried that there might be nowhere to go with their story – assuming that they could ever get out of this damn place. 'And what if it goes all the way up to the President?'

'I voted for him. I trust him,' protested Izzy.

Fergus let out a bitter laugh. Burridge – that accident-prone buffoon?

He turned to Dr Ralston. 'Does the President know?'

'Some of it only.'

'What some?' said Harry. 'Does he know about the Hubcap?'

'No.'

'Why not?'

'He's only in office for eight years at the longest. Then there's a new guy. But 51's here *all* the time.'

Harry looked at Fergus. 'You're not really thinking . . .'

Fergus nodded.

'What about her?' asked Harry, nodding at Dr Ralston.

She sneered up at him, his hypnosis clearly losing its power.

Fergus could see the problem – and punched her unconscious.

'What about her . . .?' he said.

THIRTY-EIGHT@Chapter

They reached Level Three without interference. The trio then worked their way back to the loading docks, where they had been told the Hubcap was now secreted.

Pushing through the rubber doors on to Bay 6, Fergus and Izzy saw the saucer for the first time in all its black, discus-shaped glory. It was resting on a pile of sandbags. A collection of Jeeps and Hummers was parked in a circle all around it, fortunately bereft of passengers. The Chinook had clearly flown off again and the night was surprisingly quiet – just a rustle of wind in the trees that rose up around them. The low, orange lighting was sufficient to show every detail of the compound.

'How do we get into it?' said Izzy, naturally unperturbed by this first encounter with an extraterrestrial spacecraft.

'Small hatch at the top,' said Harry. 'It'll be a tight squeeze.'

Fergus was standing motionless in silent awe. The ship was simply *beautiful*: stark, sleek, simple, stunning. He had never seen anything like it, not even in the movies – and there was nothing else he could equate it to. It was black like a Stealth bomber, but that would seem crude and angular compared to this perfectly symmetrical creation. Its purpose was obvious, yet its shape so unfamiliar to eyes used to wings and rotors and jets and tailfins. Slowly, Fergus started to smile. He had never seen anything before that looked so much like it was *born* to fly. He began to giggle – like a child receiving every Christmas present he ever desired – and then to laugh. The ship's purpose was clear and unequivocal: this was what *all* flying machines should look like. Even as Fergus found himself guffawing out loud at the absurdity of an aircraft without wings or tail, he could think of only one word to sum it up: *perfect.*

Harry nudged Fergus down off the platform and then guided them past the intermediate loading bays until they were level with the Hubcap itself.

'It's real, isn't it?' said Fergus, his amazement still growing.

'Where's it from?' said Izzy, beside him.

'No idea,' confessed Harry. He had to assume that part of himself came from the same place, but he was unable to summon up an emotional reaction to that concept.

'I'll go first,' said Harry. 'Then Izzy. Then you, Fergus.'

'I'll give you cover,' Fergus said, holding up a loaded M-16 rifle they had discovered in Dr Ralston's office.

'Do you know how to use that?' said Izzy sceptically.

'I don't even know if the thing is loaded.'

'Just point it and hope,' Harry suggested.

Fergus raised the rifle to his shoulder and peered down the sight, towards a lone tree on the other side of the compound. He squeezed the trigger and the recoil hammered his shoulder. The single shot cracked through the night like a thunderclap.

All three stared at each other in alarm, then Harry

broke for the Hubcap. Against its sheer size, he looked exactly like the small boy he was. It was a good twenty-yard run across open ground, then he leaped up on to the rim and grabbed one of the lower fins, hauling himself up until he located the hatch. Fortunately it was still open, and he leaned over to peer inside. Everything looked as it should do and he felt confident that, as soon as he took his usual seat, the controls would come on line.

He waved over at Izzy and clambered inside. Just as he settled himself into his seat, he heard more gunfire. Oh, blow. Oh, blow!

The control panel winked into life and the vision screen instantly gave him a monochrome view of the end-most two loading bays. Quickly strapping in, he brought the main drive up to lift strength, raising the Hubcap six inches off the ground and slowly rotating until he could see what was happening.

Izzy, clearly unconcerned that the ship might rise even higher, climbed on to its hull and made her way up and over the vision screen to the hatch.

As soon as Harry saw her legs dangling above him, he shouted, 'Get in. Get in!'

There was a yelp and a thump and, satisfied that Izzy had effected her entrance, however clumsily, Harry turned his attention to Fergus.

He was huddled down against the platform wall, the semi-automatic rifle trained to his right, and firing shots every couple of seconds.

Harry rotated the Hubcap to view Fergus's target. Three men were crouching low behind a Hummer, but unable to return effective fire because of another Hummer parked in between. Fergus's shots served to make them keep their heads down, but at any moment one of them could try a flanking movement.

Harry now had only one option. He skimmed the Hubcap across the compound, then raised it over the nearest Hummer, angling the craft so it hovered between the soldiers and Fergus.

The men, panicked by the sudden movement, started firing up at it. This in itself was not a problem, since their bullets would act like peas on a rhino's hide, but the increased gunfire would attract other soldiers, some of whom might get a clearer shot at Fergus.

Harry eased the Hubcap down until it crushed the Hummer's roof, then revolved his cockpit until he could observe Fergus staring dumbly upwards at the incredible manoeuvrability of the silent craft. Harry then lowered the rim until it scraped the ground.

Fergus had watched agog as the disc floated across the compound, landed on top of the Hummer, then tipped towards him so that its rim touched the blacktop only feet away. And all this without a sound. He had never seen anything so beautiful or sinister. Beauty and power, grace and terror. He was actually incapable of moving while he gaped at it.

Then he heard his name being called out. The spell broken, he noticed Izzy waving down at him. 'Get in. Get in!'

As more gunfire sounded to his side, he ran for the ship and jumped aboard, finding its surface less slick than expected. Grasping one of its thin, twelve-inch-high fins, he pulled himself up towards her. Just as he reached the narrow opening, she disappeared from view and the craft began to rise.

Oh, shit! He looked back.

Already they were thirty feet off the ground – and he had felt neither movement nor vibration! This was astonishing. It was terrifying. He hauled himself closer to the hatch.

'Wait, I'm not in yet!' he yelped, as he felt the craft sliding sideways.

Harry could hear Fergus's protests, but he could also see swarms of men emerging through three of the loading-bay doors, their M-16s aimed at the Hubcap. It was vital that he get up high enough to prevent their imminent fire from reaching the upper surface of the ship and therefore Fergus. Unfortunately, this also meant that Fergus was still stranded outside, dozens of feet up in the air.

Inside, Izzy was struggling to stand upright on the rear seat, but toppled and fell to the cockpit floor.

'Strap yourself in!' shouted Harry, aware that she wouldn't understand the Hubcap's sudden moves.

Fergus managed to get a second hand on to the hatch edge and was on the point of kicking himself inside to safety when he was buffeted by an icy blast. Glancing up, he registered a giant helicopter above the treetops, its twin sets of rotors whipping the foliage into a frenzy. Twigs and branches came smashing down on to the Hubcap.

Harry felt the down-draught power its way through the cockpit. Struggling to maintain the craft's equilibrium, he carefully revolved the tilting ship until he could observe the Chinook overhead. This one was too big a brute to assault. Besides, he still had a passenger outside. Below them, the gunfire had been called to a halt for fear of someone hitting the Chinook. But that meant only a momentary respite; already Harry could see armed men shinning up nearby trees to gain a vantage point. It would be only a matter of time before Fergus was picked off – but, as Harry could go neither higher nor lower, what was he to do?

Fergus had now lost his footing and was relying solely on his hands to keep him in place, but his right arm was hurting like the devil and he could feel his muscles starting to spasm. If only the ship would tilt the other way, he might have a chance of sliding into the hatch.

Again Harry revolved, looking for some way out. The compound was only about four times the length of the Chinook above him, so any movement he made would be easily matched by the helicopter, which now had its powerful searchlight trained on them. Two sides of the compound were solid walls, carved out of the rock and lined with brick. The third was home to the loading bays and the fourth was broken only by an access tunnel.

A tunnel?

Harry slid the Hubcap towards the tunnel entrance. It would be a narrow squeeze and he could see no light at the end, so it was either very long or, worse, there was a bend in it. But now it was their only chance.

He revolved the ship once more, eyed the men on the ground running towards the Hubcap, then glanced above, to the Chinook lowering itself towards the treetops, angling itself to aim its rocket pods. Oh, blow! No choice. Harry spun it back quickly.

As the ship revolved, Fergus felt himself sliding off.

Harry realized his mistake and tilted upwards, till the rim of the Hubcap touched the tunnel roof.

Fergus's descent was immediately arrested as he came into contact with the wet brick ceiling – then it was reversed as he fell back towards the disc's centre. Harry instantly levelled up and edged forward into the darkness.

The Hubcap had only a couple of feet to spare on each side and it took all of his concentration to keep from grazing the walls.

Suddenly he could see a light ahead of them in the tunnel, realizing too late that it was the headlights of a Jeep. As he tried to rise above it, the rim scraped the tunnel's curved sides.

As he slid inwards towards the hatch, Fergus felt the ship jerk underneath him. Then the Hubcap shuddered again – and he found himself falling through the hatch, straight on to Izzy.

Harry eased the craft forward, saw the Jeep slow to a halt. Then it began to reverse up rapidly, its driver obviously terrified by what was looming overhead.

And so this strange procession continued, for the entire quarter-mile length of the tunnel: the Jeep frantically reversing, the Hubcap floating eight feet off the ground, its front edge hovering right over the vehicle's radiator – while behind them followed a pack of armed men, firing wildly at the hovering spectre.

Finally, the Jeep breached the end of the tunnel. It swung to one side, dropping its rear into a ditch, the three desperate occupants diving for cover. The Hubcap glided past it. As Harry spotted some star-filled sky through the trees lining the road, he slowly guided the ship upwards until they were five hundred feet clear of any handgun fire.

Harry looked back at his makeshift crew. Izzy had only

managed to secure one buckle, while Fergus was still lying on the floor, his face a picture of amazement.

'Practicalities first,' ordered Harry. 'Fergus, help get Izzy buckled up.'

Realizing that the Hubcap was finally stable, Fergus pulled himself up and fastened her remaining seat belts.

'What about me?' There was no other seat.

'Best to lie down flat and grab the frame of her seat.'

There wasn't much room, but Fergus found a relatively comfortable position.

'Okey-dokey,' continued Harry. 'Number one: have you ever tried a really big roller-coaster?'

'No,' said Fergus doubtfully.

'Yes,' said Izzy. 'Great fun.'

'Well, at least Izzy's going to enjoy herself. Number two: where are we going?'

Fergus was struggling for an answer when there came a loud bang. The Hubcap rocked to the left as Harry spun them round – to see the Chinook hovering over the trees like a pregnant buzzard.

'Here we go!' he warned – and the Hubcap zipped a mile away in under five seconds. He then let it glide to a halt.

'Whooo!' shouted Izzy.

'Oh, God. Oh, God. Oh, God,' groaned a nauseous Fergus.

Harry explained, 'I can easily outrun the Chinook and its weapons. Without visual contact, their missiles are useless, since the Hubcap doesn't give off any heat. As long as they haven't got another – '

Suddenly the Hubcap dropped a thousand feet, both Izzy and Fergus screaming involuntarily as their stomachs went into free fall.

'– Apache!' finished Harry, as a Sidewinder missile boomed above them.

Fergus was completely unable to speak.

'I can outrun those too, but it's getting ahead that's going to be uncomfortable for you.'

Before Fergus could beg for mercy, the Hubcap zipped backwards at an angle of forty-five degrees. For what seemed like an eternity, Fergus's eyeballs tried to exit via his nostrils, while his breathing was cut off as his tongue became fixed to the roof of his mouth. Then the craft slowed to a halt – dropped like a stone – and stopped again – before zooming forward.

Never had Fergus experienced anything so frighteningly disorientating. It took him quite a while to comprehend that Harry was speaking to him.

'We can't be seen on radar and we're low enough not to be visible, so we should be OK now.'

'The . . . Apache?' managed Fergus.

'Now twenty-two miles away, flying the wrong way.'

If he could have spoken, Fergus would have echoed his disbelief at the distance. As it was, he was too busy trying to keep his teeth clamped shut so that the contents of his stomach wouldn't decorate the Hubcap's interior.

Harry put the Hubcap into stasis, unbuckled and turned to check on his passengers. Izzy sat wide-eyed but smiling. Fergus was anything but.

'Sorry we had to do that. I did keep it fairly slow.'

Slow?

'I can take the Gs,' continued Harry. 'Normal pilots can't.'

Fergus thought he had made this fact rather obvious.

'Okey-dokey,' said Harry. 'So, where to now? You people know the real world. I don't.'

'Can I . . . can I have a minute?' said Fergus.

'That was some rush,' said Izzy delightedly.

Silly bloody bitch, thought Fergus, struggling to pull himself upright on wobbly legs. 'Where are we right now?'

Harry checked a bright blue section of his control panel. To Fergus it looked like a lot of lights; no dials, no gauges, nothing at all familiar.

'We're twenty-six miles south-east of Down Town Two, currently at a height of 850 feet; 210 feet above the tree line.'

There was absolutely no mechanical sound. Fergus began to feel nauseous again. 'What keeps this thing up?'

'Some kind of anti-gravity drive. No one knows how it works, or where it gets its power from. All I do is direct it.'

'And that doesn't worry you: not knowing what's under the hood?'

'You drive a car, I imagine. Do you understand how the molecular structure of the gas you put into the tank gets to turn the wheels?'

Fergus shut up.

Izzy said, 'How did they keep it hidden in Nevada? This thing's so . . . so obvious.'

'Have you ever been to Rhode Island?' said Harry, remembering some of his education.

She shook her head.

'It's just a small state,' explained Harry. 'Okey-dokey, now imagine that whole state was an airfield.'

'That's how big Groom is?' said Fergus, impressed.

'No. Groom's *fifteen* times the size of Rhode Island. You could lose Rhode Island in it!'

'And this ship too,' said Fergus. 'But where do we go now?'

'You mentioned the President,' said Izzy.

'I know I did, but I don't know where to find him,' said Fergus.

'Doesn't matter,' replied Izzy. 'He'll come to us.' She swept her hand around the Hubcap's interior. 'Wouldn't you?'

'But how can we make sure he gets to us before the 51st State does? Any communication is bound to be intercepted.'

They all fell into a gloomy silence – until Fergus slapped the side of Izzy's seat. 'I think I have an idea. What time is it?'

'It's 8.16,' said Harry, glancing at a thin green light in front of him.

Fergus stared at the light. 'If you say so . . . OK, let's say we've got the whole night. We can't exactly hide this thing in daylight. But first, we need to know exactly where we are. That means finding a road and following it until we see a road sign. Then we start looking out for an expensive car driving on its own.'

'Why would we need a car when we've got this thing?' said Izzy.

'Just make sure it's an *expensive*-looking one.'

THIRTY-NINE@Chapter

It had not been a good day for Harris Rudler. Three of his afternoon's four customers had reduced their orders and the other one had switched to FFRREEKKZZ. If the week continued like this, he could kiss goodbye to half his month's commission and to the Mustang he'd had his eye on. He had hoped to finish early, and get back to Sarah and the kids, but that was not to be. It was still eighty miles to Schenectady and he felt so dog-tired he'd probably be better off booking into a motel, then swinging cross-country first thing tomorrow and catching Ed Tanzetti in Worcester at breakfast.

He drove into Leominster, NY, but, eyeing the deserted main street, decided to give it another ten miles before calling it a day. The roads were very quiet, lonely even, and he sometimes wished he had company – a truck, a Greyhound, anything to let him believe his world wasn't suddenly empty. Even the damn radio didn't work and the only tape he had was Radiohead's *OK Computer* – and he'd rather slit his wrists than listen to those boys in his current state of mind. Add to all this gloom a mortgage payment two weeks overdue; Visa and Mastercard debts up the whazoo; and, much as he loved her, a wife whose grasp of responsible budgeting was on a par with his own understanding of quantum physics.

He was two miles out of Antull and cresting a low rise on the two-lane blacktop when something ahead caught his eye. A large black shape was blocking the road. He slowed, fearing there had been an accident, then he observed the object's distinctive shape . . .

Oh, you have got to be shitting me, he thought. *It's a goddamn UFO!*

As he slammed on the brakes, his four-year-old BMW 518 screeched to halt only thirty yards short of the silent disc, whose shape was now clearly outlined in his headlights. All his life he had been sceptical about things supernatural and otherworldly – ironic for a man who made a living selling New Age paraphernalia – but even in his present exhausted state he knew he wasn't dreaming.

And then there was a tap on his window. Harris jumped and turned to see – *Oh, Jesus Christ All Fucking Mighty!* – an alien staring straight in at him.

Big grey head, big black eyes, the whole enchilada.

And then nothing, just darkness again.

So Harris didn't hear the alien's human companion say, 'Yes! He's got a cellular phone.'

Nor the female with them add, 'Even better, he's got a laptop.'

In fact, Harris Rudler wouldn't see or hear anything further until he woke up to find himself parked off the road, his Nokia phone and Texas Extensa 355 Portable PC gone – along with six hours of his life.

FORTY@Chapter

The morning turned out to be bright but cold, a stiff breeze worming its way into everyone's clothing, making their waiting even more of an endurance test.

Del Carnegie, from the *New York Sun*, swore for the fifteenth time: 'Fuck, it's cold up here.'

His photographer, Pete Buckley, reassured him for the fifteenth time: 'Yes, but you *did* say this would be worth it.'

Carnegie offered him a sick smile, then turned to scan the other reporters, cameramen, photographers. '*Everyone* thinks this will be worth it. If we can stay alive that long.'

A Channel 9 TV cameraman wandered up, sipping from a plastic cup of brown liquid. 'Forget your winter wardrobe, Del?'

Carnegie had been out at a party when the urgent call came in and had failed to pick up his overcoat. 'Sit on it, Markson,' he growled, turning back to Buckley.

'You sure Alice got the instructions right?'

'Yeah. Be here at 8.00 a.m. or else.'

He checked his watch: 7.51 a.m. Well, if nothing happened in the next ten minutes, he could head for breakfast at Harvey's.

He looked over the crowd, which was forty strong

now, with more latecomers still arriving every minute. He recognized reporters from WABC, WNBC, WCBS, WNEW and other local stations; along with CNN and Sky, who of course got everywhere, and also people from the *Times*, the *News* and the *Post*. There were agency guys, foreign press, even someone from the *New Yorker*. Quite a gathering, thought Carnegie.

Suddenly someone hurried into view, waving a sheet of paper.

'It happened. It fucking *happened*! Somewhere called Garmentine, upstate, about 5.00 a.m.'

Carnegie pushed his way over to the man. He was a reporter for *Newsweek* with whom he often downed beers in Kelly's Tavern on Eighteenth. Del grabbed the sheet of paper and began to read it.

It was a PA report, precise and unsensational, which on any other day would be spiked by all but the most desperate of supermarket-tabloid hacks as being an aberration of taste from the wire editors.

'OK, people, listen up! We've got here a Sheriff Gainsburg answering a routine call to a break-in at a copy shop. But, lo and behold, he spots this UFO hovering over his car, then like a good citizen chases it for five miles into the middle of Garmentine, where it lands on the common. Soon half the town's come out to see what all the commotion's about. Communal shitting of pants ensues, then the said UFO wings it skyward and disappears.'

At any other time, Carnegie would have walked over and stuffed the report into the top pocket of the nasty green suit belonging to MacKenzie of the *National Enquirer*, dismissing it and the man himself with a sneer. But no one gathered there could afford to be smug. Because, though often heard before, this particular account of mysterious lights and alien thingummies scaring the bejesus out of country folk was *different*. Not just because there were over 200 witnesses, but because every reporter up on the roof with Carnegie had been advised of the impending story at least two hours before it happened.

'Now, either this is all one clever hoax or something special *is* about to happen,' concluded Carnegie.

'That sounds like a line from a Spielberg movie,' muttered Ablot from *USA Today*.

'What's the nearest college to this Garmentine place?' another asked.

This prompted a short debate, until they agreed on Syracuse.

'Well, that explains it,' concluded Angela Harris from the *New York Times*. 'Remember the Lake Ontario Monster story in '94?'

There was muttered agreement all around. Many were anxious to rationalize the story – after all, the alternative to a hoax would be reality.

'So why are we all here, then?' said Matsunaga from CNN, as a gust of stiff breeze chilled them all anew.

'You get a phone call like that, what would you do?' answered Everett from *60 Minutes*.

No one had the heart to prolong the debate. Used to dealing with hard facts, they now felt lost, suspended between a story that might prove fantastic and the faint promise of something sensational. And all on the strength of a phone call made by a woman clearly reading from a script. Yet, since they were only minutes from the promised deadline, no one wanted to look a fool in front of fellow professionals. There was always just the vaguest chance that this could be 'The News Story of the Century'.

Carnegie checked his watch again, just as a dozen other reporters did likewise. It was now 7.58 a.m.

'This is ludicrous,' he grumbled, slapping at his arms to keep warm. 'One more minute,' he announced eventually. 'Then, story of the century or not, I'm going.'

Pleased that someone had taken the lead, there was muttered agreement from a good half of the fifty reporters now present.

Suddenly 8.00 a.m. arrived, its advent marked by the bleeping of wristwatches.

'Well, that's it,' said Carnegie, cupping his hands to light a Marlboro. 'Someone's probably at our homes right now, stealing our TVs and raping our cats.' He set off for the exit, his photographer trailing him. 'What a fucking waste of time.'

Then there was a yell: 'Will you look at *that*!'

Everyone turned towards the voice. It belonged to a *Newsbeat* cameraman, who in boredom had begun to take a panning shot of the city and had caught sight of something in his lens.

Those close enough followed the direction of his shaking finger – and immediately rushed to get a better view.

Within a minute all the reporters – and the three security guards – were massed at the roof edge, gaping like teenagers at a stripshow. The focus of their attention was out over the river. Immediately the punishing cold was forgotten as camera bulbs flashed and motors whirred, reporters gabbled into cassette recorders, and pencils were rapidly blunted as superlatives were scribbled frantically into notebooks.

They had been summoned up on to the top of the North Tower of the World Trade Center 'to observe an event' – and an event was exactly what they were witnessing. For slowly wheeling around the shoulders of the Statue of Liberty was a large black disc whose outline showed sharp and clear against the choppy grey waters of Upper Bay and the cloudless blue sky above.

All together, they watched in awe and disbelief as it continued to circle Liberty Island at a height of about 200 feet, seemingly without means of propulsion or support. And for once these men and women, whose very lifeblood was words, were speechless. Reporters who had braved the bullets of Bosnia, the drug cartels of Columbia, the Gulf War and LA drive-by shootings felt their bowels freeze as they watched the display in front of them.

Meanwhile, in newsrooms relaying the scene, hysteria broke out as affiliates bartered with the networks to break into their regular programming. For, hoax or not, what was flying around the Statue of Liberty in a long, lazy arc was *news.*

Already some were trying to explain it away as a Hollywood stunt to publicize an *MIB2* or *ID2* or some other megabucks sequel. Others searched the sky in vain for a helicopter that could be holding the disc up. Then there were those who simply sought comfort in Prozac and Valium. But, fake or not, it was a fantastic, wondrous sight, and even the most hardened newshounds were left mouth agape, brain on hold, as they watched the black saucer begin to wing its way smoothly across the bay towards Manhattan Island. And, as the object slid further north-west, they scrambled across the roof to keep it in view.

However, their initial reaction was nothing compared to the utter pandemonium that broke out as the craft swooped to buzz the Battery Park Ferry, then rose again to fly past Ellis Island and along the Hudson River. The disc continued 200 feet above water, gliding past the World Financial Center at about thirty miles an hour. Its speed and height did not vary as it continued up the channel separating Manhattan from Jersey City, moving parallel with Eleventh Avenue West. It then swung east over Pier 64 and from there continued to hug the shoreline. Over the heliport, past the Jacob K. Javits Convention Center, its progress was now marked by the whooping of ship sirens as astonished seamen expressed their amazement. Reaching Pier 97, it turned inland over West 57th Street, rising high above the buildings until again visible from the World Trade Center.

Some reporters had already charged for the elevators, but those who remained continued to stare intently as the black ship flew silently over the morning rush hour – its traffic only minutes away from complete gridlock.

An entire ten-block area south of Central Park came to a halt as the disc executed a graceful turn, then followed a path directly down Broadway, as if ensuring that even more New Yorkers would get to see it. Businessmen and businesswomen watched it bog-eyed, freaks freaked, shop-workers abandoned their tills, taxi drivers forgot about their fares, teamsters were lost for oaths, the religious found new faith – as did some atheists.

It cruised along by blacked-out theatres – which themselves had never managed such a well-staged performance – on past the Winter Gardens, then across Times Square, where a dozen collisions jammed the traffic solid. But the screaming and gesticulating of affronted motorists was silenced as soon as they too caught sight of the thing now hovering just fifty feet above their heads.

After this pause, it continued unperturbed down Seventh Avenue, across 42nd Street, past Macy's, past the packed Pennsylvania Station, while commuters exiting the 34th, 28th and 23rd Street subways blocked the entrances as they stopped and gaped upwards.

'It's coming back. It's coming back!' went up the cry on the roof of the World Trade Center.

As the magnificent black disc continued its journey down Seventh Avenue, the sidewalks were rapidly jammed solid with pedestrians as all of downtown New York just stood there and stared.

The saucer ignored any traffic signals and paid no heed to the panicking police cars. It was oblivious to the myriad faces cramming windows above and below it, in the buildings lining Seventh Avenue. It was indifferent to the raucous shrieks of bag ladies and winos, the screams of the terrified, the delight of children, the prayers of the godly – and even the odd stray bullet from chancers. Now at a constant ten miles an hour, it glided sedately and silently over cabs and cars, trucks and buses, past stores and delis and cinemas and clubs and offices and sweatshops.

Slowly but surely, the early-morning bustle subsided as everyone stopped to watch and wonder. It slipped through the air, its speed constant, its purpose and destination unknown. Fingers pointed, mouths gaped, feet stopped still. Eventually, only the distant rumble of trains, the hoots of ships in the harbour, the distant whine of airborne jets and the impatient sirens of immobile fire trucks disturbed the startled calm of the city's canyons.

And on it proceeded, across 14th Street, over Greenwich Village, past NYU, where hundreds of students found themselves gawping like schoolkids at its stately progress across Canal Street, past the Holland Tunnel exits and on to West Broadway. By now, those left on the tower realized they were to be its target.

Gliding between the North-East Plaza and the US Customs building, it finally came to a halt at a mid-point between the North Tower and the South Tower, right over Austin J. Tobin Plaza. As the large open space quickly filled with people, it rested there motionless, only fifty feet above Fritz König's famous bronze globe, which finally found a rival for the slow elegance of its movement. The crowds below oohed and aahed while, 1,400 feet above them, the reporters strained to get a glimpse.

As did millions of television viewers as stations across the country provided coverage from the dozens of units stationed near by.

For two whole minutes the craft hovered immobile above crowds, heads all raised to stare at the intruder. Silence reigned, as if they were trying to hear it, but it still gave no sound – nor any other clue as to its origin or purpose. Someone climbed a tree and reached up towards it, his eyes ablaze with wonder.

And then, to a gasp issuing from thousands of mouths, it began to rise up the side of the North Tower, barely feet away from the faces peering out of its hundreds of windows.

Ten feet per second it climbed, never wavering, a sleek black shape stark against the stonework, moving as steadily as a scenic elevator.

All heads craned to follow it, while both police and news helicopters hovered at a discreet distance.

Up and up, higher and higher, till its initially impressive dimensions were slowly diminished by the giant slab of the building behind it. But as it shrank in size for those in the street, all the while it was growing for the nervous reporters gathered on the roof.

At 8.22 a.m. precisely the Hubcap completed its 1,400-foot ascent and eased itself past the roof line of the North Tower, to hover thirty feet above. Then, still silent, it glided to the centre, where it gently lowered itself until only inches above the roof surface. There it stopped, as if floating on an invisible pedestal.

Not one of the reporters dared approach it. Some in fact turned and ran, overcome by its alien presence. Nothing could fly like this – not without clattering rotors or screaming jets. There was something so unnatural about its movement, something that touched a deep nerve in many. But it was this strange mix of wonder and terror, of curiosity and disbelief, that served to unite the reporters beside it with the countless millions around the world who were now watching these events unfold.

There on the World Trade Center roof, professionalism finally got the better of the remaining reporters and they fanned out in a circle around the floating object. No one even needed to worry about finding a better angle: since the thing was perfectly round and featureless, all viewing positions were as good as each other.

No one spoke. The only sound up there was the shuffling of feet and the breeze whipping through the giant antennae array.

Then a small hatch on the upper surface of the craft opened.

Cautious steps backwards were immediately taken, while commentators around the world tried to summon up the words that might ensure their own place in televisual history.

Then a young woman's head appeared. She was pale-skinned, dark-haired and attractive.

The tabloid journalists on the roof went wild with silent excitement. Flying saucers *and* sex: it didn't get much better! Maybe the *Enquirer* had been right all along.

And then she spoke, her voice clear as crystal in the eerie silence.

'Take us to your leader.'

FORTY-ONE@Chapter

As is often the case with people frequently seen on TV, President Burridge looked shorter than his reputed six foot two. Having been hospitalized five days earlier for an appendectomy, he was now still officially convalescing at his retreat in the Catskills. A widower in his early sixties, Burridge's distinguished appearance, quiet manner and sombre dress sense made him an easy target for cartoonists and comedians, though their caricatures could do nothing to dispel the man's innate grace and personal charisma. He *looked* like a president.

However, the recent illness had ensured that more than just his hair was grey: he was ashen and plainly ill-advised to venture from his bed so soon. His operation having taken place less than a week ago, he was evidently in some discomfort but had refused any medication in order to be 100 per cent alert. The extraordinary events of that morning ensured that the presidential helicopter had promptly whisked him the 110 miles to New York – to this empty office high up in the World Trade Center's North Tower.

Recently vacated by a scandal-ridden stockbroking firm, the office resembled a construction site, since the suite was currently undergoing total refurbishment. The entire half-floor was therefore bereft of furniture, except for workmen's trestles and empty wall frames hung with transparent plastic. The floor was uncarpeted and ceiling wires dangled. On two sides, the tinted windows stared blankly out over the Manhattan skyline.

President Burridge was accompanied by only four Secret Service bodyguards, although his doctor and half a dozen other agents were waiting in the marbled reception area by the elevators. The floors immediately above and below had also been occupied by FBI and NYPD SWAT teams.

Security throughout the rest of the building was formidable. All the journalists previously on the roof had been corralled down on the mezzanine, to await whatever morsels the President's press secretary would feed them regarding the meeting about to take place some eighty-five floors above them.

The President's prompt reaction was partly in response to the Hubcap's sensational arrival. He could hardly refuse a meeting, with the eyes of the world watching him. However, the other reason was straightforward blackmail.

After Izzy's initial appearance, she and Fergus had both disembarked, leaving the Hubcap still hovering twelve inches off the roof surface. They had then proceeded to hand out a twenty-page document to every reporter present on the roof. The wording had been created by Fergus on the Texas laptop PC liberated from the BMW outside Antull. It had taken him five hours to write up everything that had happened since the FAIL:SAFE list had first appeared in his e-mail. Meanwhile, using the cellular phone, Izzy had tracked down the telephone numbers of every newspaper, TV station and news magazine they could think of in the New York area. Naturally, most of those they talked to were sceptical, so Fergus had promised a preliminary display during the night at some place in the state of New York. And, sure enough, while Harry had distracted the police of Garmentine with his impromptu flying exhibition, Fergus and Izzy had broken into the local Prontaprint, downloaded the laptop to a printer and run off forty copies of his story. A story now in the possession of virtually every major news organization in the free world.

As Fergus and Izzy were shown through the door, President Burridge stood up from the trestle he had been sitting on. The door was firmly closed behind them. Burridge felt more nervous than he could ever recall, aware that they had left someone else behind inside the saucer, ready to take action if anything happened to them. So Burridge had made it plain to all of his retinue that his guests were to be treated with the fullest cordiality.

For now, at least.

Fergus crossed the long room to approach the President, Izzy keeping a pace behind him. The four agents fanned out on either side of their employer, three with eyes fixed on the newcomers, one staring towards the door they had just entered. Instead of shaking hands, Fergus offered Burridge the same twenty pages he had handed earlier to the reporters on the roof.

'I've already read this,' said the President, as he dropped it to the floor like a week-old newspaper.

Fergus handed him a further twelve pages. 'No one else's read these yet. Take your time.'

Burridge started reading silently. He edged back to lean against the trestle. As it shifted, one of his bodyguards grabbed his arm to steady him.

'I'm all right,' he said, parking his backside with evident relief and continuing to flip through the pages.

It took him ten minutes to complete his reading, during which he let out a series of quiet oaths.

He finished the last page and looked up. 'You expect me to believe this nonsense? Flying saucers? Aliens? Secret bases concealed in the woods?' He seemed to warm to his disparagement. 'Area 51? A whole complex devoted to keeping one boy in the dark? This secret organization, the 51st State, so big it has a budget bigger than . . . Frankly, Mr Kintrey, I think you've suffered one knock on the head too many.'

'That's as may be, sir, but I do believe the surest evidence is currently parked up there on the roof. Harry is out there too, waiting for us, and he means business. If he doesn't hear from us that this case is being looked into, he will fly off. Then he will not only release those same pages to the media, but will appear on live television to tell his own story, in all its gory details.'

The President cast his eyes to the ceiling. 'And if I accede to your demands?'

'Harry will return straight away to Down Town One – and nobody will be any the wiser about him.' A police helicopter buzzed by outside, momentarily distracting him. 'Harry will then continue his research with the Hubcap. Believe me, this is *his* idea, not mine. He realizes he's a freak and that, if the world found out about him, he'd never have any peace again. All he wants to do is keep on working –

which is what he was created to do. But not under the direction of psychopaths like Ralston.'

'This Harry seems a darn sight more reasonable than you are,' grumbled the President, gritting his teeth against the pain in his side.

'You've already told the media that the Hubcap's a stolen experimental craft,' Fergus continued. 'That story will keep holding water because, whatever anyone argues, they can't *prove* it's anything else. Nor will they know that Harry exists – unless he's driven to making his presence known.'

The President glanced at his bodyguards. Fergus wondered nervously if this was some kind of secret signal.

'And you honestly think you can get away with this: blackmailing the President of the United States?'

'I don't see an alternative, sir. I've been forced into this position by those very people who are supposed to protect my freedom. I'm a patriot, Mr President. I may not be a soldier or a politician, but I'm an honest man, I pay my taxes, I obey the law. I even accept that there are those who bend the rules for the greater good – doing what they must to keep our way of life safe. But this – ' he kicked his report lying on the floor in front of him ' – there is nothing that can justify *this*!'

Burridge took a deep breath and forced himself upright. 'This is very difficult.'

Izzy spoke for the first time. 'No, it isn't,' she insisted. 'It's your mess, you clean it up.' She stepped towards the President.

The four bodyguards instantly drew their automatic pistols.

'Wait up, boys,' said Burridge. 'Leave her be. And what, Mr Kintrey, will *you* do now?'

'Go back to the real world, pick up the pieces.'

Another helicopter flew past, its engine audible even through the triple-glazing.

'You've got a reputation – '

' – which you must clear, leaving me without a stain on my character.'

'I'm not sure people will believe that.'

'They'll believe what they're told. So tell them the necessary truth. And the rest of the story stays in the dark.'

'And what guarantee have I that some time in the future you won't tell your story anyway, Mr Kintrey?'

Fergus took Izzy's hand. 'Because I *want* a future.' He squeezed her hand.

The two men stared at each other for a long while: one a frightened young man, still bloody from a horrendous ordeal, the other in pain from a routine operation, his sense of responsibility to his office, his government, his country weighing on his mind every bit as heavily as Fergus's concern for his own survival.

'I believe you, son,' he finally said. 'Looks like we've got ourselves a deal.'

There was shouting outside.

'Check that out!'

The four bodyguards were already up and running, when the twin doors burst open and five people entered.

'Nobody move!' shouted their leader.

The President's people stumbled to a halt, their weapons trained on the intruders.

'Who in hell's name . . .' began Burridge.

Fergus answered the question. 'It's Dr Ralston.'

Four Paragons accompanied her. One of them slammed the doors shut again and looped some electrical cable through the door handles. Briefly visible were the unconscious forms of the six guards littering the floor of the lobby outside.

'Tell your men to lower their weapons, Mr President.'

FORTY-TWO@Chapter

'How the hell did you get up here, Ralston?' growled President Burridge.

'Badges and money, Mr President. I have top clearance and I have friends in all the right places. I have *support.* Which is more than *you* can say at the moment.'

The President studied the newcomers. Dr Ralston was an attractive woman, but with a maniacal gleam in her eye he found unsettling. Her four companions were a different proposition. They looked like four schoolboys, dressed in identical black flying suits. And each was armed with an automatic pistol that seemed absurdly large in their slender hands. But he also noticed that, despite their apparent youth, their aim was true, their arms unwavering and their eyes – *God, their eyes* – were focused with the intensity of surgeons on his bodyguards. He had little doubt, should it come to a shoot-out, these four would fire with deadly accuracy. These must be the Paragons Kintrey had described.

'Do you realize what you're doing, Dr Ralston?'

'It's my job.'

'Your job?' He almost laughed. 'You work for me.'

'I work for the 51st State. Big difference. My duty is to

defend this nation from all-comers, whether terrestrial or extraterrestrial.'

'But I'm your president.'

'And, as you've said yourself so many, many times, no man is bigger than the office he holds. I've worked through four presidents without interference so far. Down Town has existed through ten presidencies. And now, because of one little fuck-up, all our efforts stand to fail.'

'Circumstances change.'

'So do presidents.'

'As do loyalties, it seems.'

Ralston exploded. '*Loyalties?* Loyal to *whom*? You're a Maine referral lawyer. A man who'll be out of office next year – just another mister on the golf course, boring his bodyguards with the same old stories about meeting prime ministers and princes. I don't owe my loyalty to you, just to this country – and particularly to the 51st State. *That's* all that matters. Presidents and their administrations may come and go, but the 51st State lives on regardless. The work we do, the work we have done, it's served this nation in ways *you* can't begin to understand. We've played our part in every conflict, in every action involving our national security. The 51st State is what keeps this country safe.'

'Safe for *whom*?' said Fergus, anger getting the better of him. 'For Sheriff Wesley? For Deputy Lowry? For the Noltings? For that poor bastard your sister knifed at the state fair? For Harry and Philip and those fuck-ups behind you?'

Dr Ralston marched over towards Fergus. He flinched, but she smiled, then reached behind him, pulling Izzy into view. She pushed the gun under Izzy's chin, all the while staring straight at Fergus.

'Safe for those who count,' she purred, still studying the man who had murdered her sister.

'A word of advice,' intervened Burridge. 'Don't ever go into politics, Doctor.'

Ralston poked the gun deeper into Izzy's throat. 'What if I just blew her head off right now?'

Fergus was beside himself with impotent rage.

The President, however, seemed inordinately calm.

'Whatever happens, Doctor, *you* aren't escaping from this room, so tell me, is Mr Kintrey innocent or not?'

Her face turned ugly with contempt. 'In every war there are innocent casualties.'

'But we're not at war, Doctor.'

'We're always at war!' She whipped the gun towards Burridge.

Two of the Secret Service men shifted their aim.

She continued, 'We're always at war against the unknown – and it's my job to make sure we're always prepared.'

'No, that's *my* job,' said Burridge coldly.

'With respect, Mr President, you won't *have* a job fifteen months from now. I've worked on this one for fifteen years!'

'Then my successor will – '

'Will see sense.' She laughed at his naïveté. 'When Coatbridge was a senator, he worked on the Senate Appropriations Committee, the Armed Services Committee and was Chairman of the Senate Select Committee on Intelligence. He's one of ours.'

A helicopter was hovering outside. No one inside the office paid it any heed.

'So what exactly do you want?' asked Burridge.

'These two and Sixsmith eliminated, and the Hubcap returned to Down Town One. Then my work must be allowed to continue.'

'Without a pilot?'

'I've got other pilots now.'

'These?' said the President, gazing at the four Paragons. The more he studied them, the more absurd – and obscene – the scenario became. He had a ten-year-old niece who looked more substantial than these freaks. 'They don't look like pilots to me.'

'They are, and they obey orders.'

He sighed. 'More than you do, Dr Ralston. And what if I don't do as you ask?'

Ralston took a step forward, seemingly unconcerned about the Secret Service agents. 'Then you'll be attacked and killed by these two maniacs here and tragically we'll have been too late to save you – or your bodyguards.'

'You and these . . . these *children* will turn out heroes?' The President smiled indulgently. 'Dr Ralston, I think you've been underground too long. Mr Kintrey here is offering a better deal by far.'

'I think you should reconsider,' she snapped.

'And I think you should shut up, Dr Ralston!' he bellowed.

Surprised, Ralston raised her gun to his head. 'Well, you leave me no option.'

Burridge still seemed strangely unconcerned. His smile broadened. 'Before you assassinate the leader of the free world, can I say one more thing?'

She glared at him. 'What?'

'The best-kept secret is the secret no one knows, yes?'

'Precisely. *You* may be aware of most government secrets, but the 51st State maintains its own integrity.'

'How wrong you are, my dear. Has it never occurred to you that, while you were running around creating this half-alien Sixsmith and perfecting your little Paragons here, others in the 51st State might have been creating something else?'

'Like what?'

'Like a president?'

'*What?*' For the first time, doubt appeared.

Burridge rubbed gingerly at his side. 'The best way to ensure the 51st State stays secret is to ensure that those best able to pose a threat to it are kept under its control. So what if the 51st State put its full efforts into getting their own man into the Oval Office? They select him, educate him, groom him, support him until he attains office and is then in a position to ensure that the 51st State retains its autonomy and receives no undue attention.'

Dr Ralston's face was a picture.

'OK, take a young man from Maine, his father killed in Guadalcanal, educated by way of an educational grant, who works as a lawyer long enough to establish a credible reputation before beginning the long haul to become Senator for Maine. And, while in the Senate, he serves on several committees – and not just those Senator Coatbridge sits on, but also the Commerce, Science and Transportation Committee and the Government Affairs Committee. He slowly gathers influential contacts, on and off Capitol Hill. And suppose that for all that time, since he was recruited in high school, he's been working for the 51st State.

'Remember, the best-kept secret is the secret no one knows, Doctor. So you see, far from being your enemy, I'm on *your* side. I've no intention whatsoever of letting Kintrey spoil things for us – but nor will I allow you to jeopardize our position by rash and emotional responses. The death of your sister is unfortunate – as is the damage to your programme – but we can deal with it. We can cope. Trust us. Trust *me*.'

Several times, Dr Ralston looked to be about to speak, but words seemed difficult for her. Instead, she licked her lips nervously, her eyes wandering, until finally, with a shaking hand, she lowered the gun.

'I'm sorry,' she said. 'If only I'd known.'

Fergus's heart was hammering faster. Suddenly it had all gone horribly wrong. *Ralston and Burridge were allies.*

'My dear, what value *is* a secret if everyone knows it?'

Ralston still seemed lost for words. But the President wasn't.

'Kill her,' he said abruptly.

There was split second's indecision from the Secret Service men – and a flash of horrified betrayal on the face of Dr Ralston.

'No!' she yelled, raising her gun again.

The Paragons took this as their cue.

Burridge himself made no move, merely watching as an exchange of gunfire began.

Izzy, who had been standing unconcernedly beside Fergus, felt herself being hurled to the floor.

In such a confined space, the noise of nine automatic weapons was deafening: compounded by ricochets, the pinging of spent cartridges, glass shattering, screams of pain.

But the gunfire lasted only for ten seconds, then silence returned. After an agonizing minute, Fergus dared to glance up over his shoulder.

Dr Ralston and all the four Paragons were down, as were two of the four Secret Service men. Burridge had not moved, except to clasp his upper arm, where blood leaked through his fingers. The two remaining bodyguards were already on their attackers, smacking weapons away from dying hands and kicking each body to detect a response.

Outside, two helicopters hovered closer, the noise of them deafening through the shattered windows. They contained marksmen training weapons on the office interior.

From the reception area, there was hammering on the door.

The two surviving agents rolled Ralston on to her back. She was obviously still alive, but covered in blood.

'Finish her,' ordered Burridge without emotion.

They took aim at her head and both fired twice. They then swung their guns round on Fergus and Izzy.

'No!' cried Fergus.

Burridge intervened. 'Leave those two. Check on Al and Pete.'

Shaking so much he could hardly move, Fergus somehow pushed himself on to his haunches. It was then he noticed blood on the back of Izzy's T-shirt.

Easing her gently over, he located more on her front. She must have been hit just as he pushed her down with him. *Oh, God, no.*

'Al's dead, Mr President,' said one of the agents.

'Pete's got a couple of flesh wounds,' added the other. 'What about you, sir?'

'I'll live,' Burridge said. 'Damn, what a mess. Go check the girl.'

An agent knelt to feel Izzy's pulse, then ripped open her blouse to examine the damage.

'It's pretty bad, Mr President. Bullet's gone clean through. Looks like her lung – maybe worse.'

Suddenly the door smashed open and a brace of SWAT men rolled in and took aim from the floor. Burridge and his agents held their hands up.

'We're safe!' he yelled, then began to cough.

The SWAT commander stepped inside, surveyed the room. 'Clear!' he shouted, then the room began to fill with uniforms.

A paramedic stooped to tend to Izzy. As her eyes blinked open, Fergus let out a yelp of relief.

'You're going to be OK, Izzy.'

'I love you,' she murmured.

'Sssh,' said Fergus, as she squeezed his hand.

Her eyes began to blink rapidly. He felt her go limp.

'Don't die. Don't die,' he pleaded.

Izzy winced as the paramedic stabbed a needle into her arm.

'It's all right, Fergus,' she managed. 'I'm not frightened.'

Then she started to convulse and Fergus started screaming. His mind flashed back to his last moments with Cathy Farrelly. Another girl who had loved him – and who had died in his arms.

It was Burridge who finally pulled him off Izzy, guiding him away through the throng of uniforms.

Fergus paused to stare back at her. *God, she looks so . . . broken*, he thought.

'Son, let's get out of the way. Let them do their work.'

A paramedic approached Burridge, to tend his wounded arm.

'Were you telling Ralston the truth?' Fergus gasped.

'I'm a politician, Mr Kintrey. It's my job to lie truthfully.'

'So are you a part of the 51st State?'

'You'll never know, but rest assured – as long as you keep your side of our bargain, no harm will come to you.'

Fergus took another look at Izzy and stifled a sob.

Then someone shouted, 'She's arrested!'

Fergus fell to his knees, weeping uncontrollably.

FORTY-THREE@Chapter

President Burridge and Fergus were escorted through the assorted medical personnel and law-enforcement officers by a phalanx of Secret Service agents. In the crowded reception area, they waited as the stretchers carrying Izzy and the more seriously injured agent were loaded into an elevator. As the doors closed, Fergus was surprised to see the elevator was heading upwards.

'Where are they going?' he said.

'To the roof,' said someone. 'Medevac chopper. Quickest way given the chaos at street level.'

When a second elevator arrived, the President, four agents and Fergus got in. This one rose too. Burridge smiled at Fergus's growing paranoia.

'My personal helicopter, Chopper One – it's also on the roof.'

'So where are we going?'

Before the President could answer, the doors slid open.

No words were spoken as they were hurried outside.

Fergus noticed there were three helicopters. The unexpected third machine was a US Marine Black Hawk; its complement of twelve armed troops was standing in a double rank along its side.

The medevac craft took off immediately, whipping at their clothing, and Fergus watched in dismay as the one person in the world he trusted disappeared into the blue sky. It left him with a feeling of sick hollowness. He had a terrible premonition that he would never see her again, either because she would not survive the journey . . . or because he himself was about to die.

The area around the World Trade Center was now alive with other helicopters and – to Fergus's consternation – all of them seemed to belong to the military, the FBI or the NYPD. There were no TV choppers: no one to witness what was happening.

Suddenly a man ran up to Burridge. He was dressed in full combat gear, even camouflage make-up.

The newcomer saluted. 'On your order, sir,' he said.

The President nodded.

The captain ran back to join his men beside the Black Hawk. All of them donned gas masks, then fanned out around the floating Hubcap.

'Hey, we had a deal,' Fergus protested.

Burridge laughed. 'Son, what you had was a stroke of luck. With what you know, and what your Harry knows, there's no way I'm going to let – '

There was a sudden muted boom and smoke began to pour out of the hatch of the Hubcap.

'Whatever this Harry's antecedents,' continued the President, 'there's enough sleeping gas now inside that thing to bring down a class full of schoolkids.'

'You bastard!'

'Now, is that any way to be talking to your president?'

Several soldiers mounted the Hubcap's rim, pulling

themselves up towards the hatch. Into it one dropped a small camera attached to a sheathed fibre-optic tube, so the scene inside could be transmitted to a small monitor which was held by a soldier kneeling near by. After a few seconds the camera was removed. Slipping on night-vision goggles over his mask, the same soldier cautiously lowered his head inside the hatch. Four other men stood with rifles aimed over his shoulder into the Hubcap's interior.

Ten seconds later he pulled himself away, turned to his men to signal his findings.

The captain hurried over to the President. 'There's no one on board,' he announced in dismay.

Burridge turned to catch Fergus's smile. He muttered, 'I underestimated you.'

Fergus tapped his head. 'Photographic memory. On the way here from Maine, Harry showed me how to fly the thing. It's remarkably easy, if you don't move fast.'

'So how's it floating now?'

'It's called stasis – like automatic pilot. It'll continue until I change its instructions.'

The President dismissed the captain, waved away his agents and walked Fergus over to the shelter of his helicopter.

'And where's Harry now?' he asked grimly.

'That's the cruncher. I haven't a clue. We dropped him off upstate somewhere. So I've no idea where he is or what he's doing. But you can be pretty damn sure he's watching a television right now.'

The President stared at Fergus, who could not discern his mood. Finally he clapped Fergus on the shoulder and burst out laughing.

'Goddamn it, son, you should be in *my* business!' Burridge suddenly clasped his side and cursed. 'OK, let's cut the bullshit. We had a deal.'

'And what if Harry was still inside there?'

'You don't want to think about that, son. Doesn't matter how much in the right you feel you are, you don't fuck with the President.'

'It isn't just the President I'm fucking with though, is it? And what guarantee have I got that you'll keep your word?'

The man offered Fergus his hand. 'A deal's a deal.'

'We had one before.'

'We hadn't shaken on it.'

Fergus stared at the man's broad hand. It trembled slightly – though whether it was from annoyance or the pain of his operation was not apparent.

Fergus took Burridge's hand and shook it.

They then entered the presidential helicopter. As soon as the door was closed, the Sikorsky S-61 took off.

Once clear of the roof, they could see the thousands of people gathered in the streets below.

'Just how are you going to explain it to them?' asked Fergus.

The President looked down on the streets of New York, gridlocked for as far as the eye could see. 'I believe the late Dr Ralston had it covered. Badges and money, son. Badges and money.'

'That's a lot of badges.'

'And a whole lot of money too. But we can afford it.' The President leaned back, and let out a long sigh. 'Mr Kintrey, twenty-five years ago we didn't have VCRs, PCs,

CDs, cellular phones, satellite TV, credit-card calculators, ATMs, Dolby Surround Sound, ABS braking, microwave ovens, digital watches, digital telephone exchanges, the Internet, the Shopping Channel, DAT tapes, ISDN lines, laser surgery, night vision, fly-by-wire airplanes . . . So how can the US Government now be spending eight billion dollars in developing UCAVs – remote-controlled aircraft – with a delivery date of 2027?

'Or have spent fifteen billion dollars on the Aurora Mach 4 spy plane – and then cancelled it?

'Or have invested twenty-four billion dollars in Star Wars technology – and yet have only the unproven MIRACL satellite blasting laser to show for it?

'That totals nigh on fifty billion tax dollars, Mr Kintrey – a five followed by ten zeroes – spent on just *three* secret projects. Think about it. The money's all been approved and it's all going somewhere. The 51st State has all the money it needs.'

Burridge turned to stare out of the helicopter's curtained window.

Neither man said another word.

Six months later

In his office, Harry sat drumming his feet. He was strangely nervous, although he could not understand why. His testing of the Hubcap was progressing much faster than before, now there was not much reason to be secretive about it. What could anyone learn by peering at a flying disc from twelve miles away? Just about the only change locally was that the Little A-le-Inn in Rachel was doing a roaring trade in sightseers.

Occasionally he made trips to other government facilities to check on their research programmes. But otherwise he was happy to live his quiet, subterranean existence here, confident that he was doing what he was best at.

He looked up at the clock. They were late and he hoped nothing had happened to them. Time was something he was more aware of now, probably because of all the minutes, hours and days that had been squandered in his earlier life.

Another minute passed. Oh, blow, this was getting –

There was a rap on the door and a guard ushered his two guests in.

'Would you like coffee, Mr Sixsmith?'

'Yes, please. And chocolate biscuits.' Harry stood up to shake their hands. 'Good to see you again, Fergus.'

'And you. No sunglasses?'

'Hey, I'm a good boy now.' He turned to Fergus's companion. 'Izzy, you're looking much better.'

The preliminaries over, they all sat down.

'How's the Hubcap cover story holding up outside?' asked Harry.

'That the Hubcap's a US secret project and not a captured UFO?' said Fergus. 'It's holding up OK – sort of. Apparently it has "credible deniability". There's lots of rumours, but no *proof* that it's alien. So nothing's changed really. Have you made any progress?'

'I'm afraid that's classified.'

Fergus nodded, then smiled.

'And how about you?' Harry asked Fergus.

'A little pressure from the White House got me cleared. Badges and money, as the woman said. Of course, there are those who still think I'm guilty – but they're the kind of crazies who believe in wild conspiracy theories.'

They looked at one another, then burst out laughing.

'Loonies,' said Izzy.

'Weirdos,' concurred Fergus.

'And your programming?' Harry prompted.

'They offered to help, but they've messed with my mind enough. Besides, what are the odds of those lethal words ever occurring again in the correct order?'

'Eighteen billion to one,' Izzy chimed in. 'They got some English professor to work it out.'

'So what are you both doing these days?' Harry asked, as he topped up Izzy's mug of coffee.

'Cathy Farrelly left me the Ryecatcher Bookstore in her

will. I feel a bit guilty about that but, hell, I need the job. So does Izzy – no one else would employ her.'

'And the constant ears and eyes don't bother you?' said Harry, referring to the government agents assigned to follow them.

Fergus shrugged. 'Look at it this way. We're both still alive when we could well be dead. And if either of us ever gets sick or into trouble, we get the best attention immediately. I can live with that, and Izzy certainly can.'

'Don't see any problem,' she said, munching on the last chocolate finger, obviously unconcerned about her weight. 'But then I don't see any problems.'

They chatted some more, till eventually their time was up.

'We're off to Vegas,' announced Fergus, as Harry walked them to the entrance.

'Gambling?'

'Yes. We're getting married.'

'We'd love to have you as best man, Harry.'

'Except I'm not really a man,' he said sadly.

'Hey, you're as good a man as there ever was.' Izzy kissed him on the forehead. 'And don't you ever forget it.'

Harry blushed. Another new experience. 'I'm afraid they need me here right now.'

Izzy climbed into the Pinto and Fergus had to politely pull her out from behind the wheel.

'When will we see you again?' asked Izzy.

'I'm tied up for a while, but in a couple of months . . . Maybe I'll come visit you in Lewisville.'

Fergus started up the car. 'Hey, I just remembered. I

came across this quotation. I thought it might mean something to you.' He handed Harry a piece of paper.

Harry unfolded the note, to scan the handwritten quotation. It was from the English philosopher John Stuart Mill: '*The worth of a State, in the long run, is the worth of the individuals composing it.*'

He turned and watched as they drove off, dust soon obscuring the car as it headed across the airfield. A few moments later, just as expected, a dark green saloon started following at a discreet distance.

Harry stared up at the sun. Blow, it was hot outside. He headed quickly back towards the underground entrance. One of the anonymous regular passenger flights from Groom to Las Vegas and McCarran Air Force Base took off in the distance, disturbing the desert silence. He would be on a plane himself soon; and now he had some packing to do.

When he had told them he would be tied up for a while, he couldn't tell them where he was going.

First to Down Town Three, near Belport, Alaska; and then on to Down Town Four on the island of Orchua, in the South Pacific . . .

The 51st State was indeed a very large territory.